Reviews for PRINT

"Once you pick 'Print' up, you will not put it down until you've finished. And even then, you'll be pleading for more.....Lennon has a gift."

-**Jess Walton**

"Captivating. Lennon's characters grab you by the collar of your shirt and keep you there with every obsessive turn of the page."

-**Kate Leishman-Peirens**

"A twisting, turning murder mystery maze of heart pounding excitement. Print had me at 'hello'....it's the kind of crime tale you tell your friends they MUST read and then they thank you!"

-**Chris Diaz**, contributor of "winewithcheetos.com"

GUN

A Hoboken Homicide Novel

Sean Lennon

authorHOUSE

AuthorHouse™
1663 Liberty Drive
Bloomington, IN 47403
www.authorhouse.com
Phone: 1 (800) 839-8640

© 2018 Sean Lennon. All rights reserved.

Cover layout by Lucky Revilleza

No part of this book may be reproduced, stored in a retrieval system, or transmitted by any means without the written permission of the author.

Published by AuthorHouse 06/27/2018

ISBN: 978-1-5462-4889-7 (sc)
ISBN: 978-1-5462-4890-3 (hc)
ISBN: 978-1-5462-4888-0 (e)

Library of Congress Control Number: 2018907561

Print information available on the last page.

Any people depicted in stock imagery provided by Getty Images are models, and such images are being used for illustrative purposes only.
Certain stock imagery © Getty Images.

This book is printed on acid-free paper.

Because of the dynamic nature of the Internet, any web addresses or links contained in this book may have changed since publication and may no longer be valid. The views expressed in this work are solely those of the author and do not necessarily reflect the views of the publisher, and the publisher hereby disclaims any responsibility for them.

Dedication:

To Alex, my greatest creation, and Bob Lennon, this one's for you, Sparky.

Enrique Perez was both nervous and excited as he stepped through the doorway of the cold and dimly lit garage of the Academy Bus Lines Company. His cousin, Wilfredo, entered behind him, checking out his surroundings like an animal searching for prey. Inside the garage, other members of the Latin Soldados were already looking around, checking for any surprises while the members of the Hoboken Irish gang, The Jackals, looked on. Enrique noticed the Jackals' second in command, Liam Dillon, as well as the general of the Soldados, Roberto Cruz. Some of the men in his family, such as his now deceased uncle and grandfather, had been members of the main gang in Hoboken, New Jersey. The gang had made Hoboken its home since the late 70s. His father, though, was an exception. Emilio Perez was a hard-working man and pushed his ideals onto Enrique and his sister, Maritza, but Enrique saw the life that Willie had lived and the money that he had thrown around. A life of not having to bust his ass just to be middle class was extremely tempting for the teenager.

The Academy garage on Jefferson Street was lit with the occasional florescent light. The company had planted itself in Hoboken back in the 1930s when the original owner was running his lone bus route. Academy's ownership stayed in the family so that the great-grandson now ran things, bringing travelers from Hoboken to Jersey City, Union City, North Bergen and even providing charters to Atlantic City. The Soldados had made use of it from time to time, thanks to the not-so-agreeable manager of it. And being in the shadow of the Viaduct that led from Jersey City to Hoboken, it was out of the public eye. The only interruption was the recently created light rail train that went from the main station, behind the town and over to Lincoln Harbor.

Wilfredo nodded his head to the side to guide Enrique to where he should stand and be quiet. Enrique kept silent and put down the bag that he had been told to hold. Wilfredo shook his head and looked down at the bag. Enrique got the hint and picked the bag back up. Standing there, quietly, he looked around. Against the wall where the side entrance was, stood rows of shelves. On the shelves were thin plastic bins, each holding a different screw or piece of machinery that helped to make the bus engines whole. Behind him, were scattered pallets of boxes and larger parts. Near the pallets were lifts for the buses so that the mechanics could work under the vehicles. Bus seats were lined against the opposite side of the grimy and cold garage. He noticed the strong scent of the three coffee companies directly across the side street of the garage.

Robbie Cruz of the Latin Soldados walked over to Dillon and shook hands like two businessmen. It was strange for Enrique to see considering that they were both in gangs struggling to hold their own side in the riverside town. The Jackals made their entrance into Hoboken in the late 90s and at first, their appearance brought stress into Hoboken's City Hall. It was bad enough that there was one gang in what is known as the Mile Square City, but both gangs managed to be civil and divided the town down the middle. It remained peaceful between them to this day.

"Yo, s'up, D?" Cruz asked his competition. Dillon blew smoke out of the side of his mouth and shrugged.

"I don't know about you, but I just want to get this over, so I can get back."

"I hear ya. Where is this guy?" Cruz turned and looked over at Wilfredo and Enrique. He jerked his head up slightly, giving the signal to bring the sport bags that they held over to him. Wilfredo and Enrique brought the two bags over and placed them on the long wood table between the two gangs. Roberto kept the bags on their side of the table while Dillon had his men bring their two bags over.

"Who are they waiting for?" Enrique asked his cousin in a whisper.

"Guy from out of town is bringing in a shipment of guns," Wilfredo explained, "He's going to auction them off to the highest bidder."

The two gangs stood there for two minutes, talking among themselves, before the door opened and a lone figure walked in. Enrique noticed that the man wore a suit that reminded him of the men he saw walking around Wall Street. He thought it was one of those Armani suits that he heard about so much. The aviator sunglasses and the NY Yankees ball cap stood out from it.

"You the negotiator?" Dillon asked.

"Yes and no," the man answered. Cruz and Dillon looked at each other, trying to figure out his answer.

"What the fuck's that mean?" Cruz questioned him. Enrique saw Cruz's hand duck under his shirt and grab hold of the gun in his waistband. He didn't take it out, but he was ready to defend himself against the mystery man.

"Yes, I set this meeting up and no, it was not to sell guns."

"What are you talking about?" One of the Jackals asked.

"Who is this fool?" Wilfredo threw out there, interested in the outcome of the scene in front of him.

"Call me Hermes," the man said.

"Herpes? Your name is Herpes?" joked a Jackal. The other gang members began laughing. Some pointed at the stranger and made faces. The stranger began to join in and laughed himself. His laugh overwhelmed the garage until his laughter turned into a coughing fit. He hunched over, the sunglasses falling off his face. Cruz took a step forward, wondering if the man was going to fall over and die on them.

Then everything for Enrique happened in the blink of an eye. The stranger bolted up straight, in his hand was an automatic submachine gun. Enrique was surprised because the gun appeared out of thin air. Cruz, the closest to him, felt nothing as the first bullet from the Italian Spectre M4 travelled through his forehead and exited violently out of the back of his skull. The stranger moved with lightning speed, pulling the trigger over and over providing short bursts from the silencer attached to the front of the barrel. Gang members either fell to the concrete ground, dead, or scrambled for cover.

But the man barely moved from his spot. When the gun's clip was empty, it magically dropped to the ground and he slammed another clip in before the last one stopped bouncing.

"Run!" Wilfredo told Enrique. Enrique's body finally reacted, and he ducked behind one of the shelves. He turned around when he felt safe only to see Wilfredo's body on the floor. Half of his face was gone. *I have to get out of here,* he thought, unable to fight back the urge to vomit. When he finished wiping the drool from his lip, Enrique used the noise of the guns expelling bullets to run from one stray pallet to another. Although he was curious as to who was left, he knew better than to look behind him, and his fear forced him to continue running away.

He ducked behind a pallet of cardboard boxes and found a man on the ground, bleeding from the chest. It sounded as if he was breathing through the hole in his chest - it made Enrique cringe. He didn't know the man but figured he was one of the Jackals. The man reached up at Enrique, looking for help. He gurgled something that the teen could not make out.

Then Enrique saw the gun lying a few feet from the wounded man and his adrenaline took over, he grabbed the gun with both hands and turned around.

A back door! The teen's eyes glanced at his salvation, but he took the risk, running full speed to the door. He knew that just beyond it was freedom from the nightmare going on behind him. Not caring about the noise, it made, he threw himself into the door and it gave way, opening out into the cold darkness of the night. Snow was gently falling, a peaceful feel compared to what lie inside the garage.

The back door led out onto Madison Street, under the viaduct and twenty feet from the light rail tracks. Enrique headed for the tracks and decided to follow them south, out of the warehouse area and into the housing neighborhood.

Don't look back, he told himself. *Just run.*

What felt like minutes were only seconds. Enrique ran until he was about to collapse from the exhaustion. He stopped to catch his breath, feeling like he was halfway home and looked up. A hundred yards ahead of him was the 9th Street station of the light rail train. He had only run five blocks. There were still another seven blocks separating him from his home. His lungs burned from the cold air.

Enrique turned and looked behind him. The night remained silent except for his heavy breathing and the thumping of his heart in his ears. He had to keep going in case whoever shot everyone in the garage decided to come for him. But if Enrique had known that he would never make it home that night, he'd have done things differently.

One

A FINE MESS

1

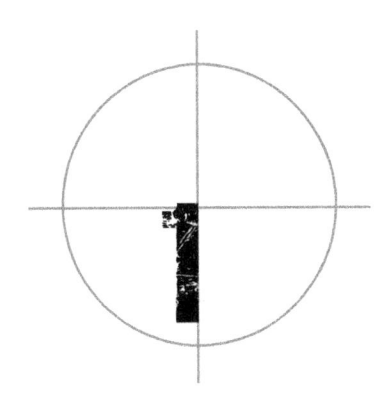

"Raghetti," Josh said into his cell phone. The Hoboken detective stood on line at Jersey City's Newport Centre Mall with his 5-year-old daughter, Tamara. He had planned to get here as early as possible, but being a week from Christmas, so did half of the population of Jersey City, Union City and Hoboken. The line for Santa Claus was not as bad as it was the night before, but it was still longer than he liked.

"Hey Raghetti, Bergen here. Did I catch you at a bad time?"

"Depends what your definition of a bad time is. I'm two people away from getting my daughter on Santa's lap."

"Where at?"

"Newport." Josh held his breath, knowing what was coming.

"A week before Christmas? What are you, insane?"

"I must be," Josh replied, looking around for a place to buy a coffee. He knew Lyndsay Bergen didn't call him for a social chat. Bergen was one of the other homicide detectives in Hoboken and they had worked together now and then but nothing big. Not since the Doug Martin case, anyway. She had previously been known to her friends and coworkers as Moskin but a couple of months ago had divorced her husband of two years when she found him in the bed of another woman. Lyndsey quickly changed her name back to Bergen and was enjoying the single life once again.

"Daddy, we're next!" Tamara giggled. She had been excited all week to visit Santa that no matter what Bergen wanted, he wasn't leaving the mall until she spoke to the jolly fat man.

"I know, honey," he said, smiling at her. The excitement on her face was worth the wait.

"Anyway, Stanton was just here in the precinct looking for you."

"Why?"

"He never said. But I think he was looking for something."

"Well, if you run into him again, just give him Foster's number. I know if I talk to him, he'll just go on and on about the latest hockey game."

"No problem. And good luck with the crowd, you nut."

"It's too late for me. I've been assimilated."

"That's too bad," Bergen joked, "All the good ones are taken."

Santa said goodbye to the child that was in front of him. Tamara smiled and looked up at Josh. Staring into her eyes, he was reminded of his ex-wife, Angelica.

He remembered that sparkle in his ex-wife's brown eyes that took him away from the job. It was one of the reasons that made him propose to her. Having Tamara was one of the greatest days in his life. But since, the job had been too taxing on his marriage and he found himself drinking to rid his head of the crime scenes and the stress.

It wasn't until last summer that he had to adjust even further. His partner, Brett Foster, had announced to him that he and Angie had recently gotten intimate after the divorce. The thought of Angie being with someone else was infuriating and he let Brett know with a punch to the face. Angie had come to him later and they had talked it out. In the end, he had given them his blessing, knowing that she was happy with his partner.

Still, seeing them together wasn't easy and being a middle-aged cop in a town of college students, bars and big families only made him lonelier. But he knew if he had been able to win over Angie, there was bound to be someone else out there willing to put up with his shit.

"Do you think he'll say I was good, Daddy?" she asked him.

"I'm sure he will, hon. Now go say hi to him."

Tamara ran up to Santa and gave him a hug. The mall Santa lifted her up and placed her on his lap. Josh stood there listening to his daughter as she gave a long speech on how she had been a good girl all year and helped her mother when it was just the two of them. The Santa laughed and finally managed to ask her what she had wanted.

"I would like the My Little Pony Play Stable!"

"Well, I think for a nice girl like you I can make that happen," said the mall Santa.

"Oh, and I would like to have a second Mommy, so my Daddy isn't so lonely." The statement shocked both Josh and the mall Santa. Santa looked up and at Josh. Raghetti, suddenly speechless, just shrugged his shoulders.

"Ummm, I will see what I can do about that," Santa replied to Tamara, "Here, why don't you take an extra candy cane for your Dad, too."

"Thanks Santa!" Tamara hopped off Santa's lap, took two candy canes from the female elf and handed one to Josh.

"Why don't we go get some hot chocolate?" he asked her, quickly walking away from the giggling crowd with his wise-beyond-her-years daughter.

An hour later, Josh and his partner, Brett Foster, walked into the bus garage, looking for Jeff Stanton from Anti-Vice. After leaving the mall, Josh and Tamara had driven to the Waterford Deli and met up with Angie and Brett. Brett told Josh about Stanton calling him and needing some help with a case that Hoboken Police Chief Christine Black assigned him. After getting Tamara some hot chocolate like he promised, Angie took Tamara home and the two detectives drove to the scene of the latest crime.

Looking around, Foster saw Anti-Vice officers, Mark Doyle and Luis Orlando. He walked over to the two and said hello. Doyle was your typical old school Irish cop: his salt and pepper hair was cropped with the old front swoop over his forehead. His thin clean-shaven face showed his dedicated years on the force in wrinkles. His mouth was usually holding a cigarette. Orlando was the opposite. His slightly plump Cuban features were decorated with a sharp mustache and goatee beard. His short hair stood up in small spikes with the help of some gel.

"Where's Stanton?" he asked.

"He had to run," Doyle replied, "Got called off for a drug overdose. Lucky bastard."

"So, what the hell happened here?" Raghetti piped up. He saw the bloody scattered bodies of gang members. Hoboken Forensic examiners, Lucky and Melvin, were collecting photos and bullet casings. Lots of bullet casings.

"Quite the shit storm," Orlando replied. He pointed to the left side of the Homicide detectives. "Over here, you've got members of the Latin Soldados. Note the black wardrobe. And to the right are members of The Jackals, wearing a lovely Shamrock green. So far, it seems that we've got a meeting gone wrong. We're still working on figuring out who shot first. But I'm not envying the M.E. He's got some overtime coming."

Brett squatted down to look at one of the Soldados members. Using his gloves, he turned the face to the side, getting a better look. "This is a pretty clean shot. Looks like he was close to whoever shot him."

"We've got a circle of shell casings here," Melvin piped up, "They all look like 9 by 19mms. Most likely from the same weapon - a submachine gun."

"I'm not finding one, though," Lucky added.

"That means we've got one guy standing right here shooting all around and then walking away?" Josh asked them.

"No way one guy could have taken out all these gang members by himself and walked away," Doyle said.

"Could have just started it and let them finish each other off."

"We'll know more once everything is recorded."

The scene ate at Foster's gut. There was something not right about it. Something was missing. He began to wander around, looking for something, anything. He peeked around the flipped over tables and the shelves, searching for a clue or a sign as to the truth of what had occurred here hours before.

"Bathroom's over this way," Luis joked.

"That's not what I'm looking for," Brett replied, straight-faced.

"What's up his butt?"

"He's working," Raghetti explained. Having been partners for so many years, Josh and Brett knew each other's styles. Josh liked to sit back and view it all in at once while Brett got his hands dirty getting right into the scene. It was from the training that his father provided to him when he had first started as a police officer in Jersey City. Blue blood ran through the Foster family.

Brett turned and walked around the pallets behind them. He slowly headed for a pallet stacked with cardboard boxes. He examined the boxes for bullet holes and found two on the north side of the pallet. Then he looked around the side and stopped. He leaned over and studied what had caught his eye.

"Hey Doyle, Orlando, did you see this?" Brett called out. His partner followed the two Anti-Vice detectives over to the pallet and looked behind it. On the ground was a middle-aged man with a bullet wound in his chest. Doyle scrunched his forehead and looked over at Foster.

"Who the fuck is that?"

2

"Hey, Melvin, can you come here, please?" Raghetti called the forensic examiner over. Melvin looked up from photographing one of the Latin Soldados members and walked over. He peeked around the pallet and saw the dead man lying alone. The man was white with a neat trim haircut. He was wearing a royal blue buttoned down shirt under a faded brown bomber jacket with blue jeans and hiking shoes. It was not an outfit any of the gang members would have been wearing.

"Who's he?" Melvin asked them.

"It's Santa," Doyle answered sarcastically.

"We were hoping you could tell us," Brett responded.

"Let me get my print kit." Melvin walked over to his Forensic case. The slim and bushy haired F.E. grabbed a small black box and returned to the mysterious body. He took several photographs of the body, preserving the scene before searching the clothing.

"He's too old to be a gang banger," Orlando observed, "And he's not wearing either of the colors."

"Innocent bystander working late and caught in the crossfire?" Brett threw out there.

"Could be. But his hands are too clean to have been working on engines," Doyle said.

"We should have one of the officers contact the owner to see if he can ID him."

Raghetti waved over one of uniformed officers that were holding the scene. A female cop walked over to see what Josh needed. Josh noticed

8

the badge read: S. KASSEN. She looked young to be a cop, Josh thought, glancing at her freckled face. She must have been one of the new officers that were just added to the force a month prior.

"Officer Kassen, we need you to contact Salvatore, the owner of Academy Buses and let him know that we need him to identify one of the victims. We believe he might have been an employee or something who got caught in the crossfire."

"Sure thing, detective." Officer Kassen turned, her long reddish-brown ponytail whipped around as she headed back outside to her cruiser.

"Wait a second," Luis said, "What if this is the lone gunman?"

"Where's his gun?"

"Maybe he dropped it somewhere around here, trying to get away."

"Where the hell was he going?" Doyle asked. Orlando pointed behind Brett to the back door that was slightly ajar, a small pile of snow gathering in the sliver of an opening.

"Hey Doyle, come with me," Brett asked, heading for the back door. Doyle followed his fellow Homicide detective to the door. Foster slowly opened the door, revealing the cold grey night sky. He saw the partially covered sneaker prints in the snow leading away from the back door headed east towards Madison Street.

"Looks like we've got a live one," Doyle muttered.

"Can you also check his hands for GPR?" Josh asked Melvin. Melvin nodded without looking up while he blotted the mysterious victim's fingertips with black ink. Gun Powder Residue could tell them whether the victim had fired a gun recently.

"Any chance I could get you to call Wogle for some help? This is a lot to cover for just two guys." Melvin asked Raghetti. Mike Wogle, head of the crime lab unit in Hoboken, was known to be a bit of a hard ass but was also to be oddly known by most of the cops in the precinct as a "Chick magnet". Josh didn't quite understand why but accepted it.

"Don't worry, I'll give him a call before we're done looking it over."

"Thanks, Raghetti."

"This doesn't make any sense," Orlando told Josh.

"Sometimes it's the ones that appear not to make any sense that end up completely reasonable."

"Yeah, thanks for the fortune cookie talk."

"Well, ok, so let's review. We've got a group of Latin Soldados and Jackals in one place. Why?"

"A meeting, of course. And a big one according to the fact that Robbie Cruz was present."

"Ok, so what could the meeting be about?"

"Um, negotiating, perhaps. Or could have been about territory crossing."

"What's territory crossing?"

"When one gang contacts another gang so that the they can briefly enter the second gang's territory to grab something or someone."

"Alright, that's a possibility. Now we throw in the X factor. Mister Bullseye. Who would interrupt a meeting between two gangs to kill them all?"

"Well, it could, um, nah." Orlando stopped.

"What?"

"A third gang? Trying to move in and take over?"

"Have you guys heard anything about something like that?"

"No, I mean it's been pretty quiet the last few weeks between these two. With the number of informants Anti-Vice has, one of us would have heard something."

"We're going to have to figure this out fast. A gang war the week before Christmas is not going to be good for the city."

"Damn," Orlando did not like the thought of that. Before the two could continue the conversation, they were distracted by shouting from the front entrance of the garage. They looked over and saw that one man was trying to get into the garage but was being held back by two officers.

"Aw, crap," Luis said shaking his head.

"What?" Josh asked.

"It's Vinnie freakin' Donnelly."

3

The two detectives followed the faint prints to the tracks of the lightrail. The further they went, the tougher it was to see the tracks thanks to the thick falling snow. Doyle zipped his winter parka up to his neck and shoved his hands into his pockets. It had been a calm winter up until two days ago when a winter chill came over the Tri-state area. The weatherman had recently warned of a possible heavy snow fall.

"This weather sucks," Doyle complained.

"I heard that up in Boston, they got hit with 3 feet of snow. Just remember that this could be worse."

"And I could be in Hawaii."

"That's what I like about you, Doyle, always the optimist."

"I do always search for that silver lining."

Foster continued following the faint tracks south along the light rail route. He was still thinking about the scene that they had just left and tried imaging what had happened there.

"You know this incident is only going to be trouble," Doyle told Brett.

"Are you thinking gang war?"

"Yep. Of course, you've got two different gangs and two different minds running each."

"How do you mean?"

"Well you've got the Latin Soldados. They're run by Julio Jimenez. Smart man, clever and strategic. He plans everything out before he does it. For him it's not about the violence, it's about taking care of their own. They're mainly focused on the families and their Hispanic neighbors.

They are willing to help them out beyond what the police can do. Thus, the name, Soldados. Or Soldiers for all you non-Spanish speaking peons. Him, I'm not worried about. He would think twice about his profits before doing anything. It's the Jackals. They're run by Vinnie Donnelly. The guy's nuts. Clinically. He'd have the whole city burned to the ground by now if it wasn't for his second in command, Liam Dillon. Dillon keeps Donnelly docile and in check. He does the dirty work. Jimenez knows that, too."

"You think Donnelly may have done this?"

"Not sure. Don't know if he has it in him to sacrifice his own men to get to Cruz. It would explain how the shooter was able to walk in without getting stopped and it would be a strong move for the Jackals, if Dillon didn't know about it."

Doyle looked up and saw the 9th Street station half a block ahead of them. He tapped Brett in the arm and pointed ahead. Brett smiled, hoping that the trail of footprints led to a parking spot. He knew the parking lot would have security cameras. If the tracks vanished they could still request the footage to see who left the trail of prints. The tracks led to the platform and then disappeared in a dry area. Brett and Doyle looked around and were unable to discern the specific tracks from the numerous ones made in the last few hours.

"That's the end of that. At least we can get the footage to see who walked away from the shootout." Brett looked up and smiled at the camera pointed in their direction.

"Talk about luck," Doyle added. Brett pulled out his iPhone and dialed the front desk of the precinct. After a few rings, the new desk sergeant, Danny Hines, answered.

"Hey Hines, it's Foster, I need the number of the head of Lightrail security."

"Hey Foster. Yeah, give me a minute and I'll look that up for you." Brett waited and listened to the tapping of the keys while Hines accessed the information. Hines began singing in a whisper to himself one of the classic songs from the 1950's that he was known to hum while working the desk. Even though Foster was in his early 40s, the songs that Hines belted out were unknown to him.

"Here we are," Danny said. He provided the number to Brett.

"Thanks, Danny."

"Anytime, Brett!" Danny said before hanging up.

"That Hines is too damn happy to be a cop," Doyle joked.

"Tell me about it." Foster dialed the number and spoke to someone to request the footage for the 9th Street station. The head of security informed him that the footage for all the cameras ran on a 24-hour loop, giving Brett surveillance of the station from yesterday afternoon to that moment. That was perfect for seeing who was on the platform last night. He jotted down the address of where the tape could be picked up and thanked the guard.

"I'll swing down there after we get back," Foster told Doyle.

"Better head back and see if they found anything else." Foster and Doyle walked back the way they came. "How's that whole thing with Raghetti's ex going?"

"It's not as awkward as it sounds. Josh has gotten used to it, were just worried about his daughter and her reaction to it."

"Must have freaked her out."

"Surprisingly, no. She's pretty smart for her age. Sometimes a little *too* smart."

"Yeah, wait until she hits her teens. Those are the 'fun' years," Doyle reported sarcastically.

"It's actually not too bad being a 'second father'. A year ago, I would have told you that I'd never had kids in a world like this. But I've changed since Angie and I have gotten together."

"It's a different story when they're yours, though. You try to make up for the things your parents did but only end up realizing that you're just like them. And then you see that they were doing what's right."

"Well it's only been a few months since we first started this relationship, so the future hasn't been brought up, but it's better than going home to an empty apartment every evening."

"Very true."

The two turned the corner to the block of the garage and Doyle stopped short.

"Aw, shit," he said, running his hand across his balding head.

"What?" Brett looked over at the garage, wondering what Doyle had seen that he was missing.

"See the green Cadillac over there?"

"Yeah, who's it belong to?"

"Vinnie freakin' Donnelly."

Brett and Doyle walked into the garage and the yelling match between Donnelly and Raghetti and Orlando. Vinnie Donnelly was slim, wearing a green leather jacket and long droopy jeans that revealed the top of his plaid boxers. Brett saw the bulging veins in Donnelly's neck and the red coloring of his face below the blonde crew cut and realized the frustration that Doyle conveyed when he saw the car. Donnelly was definitely going to be trouble.

"Hey, hey, hey," Doyle shouted, "Enough! Vinnie, what are you doing here?"

The trio quieted down like children that were in trouble. Vinnie took a deep breath and then turned to Doyle.

"I was looking for my guys and I'm now wondering who did that to them," he said, pointing at the dead Jackal members.

"First, you're not allowed into the crime scene until after we've examined the area. Secondly, shouting at us isn't going to get you answers."

"Yeah well if these two weren't trying to knock me down when I walked in –"

"Actually," Luis interrupted, "House of Pain here came barging in and knocked over one of the officers at the door."

"Whatever happened, you still know better Vinnie. Now, are you by yourself?"

"Yeah."

"Okay, and where's Liam?"

"He's right over there," Vinnie pointed to one of the dead bodies lying on the floor twenty feet away.

"Oh crap," the four detectives said in unison.

4

"Maritza! Please let the dog out! I'm trying to make some enchiladas for the bake sale tomorrow." Carmen Perez yelled to her daughter from the kitchen of their home on Garden Street. Their dog, a Bischon Friese named Gizmo, sat at the back door in the kitchen, yipping every few seconds to get someone's attention. The house sat in the middle of the block among the other two-story homes. Her red brick with white trim house had been in her family since her parents had bought it when Carmen was a teenager. They had left her the home in their will. Carmen was grateful that she and her husband could move into from the tiny apartment that they were in at the time.

"I'm busy! Tell Enrique to do it!" Maritza yelled from her bedroom. Carmen sighed. Maritza had been recently hanging out with the popular girls in her class and has been trying on makeup and shrinking her clothes, so they were tight. *Where did I go wrong?* She thought. When she was young, it wasn't all about tight clothing and how much bare skin you showed. Raising children in today's world was more work than enjoyment.

"Enrique is still sleeping. It's not going to kill you."

"Mom! Jesse is telling me what happened with her boyfriend! God, why do I have to be the servant around here?"

"Dios mio, give me strength," Carmen sighed, looking up to the ceiling.

Her husband, Emilio, entered the kitchen, still brushing off snow from his coat. The tall bulky man leaned over and opened the back door for Gizmo. The dog bolted out the door and into a snow drift, digging his way through the white powder.

"It's starting to come down harder," he told her, "I'll probably have to shovel again by dinner."

"You should ask Enrique to help you. You know what that does to your lower back."

"Is he still sleeping?"

"He hasn't poked his head out of his room since I woke up."

"He'd sleep until 4P.M. if we let him. I'll get him up." Emilio took off his coat, placed it on the back of a kitchen chair and walked back to the living room and up the stairs. He had worked hard to have a home of his own where his family did not have to worry about hearing neighbors through the walls. His job with the city wasn't the best paying, but it took care of the bills.

He knocked on Enrique's door and waited, allowing his son the respect of privacy that most parents did not give their kids. The room beyond the door was dead silent. It was then that he realized that he did not remember hearing Enrique come home last night.

Emilio knocked again, harder and gave him a few seconds to respond. Still no reply from inside the bedroom. He turned the knob and called into the room, "Enrique, it's time for you to get up." Again, no answer. Emilio opened the door wide and saw that the bed was empty. Where was he? Emilio returned to the kitchen.

"Did you hear Enrique come in last night?" he asked Carmen.

"No, I went to sleep before you did, why? Where is he?"

"I don't know. Where's the phone?"

"Over there," Carmen pointed to the far corner of the kitchen counter. She began pacing around the kitchen. She did that whenever she became worried or stressed. Noticing it and thinking that she was worrying over nothing, Emilio grabbed the cordless phone and pressed the talk button. The phone beeped once, informing him that the line was already in use. Maritza was on the phone again.

"Mari! I need to use the phone!" he yelled to the second floor. He was answered with a slam of her bedroom door. Carmen sighed. "That girl is looking for a grounding," he growled.

Emilio reached over to his coat and pulled his cell phone out of the front pocket and called Enrique. He listened to the ringing and ringing with it eventually reaching his voice mail message. He looked over at Carmen and saw his wife's worried face waiting for good news. He ended the call without leaving a message.

"No answer."

"Where would he be? Do you think something happened to him?"

"I don't know, Mami." Emilio kept his concern hidden from Carmen, he didn't want to worry her even more. This wasn't like his son. Something had happened to Enrique. Carmen's panic began seeping into his head.

Emilio placed the phone on the kitchen table and silently returned upstairs. Without knocking, he opened the door of Maritza's room and walked in.

"DAD! I'm on the phone!" Maritza was draped across her bed, but suddenly shot up in surprise. Her father had never just barged into her room before.

"Where is your brother?" he asked her sternly.

"I dunno."

"Call his friends and find out."

"I don't know his friends. They're all dorks."

"Then give me the phone."

"But I'm talking to Jesse."

Emilio reached out and wrestled the phone from her hands. He hit the END button on it and began going through the Caller ID to see if Enrique had called. There was nothing.

"Ow, what the hell?"

"Where does he hang out?"

"What? Why? What did he do?"

"Tell me!"

"Geez, calm down. My God."

"Your brother did not come home last night. Tell me where he went."

"Wait, what?" Maritza then stopped arguing, realizing the seriousness of the situation.

"Where was he going last night?"

"I don't know, for real."

"Emilio?" Carmen said from the doorway of her daughter's bedroom.

Emilio refused to turn around to face her. They all stood there in silence, unsure of what to do or say.

The phone in his hand broke the silence with a ring. He looked down at the phone, afraid of it and the news that it may bring. The Caller ID read UNKNOWN. The ringing continued as Emilio fought for courage to press the TALK button. It felt like an hour in-between each ring. If he didn't answer, it would just go to voice mail. He was afraid of who was on the other side of the call. Was it someone telling him that Enrique had been taken? Was it someone calling to inform him that his good son was dead? Dozens of scenarios ran through Emilio's mind. He pictured Enrique alone, injured, needing his help. Emilio had never felt this helpless before. He pressed the button and brought the phone shaking to his ear.

"Hello?" he asked into the phone. There was a moment of silence on the other line before a voice spoke into his ear.

"Dad?"

5

Jacob Scott exited the elevator of the Harborside Financial Center building where his law firm resided on the riverside of Exchange Place in Jersey City, just south of the Newport Centre Mall. It was a grey Monday morning; the snow having stopped overnight. Jacob walked up to the front desk where the main receptionist, Abigail Jamison, sat with a smile. Abigail was a mousy woman with dirty blonde hair and dressed in outfits that Jacob had thought a school teacher from the 1920s would have worn.

"Good morning, Jacob. I've got a message from Chris Thompson for you. He's waiting for your call." She reached over the desk and handed him the yellow message slip. He took it from her and nodded.

"Morning Abby, thank you. How was the drive in this morning?"

"It wasn't so bad. But I heard that there's going to be lots more snow falling later this week."

"Funny how as a kid you look forward to the snow but as an adult you end up cringing at the mention of the word."

"You never had to dig your car out of a bank when you were a kid."

"Good point. Have a good morning."

Jacob continued to his office and was halted again by Christopher Delgado, the fellow lawyer turned recent partner who Jacob was working under now. Delgado had a smile on his face, which to Jacob was an abnormal thing. Delgado was all about business. He stood there, slightly shorter than Jacob, with a permanent five o'clock shadow, dark close-cut hair and a stare that only a hard ass boss could have been born with.

"Jacob, good morning. I want to introduce you to our new member of the firm, Ronald Price. He'll be taking over Doug's office and will be helping out in any way possible." Delgado patted Price on the back while he said this.

"Welcome to the firm, Ronald. We're always looking for new and bright talent to join us in our crusade." Jacob shook the hand of the young man in front of him. Ronald Price had a model face. His smooth skin had not a hint of facial hair and the hair on his head was teased just enough to still look professional and rebel-like. Jacob also noticed the slight bulge of muscles under the sleeves of Ronald's suit jacket.

"Thanks, Jacob. Chris has told me a lot about you."

"I'll tell you all of the good stuff later," Jacob joked. Ron laughed, and Delgado scowled at Scott.

"Price. Why does that sound familiar?"

"You've probably have heard about my father, Donald Price. Police Commissioner of Hoboken? His Take Back Your City Initiative?"

"Yes," Jacob replied, "I have. He may have something good there for the city."

Donald Price had been the Police Commissioner of Hoboken for the past six years, preceding the now retired Earl Lisbone. Price had quickly jumped into the shoes that Earl left and helped revamp the police force in the small city. Hoboken Mayor Ray Victor had been pleased with the changes and its results. Since then, Hoboken had flourished, bringing in more families and changing the stereotype that the city was a college town, while Steven's Institute of Technology still called Hoboken home and thrived. Recently, Price had decided to work on ridding his city of the gang population. With Ray Victor's help, they came up with the Taking Back Your City Initiative. It allowed Hoboken residents the ability to help police by informing a hotline of any crimes and/or gang activity.

"He's very excited about it and is hoping it catches on with the number of families that live there now."

"Right, not so much a College Bar town anymore."

"Jacob, I'd like you to look over your caseload and see if there is anything that Ronald can assist you with," Delgado broke into the conversation. "You know, so we can have him dive right in."

"Sure. I'll have Robin go through what I currently have going."

"Well, I'm sure you have cases to deal with, I'll let you go. But I look forward to working with you."

"Thanks Ron, enjoy your day." Jacob winked at Delgado and Chris paused, not sure how to take the wink. Jacob walked away, letting it sink in. He enjoyed teasing Delgado. It made the day more enjoyable.

Reaching his office, he found his legal assistant and present girlfriend, Robin Masters, hard at work. Robin was typing away a letter for one of his clients that were coming in tomorrow. She had her shoulder length blonde hair in a bun this morning revealing her slender neck. Jacob always found it sexy.

"Missed you this morning," he said, approaching her desk.

"I knew if I stayed, we'd both still be there right now, and you have a full day ahead of you that you can't miss."

"Well, you can't say you wouldn't be enjoying the day off." He smirked. She gave him a sultry look from the side and then continued the letter.

Jacob's life in the last few months had gotten better after the incident with the Craig Waterford case. An old friend from college, Craig was framed for murder. The web of deceit led to the law firm, Hoffman and Reynolds, as Reynolds, now dead, had worked with the previous governor to ruin Craig's life. And with the opening of the partner spot, the remaining partner, Hoffman, gave the spot to Delgado, telling Jacob that he wanted him on the front lines because that was where he'd continue doing the best he could for the firm.

Jacob's relationship with Robin began during Craig's case and had gotten serious since. Robin was spending more time at Jacob's place and they were talking about her just moving in. Robin had no problem giving up her apartment to stay in Jacob's nice home.

He sat down at his desk and placed the day's events out in front of him. There was the case of two neighbors and the demise of one neighbor's faithful Rottweiler. There was the case of Miss Page and her stolen personal property that had been found in the shed of her co-worker. And finally, a molestation case that was open and shut thanks to a video tape showing that the accused was mistaken for someone else.

Jacob opened the first file with the two neighbors and looked it over for court this afternoon. He managed to get through the first page of the file before his phone rang. He glanced over and saw that it was Kristie Marks, ex-paralegal for friend and co-worker, Doug Martin.

"Morning Marks."

"Yo Scott. We still on for the last-minute cram session?"

"Absolutely, Robin and I are looking forward to having you, Dean and Connor over for dinner and then we can go over whatever you're needing help with for tomorrow."

"That'll be a big help. I'm so nervous."

"Everyone going for the Bar is a nervous wreck. As long as you know your stuff it'll be fine."

Jacob was kind of proud of Kristie and how far she'd come in the last several months. After the lawyer she worked for was murdered, Kristie came into her own and decided to make more of her life by taking the next step and was now taking the Bar. Dean, her fiancé, and Connor, her son, were behind her all the way. And with Jacob and Hoffman's help, she would be ready for test day. She had told them to not hold back and so he would honor her request and push her to be the best.

"Awesome. Thanks Jacob, you rule."

"Yeah I know. Just don't let anyone else know that."

Jacob hung up the phone and returned to the open case that lay on his desk. He read about how Mr. Court had owned a Rottweiler and had left his dog in the backyard overnight, where it's continuous barking had annoyed his neighbor, Mr. Hansen. Mr. Hansen had filed several complaints with the police but after filing his fifth and seeing that Mr. Court was only being fined for the late-night disturbing, he decided to take matters into his own hands. The next morning, Mr. Court went to bring his dog in and found it lying dead on the back porch. A local vet confirmed that the dog had ingested small meatballs laced with rat poison. Heartbroken, Mr. Court walked into the newly named Hoffman and Delgado the same day to sue his neighbor.

Jacob noticed that the statements showed that Mr. Hansen said that he had made five calls to the police, but he only had two complaint forms in the file. He stood up and stepped out of his office to speak to Robin.

"Hey Robin, can you please contact the Hoboken precinct and find out how many official complaints they have on file for Mr. Hansen about Mr. Court's dog?"

"Sure. Give me five minutes and I can do that."

"Thanks." Jacob went to turn back into his office but saw Allan Hoffman, the senior partner of the firm, walked past his office. Hoffman stopped when he saw Jacob and entered Robin's area. He smiled gently and reached out to shake Jacob's hand. Allen Hoffman was a short Jewish man who normally had a warm smile on his face outside of the courtroom. He always looked out for his employees and made them feel valued at the firm.

"Hello, Jacob, how was your weekend?"

"Good morning, Mr. Hoffman. It was a nice quiet weekend, thank you."

"All ready for the holiday?"

"Surprisingly, yes. Miss Masters here has no idea what she's getting." Robin looked up at the two men and smiled.

"The same goes for Mr. Scott, too" she added. Hoffman laughed.

"You two remind me of the wife and myself when we were young. That was 48 years now. And I still get that flutter in my stomach when I look into her eyes. Never take what you have for granted," he said, pointing at the two of them.

The moment was interrupted by a burly middle-aged man following Abigail. It appeared to Jacob that the man had walked past Abby and was looking for someone or something. He had a panicked look in his eyes and Jacob wondered if they were in danger.

"Are you Jacob Scott?" the man asked through deep breaths. Abby came from behind the man and stopped.

"I'm sorry," she told him, "He was adamant about seeing you."

"That's fine, Abby. Yes, I am Jacob Scott. Is there something I can do for you?"

"My name is Emilio Perez. Please, my son needs your help."

6

"Okay, Mr. Perez, why don't you come into my office and I can see what I can do to help your son."

"I'm sorry, but I don't know what else to do."

"That's fine. Did you want something to drink?"

"Just some water, please."

"I have some inside." Jacob motioned to Emilio to enter his office. As he did, he looked over at Robin and she tapped her ear twice. It was code for her to keep an ear out for the safety word if something were to go wrong whenever Jacob was in his office with a possible hostile client. It was something they had worked out when Robin was hired. Jacob's job and the location of the firm gave many people reason to assault him. Jacob looked back at her and shook his head. He did not know Emilio Perez or his son, but he felt that he was not in any danger from the beefy man.

"Need anything?" Hoffman asked Jacob. Jacob smiled and gave a thumbs up to the senior partner. Hoffman nodded and watched Jacob follow Emilio Perez into his office. When the door closed behind them, he turned to Robin.

"Please let me know if everything goes ok."

"Absolutely, Mr. Hoffman," she replied, hoping the same thing.

Inside, Jacob provided a chair for Emilio and poured a glass of water before sitting down himself. Emilio took a long drink before he began explaining everything.

"My son has been arrested, Mr. Scott."

"What's the charge?"

"They said that he carjacked some woman with a gun, but Enrique isn't like that. He's a good kid."

"Was he found in this woman's car?"

"Yes, the police only found him because they caught him running a stop sign." Emilio went into detail about what the police told him when he arrived at the police station yesterday after getting the call from Enrique.

"Did your son say why?"

"No, he's not saying much. There's something wrong, but I can't tell if he's scared from being arrested or if it's something else."

"What makes you say that?"

"His eyes. When they finally allowed me talk to him, he was scared. I've never seen him that scared before. The only thing he said to me was that he wanted me to make sure his mother and sister are safe."

"He didn't say why?"

"No, he refused to explain himself. I told him that it would be better if he worked with the police and just talk to them, but there's something he's not telling any of us."

"Ok, well, if the police caught him with a weapon in a stolen car, regardless if it's his first offense, there's not much that can be done. He was caught red-handed. I can represent him if you'd like, to try and play on the mercy of the court if he is a decent kid. I would need to get some background on him. School records, hobbies, community activities, that kind of thing."

"I can get that for you." A glimmer of hope appeared in Emilio's eyes.

"The main thing you need to do is, if there is more to this story, get him to talk. Cops like it when they have someone who is willing to cooperate. If he can provide info on this something bigger you think he knows about then it may help him get a reduced sentence."

"I'll try again. I don't understand, he's never been in any trouble before."

"Kids have trouble doing the right thing sometimes because they don't have much experience of trouble or what to do in an emergency. Did he at least say where he got the gun?"

"No, but he did tell me it wasn't his." Jacob thought for a minute. An idea came to mind.

"Mr. Perez, could you give me a few minutes? I want to try and see if I can get a favor from one of the detectives at the precinct where he's being held."

"Absolutely. Thank you, Mr. Scott."

"Don't thank me just yet," Jacob told him exiting the office. Robin looked up from her computer screen and breathed a sigh of relief.

"You're ok?" she asked.

"Yeah, he's harmless. Interesting case though. I'll be taking it. I need you to give a call to Detective Orlando over in Hoboken. Tell him I may need his help on this case and see if he's available to stop in for a visit."

"I'll call him right now."

"Thanks Robin."

Jacob wondered if what he was thinking would work out for Enrique Perez. It was just a matter of waiting to see.

7

"Daddy!" Tamara shouted. She ran for her father and wrapped her tiny arms around his waist, squeezing as hard as she could. Josh bent down to scoop her up in his arms. She stopped to bury her face in his jet-black hair. She had always loved the smell of his shampoo.

"Hi sweetie, ready for school?"

"Yep! And do you know what today is?"

"Um, pepperoni day?"

"No silly, it's Show and Tell day!"

"Oh wow, that's great. What are you bringing?"

"My picture with Santa!"

"That's a good idea. You can tell them all about the line and what you asked for."

"Oh, I will."

Angie walked over to the front door with Tamara's Shopkins backpack in hand. She was wearing her sleepwear, consisting of a spaghetti strap tank top with grey cotton shorts. Josh looked over at her and, with raised eyebrows, smiled. Even though it had been some time since they were an item, he still found her beautiful. Any man that laid eyes on her would. Her wavy brown hair, long slim legs, flat stomach and a backside that was firm but very spankable in Josh's eyes were reasons enough to fall for her. He had understood her decision to end it with him, though. He didn't make life easy with his late nights and new drinking habit.

It was almost three years ago, when it all began. The job was taking its toll on him and he saw how other cops found a way to deal with the stress by drinking it away. He remembered the night he first started drinking. It felt wrong being at the bar and ordering something that he had never tried before, but he did it anyway. The burn of the liquor going down and the eventual numbness after several glasses got rid of the knot in his head. Going home a few hours later, he finally found the deep sleep he had missed. Angie knew right away what was coming and did what she could to keep the marriage stable. She had fought for them. After trying to talk to him and seeing someone for advice, Josh had ended up pushing her away. He delved deeper into the bottle.

Having no other choice, she approached him with the divorce papers, agreeing that if he were to clean himself up, she would share custody of Tamara. Realizing that he was too late to save his marriage, he did all he could to avoid losing his daughter as well. With Brett's help, he joined an AA group and stopped drinking. He began letting out his frustrations at the gym. It was therapeutic and didn't destroy his body from the inside.

"You've got that look in your eyes," she said, staring at him, "The same one that Brett had last night."

"Well, if I were a mirror, you'd know why," Josh smirked.

"Behave," she told him, "Everything else okay?"

"It's just this case that we're on. Something about it just doesn't fit."

"Well, just don't allow it to interfere with tomorrow night."

"What's tomorrow night?"

"My school Christmas play, Daddy!" Tamara told him, excited.

"That's right! How could I have forgotten?"

"It's okay, Daddy. I know. Mikala's dad told her that policemen always forget stuff."

"Oh, he did, huh?"

"Yes, so that's okay."

"So, what are you going to be in the play?"

"I'm an elf."

"I think you'll probably be the best elf in the play."

"I know all my lines. You have to if you want to be a movie star."

"That's right, you do." Josh smiled at Angie and she shook her head in return.

"And Brett said that he's going to be in the front row watching. Will you be there too?"

"I'll be right next to him, taping the whole thing. I promise."

"Can we post it on Youtube, so it can go viral?" Tamara asked, astonished.

"We'll have millions of views!"

"Billions," Angie added.

"Is that a lot?" Tamara asked her mother.

"It is."

"Let's get billions then!"

"Let's get you to school before you're late, ok?"

"Okay, Daddy." Tamara hopped down from Josh's arms and ran down the front steps to his car.

"Brett still here?" he asked Angie.

"No, he's still not comfortable staying the night just yet. He's afraid of freaking out Tamara."

Raghetti remembered the night that Brett revealed the sudden relationship that he and Angie had fallen into. Josh was furious that Brett had hidden it from him for days before coming clean. It was a betrayal from both ends as he had considered talking to Angie about trying to work things out. After Angie talked to him, he realized that, even though she still cared for him, she had moved on. He couldn't blame her after what he had done. It made things somewhat easier knowing that she didn't hook up with some loser, but he would try his best to never picture her and Brett in bed together.

"Give him time. He'll come around. He's just a big boy scout."

"I know. That's why I haven't said anything."

"Well, you should get back inside before you freeze those legs off."

"Thanks. And Josh? Good luck with the case." She gave him a peck on the cheek and headed back inside. Raghetti smiled, feeling loved and alone at the same time.

8

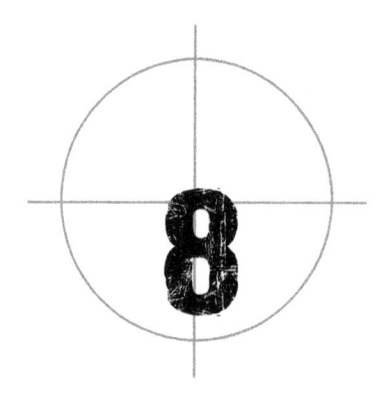

"I am in need of some coffee," Melvin said to Lucky, "It's way too early for me."

"Hey, I'll cover for you, if you run and grab me an espresso at the café."

"Deal. Want a bagel too?"

"Yeah! Toasted with some cream cheese!"

"Got it. Watch out for Wogle, though. Hines told me he seemed grumpy this morning." Melvin threw his coat on and headed out of the lab, running into Foster as he did.

"Hey Foster, I'm going on a Dunkin Donuts run, want a coffee?"

"No thanks, Melvin. I'm good," Brett said, holding his coffee cup up to show. Melvin left, and Brett walked over to Lucky.

"Hey Brett, looking for an update?"

"If you've got anything that will help me."

"Not as much as I hoped to by now, but I can show you what we have found. Over here," Lucky brought Foster over to his computer. He hit a few keys and the screen came to life with information.

"Melvin's still running the print of your mystery man, but the owner confirmed that he is not an employee of the company."

"Then what the hell was this guy doing there?"

"Still unsure right now but we're hoping that his prints bring something to the table that will help with your question. He did have some gunshot residue on his left hand. Meaning he did fire a gun. We found a casing near the body too. But there was no gun anywhere near the body."

"Could the shooter have taken it?"

"Possibly, or whoever it was that had left tracks out the back door. Speaking of which, The Lightrail security guys brought over the video footage of the parking lot for the 9th street station. I'll be going over it later this morning."

"What about the bodies and the pile of cases that the shooter may have left?"

"Aaron should be bringing up his results on the bodies a little later. As for the pile of casings, we've gone over all of them and there are no prints on any. I've got one of the casings running to see if the bullets in the bodies match the casings."

"Any info on the gun used by the shooter?"

"Well, with this kind of bullet, we could be looking at a submachine gun or a hand pistol. Either way, the 9x19mm bullets were designed to be lethal up to 50 meters and can still do damage at farther distances."

"Let me help out. I can review that video from the train station. Hopefully that will bring us a lead."

"Yeah, sure! That's a big help. There's hours of footage to watch because I still waiting for the time of death on any of the gang members yet. With that we could pinpoint a smaller frame of time to view."

"That's fine, I can always head down to Aaron for any findings."

"Somebody call for me?" said a voice in the doorway. The two turned to see Aaron Greene, head Medical Examiner for the Hoboken Police. The examiner covered his teddy bear physique with the typical stained white lab coat. His smile through the brown beard gave people who dealt with him a sense of security. How he ended up as a medical examiner instead of a school teacher was beyond Foster.

"Hey, Aaron. I was just about to head down to see you," Brett told him. He shook hands with the examiner and Aaron handed a transparent baggie with several bullets inside to Lucky. Then he handed a file folder to Brett.

"Lucky, here's some bullets from several different members of both the Latin Soldados and the Jackals. Same gun was used to fire all of them. Same grooves on all the bullets I've retrieved so far. Looking at the photos of the scene and the trajectory of all the bullets, it's conclusive that all the shots came from the same place, that pile of casings you found. And seeing how they all hit their marks, I can confirm that this shooter knows how to aim and fire a gun. He's had some practice."

"So, all those gang bangers were shot by one man?" Brett asked.

"That's how the evidence shows it."

"This guy must be the Punisher?" Lucky joked.

"Who?"

"The Punisher, it's a comic book about one guy whose family is wiped out by the mob, so he makes it his life's purpose to kill all criminals and mobsters in New York City. He's unstoppable and wears a shirt with this skull design on it."

"Great," Brett thought aloud, "That's just what this town needs, a vigilante taking matters into his own hands."

"I'll take a look at one of these and see if I can match the grooves in the casings with the bullets just to make sure. Then I'll run the grooves to see if we have the gun used in our database. Give me to the end of the day to get back to you on that. Melvin will also call you or Josh about the prints if anything comes back soon."

"Thanks guys. And try to keep it hush about the vigilante thing. I don't want that getting out in the papers. It'll only cause a bigger panic than the oncoming blizzard during last-minute Christmas shopping has caused already."

"No worries, Brett."

"And all my findings are in that folder, Brett," Aaron told him.

"Thanks, Aaron." Brett walked out of the crime lab and saw Mike Wogle walking down the hall towards him.

"Hey Brett," Wogle said, "What's new, what's exciting?"

"Just trying to close this case I'm on by the end of the week. I hate having a case carried over a holiday."

"Is that the gang shootout case I've heard so much about?"

"That's the one."

"Lucky was telling me about that. I've actually gotten them some help on the case because of the amount of evidence they had to collect. You need anything, let me know and I'll do what I can to have it rushed."

"Thanks Mike."

Mike continued down the hall to Lucky and Melvin's lab. He poked his head in.

"Hey Lucky? Got a few minutes?"

"Sure Mike, what's up?"

"I've got a new lab tech that I'm about to interview to help with the workload. I wanted you to join me with the interview process. After all, you and Melvin will be working with her, so I want your take on it."

"Now?"

"If you can."

"Now's a perfect time. Just waiting on the results of the prints on our mystery guy and the matching of the casing grooves from the gun used."

"Great, her name is Maura Alvano. She's full of knowledge on several topics of forensic examinations from what her previous employer explained to me." Mike and Lucky left the lab and headed to Wogle's office for the interview.

The silent lab left behind remained so for all of one minute. Then the computer on Melvin's side beeped with results. The screen flashed quickly, and a picture of the shootout's mystery man appeared and in bright green letters above it, stated MATCH CONFIRMED. Below the picture was a name and more information on the man in the picture.

9

Josh walked into the Homicide area and found Brett at his desk reviewing the folder that Aaron had given him. He took his coat off and hung it on the back of his chair. Raghetti sat down with a deep sigh at his desk that was adjoined with Brett's. Brett looked up at the sound of the sigh. The pink sparkling sticker that read 'Princess' hanging from Josh's hair made his partner chuckle.

"Morning Princess," Foster joked.

"What?" Brett took a second to decide whether he planned to tell him about the sticker.

"Nothing, what's wrong?"

"I'm just worried that I haven't gotten enough presents for Tamara."

"You want to take a break to go shopping, go ahead. I'm just waiting for the lab to give us something to work with."

"Really?"

"If anything comes up, I'll buzz you."

"Cool beans. What has Angie gotten her already?"

Brett rattled off the items that he remembered Angie picking up at the Toys R Us store in North Bergen two weeks ago. Angie was super excited to know that she now had a place to hide the presents besides her home so that Tamara wouldn't find them.

As Brett was listing the presents off, Lyndsey Bergen and her new partner, Danica Page, walked past. Page had transferred from Bergen County after moving to Hoboken shortly after Halloween. She was the opposite of Lyndsey in almost every way. Where Lyndsey had glasses,

Danica did not. Where Lyndsey was taller, Danica was shorter. Where Lyndsey had long brown hair, Danica had short blonde hair. But the two of them had been paired up and immediately became close. They had a connection that few partners had right away.

Danica noticed the princess sticker and stopped short. She grabbed Lyndsey by the arm and tilted her head over to Raghetti. Lyndsey tried hard not to burst out laughing and decided to have a little fun. She turned and walked over to Josh's desk.

"Hey Raghetti, how's it going?" The conversation between Brett and Josh paused to include her.

"I'm doing okay. How's the Roy case going?"

"Not bad. I had to come over to let you know that you look fabulous." Lyndsey gave him a sultry stare. Josh, unsure of what's going on, raised his eyebrows.

"Thanks?"

Danica laughed and Raghetti looked over at her. Lyndsey joined in and began laughing as well. Josh was still in the dark and looked to Brett for help, only seeing that his partner was trying to look away and hold in a laugh.

"What am I missing?" he asked them.

"Just keep sparkling, sweetie," Lyndsey told him with a wink of her eye. Brett finally reached over and pulled the Princess sticker from the side of Josh's head.

"You should really check yourself before leaving Tamara from now on."

"I was wondering why Emerson kept calling me, 'Your Highness'."

"Just be glad I didn't let you walk out with it still on."

"Asshole."

Brett sat back and paused. Then he said, "Actually, come with me for a minute."

"For what?"

"Some entertaining TV." Foster picked up the tape that Lucky had given him. Josh followed him to the break room and Brett popped the video cassette into the ancient VCR that sat on a rolling metal cabinet where a 32-inch tube TV rested. Turning the TV, he pressed the PLAY button. The screen flickered and suddenly a view of a parking lot and most of the 9th Street lightrail station appeared.

"Do we have a timeframe on the shootout?" Josh asked.

"Aaron just gave me the report. He said that the time of death occurred about 11:45PM Saturday night." Seeing that the time at the beginning of the video was 12:10PM, he hit the FAST FORWARD button and let it run until it reached 11:30PM. Pressing PLAY again, he grabbed a chair and sat down, watching the video closely. The two detectives remained silent for a few minutes as the screen flickered the dimly lit scene.

"They should have brighter lights at these places," Josh complained.

"Tell that to the mayor. Maybe he'll consider it and then throw the idea out the window like all the other ideas."

The time slowly reached 11:45PM. The two moved their chairs closer, waiting for the reveal of the person who left the tracks from the bus garage. The screen showed the snow slowly fall on the cars and the lot, itself. No one entered the screen. The lightrail train appeared and rushed past the station, not stopping for anyone.

"At least they didn't get a ride on the train." Another minute past before someone ran onto the station platform from the direction of the Academy Bus Garage. Brett clapped his hands and leaned forward, looking closely.

"It's a kid."

"One of the gang members got away?"

"Seems like it. And from the dark colors, looks like one of Jimenez's boys too. Now if he would just look at the camera."

"Looks like he's carrying, too." Josh pointed to the kid's right hand. Brett saw the gun shine in the florescent lights.

"Our mystery guy had GSR on his hand, but no gun was found near him. I'm thinking this kid must have grabbed it as he ran out the back door. But where did he go?"

They kept watching. The kid looked right and left while on the platform. No train was in sight. Then he moved to the few cars in the lot, trying the door handles on several, seeing that they were locked and then he ran off camera and disappeared. They sat and waited for him to return. After four minutes, they cut their losses.

"Crap, that's it? Where the hell did this kid go?"

"I don't know but I think we can get a good shot of his face after he tries that second car in the lot. We could use that to get the boys upstairs to enhance it and provide us with a photo. Then we could take it to Jimenez. See if he can identify this kid." Foster took the tape out of the VCR and they headed back to their desks. Foster's phone rang, and he picked it up.

"Brett, it's Luis. I've got some good news for you."

"Is it about the Academy shootout?"

"Damn straight it is."

"Don't keep me hanging, Luis. What do you have?"

"One hell of a lead. Get your butt over to the Harborside building in Exchange Place." Luis provided him the floor and person to see when he got there. Brett hung up and grabbed his coat off the back of his chair.

"Scratch your shopping trip, we're going to visit someone," he told Josh.

"What? Can't we visit this person after I shop?"

"No. But you can shop after the visit. If we have time."

"Dammit."

* * *

Enrique Perez sat downstairs in the basement level of Hoboken's Chief Crummins Police Headquarters in a holding cell of his own. He had been there since Saturday night when the police caught him for stealing the car from that innocent woman. But it was the fear that made him do it. It was all because of what he had just gone through. He had just wanted to get home as quickly as he could no matter what he had to do to get there. It was the place where he knew he would be safe. A place where the evil that happened before his eyes couldn't reach him. Where Wilfredo didn't have half a face. Every time he closed his eyes that was all he could see. The flashes of gun fire. The blood drops flying through the air. The stranger on the floor gasping for air, reaching out for him. He had barely slept. The cot was uncomfortable enough, but the silence was deafening.

That was until earlier this morning. A Jackal member had been brought in and placed right in his cell. The officers that kept an eye on the cells thought it would be entertaining to have the rivals together with no escape. He realized that he was still in the black clothes that the Soldados wore. But he wasn't a true Soldados. Nor was he now wanting to be.

"Yo, what you in fo'? Stealing candy from a baby?" the Jackal laughed. Enrique did what his father had told him over the one phone call that he was given. *Don't get sucked in by the others. Keep quiet in the cell but if the police ask you anything you answer and end each sentence with 'sir.'*

His father had pressed him for details. Enrique had hated holding back from him, but he knew better. He knew that his family would be safe as long as he kept quiet. The only thing that worried him was when. When would he come for Enrique? No one was supposed to walk out of that garage Saturday night. And no one else was supposed to see what he saw. *The face of the man in the Armani suit.*

10

Luis Orlando walked up to the front desk and flashed his badge. The young woman behind the wide desk looked up from her screen and smiled. Examining the badge, she asked what she could do for him.

"I just received a call from Jacob Scott. He's expecting me."

"I'll let him know that you're here, Detective." The woman got on the phone and punched a few buttons. "Hi Mr. Scott, a Detective Orlando is here to see you. Yes, sir, I will. Mr. Scott will be here in one moment."

"Thank you." Orlando looked around the front lobby and wondered if there could be any more glass objects placed there. The reception of Hoffman and Delgado was classy in his eyes. Having grown up on the streets in Jersey City, he was more used to old run-down things instead of the professional rich styles of the Harborside Financial Center.

Strolling back and forth, waiting for Jacob, Luis heard a voice calling his name.

"Detective Orlando," said Chris Delgado, "I see they'll let anything through the security desk downstairs." There was a look of disgust on Delgado's face, as if he had just eaten something sour. Luis looked over and smiled. He saw a moment of opportunity and took it.

"Mr. Delgado, I was wondering what that stench was. Seeing that your mouth is open, it makes sense, considering your kind is always spewing bullshit."

"My kind? Is that some kind of racial remark? Not the kind of thing you want to say on a floor of lawyers."

"Racial remark? We're both Cuban, you moron."

"Typical of you to resort to name calling. Very mature."

"Stop me if you've heard this one before, what's the difference between a vacuum cleaner and a lawyer on a motorcycle? The vacuum cleaner has the dirt bag on the inside."

"Very classy. Especially from someone attempting to resemble a homeless person," Delgado said, pointing to Luis's beard.

"Aw, tell me you didn't disrespect the beard." Luis looked over at Abigail. "Hey, do you know how many lawyer jokes there are? Only three, the rest are true stories."

"I'm not going to waste my time with you. You're petty, tasteless and only good for passing out parking tickets." And with that, Delgado turned to walk away. He passed Jacob and stopped briefly, "I'd prefer you not invite him in here anymore."

"Wait, no man hug?" Orlando called out. Jacob furrowed his brow, unsure of what he missed. Delgado quickened his pace walking back to his office.

"I don't think I want to ask what that was all about."

"Oh, Mr. Delgado and I go way back. Best of friends."

"Okay. Thanks for coming by the way. I need your help with a case that just fell in my lap."

"Sure thing. What is it?"

"Gentleman walked in an hour ago, asking for my help." Jacob gave Luis a quick recap of the situation that Emilio Perez' son was in. "I was hoping you could talk to the son and see if you could get anything out of him. He was tight lipped with his father, but I think he might open up to you."

"Doesn't seem too hard. Mind if I talk to his father first? I just want to get some background on the kid before I speak to him. The more I know about him, the easier it will be getting him to open up."

"Absolutely, my office is over this way." Jacob brought Orlando back to his office and introduced him to Emilio. "Mr. Perez, Detective Orlando is here to help your son and see if he'll talk to him. But he just wants to ask you a few questions first if that's alright with you."

"Yes, it is fine."

"Thank you, Mr. Perez. First off, I want you to know that my main concern is to make sure that he is okay. He's safe where he is right now. Can you tell me what kind of a boy Enrique is?"

Emilio began talking, explaining what hobbies Enrique had, what he liked, and the type of things that interested him. With every piece of information, Emilio's shell cracked. Soon, he was bawling like a child. Jacob couldn't help but look at the big man and wonder if he would act the same way if and when he had kids.

Luis consoled him with a soft hand on the shoulder. He knew enough about the boy. It was time to get the facts.

"Now can you explain to me where your son was when he carjacked the victim."

"I don't know. He won't tell me anything about where he was before that. But I noticed him wearing all black. I warned him about getting involved with the Latin Soldados, but he doesn't listen. Now he's in jail because of them."

"I'm sorry, you said that he's in with the Latin Soldados?"

"Yes. I tried to warn him about the gangs. His uncle and my father died because they were members. I vowed to my mother that I would stay away from that life and I will be damned if my son dies because of them."

"And when was he arrested?"

"Saturday night. My wife and I found out the next morning that he never came home."

"And he's refusing to say anything about that night?" A lightbulb went off over Orlando's head. Emilio saw the thought in the detective's eyes.

"That's correct. Do you know where he was?"

"It's a long shot. Give me one minute." Luis pulled out his cell phone and dialed the precinct. "Hey Hines, can you do me a favor? Punch the name Enrique Perez into the system. That's right. Ok, great. Can you tell me where the police statement says that the carjacking took place? 8th and Madison? That's what, two or three blocks from the 9th Street station? Great, thanks, Danny. Before you go, can you transfer me to the lab?" The detective took a deep breath.

"What is it?" Jacob asked him.

"I think I may be able to confirm where Enrique was Saturday night. And if I'm right, that kid's in bigger trouble than we think."

11

Saying that Julio Jimenez was furious was an understatement. He was beyond furious and he was looking for someone to pay for what they did to the members of his gang, and most of all, what they did to Robbie. He sat in his home on Castle Point Terrace, just next to the tennis courts overlooking Sinatra Drive, going over the information that his men had found out so far. Something told him that Donnelly was involved in this. He was unstable and dangerous to even his own gang. How Liam Dillon didn't manage to overthrow him was beyond Julio. Although maybe Dillon had tried, as he was among the dead in Saturday's mass shooting.

Something didn't make sense to Julio, though. Both gangs had received word through the grapevine that there was someone looking to get rid of some weapons and were willing to hand them off to the highest bidder. Julio contacted Dillon and talked it over. They decided to play it like an auction.

No one had survived the shootout, he had been told, but he knew that to be a lie. There would have been one person to have walked out of there alive, the last one standing. And he knew that was the gun runner that set up the meeting. But why? Was he part of another gang, looking to take over Hoboken? He needed to get his feelers out there. That's why he contacted his best men to meet him at his home this morning.

There was a group of seven of his best men, all with the smarts and the contacts that was needed for this mission. Robbie would have been the eighth if he wasn't now in the city morgue. And Julio would be damned if he would allow anyone to come in and take over what he had worked so hard to obtain. This was his town, his home, his birthright.

"Thank you for coming. You all know what this meeting is about, so I will just cut to the point. We were wronged. Someone attacked our family and I want to know who and why. You have been chosen to locate this information for me. Now, I'm just asking you for the info. I don't want you taking matters into your own hands, as much as I'm sure you'd like to. These men were your brothers as much as they were mine. But, I will resolve this on my own. And this is not a race, either. There is no punishment for those who are unable to locate the shooter, but there is a gracious reward for the one that does."

"Excuse me, Julio. I actually think I have something that you may want to know," Ryan Mendoza said, partially raising his hand.

"Is it about this topic?"

"Absolutely. One of our guys escaped that shootout."

Julio sat up in his chair. He had not heard about this. This was what he needed to get vengeance on whoever murdered his men.

"Why am I just hearing about this now?" he asked.

"I was just told about it this morning, myself."

"Who escaped and where are they?"

"Some new kid named Enrique Perez. Wilfredo's cousin. He got arrested trying to carjack some woman a few blocks away. They've got him down in a holding cell at the precinct. My guy thinks the Jackals know about it too."

"Perez. He's related to Wilbur Perez, isn't he?"

"I think so. His nephew or something."

"Find out all you can about Enrique immediately. I want to know that he's safe if the Jackals are after him. Get a hold of my guy in the precinct. Everyone else, I want you to stay on finding out about this gun runner that set up the meeting. Our blood has been spilled and it will not be the only blood seeping into the dirt. Now go and contact me if any of you hear anything. Ryan, please stay for one minute." The remaining six members of the Latin Soldados dispersed and left Julio's home in search of any information that would lead them to the mystery shooter. Julio motioned for Ryan to sit down, which he did.

"Here's what I'll need you to do for me," Julio explained, "Go down to the precinct, ask for Officer Darren Sheridan, tell him you're there to see Enrique. He will get you in. Talk to Enrique and see what he knows and if he's spoken to the police about it yet. They may not have made the connection yet if he was arrested for carjacking. Then have Officer Sheridan provide you with how much the bail is going to cost and come right back here."

"Understood, Julio." Ryan stood up and left as well.

Julio sat back and thought it over. If Donnelly or the gun runner knew about Enrique, the boy would not last past Christmas Eve. And that was five days away. He reached out to pick up the cordless phone on the side table next to him. He dialed #2 and waited for Donnelly to answer. When he did, Julio took a deep breath.

"Hello, Vincent. How are you doing?"

"How the fuck do you think I'm doing? Several of my men, including Liam were shot like dogs!"

"Now now, calm down. My men were slain as well. Roberto is dead. We have the same enemy. If we are to find out who did this, we must work together. I was hoping we could meet in an hour to discuss this."

Vinnie paused for a moment, thinking. Then he replied, "Sure, but if this is a set up."

"No, this is not. I'm just looking to talk. I'll see you in an hour." Julio hung up and did not feel any relief in that call. He was trying to prevent the possibility of a gang war in his town. But since the shootout, he'd felt it looming closer and closer.

12

The three detectives were guided to Jacob's office. Foster remembered the last time they had worked with the defending lawyer. It was the Doug Martin case: the lawyer had been murdered in his home and an innocent man had been framed for the crime. The case had made a sharp turn when they had realized who Craig Waterford was and why he had been framed. Standing in the reception area was Jacob, his assistant, Robin, Orlando and another man with a worried look on his face.

"Mr. Scott, good to see you again."

"Same here," Jacob said, shaking his hand, "Just wish it was on better terms."

"No rest for the wicked," Josh added.

"Unfortunately, that is completely true. Please come on in and Detective Orlando and I can explain why you were called here. Does anyone need some coffee?"

"I'll take one black, two sugar," Doyle responded. Josh and Brett denied the offer. Robin nodded and walked out to the coffee room to grab Doyle's cup. They all entered Jacob's office and Jacob sat on the edge of his desk, folding his arms in front of him.

"We've got a lead on the shootout," Luis explained.

"Is it about the shooter?" Foster asked.

"No, but it could help identify who was there. Let me explain." Orlando went over everything that Jacob and Emilio Perez had told him. He remembered the sneaker tracks that led from the back door to the train station. He figured that Emilio's son and the escapee could be one in the same.

"Is he slim with short hair and a strong jawline?" Brett asked Emilio.

"Yes, that sounds like Enrique."

Brett looked over to Jacob and Luis, "We just reviewed the camera footage from the station's parking lot on Saturday night. It's him."

"So, you're saying that we've been looking for this kid all weekend when we already had him? Figures." Doyle took a deep breath and shook his head.

"He was in a shootout?" Emilio asked.

"Sorry, Mr. Perez," Raghetti explained, "Your son was at a meeting between the Latin Soldados and the Jackals on Saturday night. Something happened at the meeting and all the members are dead. Except for your son, he managed to get away. Only problem is that by now, we're sure that the gangs are aware of this and looking to get revenge. Your son is the only one who really knows what the hell happened at this meeting, so that makes him very important to both gangs."

"But," Emilio looked to Jacob, "He's not really saying anything about where he was on Saturday."

"That's fine, we know the where, the when and the how. We just need to know who started the shootout and why. We'd need your permission to speak to him, of course," Brett explained.

"Will he still have to go to jail for the carjacking?"

"Actually, Mr. Perez," Jacob explained, "If your son helps the police solve this case, I'm sure they would make sure that his sentence was greatly reduced because of his help."

"If he can direct us to the person that started all this, I'll make sure all the charges are dropped."

"You can do that?"

"I'll pull some favors, but yes."

"Thank you, Detective. Yes, speak to my son. He's a good kid, I don't understand why he was there with those gangs. I've told him over and over how his grandfather and uncle died because of the Latin Soldados. My brother was one of them and several years back he was shot during a drive-by."

"Sometimes, kids get sucked in to gangs because of the way that they are portrayed in the media. Once they see the dangers of it, most quickly jump ship. I'm sure Enrique is one of those kids."

"Why don't you come with us to help get your son to talk? Mr. Scott can join us as well. It will help your son relax knowing you're there to help."

"Yes, can you still help us, Mr. Scott?"

"As you have asked me to help represent your son, I can't deny you representation. You and your son have a strong case and I am here to do everything I can to help."

"Thank you. Thank all of you. It means a lot."

"You're welcome. Now let's head down to the precinct so we can get this all taken care of." The group of men walked out of the office and Jacob followed. He stopped at Robin's desk to give her an update.

"Can you please call back Mr. Hansen and see if he can move the appointment to this afternoon? Actually, ask Chris if he can have Ron take the case off my hands."

"Everything ok?" she asked, concerned. Jacob saw the look in her eyes and knew that she was thinking that this was another dangerous case that dropped in his lap. Just like when Doug was murdered.

"Yeah, this case just got even bigger." Jacob filled her in quickly and assured her that he was going to be just fine. And just as he turned to leave, he placed a quick kiss on her lips. "For luck."

Ron walked over to the office as Jacob left. He watched the group of men walk towards the elevators.

"What's with the security detail?" he asked Robin.

"What security detail?"

"The cops with Jacob."

"Oh, it's a case that they're working on together."

"A juicy one, I take it?"

"There was a gang shootout on Saturday and Jacob's client's son witnessed the whole thing."

"More gang violence," Ron said, shaking his head. "I now see why my father is so headstrong about promoting his whole Take Back Your City Initiative with the mayor." Don Price thought the start of the holiday season was the perfect time to start it as it would motivate residents to get out, shop and celebrate the holiday and the town's community activities while feeling safe about their city. The Mayor of Hoboken thought it was a great idea for his father to pitch and set up a press conference to announce it over a week ago.

"Well, it seems like it was the gangs that were the victims."

"The police were involved in the shootout?"

"No, but they are not sure who was responsible. There's a chance that it's another gang trying to move in."

"Oh, no."

"What?"

"Well, if there is a third gang trying to move in on Hoboken, then the media may think they were motivated by my father's press conference."

"Oh," Robin said, "I didn't think of that."

"That's the last thing he needs. He was hoping to use this as a platform for running another term. I'll have to call him. He won't be happy about it but he'll at least have time to come up with a comment for the news." Ron pulled his cell phone from his pants pocket and started to dial as he began walking away.

"Oh, Ron, wait a moment. Jacob was wondering if you could help him out with his case load. With this new case that fell on his lap, he's a bit overloaded. It's a simple open and shut case. All the notes are in there and if you have any questions, I could answer them."

"Sounds good. I was hoping to be able to get something to work on. There's only so many times you can organize your desk before you come up with every possibility." Laughing, he plucked the folder from Robin's hand and continued contacting his father.

Robin watched Ron walk away and felt her stomach twist, thinking about Jacob and the danger that he may be putting himself in with his new gang case.

13

"What is this, a testosterone parade?" joked Danica, watching all four detectives walk past her and down to the holding cells. No one said a word to her, creeping her out. She looked over to Lyndsay for an explanation, but her partner just shrugged her shoulders. The two females continued to watch them disappear down the stairs.

The staircase led down into an open hallway. If one headed right from the bottom of the stairs, they would be taken to the morgue, where Aaron did all his work. Heading to the left led one to the area where the holding cells were located. Brett, leading the group of detectives, stopped at the desk and looked at Officer Katie Peters.

The slim woman with the long flowing brown hair was the least intimidating officer on the Hoboken force, but Brett knew better. A few months ago, Anti-Vice detective Stanton had tried hitting on her. She ignored his advances until he placed his hand on her shoulder, and before anyone in the room could react, Peters had grabbed Stanton's wrist and had flipped him over onto his back, twisting his arm in a way that would definitely break some bones if either of them moved. Ever since then, Katie would always wink to Stanton when she saw him and ask how his arm was.

"Hey Katie, we need one of your guys in there."

"Feel free to take the one in the green wife beater. He hasn't shut up since they brought him in."

"Not him, the kid in the black." Brett pointed to the teen that he had seen on the video, who was in the farthest cell from the front.

"Okay, sign your name and he's yours." She slid the clipboard around to him and dropped a pen onto it. Foster checked the time and signed Enrique out for questioning.

"He's all yours." Katie stood up from her chair and flipped through the small collection of keys on her hip key ring.

"Thanks." Brett followed her over to the cell where Enrique was held. Katie waved her hand forward, shooing the other detained guy away from the cell door.

"You know the drill. Move it back." She opened the door and pointed to Enrique. "Ninja boy, it's your lucky day." Enrique looked up from the concrete floor and saw Brett. He stood up, hesitant, unsure if he should come forward.

"Come on," Brett assured him, "It's okay, I just want to talk to you. Your father is here with my partner back there." Brett pointed behind him and waved Enrique to him. Enrique looked at the back where Brett pointed and didn't see anyone.

"Don't do it, man. It's a straight up trap," piped up the skinny guy in the green shirt.

"Zip it, string bean," Katie threatened, "No one's asking for your opinion."

"Well, if you ever want my opinion, sweet thing, you let me know. I'll give you all 10 inches of it." Several of the other detainees in the adjoining cells snickered at the comment that they knew was a big fat lie.

"Really," Foster told Enrique, "I'm not pulling anything funny. We're just needing some help."

Enrique paused, thinking of his options. Then he walked forward, getting close to the cell door and Brett. "I'm sorry about this," he whispered to Foster.

"About what?"

Enrique looked Brett in the eyes, then threw his eyes in the direction of the String bean guy. Brett wondered what Enrique was getting at. He had no time to react to the glob of spit that Enrique fired onto his face. He stood there for a few seconds, stunned, as Katie stepped forward to swing a punch at Enrique. Brett held his arm out, holding her back.

"No," he told her in a growl, "He's mine." Foster grabbed Enrique by the back of the neck and yanked him out of the cell. String bean laughed at the glob, still on Brett's face.

"Boy's got balls after all!" Katie flinched in String bean's direction and he shirked backwards onto the dirty cot.

Once Brett knew they were out of the view of anyone in the holding cells, he let go of Enrique and wiped his face. Emilio came from around the corner and wrapped his arms around his son and held him tight.

"Dad, I'm sorry. I didn't know. I didn't."

"Shhh, it's okay, you're safe," Emilio replied.

"I don't mean to break this up but the sooner we get the information that your son has, the faster we can wrap this case up before it gets worse," Raghetti told them. Emilio let go and took a step back.

"Enrique, you need to talk to these detectives. They can help you with the carjacking charge."

"I don't care about the carjacking. If they want anything, I need them to take care of something else."

Brett closed the door of the interrogation room behind him. Josh stood over the table in the middle of the room and Enrique was sat on the other side of the table. On the east wall was a two-way mirror. Behind the mirror, Luis, Doyle, Jacob and Emilio stood and watched the scene before them. Foster scratched the stubble on his chin and looked down at the teen. He was smarter than they thought of him earlier, but he was the only obstacle in their way to solving this murder. They had to come out of this room with something or else this whole day would be a waste. And the town would come that much closer to a gang war.

"Look," Josh began, "We know that you were at the bus garage Saturday night. We've got proof. And we know there was someone else that was there who wasn't a member of either gang. Who was he?"

"Kayne West. He was looking for some people to hire for his next video."

"Fine, be a wiseass. Maybe you'd like to go back to the holding cells with your buddy in green shirt?" Brett opened the door to the room and stepped back. Enrique stared down at the table. He shook his head in silence. Foster closed the door again.

"I get how you're feeling. You're trying to be strong in front of your father," Brett pointed to the mirror, "But deep down, you're scared out of your mind. I can see that. And if I can, so can those other gang members. I can guarantee that they know just as much as us by now. And they're going to be trying to get to you first. Now you can tell us what we need to know, or you can kiss your father goodbye. Because when Julio Jimenez or Vinnie Donnelly get a hold of you, they're not going to be as kind asking you the same questions. Your choice."

"I was telling the truth earlier. I don't care about the arrest for the carjacking. I made a dumb mistake. I was scared. But if I'm going to help you, you need to help me with something else."

"And what, pray tell, would that be?" Josh asked, folding his arms and leaning up against the wall in annoyance.

"You need to make sure that my family is kept safe from them. When I see that they are, then I'll talk."

"You need to give us something if you want us to protect your family. Did you see this lone guy shooting everyone?"

"I may have." Enrique looked up at Brett. Brett noticed something in the teen's eyes. He saw the recalling of the night and the horror that he experienced first-hand. Brett knew that this kid was smart. He knew that if he made the kid seem smarter than the two detectives in the room with him, he may get cocky and slip with giving some information.

"Did he give a name? An accent when he spoke?"

"Nah, no accent. He sounded local. And he wore one of those fancy Armani suits. Oh, he did give a name too, but I don't think it's his real one."

"What did he say?" Josh stood up and stepped forward, now interested that they were getting somewhere.

"He said that we could call him Hermy."

"Hermy?" Brett and Josh looked at each other.

"Yeah, it was something like that."

"Hermy? Hermy." Brett repeated the name trying to think of what it meant or if he had heard of a Hermy before.

In the viewing room, the four men were also stumped.

"Maybe Hermaphrodite?" joked Orlando.

"You dumb asses," Doyle muttered, throwing Luis a look while motioning over to Enrique's father. He pulled out his phone and typed something into it. Then he hit the SEND button and tapped on the opposite side of the mirror. Brett looked up and felt the vibration on his hip. He looked at the screen and then looked back at Enrique.

"Could it maybe have been Hermes?"

"Yeah, that's what he said." Enrique sat up more alert now that he remembered the name that the man in the Armani suit gave.

"Who's Hermes?" Josh asked Brett at the same time as Orlando, Jacob and Emilio asked Doyle.

"Am I the only one that learned anything in school?" Doyle asked. "Hang on, I'm only going to say this once." He knocked on the mirror again three times. Brett and Josh took the code to join them and left the room to enter the viewing room.

"What do you know about Hermes?" Brett asked.

"Hermes is from Greek mythology. He was one of Zeus's sons, known as the messenger of the Gods. His job was to herald the dead and guide their souls to the underworld. From the stories, he was described as cunning and shrewd."

"So, this guy thinks he's a god?" Orlando asked his partner.

"I don't think he's referring to himself as one. I think he's seeing himself as the one person whose job is to send these gangbangers to hell."

"Great. He's a vigilante." Raghetti threw his hands up in the air.

"Hang on," Brett explained, "Before we make judgments, let's find out more about this guy." He and Josh returned to the interrogation room.

"Okay, so he calls himself Hermes. What does he look like?"

"Nuh-uh. That's all I'm saying until you get my family to a safe house or something. Let the Soldados and the Jackals come for me, but I'm not putting my family in danger, too."

"Listen kid, that's all brave and everything but it's not just you and your family. If we don't find this guy before the gangs do, they will tear this town apart looking. And that puts everyone in danger. Are you ready to have that much blood on your hands?"

Enrique remained silent. He thought it over and wondered if the detective was just trying to scare him or if he was telling him the truth. The guilt would rip him apart from the inside. But it was like his father taught him, family always came first. A vision of Wilfredo's one remaining eye staring up at him came flooding back and he almost gagged at the image in his head. He had to help give justice to Wilfredo's killer. But he had also had time to plan it while in the holding cell over the weekend.

"Get them to a safe house then you get what you want. That's all I'm saying for now. Wait, I have one more word for you. Lawyer." Enrique pushed back from the table and slouched in his chair. Josh gritted his teeth at the teenager's wiseass attitude. Brett threw up his hands and turned to leave.

"Let me speak to him," Emilio said, "I can convince him to tell them what they need to know." Jacob stopped him from leaving the room by holding up his hand.

"No, Mr. Perez. If he sees you right now, it will only strengthen his determination to keep you safe. As his lawyer, let me see what I can do." Jacob left the room and met Brett and Josh in the hallway. Josh was running his hands through his black wavy hair while Brett was staring down at the tiled floor.

"Why am I the only one who can feel the shit storm coming?" Brett muttered. Jacob hoped that Foster's gut was wrong, but he knew from the interaction that he had previously with the homicide detective, the town of Hoboken was looking at a holiday in hell.

14

A brunette with an athletic build walked into the lobby of Hoboken's One Police Plaza and approached the front desk where Danny Hines sat, dealing with an irate citizen. The large wooden counter made Danny look smaller than he really was. An older Scottish man, he had been planted behind the counter for as long as the building itself, as per most of the officers that currently populated the police force. Anyone and everyone who worked in the building never entered without a happy greeting from Hines. But get on his bad side and one would certainly find that there was a wrath quietly boiling in the smiling old man.

"I am telling you, officer. I am sick and tired of these hoodlums terrorizing everyone in my neighborhood. Something must be done about it."

"I understand, Mr. Bennett. And your complaint has been entered into the system. I will have some of our officers take a drive over to take care of it."

"You said that last time and they still came back. This police force is a joke. I'll have to take care of it myself."

"You don't wanna do that, sir," Hines said, trying to calm the man down.

"What? Are you going to ticket me? Whatever." Mr. Bennett waved his hand in the air, dismissing Danny. He then walked out of the police station as angry as he was when he entered.

She noticed him staring at her and looked up. The angry look in her eyes made Danny aware that she was not here for pleasure. She was all business.

"Good afternoon, miss. How can I help you?"

"Yes, desk sergeant…Hines. I would like to see your chief of police, please."

"Um, ok. Is she expecting you?" Hines wasn't used to civilians just demanding an audience with Christine Black, the Chief of Police. He wondered if there was more to this woman that he was unaware of.

"No, but I don't have a whole lot of time. So please go get him or her."

Danny was taken back by the woman's attitude. As beautiful as she was, she did not have much in the nice department. He nodded and stretched his arm out to the left.

"Please take a seat and I will contact her right away."

"Thank you." The woman turned and took a seat, staring straight ahead of her. Hines shook his head and looked around. He was hoping to find someone to get Chief Black because as the desk sergeant, he was unable to leave his post.

He noticed the unkempt and unfriendly officer Darren Sheridan speaking to someone in civilian clothes. Hines figured that he was not busy and shouted over to him.

"Hey Darren, can you go get a hold of the chief? I've got someone here looking to speak to her."

Darren stopped talking to the stranger he was standing next to and looked over at Danny. "I'm busy. Find someone else."

"Great, thanks," Hines replied sarcastically. Having no choice, he picked up the desk phone and dialed the Chief's extension. He stared as the determined woman as he waited for her to pick up.

Christine Black, the Hoboken Chief of Police, sat in her office with Don Price, discussing his initiative for the city and the upcoming press conference he had scheduled. Black relaxed in her chair sipping on a fruit smoothie from the café a few blocks away on Washington Ave. Don enjoyed a cup of coffee from the Waterford Deli and leaned forward.

"You know, I used to have an assistant by the name of Kenny, who used to drink one of those. It was, like, a spinach flavored one. Looked like the stuff that the girl from the Exorcist spit out before her head twisted around. Worse part was after an hour of having drank it, he always had to use the bathroom. Stunk it up like a garbage dump on a hot summer day." Black looked at her smoothie and placed it on her desk.

"Thanks for that, Don. What is it you wanted to discuss?"

"I wanted to get an update on that shootout your men are investigating. My son told me earlier that they're thinking it was another gang? If this is true, then we have a bigger problem on our hands then I expected."

"We haven't come to any conclusions at this time," she explained to him, "We've got a few leads that they are working and as soon as something concrete comes our way, I will call you personally."

"That's great and all but do you think you could have them keep it quiet on the gang violence possibility? If the media gets word, the mayor is going to come straight to me and my plan for the citizen patrol this holiday is going to get shot down as fast as a fat girl in a speed dating service." Black looked down at her desk, no longer shocked by the expressions that Price threw out into the air, but she still shook her head over it. Regardless, she still agreed with his new initiative.

"Well, we don't want that now," Christine said, "I'll have a talk with my detectives. They're also considering it may be a bold move for a gang war by one of the gangs."

"Perfect. Just what this town needs during Christmas week. Just please keep me updated on what they find?"

"I will, Don." Her desk phone rang then, and she secretly thanked the caller before she picked up.

"Hi Chief, it's Hines. I've got a woman here asking to see you."

"What's her name?"

"I dunno. She won't tell me what she wants or who she is, just asking for you."

"Can you tell her I'm in a meeting?"

"I can, but I don't think that will send her away."

Black sighed. This day was just getting better and better for her. She considered turning the woman away, but she decided to see what she wanted. She told Danny that she would be there in a few minutes. Then she hung up.

"Sorry Don, but even though it's the giving season, we're still extremely busy."

"No worries, Christine. I understand." Don stood up and put his winter coat back on.

"I'll walk you out," Christine said, opening the door to her office with a slight smile on her face. *Thank God, this meeting is over*, she thought.

At that moment, Homicide detectives Kylee Fernandez and Russell Emerson walked in with a member of the Latin Soldados. They had caught him trying to relieve an elderly woman of her purse. Fernandez's short stature did not diminish her attitude. She was feisty, aggressive and had a mouth like a sailor's. Most of the cops in the town nicknamed her the Wolverine because of her personality. Emerson, on the other hand, was timid and always analyzed a situation before diving head first into it. Chief Black had teamed them up because, combined, they were one of the best teams on the force. And after being partners for the past four years the two had grown together in the bedroom as well as on the street. Even though the others had continuous asked him about Fernandez's bedroom personality, Emerson was not one to kiss and tell. And Kylee had respected him for that.

"I'm telling you, I bumped into the woman. I swear. I was just trying to give her back her purse. C'mon guys, it's Christmas."

"Shut it, fucktard," Fernandez snapped.

"This is bullshit, man."

"What do we have here?" Hines asked the two.

"Purse snatcher," Emerson replied, pushing his glasses up the bridge of his nose. "He says that he was only returning it but somehow got lost and was running to return it in the wrong direction."

"It's snowing out there! You tell me if you can see anything past those big snowflakes!" Hines shook his head and tossed a thumb over his shoulder in the direction of the stairs leading to the holding cells and handed some paperwork to them. Russell let go of the perp to take the forms they needed to fill out. The purse snatcher took advantage of the moment and yanked his arm from Kylee's grip. He broke free and took off, running full speed, further into the police station instead of out the front door. It was at that same moment that Chief Black and Commissioner Price turned the corner and into the purse snatcher's path.

"Oh, damn," Emerson muttered under his breath.

15

Black's eyes grew at the sight of the oncoming criminal. Price took the few seconds left before the criminal hit them and stepped in front of Black, protecting her from the impact. He braced himself, placing his right shoulder forward and tucking his head.

But the purse snatcher did not get the chance to slam into the Commissioner. The woman who was patiently waiting for Chief Black had jumped up and sped forward into the criminal's back. He jerked back and fell full force into the blue tiled floor, as if he were tackled by a giant freight train. His face smashed into the tile and they saw the blood immediately begin gushing from his nose. A moan of pain crawled through his lips.

The woman stood up and grabbed the short chain in-between the cuffs around the criminal's wrists. Yanking him back up to his feet, he turned to look at the female stranger.

"Ou broke ny fuckin' ose!" he yelled at her, spitting drops of blood at her as he did.

"You shouldn't have tried to run, then." Pulling his by his wrists, she passed him back to Fernandez. The short haired brunette then slapped him in the back of his head.

"That's for the dumb attempt," Kylee said. Then she slapped him again, causing him to cough. "And that's just for being an asshole and not running for the door like most people with a brain would have done."

Emerson apologized to Chief Black and Commissioner Price. Then they dragged the perp down to the holding cells for Katie to deal with.

"That was quite the brave move, Miss." Price stretched his hand out in thanks. The woman shook it and nodded.

"Nothing that I wasn't trained for, Commissioner. Chief Black?"

"Yes, are you the woman asking for me?"

"Yes, ma'am. My name is Amanda Fenton." Fenton shook Christine's hand as well.

"Well, thank you Miss Fenton. What can I do for you?"

"I just wanted to talk to you about something." Amanda reached into her coat's inside pocket to grab something. As she did, the group of Orlando, Doyle, Raghetti and Foster came from the hall that led to the interrogation rooms. They all saw Chief Black at the same moment and all began talking at once to her, trying to inform her of the latest. Black leaned back from the four detectives, overwhelmed by all the noise. Foster stopped and managed to quiet the other three to explain what they had just learned.

"Sorry Chief, but we've learned that the teenager that Officers Kassen and Scheibel arrested in the car-jacking from Saturday night is actually the same kid that escaped out the back of the Academy Bus garage. We just finished questioning him. Unfortunately, he's not saying anything until we move his family into a safe house. This kid is scared and he's pretty damn smart."

"Did you inform him that he's putting the city in danger by keeping quiet?" Price interjected.

"Yes, Commissioner. But this kid's stubborn. Do we have anywhere to place his family, so he'll start talking?"

"Let me check with the state. I know that they have one up in Fort Lee, but I don't know if it's being used," Black told her detective.

"The sooner we can get this done the better a chance we'll have to wrap this up before Christmas Eve." Brett realized how few days were left until the actual holiday arrived.

"I know."

"Allow me to pull some strings and call in some favors," the Police Commissioner told them.

"Thank you, Commissioner."

"Don't thank me; I'm just looking out for the city like you all are."

More like looking out for himself, thought Chief Black.

Raghetti and Orlando noticed Fenton standing there, not recognizing her. Orlando nodded to her with a smile, smoothing out his beard. Fenton rolled her eyes.

"Sorry to interrupt, Chief Black," Fenton said, "But I think I may be able to help with this case." The group turned their heads to her and raised their eyebrows.

"Please tell us you know the shooter," Doyle begged her.

"Well no, but I think I may know someone who does."

Before she could explain further, Melvin hollered to Foster from the main staircase in the front of the lobby that led to the second floor. Upstairs was home to the Homicide department, Child Services, Anti-Vice and the Forensics lab. He was running as fast as he could down the stairs, waving a piece of paper in his hand. Josh thought for sure he was going to miss a step and fall horribly. When he reached the group, he stopped and bent over to catch his breath.

"I hope that's not spoilers for the next Walking Dead episode," Raghetti joked. Brett threw him a look and asked Melvin what was wrong.

"No," Melvin answered Josh, "but I read the comics, so I know what's going to happen."

"Melvin, focus." Brett waved his hand to get the lab tech's attention.

"Sorry. I've got it."

"Got what?"

"The prints of our mystery guest to the gang meeting. They found a match. You're not going to believe this."

"Just spit it out."

"The guy's name is Thomas Ketchum."

"And who is Thomas Ketchum?"

"Actually," Amanda Fenton interrupted, "that's why I'm here."

16

"ATF, huh?" Raghetti said, impressed by the attractive woman's title. Amanda nodded and took back her Alcohol Tobacco and Firearms badge that she had handed to the group. Placing it back into her coat pocket, she went into further details. The group took the information in.

"Thomas Ketchum was my partner. We've worked for the Newark field office for the past five years."

"You say he *was* your partner."

"Well, Last Thursday, I had a family emergency. I had taken off for a few days. When I got back on Sunday, I called him to tell him I was back. Normally, he calls back within a couple of hours, but he hadn't. And when I came into the office this morning, no one had heard from him. It was then that I knew something was wrong. An hour later, one of our guys noticed that his prints were run from here. So, I came down here to find out what happened to him."

"You knew he was dead?" Orlando asked.

"Why else would you run his prints?"

"Good point."

"I'm sorry about all of this," Brett told her.

"Can I see his body?"

"Absolutely. Foster, Raghetti, please take Agent Fenton down to the morgue." Chief Black guided them to the stairs. "I am terribly sorry for the loss of your partner."

"Thank you, Chief Black. I just want to know what happened."

"We can go over that on the way," Foster explained. They walked down the stairs and Brett went over what they had learned so far about the case. He told her about the shootout, their witness, and the fact that he had been found with no ID or weapon.

"He normally left his ID in his car. But he always had his weapon on him."

"Well, he did have his gun on him; it was just that the only living witness took it in panic and ran off. We've retrieved his gun and had it logged into evidence."

"Good, I'd like to bring it back to headquarters if it's possible."

"Of course, we'll head over there after we stop off at the morgue. I'm just curious why he was there that night."

"One of our fellow agents told me that he had gotten a call from his Confidential Informer in town. I think it may have led him here. You said it was an arms deal?"

"That's what the gangs are telling us. We believe the man who set up the meeting is the one that killed them."

"One man shot all those gang members?"

"As impossible as it sounds, that's what we're being led to believe. Especially with the evidence at the scene."

They reached the morgue and walked in, looking for Aaron. Next to the entrance of the morgue was Aaron's small office, where he did paperwork. Just beyond that was the examination room followed by a restroom and refrigeration unit. They found Aaron working on another body that had been brought in by Danica and Lyndsey. He looked up at the sound of the door and saw the three of them standing there. Aaron smiled and took off his goggles.

"Hey Brett, Josh. What can I do for you?" "Hey Aaron, can you show us the John Doe from the shooting?"

"Sure can. Follow me." Aaron led them into the back where the refrigeration unit was. The small square doors covered the metal back wall. He walked over to the second row from the end and opened the third door, which was at thigh level. He slowly pulled the table from inside of it and gently folded back the sheet.

Amanda looked down at Thomas. His pale skin and blank face brought a lump to her throat. Her best friend was dead. And the man responsible was not caught yet. She brought two fingers to her lips, kissed them and placed them on his cold cheek. She had to help the two detectives, she thought. She knew if the role was reversed, Thomas would have done the same for her.

"It's him," she said softly.

"Again, I'm sorry."

"What was the cause?" she asked Aaron.

"The internal bleeding caused by the bullet that entered his chest filled his lungs. He drowned in his own blood."

"It wasn't quick?"

"It may have taken a couple of minutes." Aaron bowed his head in apology.

"Thank you for your time." Amanda took hold of the sheet and covered his torso and head again. Then she walked out of the morgue. Brett and Josh thanked Aaron and followed after her. She was standing by the stairs, holding herself tight.

"Do you need a minute?" Josh asked her.

"No, I'm good," Amanda lied, "But I'm going to be making a call to my supervisor. I'll be staying here a few days to help with the investigation if that's all right with you and your chief."

"You're more than welcome to join us. The more people we have, the faster we can close this case."

"I think we should talk to his CI first." Amanda took a piece of paper from her pants pocket and handed the name of Ketchum's confidential informant. Brett looked at the name and shook his head.

"Kevin Finnegan? I don't know of him. But we can ask the Anti-Vice guys that are helping us. One of them should know him."

"Well, let's not wait." Fenton climbed the stairs back to the main floor. Doyle and Orlando were still there, talking to Chief Black.

"Hey, Doyle," Josh asked, "You've ever heard of a Kevin Finnegan?"

"Finnegan? Of course. He's one of Donnelly's guys. What do you want with him?"

"He was Ketchum's CI. He called Ketchum about the meeting," Brett explained.

"Do you know where he lives?" Amanda asked the older detective.

"Yep. He's not too far from Donnelly's place. Just across the street from Church Square Park."

"Can you take me there? I want to question him about what he told Thomas."

"Yeah, just give me a minute to use the little boy's room and we can head over there."

"I'll take care of the paperwork," Luis told him.

"I think we should go grab something to eat and go over the evidence again. There's something there that's bugging me about it. But I can't put my finger on it." Brett scratched his chin, hoping to think of what it was.

"Can I look it over when we return?" Amanda asked.

"Sure. A fresh pair of eyes may be able to find what I can't."

"Thank you, Detective Foster and Raghetti." Fenton shook their hands and stepped out into the cold afternoon. Brett headed back to his desk to grab his coat while Lyndsey approached Josh.

"Who's the tall brunette?" she asked him. Josh told her about Agent Fenton and who the John Doe at the gang shooting really was.

"That's sad. I couldn't imagine having one of us dying on the job."

"I know what you mean. It's like my other family here."

"I must be the hot second cousin," Lyndsey smiled. Josh laughed and noticed the sparkle in her eyes. *Could Bergen be flirting?* he thought. He paused for a second and decided that it was his loneliness talking. But then again, he could use the company.

"Hey, would you like to go grab some lunch?" He was as surprised by the question as she was.

"I'm actually supposed to go question a suspect with Page. Maybe some dinner?"

"Oooo, not possible. Tamara's Christmas play is tonight."

"What about lunch tomorrow?"

"Sounds better," he smiled.

"Wear the blue shirt," she said, winking as she walked away, "It brings out your eyes." Josh stood there, with his mouth opened, wondering if that all really just happened.

17

Vinnie Donnelly smacked the table in front of him with his hand and cursed under his breath. He hated being in the dark like this. He was no where close to finding out who shot Liam and the others, and he didn't know what the police or Julio knew. It was driving him insane. Not that he wasn't already.

Donnelly was born in Jersey City and at the age of five, his parents moved the foursome to Hoboken. He had grown up happy. Then, on his thirteenth birthday, he and his older brother were on their way to the park to practice baseball pitches. With only one block to go, Vinnie dropped the ball and it rolled under a car on the other side of the street. He ran over to get it and did not see the Cadillac with three old school Latin Soldados members inside. The gang members couldn't stop soon enough. He slammed onto the hood and his skull shattered their windshield.

The three gang members got out and started screaming at each other. Vinnie's brother ran over to check on his younger sibling. The gang members blamed the damage to their car on Vinnie. Vinnie's brother argues, so the driver shot him in the head point blank. They tossed Vinnie off the car and sped off before the police could arrive. Neighbors on the street came out once the gang members were gone and called an ambulance for an injured Vinnie.

The impact of the windshield on his skull had rattled his brain. He was in the hospital for five days before he gained consciousness. It only took his parents five minutes to realize that the impact had affected the part of his brain that controlled his thought process. There was no recognizing the difference of right and wrong after that. The knowledge of his brother's death only made it worse.

As an act of revenge, he gathered some of the other Irish kids in the neighborhood and brought the Jackals to life. And now that Liam, his 'brother from another mother', had also been killed, he felt the need for vengeance returning once again.

"I know that mutha, Julio is behind all this!" he shouted to his men sat around him. There was no meeting table in the main headquarters of Jackals. There was barely a table in the kitchen area. Instead, there were several couches in the living room area of the house that the group had taken over just north of the train tracks that separated Hoboken with Jersey City. The couches all pointed in the direction of the 60-inch LED television, complete with game consoles and Blu-Ray player. That was the only decoration that Donnelly thought it needed. Liam, on the other hand, thought it made them look like animals and tried to spruce the house up with lamps and small paintings. There was a painted landscape of Ireland, one of New York's Times Square and a poster of the group House of Pain. And each room was painted a different shade of green.

"He had me meet him to be all nice and tell me that he wants to find out who did this as much as I do. All lies!"

"Why would he kill his own right-hand man?" one Jackal asked.

"It throws the suspicion off him! He's such a smart snake. He knows that the police would never suspect him if his own men were killed in the same act. But I know better. I know that they've been trying to get rid of me all these years."

"Yo, he'd be nuts to try and take you out, Vinnie."

"Oh, he had tried once before. They couldn't kill me then and they certainly won't be able to now. I'm bulletproof!" He pounded his chest in fury. Taking a breath, he looked around him at his gang. He knew it was finally time to let loose, for Liam was no longer around to hold him back.

"It's time to show Julio and his boys that we will not be stopped. There's a briefcase with a whole lotta cash for the Jackals that brings me the man who killed Liam and our fellow gang members. Now get out there and tear this town to pieces so we can find them! No. Holds. Barred!" He threw his arms in the air and spun around. The gang hollered in agreement. Then they began to disperse, talking among themselves as to where to look.

Vinnie took hold of a bottle of Heineken and drank it deep. Then he tossed it to the side, still half full, and wiped his mouth with his arm. He looked around and frowned. Donnelly grabbed the arm of the nearest Jackal. It was Brian Murphy.

"Hey, Vinnie, what's up?"

"Where's Kevin?"

"Ya got me. I haven't seen him lately. Want me to give him a call?"

"Yes please. I've got a mission for him. Tell him to come see me as soon as possible."

"You've got it, Vinnie." Brian started texting Kevin and Donnelly stopped him.

"What about Walsh? Has he called in yet?" Donnelly had sent Marc Walsh out to get himself arrested in the hopes that he could be paired in the same cell as Enrique Perez, now that he knew where the kid was.

"Nah, Marc told me that they haven't allowed him to call yet."

"Let me know when he does, please." Vinnie flashed Brian a friendly yet creepy smile. It made Brian even more uneasy.

"Right away." Vinnie let go of Brian and dropped onto the couch to his left. He propped himself up on his elbow and watched the local news reporting the Christmas crowd at the Newport Mall. They interviewed someone who was telling the reporter that this year was going to be a year that his family would never forget.

Vinnie laughed to himself. Little did the guy on the TV know, but he was completely right. The residents of Hoboken were going to have one hell of a holiday. And he would bring it to them. In blood.

18

Robin sat up when she saw Jacob walk in from the elevators with an exhausted look on his face. He was alone, and his slouched shoulders hinted to Robin the tiredness that she had seen whenever he would get stumped on a case. Jacob sat down on the small couch next to her desk that was for clients waiting for an appointment. He placed the courier bag on the floor next to his feet and placed his face in his hands.

"Are you ok? Did something bad happen?"

"Yes, Emilio Perez walked into my office," he replied through the fingers.

"Did it go that bad?"

"Oh yeah." Jacob described the questioning of Enrique and the deal he was trying to get for his family's safety.

"Can the police get them that?"

"They're looking into it. There's a safe house in Fort Lee, but they have to see if it's currently available for them to use."

"All the way up in Fort Lee? That's pretty far."

"I know. I tried to get Emilio to help convince his son to just tell the police what they need to catch whoever was behind this, but he was no help. His appearance there just made Enrique more stubborn. I don't know what to do. The police were pressuring me to convince him to talk and to stop being such a teenager."

"Did they tell him what could happen to him if he didn't tell the police about the shooter?"

"They threatened him, verbally abused him and even sat him down to explain the viciousness of these gangs, but he didn't even flinch. This kid is going to be impossible to work with and when he's going to have to be in court for the carjacking, the judge is not even going to bat an eye at being lenient. I would feel a lot better if my head was doused in gasoline and set on fire."

Robin sat down on the couch next to him. She rubbed his upper back and placed a gentle kiss on his temple. "I'm so sorry this is happening. There's got to be some way to get him to talk without anyone getting hurt. I'm sorry, but I have no experience with teenagers. I would strip for him if I knew that would help," she joked, trying to lighten the moment.

"Would you?" Jacob played back, "Maybe getting to him through his other head would do the trick. You could do that sexy whispering in the ear thing that you always do."

"You're going about it all wrong," said Kristie from the hallway outside the reception office as she headed back to her desk from Hoffman's office.

"You know how to talk sense into a teenager? Is that even possible?" Jacob asked.

"There's only one person who could break a teenager. Their mother. It's their kryptonite."

"Would that really work?" Jacob asked, interested. Kristie had gotten his attention.

"Hells yeah. I can get Connor to cave in for anything. And it's actually kinda fun too."

"I'd sell one of my kidneys if it gets him to talk."

"Yeah, I don't think that would," Robin told him.

"Well, if you think bringing his mother in will work, I'll give it a try. I'll call the Perez home tomorrow and try to convince his mother to come and talk to him down at the precinct."

"Let me know if you want any help with it," Kristie offered.

"Oh, I'll be taking you up on that."

Robin's phone buzzed, and the intercom flashed. Robin stood up and walked over, pressing the speaker button.

"Hey Abby, what's up?"

"Hi Robin, is Mr. Scott available? There's a Mr. Jimenez here to see him." The trio froze where they stood. Robin looked back at Jacob and

Kristie brought a hand up to her mouth. They all knew that an appearance by Julio Jimenez was never a happy one for the person he was visiting.

"Um, did you say Jimenez?" Jacob asked from across the office.

"Yes sir. He was asking to see you for a few minutes. He wanted to help with the Perez case."

"Shit," Jacob said lowly.

"I'm sorry?"

"Uh, nothing Abby. I'll be right there. Thank you." Abby disconnected the intercom and left a hanging silence in the office.

"I think we may have to scratch the study session tonight. I'm sorry, Marks."

"Hey, don't apologize. If I'm not ready by now, I shouldn't be going tomorrow. Just make sure you're careful with him. Good luck." Kristie headed back to her office. Robin looked over at Jacob with worry.

"Stay here," he told her, "I don't want him to learn anything about us being a couple and use it for leverage in the future."

"But,"

"No, please. Just stay here. I'll be okay. I promise." Jacob kissed her soft lips and brushed a rebellious strand of blonde hair from her face. Then he headed over to the lobby. Just before he turned the corner to where Abby's large wooden desk was, he stopped and took a deep breath. Nothing could prepare one for a meeting with the leader of the Latin Soldados. Turning, he saw Julio stood there in a black suit, wearing a bright red shirt. Jacob thought he appeared like a typical villain from some spy movie. There were two other men with him. His guards, the lawyer figured. Julio saw Jacob approaching and smiled.

"Mr. Scott, a pleasure to meet you. Any man who is willing to help any of my friends is considered a friend as well."

"What can I do for you, Mr. Jimenez?"

"I'm glad you asked. May we?" Julio motioned back to Jacob's office. Jacob refused to allow the gang leader to sit and relax in his office.

"I'm sorry, my office is a mess right now. We can take a conference room over there, if you prefer."

"That would be fine, thank you." Julio turned and raised a hand to the two guards. They both nodded and remained there, hands clasped together in front of their waist. They weren't as dressed up as Julio, but they were definitely better attired than the Jackals. Jacob guided Julio into conference room 1 and shut the door behind him.

"I apologize for the late visit, but I knew I would need to talk to you first."

"Okay, talk away." Jacob sat on the opposite side of the conference table. This gave him some distance and an obstacle in the event that Julio attacked him in his own law firm.

"I was notified by some of my gentlemen that young Enrique Perez had been arrested for carjacking."

"That's correct. And I have decided to represent Enrique as per his father's request."

"That's very noble of you. Now I know Enrique. He's a good boy. Very family oriented and smart. This carjacking does not seem like him. I'm sure that it was a silly teen mistake. I want to be able to give Enrique the help that I didn't have at his age."

"And how were you looking to help him, if I may ask?"

"Simple. The boy shouldn't be forced to fester in a jail cell until his case gets brought before a judge."

"What are you saying?"

"I want to post bail for Enrique. I know he realizes the error of his ways, but he should be able to see his family without them having to sign in. And I would take total responsibility if he ends up being a flight risk."

"Um, ok. If you leave a number that you can be reached at, I will contact the precinct and gather the information for you."

"Thank you. And the sooner we can get him home, the better it would be for all involved."

Jacob nodded in reply. Even though there was no hint of malice in Julio Jimenez's voice, he had heard the threat loud and clear.

19

"It's this building right here," Doyle pointed out to Fenton. An older apartment building off the corner of Hudson and Thirteenth street, it was part of a long line of apartments that took up half the long street block. Reaching a total of five floors, it once overlooked a riverside factory. But in the last ten years when the plans to renovate the city began, the unused factory was torn down for bigger apartment building providing a better view of the Hudson River and New York City. Now, the older apartment building looked over a new liquor store that contained beers that Doyle had never heard of, nor would want to.

He pulled the car into an available spot down the block from Kevin Finnegan's home. In Hoboken, a parking spot near your destination was like seeing Bigfoot. If you had one, you were one of the chosen few. Doyle got out and looked around, checking the scene like he had always done. His father had been a cop before him and had died on the job. He was in the middle of collaring a pickpocket when the pickpocket's sidekick came up from behind and plunged a switchblade into his right kidney. His father had bled out before he could get to the hospital. Doyle vowed never to let someone get the drop on him.

Amanda got out of the car and checked her weapon. Then she wrapped her coat around her torso and looked up at the grey sky.

"It's only going to get worse the closer we get to Christmas," he told her. She looked at him in confusion. He pointed up to the sky saying, "The weather, not the crime."

The two walked into the small enclosure just inside the building's entrance and looked over the thin mailboxes. Doyle located Finnegan's apartment number and pressed the bell buzzer. He held it in for the annoying effect.

"You're enjoying that, aren't you?" Fenton smiled.

"Always do," he said with a shit-eating grin.

They waited for a little over a minute and no response came. Doyle was afraid of this. Finnegan may be hanging out with the gang and not home. Tracking him down would be a problem. Amanda noticed the frustration on his face.

"He's not home?"

"Probably not." Doyle looked around and got a new idea. "Well seeing how we're already here, why waste a trip?"

He pressed the buzzer for the Superintendant's apartment. He was a little less annoying this time. The superintendent opened the door just inside the enclosure and poked his head out. The older, balding man looked at them, expecting someone else. Doyle took his badge out and held it up to the glass door. The older man shuffled out in sweats and slippers to open the door.

"Who called you guys now?" the superintendant asked.

"We're just here to question one of your renters. They weren't answering, and we thought they may be in a little trouble," Doyle lied.

The superintendant licked his lips at the sight of the tall Amazon standing next to Doyle. Doyle snapped his fingers, getting the older man's attention back.

"Yeah, sure, go on." He waved them in and shuffled back into his apartment. Just before he closed the door behind him, he turned and told the two, "No shooting this time. It's a pain in the ass filling in those holes perfectly."

"Cross my heart," Doyle told him. The older man got in one more look at Fenton and headed back inside. "I think you may have a fan," Doyle joked. They headed over to the skinny elevator located opposite to the staircase and pressed the UP button. A ding called out the arrival and the two stepped in, the space between them was thin. Doyle hit the button and moments later they stepped out onto the 3rd floor. Doyle pointed to his right and they walked down to apartment 322. Doyle knocked on the door hard and fast. There was no response behind the door but next door over opened and a short woman in a housedress stepped out.

"Are you here about the complaints?" she asked them.

"What complaints are those, ma'am?"

"I called you guys Saturday night about the noise over there. If you're not here for that, why are you here?"

"Saturday night? What kind of noise did you hear?"

"A lot of slamming and breaking glass. It sounded like that TV wrestling my son-in-law watches. My God, that stuff is worse than my soap operas."

Doyle and Fenton looked at each other and suspected that whatever this neighbor was talking about from Saturday night would be linked to the shootout. Doyle took a deep sigh and held his hand up to the woman.

"Ma'am, I'm going to have to ask you to return into your apartment, please."

"Are you going to arrest him? Good, cause, he's been nothing but disrespectful to the rest of the people on this floor. Take him away and don't bring him back!"

"Ma'am, please."

The neighbor threw her hands up and closed her door. Doyle unhooked the strap on his holster and prepared himself for entry into the apartment. He motivated himself to kick in the door and took a step back. Taking deep breaths, he held his left shoulder and arm towards the door and stared at it. Fenton stood back and watched. He then drove his body into the door and was knocked back by the resistance. Doyle struggled to keep his footing and prevent falling in front of the attractive ATF agent. He cursed under his breath and prepared himself again.

"Hang on," Fenton asked him. She leaned in and took hold of the knob. It turned easily in her hand and the door slowly opened. Doyle felt himself blush in embarrassment. He took his gun out and flipped the safety off.

Walking slowly into the apartment, he turned back to her and said, "Not a word about that."

"My lips are sealed," he told him, twisting two fingers in front of her smiling mouth.

Doyle continued in and was hit by a foul stench. He couldn't put a finger on it, but it smelled more like garbage than death. He looked around the living room. There was fast food wrappers and dirty laundry littered over everything. One of the fast food soda cups had eroded on the bottom and the soda had leaked out onto the table, soaking the garbage around it. The glass coffee table was shattered, and a couple of chairs had been overturned. Doyle knew the signs of a struggle when they screamed out in front of him. This was not a good sign.

"Must be the maid's week off," Fenton joked, covering her mouth and nose with her coat.

"A pigsty like this, yet he's got a bigger entertainment system than I do. Where's the justice?"

"Obviously we're in the wrong business."

Doyle headed into the kitchen and the stench of rotten garbage only got stronger. He denied himself the luxury of seeing what was in the fridge. Fenton turned to the left and headed down the hall to the bedrooms in the back. She slowly pushed the partially opened door. Inside was a bedroom made into a storage/ workout room. There were garbage bags of items in a corner with a workout bench and treadmill on either side of the room. She stepped in to get a better look around and saw no one inside. Stepping back into the hallway, she continued down to the second bedroom door. This one was latched. She held her gun up to her face and stepped to the side of doorway. It was then that she smelled something else other than foul garbage. Slowly taking hold of the doorknob, she opened the door and pushed it open gently. The door opened halfway and stopped as if something inside had blocked it.

"Police!" she said into the darkened bedroom. Nothing inside replied. Doyle entered the hall behind her to provide backup. She nodded to him and swung into the room. Holding her gun out, she swung it behind the door and released the tension in her body. She put the gun down and waved Doyle in.

"Please tell me this is not Kevin Finnegan," she asked him. He poked his head in around the door and saw a body on the floor, dressed in the usual green articles. The face was partially covered by strands of red hair. He leaned down and brushed it away with a finger. The bruised face of Kevin Finnegan stared back at him. Doyle noticed the slit throat under the handlebar mustache and stubbly chin.

"Dammit. Call it in. We've got a dead end here." Fenton cursed in frustration. They were not getting any closer to this Hermes and they were running out of time.

20

The snow, getting thicker, made it harder to see outside. Brett and Josh walked down Washington Street, hoping to clear their heads and then return back to the precinct for an hour before heading to Tamara's Christmas play. Brett zippered his coat all the way up to his chin, wishing he had a hat to cover his ears. Josh walked along his side, with his coat open and his short-cut thick black hair covered in large white specks.

"How you can walk around like that in this weather confuses the hell out of me," Brett told him.

"It's the Italian blood. We're a hot-blooded nationality. Hot pasta, hot sauce, hot bodies. I can't help it."

"Hot bodies? You obviously don't have a mirror in your apartment."

"Don't hate the player, Foster." Brett looked over at his partner with a quizzed expression.

"Okay, what'd I miss?"

"Huh?" Raghetti looked over at him.

"Why in such a good mood? Might I remind you of the case that we're working? The one that may cause a shit storm to hit this town?"

"I just have faith that we'll figure this out before it's too late."

"And does this Faith have a last name too?" Brett asked, leaning in.

"What? No."

"Fine. You're acting weird, even for you."

"You're over-thinking things. Just kick back for a few. Remember, Tamara's going to be looking at us."

"I know."

"Hey, we've got time before the thing starts. I could go for a nice thick milkshake." Josh stopped in front of Johnny Rocket's, a franchise in New Jersey that was designed like an old 1950's malt shop. They were known for their surprise entertainment, where the waiters and waitresses would stop everything and break out into a classic song, and their thick milkshakes.

"I wouldn't mind a Rueben sandwich." Brett said, agreeing to Raghetti's choice. The two entered the restaurant and were sat at the counter. After a few minutes, they both ordered and awaited their food.

"So, who's got the best motive to have taken out those gang members?"

"Who doesn't?"

"That's the problem. Everyone involved does. Donnelly had Dillon keeping him in check. He could have taken him out just for that. Jimenez could have set everything up to make it seem like Donnelly just, so his competition could be taken off the board and then the whole town would belong to the Latin Soldados.

"Or it could have been a new player, trying to take over Hoboken's turf," Josh added.

"Or it could be a vigilante motive. Hell, who knows, the Commissioner could be behind all this with that Initiative thing he's got brewing."

"How bad would that be?" Josh wondered, "First a crooked Governor and now a vigilante Police Commissioner."

"Don't say that too loud. You never know who's listening." The waitress came over with their orders. Josh took his milkshake and drank it in. He smiled and wiped the milkshake mustache from his face. The bell on the inside of the door jingled and the detectives glanced over to see who was coming in from out of the cold. Josh rolled his eyes and Brett shook his head when they saw that it was two members of the Jackals. The two gang members walked in and looked around for a spot to sit. Then they looked upon the detectives and laughed.

"Hey, Murphy, look, it's Riggs and Murtaugh. A couple of lethal weapons," one joked.

"Who?" Murphy asked, unaware of the movie reference. Josh felt it was a sad day when a Lethal Weapon reference to a young adult fell flat.

Josh looked over at Brett and said, "I guess because of my Italian heritage that makes me Murtaugh?"

"You do have a darker tan than me."

"An albino has a darker tan that you."

"Yo, cops. You the ones looking for the asshole who shot our guys?"

"Yeah. Why, you have something for us?"

"Hell no. We just want you to know that we're going to do your job for you and find the guy first."

"Go ahead. And then we can arrest you for the laws you'll break getting there."

"You think you're funny," Murphy said, walking up to Josh.

"No," Josh replied, "I'm the cute one, he's the funny one."

"Keep joking," Murphy said. He leaned in and got close to Josh's face. Josh did not flinch. "We'll show the people around you how much of a joke the police department here is. And then I'll be the one laughing."

"Step back," Josh told the one named Murphy.

"Make me, piggy."

Josh stood up and looked the Jackal in the eyes. Brett knew if he allowed it, this face-off would end in property damage and some bloody faces. He stood up and squeezed a hand in between them.

"Take it elsewhere," he told Murphy. "It won't end well for you. Trust me, I've seen it before." Foster remembered feeling the right hook that his partner had given him when he had first told him of the relationship that had evolved between him and Josh's ex-wife.

"Yo Murphy, we're wasting time. Let the piggies stuff their faces. Donnelly wants us to go check on Jimenez."

"What, why would he want to check in on Jimenez?"

"Wouldn't you like to know? It's gonna be a hell of Christmas in Hoboken, bacon boy." The comment sent a shiver down Foster's spine.

"Tell Vinnie to watch himself. He tries anything, and he'll have more than Jimenez and the Soldados to worry about."

"Please, you think he's worried about you guys? Bitch, the man has lost his mind. Liam ain't around anymore to hold him on a leash. This is our town now. And there's nothing you or the Soldados can do to stop him."

"Back off now, before this ends in the death of too many innocent people. Leave Donnelly unleashed for too long and he'll find an insane reason to come after you, too. Remember that."

"Whatever, man. You'll see." Murphy waved his hands around the restaurant. "You'll all see what it's like to mess with the Jackals." Murphy and the other Jackal turned and swung the door open to leave. A cold snowy gust came into Johnny Rockets and chilled everyone in there. When they had left, and the door had closed, Brett was still staring at the door.

"Hey, let it go. We'll stop this."

"Will we? Every day that passes without finding out who's behind this is only going to bring this closer to war between those two."

"You've got to be positive, dude. Trust me. We love this city too much to let them burn it to the ground. Now come on, let's finish eating and then we'll go see Tamara's school play. Then we can get back to protecting our city. And maybe getting that Christmas shopping done while we're at it."

"God help us all if we fail."

21

Enrique sat in the corner of the jail cell, wishing that he was home with his family, under a warm roof. Instead, his mistake had landed him here with half the town looking to learn what he knew. It was amazing what a difference a few days made in a kid's life. He wished that this was all a bad dream and he had never followed Wilfredo to that bus garage. He should have just gone home, and he and his family would be safe to enjoy Christmas without any worry.

"Hey Latin boy," Stringbean called out to him from the other side of the cell. "What 'cha thinking about? Your mommy?"

"Shut up."

"I'm sorry, what?" Stringbean stood up and walked over to Enrique. He loomed over the teenager like a corn stalk. Enrique didn't find the gang member threatening at all, but he still didn't want any trouble.

"Just go away."

"Nah, I don't think so. Let me tell you something junior. You're in over your head. You have no idea what you're involved in."

"I don't know what you're talking about." Enrique refused to look up at the Jackal.

"Oh, I think ya do. I know that scared look. I've seen it a bunch of times on the guys I've killed."

"Yeah, right."

"Son, haven't you learned by now? That mouth of yours has gotten you in enough trouble. You can keep the act up all you want but I know you.

You're wet behind the ears and you and your family are only going to end up another casualty in this gang war that *you* started."

"What are you talking about?" Enrique finally looked up. The mention of his family dying caught his attention.

"You've been holed up here for three days down. You have no idea what is going on out there. That meeting that you were at? It was a set up. Both gangs know that now. But the only person alive that knows who set the trap is you. And you're not talking. So, everyone outside of this cell is blaming the other. The cops, the Soldados, the Jackals, they all think they're the target. But you know that's not true. They're all looking for the proof. The person who killed those gang members, whoever it is, they're smart. They covered their tracks. And they left you to be the scapegoat. Everyone wants you. They want to convince you to tell them, so that they have the upper hand in the coming war. You think I'm stupid enough to get caught for something petty? Hang on a minute." Marc Walsh walked over to the bars and shouted to the night officer.

"What the hell are you yelling about?" the officer asked, walking over.

"Can you be a gentleman and remind me what I'm in here for?"

The male cop that took over for Peters looked at Walsh, trying to figure out what he was up to.

"Why?"

"I just want this young man to know who he's dealing with."

The cop rolled his eyes and asked, "Name?"

"Marc Walsh. With a C, not a K." Walsh leaned back and waited for the answer as the officer went back to his desk to look over the clipboard with all their names on it.

"Walsh, charge of shoplifting, one count of assault and resisting arrest. You're dealing with a real killer, kid," he said to Enrique. Then he looked over at Walsh and added, "Now shut it."

Walsh walked back over to Enrique and smiled. He crouched down to meet the teen at his level.

"See, shoplifting. Who really gets jailed for shoplifting anymore? See, my boss told me to do what I needed to get in this jail cell. You know why?" Marc poked his finger into the tip of Enrique's nose.

"Why?"

"You're the big Christmas gift that Santa has nicely wrapped for the lucky kid that finds you."

"Yo, Perez," called a voice from the next cell over. Enrique and Hannigan looked over to see Carlos Cruz peeking through the bars. "You better not tell him anything. Soldados takes care of their own. Unless they're snitches."

"You know who that is? Carlos Cruz. His older brother was there that night. He's dead. You think Carlos is here because he made a mistake and got caught?" Hannigan shook his head and pointed at Enrique.

"Just leave me alone."

"Your choice," he replied holding his hands up in defense, "But remember this when Donnelly or Jimenez get their hands on you: if you don't fess up to what you know, they'll kill your family first before they even think about touching you." Hannigan stood up and returned to his cot, a big smile on his face. Enrique stared down at the concrete floor, more scared now than he had ever been.

22

Angie met the two men in her life inside the front entrance of the school. She waved and got Brett's attention. Brett patted Josh's arm and pulled him in her direction. The two had returned home to get changed for the play and then hurried to the school, knowing that they'd have to park blocks away.

"Just in time," Angie said, "The play starts in five minutes. I've saved some seats for us in the front. Come on." She took Brett's hand and guided them to the auditorium. There was a teacher at the entrance handing out programs. Angie and Josh took one each. Brett felt out of place, not having an actual child of his own, but it didn't seem to faze Angie. She had already been bugging him to stay the night, even though he was unsure of how Tamara would take it. He didn't want to seem like he was replacing Josh.

The trio found the seats that Angie had covered with her and Tamara's coats. Angie sat on one end, leaving Brett in the middle with Josh on his other side. Angie wrapped her arm around his and clasped his hand in hers. He looked over and saw the excitement on her face. She was happy to have him there next to her. It was an odd feeling for him, knowing that he could make someone this happy by being there. Regardless of his looks, he wasn't much of the ladies' man. But he was one of the few who always would lend a hand for someone he considered a friend.

She glanced over to him and saw the look in his eyes. She tightened the grip on his hand, calming him.

"Hey, smile. It's time to take a break from the case and enjoy time with us."

"You're right, I'm sorry." He smiled to her and felt some relief. Distracting himself, he turned to Josh and leaned over. "So, who is she?"

Josh, caught off guard, looked over with his mouth open.

"You're horrible at hiding stuff."

"You're spending too much time snooping."

"Maybe, but you haven't answered the question."

Josh looked around them, as if someone else they knew might be listening. Brett laughed at the awkwardness.

"Bergen," Raghetti replied.

"You slept with Bergen?"

"What? No, I didn't sleep with her. I just asked her out."

"You've only asked her out and you're gleaming like a schoolgirl with a crush?"

"What can I say? I'm smitten."

"Smitten. This is new. You've worked with her for this long. Why now?"

"I dunno. I think I've just realized that Bergen and I have flirted with each other for the last year. It's been two years since Angie and I got divorced. I'm just at that point where I need to move on. I'm divorced, she's now divorced, why not?"

"I take it she said yes."

"Tomorrow I take her out for lunch."

"Well good for you," Brett said, "I'm glad to see you moving on. Nice choice, by the way. She's quite the catch."

"Did you say something?" Angie asked, listening in. Josh noticed Angie giving his partner the eyebrows. He knew better to interfere when she gave the eyebrows.

"What? Oh no, I was just asking Josh what to expect from a Christmas play."

"Oh, right," she smirked. Brett smiled back and snuck a thumbs up to Raghetti.

The principal of the school walked to the front of the stage and tapped the microphone in his hand. The crowd quieted down, and he thanked all the parents for showing up. Then he waved his hand at the curtain and it began to rise. The lights over the audience dimmed and the lights directed at the stage turned on.

The stage had a house setting backdrop. There were a number of children on the stage, several dressed in pajamas and one in a Christmas tree costume. The play began, and the trio watched, waiting for Tamara's moment of stardom. Josh held his camera up, recording the entire play.

The play began with the kids in the pajamas waiting anxiously for Santa. A few holiday puns were thrown into the script, provided by the kid as the tree. After a few minutes, Brett forgot all about the case and the danger that loomed on the horizon.

The play continued as the kids fell asleep one by one. The stage lights dimmed slightly and then off stage the jingle of Christmas bells was heard. A kid dressed as Santa and two of his elves came onto the stage, ready to drop off presents for this home. Tamara looked out into the crowd and saw Josh, Brett and Angie sitting there together. She smiled and waved her hand at them. They all smiled and waved back. Brett thought that she could not have been any happier, seeing the three she cared about together for her. *I could get used to this*, he thought.

A minute or two later, Tamara stepped forward. The smile left her face and Josh saw the concentration take over. He nudged Brett, knowing that this was her moment.

"Christmas Tree," Tamara shouted as loud as she could so that everyone in the auditorium could hear, "Can you tell if Santa is on his way?"

"With my Santa locator, I see that he is getting near," the kid in the tree outfit replied.

"Do you know if he's planning to give all Christmas bonuses this year too?" she asked. Before the tree kid could answer, Tamara leaned towards the audience and winked at her parents. The crowd laughed at the adorableness of it all.

With a huge smile, Josh looked over at the stranger to his left and said, "That's my girl. A real actress, huh?"

In the back of the auditorium, a young man by the name of Brian Murphy, stood keeping an eye on Foster and Raghetti. He noticed the girl elf on the stage, waving to them. He leaned onto the back wall and sent a text to the leader of the Jackals. He would stay there until the play was over, then he would slip out of the school and continue the job he was given.

23

Maritza sat on the couch opposite from her mother, while Emilio sat in his comforter chair. They remained silent, slowly eating dinner while the TV showed yet another Christmas movie. No one felt comfortable eating at the dinner table without Enrique. It didn't feel right. They all worried about him. Emilio had arrived home a few hours earlier and explained to Carmen what had occurred that day.

"Why is he not talking to them? Doesn't he know that he could be home if he had?"

"Yes, Mami. I told him that, but he's got this protecting us in his head. I'm afraid for him. He's too young to understand what's really going on."

"And what is going on?"

"He's the only witness to a mass shooting. He thinks the one who shot everyone is after him. The police believe he saw the man's face, but he won't say anything until they get us in a safe house."

"Then why don't they move us for a few days?"

"It takes time to get a safe house set up, I guess. The police asked me to talk some sense into him, but he wouldn't hear it." "What horrors has that boy seen to make him act this way?"

"I don't know, but he's scared. I could see it in his eyes. I feel so helpless not being able to get him out of this mess."

"You're doing what you can, Emilio. He needs to learn."

Maritza entered the kitchen and asked about her brother. Emilio explained a second time to her.

"Why is he being so stupid?"

"Your guess is as good as mine, Mari."

Carmen served up dinner for the three of them with an extra plate on the table for Enrique before she realized her mistake. She quickly put the plate back in the cabinet.

"It's weird how quiet the house is without his stupid comments," Maritza mumbled.

"Mari, please, it's not nice to talk bad about your brother. He's in jail trying to keep us safe."

"Yeah, but he'd be home right now if he had told the cops about the guy."

"Unless the man who shot those gangs was a cop?" Emilio said, thinking out loud.

"Do you think the man is a police officer?"

"Maybe I'm just watching too many cop shows, but why else would he be scared to tell anyone anything?"

"Yeah but if the guy was a cop, wouldn't he still be able to get to us if we're placed in a cop safe house?" Mari interjected.

"Good point. Maybe it was one of the gang leaders."

The night continued with discussion of what was running through Enrique's head. They couldn't figure out why he was keeping silent when the police could have caught the man already. After they had finished dinner, Emilio gathered up the dirty dishes and washed them for Carmen. She thanked him and gave him a kiss. Maritza came down the stairs after being up in her room for a few minutes. She had her coat on and was putting on her new boots when Emilio noticed her.

"Where do you think you're going?"

"I'm going to Jesse's."

"I don't know if that's a good idea."

"Why not?"

"Because what if Enrique's right? What if we are in danger? Going out on your own in weather like this isn't smart."

"Do you expect me to stay home until he decides to smarten up and tell the cops what they want?"

"Let me drive you, then. That way you're not alone."

"Dad, that is lame."

"Either I drive you or you spend the night here with us. You decide."

"Ugh, fine, let's go." Emilio got his coat and boots and heated up the car while brushing off the collection of snow. He honked the horn when he was ready, and Maritza came out and rushed into the car, in case any of her friends were walking by. Emilio pulled out of the parking spot and drove down the street. Carmen watched them from the living room window, saying a prayer that both remained safe.

But she was not the only one watching them drive away. Several houses down, sitting in his Le Baron, Vinnie Donnelly wrote the car's make and license plate number on his hand. Then he made a call on his cell phone.

24

"Russell," Fernandez whined, "Can you rub my feet?" Emerson looked up from his paperwork.

"Now?"

"I'll make it worth your while when we get home," she said, winking seductively. He sighed, being the nice guy, and wheeled his chair over to her side of the desks. She smiled and kicked off her shoes. Placing a foot on his lap, he began helping his partner/girlfriend relax. Lyndsey and Danica walked into the room and saw the two kicking back.

"Can I be next?" Danica joked.

"Nope, sorry," Kylee replied, "He's my partner and my slave. You should ask Lyndsey."

"Um, don't swing that way," Lyndsay told her.

"Oh, we know."

"What's that mean?"

"Hines overheard you and Raghetti chatting like a couple of high school sweethearts."

"Wait," Danica said, "You and Josh? That wasn't just playful flirting?"

Lyndsey sighed, "How did this turn into a soap opera?"

"The moment he asked you out."

"But what about you two?"

"Me and Russell? That's simple. We didn't hide it. I don't give a fuck what anyone thinks. And Russell cares about me, so he ignores all the ribbing."

"Fine," Lyndsey said, giving in, "I mean he's kind of cute in a rugged way. And I've seen him with his daughter. He's responsible and now that we're both available I thought I'd give it a try. For the record, though, he asked me out. I just jumped at the opportunity."

"Fair enough," Kylee said, switching feet.

"Does this mean you two are going to be partners?" Danica asked. "Don't make me partner up with Foster. He's too serious."

"Don't worry, I'm not going to trade partners. You're still my next maid of honor."

"Thank you!"

"I've never realized that this place could actually be this quiet," Russell finally added to the conversation.

"It's the calm before the storm," Kylee explained, "Christmas is right around the corner and people always get crazy around the holidays. Take advantage of it while it lasts."

"Brett! Josh!" a voice from the hallway called out. The detectives looked over and saw Lucky come speeding around the corner, almost tripping himself up and falling forward.

"See? Told ya," Kylee said.

"Hey Lucky, you need to be more careful," Danica said.

"Thank you. Where's Brett and Josh?"

"Josh's daughter had a school play tonight," Lyndsey told him.

"I've got to call them. Foster is going to flip."

"Why?"

"I've been running a search on the bullets and the casings that came from the lone shooter. And it just came back with a match!"

"Let me see," Lyndsey took the paper from his hands and read the results. "Oh my God."

"See? I told you!"

"Let me call him," she told Lucky. She grabbed the phone off her desk and dialed. She stood, waiting for him to pick up. There was no answer.

"He must have his phone off. Danni, let's go find them."

"But what's it say?"

"I'll tell you on the way." Lyndsey and Danica put their coats back on and left the room.

"Is someone going to tell me what the fuck the results were? I'm curious too" Kylee asked annoyed. Lucky walked over to her to explain.

"There's a reason why the search took so long. I had running the search using only the criminal database. But one of the guns used by our mystery man wasn't in that database because it wasn't used by a criminal."

"Well, if it wasn't a criminal, then who shot all those gang members?"

"Tony Hughes."

"And who is Tony Hughes?"

"He worked Anti-Vice here for a good twenty years, but he retired six years ago."

"So, a retired cop killed those gang bangers?" Russell asked the crime lab tech.

"Not quite."

"Lucky, if you don't tell us I will cut you like a bitch."

"Tony Hughes died of a heart attack seven months ago."

"Then who used a cop's gun to kill a bunch of gang bangers?"

Lucky didn't have an answer to that.

25

Doyle walked Amanda Fenton to her hotel, the W Hoboken. Located on Third and River Street, the W was a ritzy hotel built back in 2009 along the riverside, that gave their guests a beautiful and pricey view of Manhattan.

"Quite the fancy spot," Doyle said, "You ATF agents have it made."

"Oh no, this is coming out of my pocket."

"Really? They won't pay for a hotel when you're on a job?"

"I'm not really on an official job. I came down here to see where Thomas was. I haven't notified anyone."

"Well, I'm sorry your partner was murdered. How long are you planning on staying here?"

"Until we find the guy. So that I can get some closure and make sure that son of a bitch pays for what he did."

"Don't you have anyone waiting for you back in Newark?"

"Not really. Haven't found the right guy yet. And the job doesn't give a person much time to look either."

"Yeah, I understand. My wife died a few years ago and I haven't really try to replace her. It's a bit different for me though. We were married 26 years."

"Oh, I'm sorry."

"Ah, it's not your fault. She had a heart disease. She cared too much I guess. She's better off now."

"Must make this time of year hard on you, huh?"

"Nah, it's not so bad. I've come to accept that she's gone."

"Times like this reminds me of my father. He passed away five years ago on the job in Union City. He apparently had crossed the wrong guys on patrol one night and they gunned him down in an alley. They never did find out who did it. It just makes me strive harder to make a difference for him."

"Sorry, kiddo," Doyle said, unsure of what else to say to that.

"Do you have any kids?"

"Just one, a daughter. The doctor had told me that I was shooting blanks in that department, but when my wife became pregnant, it surprised us all. She's married and lives up in Englewood, though. I visit them from time to time when I have the chance."

"Well at least you've got her."

"Yeah. I just haven't figured out what I'll do when they make me retire. I'm not the Florida retirement type. This is my home, always will be. I'm just old school like that."

"Even though I've only been here for less than a day, I have to say, it seems like a nice place."

"Yeah, it ain't the Hamptons but that's okay. I can't stand those fake snobby types."

"You're not the only one," she laughed. They walked into the hotel lobby and Amanda stopped. Doyle was stunned by the stylish lobby.

"Here I am," she said.

"Now you should go get some sleep. Who knows what tomorrow will bring."

"Thanks Doyle. Have a good night."

"Yep, you too." He tipped his hat to her and watched her walk past the registration desk and over to the elevators. Nice girl, he thought. She had reminded him of his wife, that caring look in her eyes. He remembered seeing that look whenever he came down with a nasty head cold. She would get him to sit down and relax with some cough medicine and a hot bowl of soup. The thought of the soup made him hungry.

Heading back to Washington Street, he stopped over at the Subway to get some dinner for himself. The sandwich shop was quiet. It normally happened that way when the weather got bad. No one wanted to be outside in this.

There was a younger guy standing behind the counter, wiping the top down. He looked up and smiled at Doyle.

"Hey there, sir. What can I do for you?"

"Yeah let me get one of your meatball sandwiches. On that parmesan bread." The kid looked into the bread heater.

"Hang on one second," he said to Doyle, "Larry! Hey Larry! We need some more parmesan bread!" Doyle rolled his eyes. A few minutes later he had his dinner and was back out in the cold, headed down 6th Street to Willow Avenue. He was two blocks from his home when he passed an alley. Through the wind and noise from Washington Avenue, he heard something. Doyle paused, not sure if what he heard was his imagination. The area went silent and he continued to listen. Doyle's instinct screamed at him.

Then the sound came again. It was a man's scream. Doyle turned trying to gather where the scream came from. The alley to his left seemed like a good idea. Removing the gun from his holster, he slowly crept over into the alley. Squinting his eyes, he was able to see two figures in the darkness beyond. One was on his knees with his hands up while the other stood over him, dressed all in black. A hoodie covered the standing man's head. Doyle was still able to see the gun in his hand.

"It's too cold for this shit." Doyle moved in closer and began to listen in on what was going on.

"Please, man. Don't shoot. I swear I give it all up."

"It's too late for that. You and your buddies have turned this town into a shithole."

"No, really, I'll talk to Julio. You'll see. It's the Jackals that are the problem. That Donnelly guy is a psycho."

"Donnelly will be taken care of, too. When I'm ready for him. But your boss needs to know that he's not untouchable. And you're going to send him that message for me."

Doyle didn't recognize either of the voices. Could this be the Hermes that they were all looking for? He couldn't let him get away. He had promised his wife on her deathbed that he would keep the town safe from people like this. It was the least he could do for the woman that he loved, who had died of something he could not stop.

The figure he believed was Hermes raised his hand. In it was a gun.

Doyle had to make his move now. He placed the dinner on a garbage bin next to him and stepped out into the middle of the alley.

"Police!" he yelled, "Drop the weapon and put your hands up! Both of you!"

Hermes paused, turning his head slightly. Doyle couldn't see his face under the dark hood. The man on the ground threw his hands up.

"Oh God," the Soldados member said in relief, "He was gonna kill me, man!"

"Not anymore." Doyle slowly approached the two men. Hermes did not move, nor did he place the gun down. Doyle had a bad feeling about this.

"Yo man," the Soldados member said, "He said to put the gun down. You should really listen to him." But Hermes remained stiff, as if he was calculating his odds. It made Doyle and the gangbanger nervous.

"Listen," Doyle told him, "I was on my way home to eat my Meatball sandwich and watch a What's Happenin' marathon on Nick at Nite. I *really* like What's Happenin'. Missing an episode makes me grumpy. This snow is bad enough, are you going to make me miss a show?"

"Which one are you, detective?" Hermes finally spoke.

"Which what?"

"Your name."

"Detective Doyle, Hoboken Anti-Vice."

Hermes' head dropped slightly. He shook it gently, as if disappointed in the detective's name. Doyle's nerves were on edge. Even though it was snowing and windy, he felt a drop of sweat trickle down his forehead.

"You've been slacking on your job, Detective. These scurrying filthy rats are turning the city into a garbage barge. Why are you allowing this to happen?"

"The hell you say. I do my job. Gang activity was down this year."

"And it will be even lower thanks to me. I only have so many days left in this year. Arresting me is not going to help you get rid of filth like this."

"Killing them only makes you as bad as them," Doyle explained, "Is that what you want?"

"It is the only way to clean up this town. You've failed to do your job. Now it is up to me. Please continue on your way home. You will if you know what is good for you, detective."

"Sorry, I'm not one for taking orders from some scumbag. Now put down the gun or I will put it down for you."

Hermes stood there, considering his options. Then Doyle saw the arm holding the gun lower. Doyle took a sigh of relief and relaxed slightly. As he did, Hermes raised his arm with lightning speed and fired the gun at the Soldados member. Doyle saw the explosion of the gang member's skull as the bullet traveled through it. He recovered, gripping his gun with both hands and fired at Hermes. Hermes jerked forward, stumbling from the shot to his back. Then he fell over.

Doyle didn't move for a minute, not sure of what had just happened. When Hermes did not move, he lowered his own gun and walked closer to the vigilante. When he was a few feet away, Hermes moved. He did more than move. He got to his feet.

"What the hell?" Doyle said to himself. Before he could raise his gun, Hermes aimed his at Doyle's face.

"Have you ever been shot, detective?"

"No."

"Well, let me tell you, it really does hurt. Even with protection on." Doyle realized why Hermes didn't stay down. He was wearing a vest under the thick hoodie. Where the hell did he get a vest? Doyle thought of the possibilities and dismissed them, as they didn't seem right.

"You do realize that your actions are going to cause a war in this town, right?"

"I do. That was my whole plan. Let the vermin take themselves out. Saves me the trouble of doing it all myself. And when the smoke clears, I move in and take down whoever's left."

"You're friggin' nuts, you know that?"

"Yes, but it's the crazy ones that make the most impact on society. Nicolai Tesla had OCD. He always had to walk around the block three times before he allowed himself to enter a building. Pythagoras, the Greek Mathematician, believed that beans were evil. And the great poet Lord Byron kept a bear in his dorm room at school as a pet when they told him his dog could not stay. I consider myself quite sane compared to them."

"Look, let's just go down to the precinct and we can all talk about this."

"I will not let you and your fellow detectives stop me until I am done with what I need to do."

"Fine. But there's no need to shoot me. I'm one of the good guys, remember."

"Yes, detective, I do. You have done some great things in your career as an officer of the law. You have earned my respect."

"Then just put the gun down. Let's just talk about this."

"Are you going to give me advice?"

"Well, not really. But I was hoping to convince you to stop doing what you're doing."

"And how are you planning on doing that?"

Doyle planned out his words out gently. "This war that you'll start will get innocent people hurt. You've had to have realized that."

"I did. I spent a lot of time thinking this over. I examined every option. But if I didn't do what I have done so far, it would only cause more innocent lives to be snuffed out because of these two gangs."

"So, you're just going to let a couple of civilians die for the betterment of the rest?"

"See, I knew you'd understand me, eventually."

"It's still wrong."

"For the present, maybe. But so much better for the future."

"You have kids?" Doyle asked. Hermes fell silent. He thought that he had hit a sore spot with the question.

"Don't try to get in my head, detective. You won't like the visit."

"Look, enough. I'm too old for this shit. Either shoot me or leave."

Hermes stood there, wondering what he should do. Detective Doyle knew too much now. He raised his free hand and pushed back the hood that covered his face. Doyle looked at Hermes and the recognition in his eyes gave it away.

"You're Hermes? Why?"

"I'm sorry, detective. But I thought you should see the face of the one who kills you. It's only out of respect. I'm terribly sorry. I can't have you and your fellow officers stopping me before I'm done."

"Look, come on," Doyle began to say, but the shout of the gun cut him off. The bullet pierced his chest and lodged itself in one of his main arteries. Doyle jerked back from the force of the bullet and looked down at his chest. A blooming circle of red grew on his white button-down shirt.

"I am truly sorry," Hermes told him. Doyle fell to his knees and slumped over. Hermes crouched down and placed a gentle hand on the dead detective. He whispered a prayer that no one heard over the howling wind. Then Hermes stood up and walked off into the night.

Two

WAR

26

Raghetti and Foster walked onto the scene an hour after the two bodies were found. Officer Kassen stood at the yellow tape, keeping back the gawkers wandering past. She saw the detectives and nodded, lifting the tape up to allow them into the crime scene. Josh nodded back and looked over at Melvin, who was hovering over Doyle's body, examining the body before Aaron took him away. Brett glanced around and saw a Subway bag resting on the top of a garbage can near the entrance of the alley. It didn't have as much snow on it as most of the other objects around it.

"Hey Melvin, do we have anything that tells us who did this?"

"I'm sorry, guys. We've got a single gunshot wound just below the collarbone. Exit wound out the back means that the shooter was up close, almost point blank."

"Did he suffer?" Brett asked.

"Doesn't look like it. With the trajectory from the entrance wound and the exit wound, it would have punctured his heart, so no, he didn't."

"Do we have the bullet?"

"Still looking for it but we do have the casing, so we can use that to match it with the other casings from the garage shooting."

"Did he at least get a shot off?"

"I've haven't checked for GSR on his hand or sleeve yet. I was about to. I've only gotten here about twenty minutes ago."

"And the other guy over there?" Josh pointed to the faceless Soldados member. Melvin shrugged his shoulders.

"Gunshot to the face. I'm guessing that's what killed him. Haven't gotten to him yet either, I thought Detective Doyle took precedence."

"Thank you," Brett said, looking at the lab tech. The two left Melvin to finish what he was working on and went over to the dead Latin Soldados member. Luis was standing there looking down at the body. He noticed the two approaching and shook his head.

"This pendejo is attacking us now?" Luis asked them. The others could tell Orlando was furious when he spoke a mix of Spanish and English.

"Looks like Doyle may have just come across the attack on this guy and the shooter. There's a bag from Subway over on that garbage can. You know how he loved those meatball sandwiches," Brett explained.

"Nice catch," Josh added.

"No ID on this yet, if that's what you're wondering," Orlando answered before the two could ask him.

"Black's not going to be happy losing Doyle to this prick."

"Wow, Raghetti, you really are the master of the obvious."

"Bite me," Raghetti retorted.

"Cut it out you two," Brett said, annoyed, "We need to start banding together on this. For Doyle." Luis and Josh realized that Foster was right and they quieted down.

"He's showing us that he has no intention of slowing down, even if we get in the way."

"Then we bring out the big guns and mow this fuck down." Brett paused and considered at what his partner had just said.

"You might have an idea there."

"Huh?"

"About getting out the big guns." Brett reached into his pants pocket and took out his wallet. Poking around in it, he retrieved a card. Then he dialed the number on the card.

"Sorry for the late call, Agent. It's Detective Foster. I was wondering if you wouldn't mind coming back out in this harshness. I think I know how you may be able to help us with taking down the man that killed your partner." Foster gave her their current location and thanked Fenton before hanging up.

"What's that all about?"

"Well, right now we're outnumbered. We've got the Soldados, the

Jackals and this mystery guy all against us. It's time we got some backup for our side. If we don't now, when the shit hits the fan, and it will, then we really won't stand a chance protecting this city from them."

"You really think it's going to get that bad?" Orlando asked, afraid of the answer.

"Yeah, and that's what I'm afraid of the most. Because then Doyle won't be the last of us to fall."

"So, what's the plan?"

"Agent Ketchum got involved in that gang meeting because one of his CIs told him about it."

"Yeah but we found out the CI's dead. What help is that to us?"

"Yes, but local police or ATF agent, the relationship between Finnegan and Ketchum should have been documented regularly. Ketchum's boss should have something on file about the conversation those two had regarding the garage meeting."

"He's got a point," Luis said.

"That's the only solid lead we've got right now. Not using it is a waste. If Agent Fenton wants to help us, I'm going to use all the help she can give."

"Yeah, but what if Ketchum was told right before the meeting went down and he never had time to make any calls or document it? He was there on his own, remember? No backup. That's not normal for any cop."

"Well, then we're back at square one."

27

The lawyer and the head of the Latin Soldados gang walked into the police precinct late that evening with one thing on their mind. Hines peeked up from his keyboard behind the large desk and almost fell off his chair at the sight of Julio Jimenez walking in. Julio noticed it and smiled to himself. Jacob muttered something under his breath that Julio knew was a curse about his current situation, but Jimenez didn't care. That's what gave him the power that he had to run his gang in this town. It was what forced them to respect him.

"Good evening, sergeant. We're looking to post bail for an Enrique Perez, please," Jacob said to Hines. Hines didn't take his eyes off Julio to talk to Jacob.

"Bail agent is on the second floor. Take the stairs, turn right and it's the third door on the left. Room 204. Better hurry though, he should be leaving for the day."

"I know, thank you." Jacob motioned to Julio and the two headed for the stairs. Jacob could feel the burning stare of Hines on his back. Once they hit the second floor, they turned to the right and walked over to the door leading to room 204. Julio noticed the Hoboken Police Museum display on the side.

"Ah, I've always wanted to see this display, but I just never got around to it. Never thought they'd let me past the front door."

"Come on," Jacob said, shaking his head, "If we miss him, we'll have to wait until tomorrow morning. I'm sure Enrique would love to be home again."

"Very true, Mr. Scott."

Jacob knocked on the door and could hear some scuffling around inside. He sighed, knowing that he wasn't late, and that Enrique had a chance to make it home tonight. Although, he wasn't sure what Julio had planned for the boy. A man in his fifties opened the door and looked at the two men in the hall.

"Hey there, I'm just on my way home for the day. Sorry but it will have to wait until tomorrow. I'm here at 9a.m." the man said.

"That just won't do," Julio told him. He stepped forward and entered the room. The man stared at him and gave Jacob a look. Jacob just tried to smile and shrug.

"Yeah, sure, come on in. Make yourself comfortable," the man said sarcastically. Jacob entered the room, seeing that Julio had already found a seat. The man closed the door and sat behind the desk in the small room. Jacob decided to start immediately so that this awkward meeting could end as soon as possible.

"My name is Jacob Scott, this is Mr. Julio Jimenez and we are looking to post cash bail for an Enrique Perez, please."

"Perez. Sounds familiar. Wait, that's the kid that was talking to the Homicide detectives earlier. Let me get his file." The man stood up and walked over to the filing cabinet in the far corner. He pulled out a file from the third drawer and opened it on the desk. "Here we are, the charges are carjacking, possession of a weapon, and assault. Kid's looking at about fifteen grand, even though it is a first offense. You want to make that check out to Hoboken Department of Bails."

"A check won't be necessary," Julio told the man. He reached into his inside coat pocket and removed a wrapped wad of bills. Jacob could notice the top bill was a hundred-dollar bill. Julio opened it up and began counting. He placed most of the wad on the man's desk.

"Fifteen thousand. Feel free to count it."

The man stared at the pile of bills and then up at Julio, "Um, no that's fine. I trust you." Then the man took a form from his top desk drawer and began filling it out. Jacob looked over at Julio and saw the small smile on his face. After a few minutes of silence, the man turned the form around to Julio.

"I need your name and address up here. Then sign here and initial there and then I'll write up a receipt. If Mr. Perez shows up at his hearing, the funds will be refunded back to you at the address provided."

"Thank you," Julio said, filling in his information onto the form. The man took the form and wrote up a receipt. He tore it off the book and handed it to Julio.

"Take that down to the desk sergeant and he'll have Mr. Perez brought upstairs."

"That'll be fun," Jacob said lowly.

"I'm sorry?" the man asked.

"Nothing, thank you, sir." Jacob and Julio stood up and walked out of the room, leaving the bail agent with the pile of bills still on his desk. Downstairs, Hines was clearly waiting for the two of them to come back downstairs. He noticed the receipt in Julio's hand and made a face. Julio handed the receipt to Hines and smiled. Danny picked up his phone and made a call down to the holding cells. He told the night officer to send Enrique upstairs.

A few minutes later, Enrique was escorted to the front desk without any handcuffs. Enrique saw Jacob and smiled. Then when Julio stepped forward, the smile faded, and disappointment took its place.

"Enrique, my boy! It's good to see you again. Let's get you home." Julio gave the boy a hearty pat on his back. The escorting officer handed Enrique a large paper bag, containing his things that were taken when he was brought in. Enrique put his coat on and zipped it up, looking at the large flakes falling outside. Jacob thanked Sergeant Hines and walked Julio and Enrique to his car. Julio's bodyguards, standing in the lobby the whole time, stepped outside to open the door of Julio's chauffeured vehicle. The leader of the Soldados got in and the guards motioned to Jacob and Enrique to get in as well. Jacob did as he was told and the two joined Julio in the back. One guard held his hand out at Jacob. Unsure of what to do, he looked over at Julio.

"Give him your car keys and he will take your car over to Enrique's home."

Jacob handed over his keys and they drove off to the Perez home. The ride started out quiet, but Julio didn't waste any time in getting what he was there for.

"Did you see the man who killed several of my men?"

Enrique kept quiet and looked down at his hands. Julio knew the answer to the question he had just asked. Now it was just a matter of time to get the one thing he wanted.

"No. I was too scared." Jacob was almost surprised by the boy's voice.

"Are you sure?" Julio pressed.

"He said no," Jacob interjected, "As the boy's lawyer, I have to insist that you refrain from pressuring my client." Julio looked over at Jacob and smirked. Jacob knew that Julio could have him killed with a snap of his fingers, but he was not one to back down from a fight, especially when a client was involved. The rest of the ride was silent.

28

Don Price hung up the phone and rubbed his temples. The headache from the phone call was beginning to form. He had just been told by Christine Black of Doyle's death. It was a horrible feeling when a cop under his command was killed in the line of duty.

He remembered the days when he was growing up in Hoboken and how it seemed so big and lively. The town had grown since then; with the renovations of Hoboken Transit Terminal and what is now known as Frank Sinatra Park, and the Lightrail line that ran through the town from the Harborside Financial Center all the way up to the north end of Union City. He was happy to see how far the town had come over the years.

Mayor Raymond Victor had played a major part in the turnaround of Hoboken in the past few years. He had worked with Price and Black to help make the town more of a family and tourist town instead of the college party town that it was once known as. Victor had even signed the authorization forms for the TLC channel to film in Hoboken, although he wasn't much of a reality TV show fan.

Don poured himself a splash of bourbon with some ice, wondering what he could do for Detective Doyle's death. Leaning back in his office chair, he pondered the thought. He dialed the cordless phone and waited for the other line to pick up. When it did, he threw back the bourbon and cleared his throat.

"Raymond, it's Don. Have you heard about Detective Mark Doyle?"

"I just got off the phone with Christine."

"It's a horrible shame that this had to happen."

"I don't like it any more than you do, but I've been thinking that your plan for this war on crime initiative needs to be out there as soon as possible."

"I was thinking the same thing. That's why I'm calling. I spoke to the tech guys at the precinct earlier today and they've got everything in place for the tip app. We could get that running tomorrow morning. The rest of the E.T.C. program can be explained in a press conference if we can get one set up."

"I'll give my assistant, Carol, a call and have her set one up in front of City Hall tomorrow around noon. Just make sure you include Detective Doyle's passing in it to help bring some seriousness to what we're trying to accomplish."

"Understood. Thank you, Ray."

"Anything to help clean up this town for the people. I'll talk to you in the morning. I've got family here right now."

"Give my best to Marianne. And Merry Christmas."

"Same here."

Don hung up the phone and looked out into the darkness just outside his den's window. His plan was finally going to see the light of day. All the years of hard work he had put into the position was paying off. He raised the glass in his hand up and looked at the ceiling.

"This one's for you, dear." He smiled remembering his wife of 24 years. Bethany Price had died four years ago of breast cancer. Not one for showing his emotion, Don dug himself into his police work, grieving only in private. He made a large donation every Christmas to the Cancer Society in her name. He knew that even though, he, himself, couldn't do anything to end cancer, he had promised her that he would do what he could to keep her hometown safe and family friendly.

The thought of Beth brought his only son, Ron, to the front of his mind. He and Ron didn't talk often. In fact, the last time they spoke was when Ron called to announce his acceptance to Hoffman and Delgado law firm. It had made Don proud. Now that Christmas was only a few days away, he thought of spending some time with Ron to make up for all the years that he was too busy working his way up the ranks. He could hear Beth pestering him in his ear, *give him a call. Let him know you care.*

Don picked up the phone again and dialed his son's number. After a few rings, Ron picked up.

"This is Ronald Price."

"Hello, son. How is the new job?"

"It's pretty great, Dad. Allen is very welcoming and the whole firm is friendly. I've already been handed some cases to work on."

"That's good to hear. I knew Allen would be great to work for." Don had known Allen Hoffman for many years. The friendship between the two older men wasn't a close one but it was strong, nonetheless.

"Yeah, I can see myself here for a long time."

"That's fantastic."

"Now, why are you really calling?" Ron asked his father.

"Can't pass anything by you, can I? Just like your mother. She always knew whenever I was hiding something."

"You're missing her, aren't you?"

"A little. The holidays are always tough. You know that."

"I do. How about I finish up here and we can go out for dinner?"

"I'd like that." If anything, Don Price knew that he had raised his son right. Now if he could only get the city to go the same way.

29

By the time Amanda arrived at the crime scene where the detectives were waiting, Doyle's body had been taken back to the morgue for autopsy. Josh got her through the barricade and brought her over to the other detectives.

"Agent Fenton, thank you for coming out in this."

"Did this Hermes attack again?"

"Yes, and Detective Doyle came across them when it happened."

"So, we've got him?"

"Unfortunately, no. Detective Doyle was shot. He died before anyone could find him."

"Oh God." Fenton covered her mouth in shock. Brett looked down for a moment, giving her a moment to take in the news.

"We're done playing around with this fuck," Josh told her, "We're asking for your help in getting any information that Agent Ketchum may have received from his informant. A name, a description, anything."

"I was going to call my supervisor tomorrow, but I'll give him a call tonight. I just hope Tommy told him about the call before he went running off. He was always reckless and eager in getting things done. Is there anything new from your witness?"

"No and we can't wait for the kid to wake up. Not anymore." Brett looked over at the spot in the alley that was covered in a pink mix of blood and snow.

"Give me a few minutes and I'll see what I can find out." Fenton took out her phone and pressed a few buttons to dial her supervisor's number.

She walked over to the side and Brett and Josh waited for her to finish the call.

"Josh," called out a voice. Raghetti turned and saw Lyndsay approaching him. She had tears in her eyes. He knew that the word was now out and everyone on the force would be feeling the loss of a brother in arms.

"Hey," was all he could say.

"I can't believe he's gone." She wrapped her arms around his chest, digging her face into the crook of his neck. It surprised Josh but he followed up with placing his arms around her shoulders. Despite the solemn situation, it felt good and right at the same time.

"We've got Agent Fenton looking into any information from her boss. I hate that we don't have more to run with at this time."

"But we do," She said pulling back, "Lucky identified the gun that was used."

"He did? Who's it registered to?"

"A retired Hoboken detective named Tony Hughes. The bad news is Hughes died a couple of years back from health issues."

"Did anyone follow up on this?"

"Chief Black assigned me and Danica to go visit Hughes' widow. We're hoping to get something from her."

Josh called Brett and Luis over to explain to them what Lyndsay had told him. Their faces brightened over the news.

"Wait, I don't see an elderly woman pulling this off and getting the jump on Doyle," Brett said.

"Who's to say that she still has it? She could have sold it or given it away."

"Let us know what you find out," Foster said to Bergen, "We're going to head back to the stationhouse in a few. We've got everything from the scene that we need."

"Danica and I will call when we're done." Lyndsay turned to Josh, "Looks like that lunch date will have to wait."

"That's fine. There's always tomorrow."

"Be safe," she said, looking into his eyes and smiling gently. Josh thought he could get used to dating again.

"You too." Lyndsay and Danica left in their unmarked and Fenton returned to the trio after a few minutes, still on the phone.

"Hey guys, what's your email address?" she asked them. Brett gave it to her and she repeated it to the phone. Then she thanked her boss and hung up.

"Good news, Tommy handed our boss a recording of the conversation. He's headed back to the office to email it over to you. I'm hoping that there's something in it that you can use."

"It's worth a try," Luis told her.

"Anything to get this guy."

"I'm going back to the stationhouse to wait for the report and to see if Aaron or Melvin found anything," Brett told them.

"Why not just go see Angie?" Josh asked him. "I'll go back and when we get something, I'll call. Tamara told me that she was making her some paintbrush cookies. Go spend some time with them."

"Are you sure?" Brett asked.

"Yeah, I've done the paintbrush cookie thing. And little Miss Independent will have fun teaching you how to paint them. Besides, this will give me time to shop for those gifts."

"Christmas shopping a couple of days before Christmas?" Luis asked, "You're crazier than I thought."

"Alright, I'll drive you two down there and head back, but call me the moment you hear anything."

"I know what'll happen if I don't," Josh joked to Amanda, "He gets this frumpy look on his face for a couple of days after."

"Very funny. And for that, it's the Christmas music channel for you."

"Damn. Ok, I'm sorry."

"Too late," Foster grinned.

30

He sat back, feeling proud of the evening's accomplishment. The dim light faintly illuminated the room. He loved his place like that, just bright enough to see but low enough to feel the darkness around him. He leaned his head back on the head rest of the lounge chair and took a deep breath. The expanding of his lungs caused a painful throb in his back. He sat up and opened his hoodie, revealing the Kevlar vest that he had obtained from the home of a Jackal by the name of Kevin Finnegan.

He had followed the Jackal home after Finnegan had spoken to the ATF agent and had posed as a new neighbor to get into Kevin's place. Once inside, he attacked the Jackal and made sure that there were no loose ends. He had had no choice but to kill Kevin. After he did, he searched the apartment for any evidence of their chat. That was when he found the bulletproof vest. Knowing that he would need it in the future, he had wrapped it in a blanket and taken it with him.

Tearing at the straps, he slowly removed it and slouched back in the chair. He never went on a hunt without the vest. His prey was always packing and never hesitated to fire at him.

The man known as Hermes to the local police grimaced. He examined the bruise on his back in the mirror. It was tender but would have been a lot worse if that cop had shot him elsewhere. He didn't want to kill the detective, but he had had no choice there either. It was clear that the detective might have seen part of his face and could have identified him before his work was done. He couldn't have allowed that to happen.

He rose from the chair and walked over to his kitchen. He poured himself a glass of milk and drank it down quickly. The cold liquid cooled the heat of the adrenaline. So far it had all gone well. Now, it was time to ramp things up if he wanted it all to come to a head before Christmas. He had more in store for both gangs before he could sit back and watch the fire catch and spread throughout the city.

He had first thought of his plan to take out the gangs several months ago. He was walking alone along Sinatra Drive as the sun was setting over the Hoboken buildings, bringing the lights of New York City to the skyline. The winter wind was slowly sneaking in at the end of fall, but the view of the city that never slept was too beautiful to let the cold breeze bother him.

Two female joggers came heading his way. Both were lost in the music coming from their iPods and weren't aware of the three gang members that were strolling behind him.

"Hey sweet thang," one of the gang members called out to a jogger, "I can give you a *real* good workout." He made some kissing sounds at her.

Hermes knew that the jogger could hear him, but she pretended not to. The gang member was laughed at by the other two, which made the flirty one angry. He reached out and grabbed the jogger's arm. Both joggers came to a stop and pulled the ear buds from their ears.

"What? You didn't hear me?" Cupid asked the jogger.

"I'm sorry," she said, "I listen to my music loudly."

"Why don't you come over here?" Cupid asked her. He yanked her over to the side of the path. It was at this point when Hermes had reached his boiling point.

"That's enough," he said to Cupid, "Let her go."

"Hey, boy scout, mind your business," one of the other gang members said to him. Still, Cupid tightly gripped the jogger's arm. Hermes lunged forward and landed a punch on Cupid's jaw. The gang member fell to the ground. With a surprised shriek, the jogger and her friend took off, leaving him to deal with the other two gang members.

They came at him with full force, giving him little chance to run off, but he had had no plan to do so. He attacked them as well. An hour later, he returned home with a black eye and bruised ribs. He also arrived home with an anger that fueled him to give birth to his current plan. By the end of it all, the city would be a better place to live. And it will all be because of him. He'd show them. They would all bow down to his genius.

31

Enrique looked out the back-passenger window of Jacob's car at the home that he thought he'd never see again; he yearned to open that front door and walk into the warmth that he had taken for granted. Surprisingly, he even couldn't wait to hear his sister complain about something. He had been told in school that jail time changes you. They had been right. If only in a holding cell for about two days, he now had a taste of what the path he had tried going down would bring him. He no longer wanted that life. Between what he had gone through and seen in the past 72 hours, he just wanted to go back to hanging out with his friends and hitting on girls.

"Ready?" Jacob asked him, putting the car into park and looking over to him. Enrique continued looking at the house and nodded. He was afraid if he looked away that it would be taken away from him again. Freedom was a gift. And he wasn't going to give that up ever again.

Jacob and Enrique got out and walked up the steps to the small porch in front of the house. Jacob knocked on the door, suddenly realizing that he had forgotten to call Enrique's parents about what had just happened with Julio Jimenez. Julio had dropped them off at the precinct, leaving the two next to Jacob's vehicle, parked outside the precinct's parking lot. Julio had winked at Enrique before he got out and told him that he would see him tomorrow. Enrique didn't respond to the statement, he kept his head down, looking at the floor of the car.

The door opened, and Maritza's face appeared in the crack. She looked at Jacob, not seeing Enrique at first. Then she turned to see her brother standing there. Upon seeing him, she did something that shocked her brother: she wrapped her arms around him and hugged him tight. Enrique's awkwardness melted, and he hugged her back. After what seemed like minutes, she pulled back and began a tirade about him being stupid and worrying their parents all weekend.

The tirade brought the attention of Emilio and Carmen. When they saw that it was Jacob and their son at the door, they did the same. Wrapping their arms around Enrique, Jacob smiled. Carmen hurried them inside and closed the door from the cold outside. Jacob smelled the aroma of Carmen's home cooking and noticed that he hadn't eaten anything since breakfast this morning.

"Thank you for bringing him home," Emilio said to Jacob. Emilio grabbed his hand and shook it firmly. A smile on the father's face showed much appreciation.

"Don't thank me just yet," Jacob told him, "It was Julio who paid Enrique's bail. I just helped get it done."

At the mention of the Soldados's leader's name, the excitement and happiness on Emilio's face cracked, revealing disgust that a known criminal had helped his family. Jacob could see the anger of now being in debt to Julio flare in the father's eyes.

"Never mention his name or what he did for Enrique in this home again. Understand?"

"Absolutely."

"Thank you," the big bear of a man said to him, relaxing once more.

"Oh, you must be starving!" Carmen said to Enrique, "Come sit down I just finished a pot of Arroz Con Pollo. I'll get you a nice big plate of it. Mr. Scott, please join us."

"Oh no, I couldn't intrude. Besides I've got my girlfriend at home waiting."

"Then let me get you some to take home. Please." Jacob looked over at Emilio who raised his eyebrows and smirked.

"Agree, because you'll never leave this house without some. She will break you eventually," he joked. Jacob nodded.

"That actually sounds great. Thank you."

Carmen pulled several large plates from her cabinet and placed them in front of the chairs at the kitchen's dining table. She had Maritza get the utensils and glasses. She scooped with a spoon so large, Jacob thought it was made for giants. The mother plopped hearty helpings onto each plate. Jacob took the happy diversion as an opportunity to talk to Emilio privately. Emilio looked concerned but followed the lawyer. When Jacob believed that he was far enough for the others not to hear him, he explained Enrique's situation to Emilio.

"Enrique needs to come clean about what he saw that night. He needs to tell the police before Julio or even Vincent Donnelly forces him to tell his secrets. He's not safe until he reveals what he knows."

"I understand," Emilio said, "And you're right. But he won't listen to me."

"Then who does he trust enough to convince him it's the right thing to do?"

Emilio looked over at his wife and tilted his head towards her. Jacob looked over and saw that Enrique was already digging in at his plateful of dinner. He noticed the quick glance that Carmen made at her son. Her eyes were full of happiness and love. The look made him think of Robin and the night he told her that he loved her.

"Have her talk to him tonight. The sooner he gets down to the station to make a statement, the sooner this can be put behind you and your family."

"I will, Mr. Scott. And please let me know if there is anything I can do to make up for you taking care of my son. You are always welcome here."

"Just convince him to talk to the police and we'll call it even."

"I will."

Carmen walked over to the two men and handed Jacob a shopping bag with overloaded, plastic-covered plates of food for Robin and himself. Jacob took the bag and thanked her again. Carmen gave him a great big hug and the lawyer headed home. Emilio stood there, not moving, staring at his son enjoying his mother's dinner. Jacob Scott was right. His son would not be safe, even at home, until he talked to the police. Both gangs were dangerous in their own ways and they would be targeting Enrique until the man who had shot everyone at that bus garage was either behind bars or dead himself.

"Papi, come sit down with us," Carmen said to Emilio, reaching out to him.

Emilio leaned over to her and lowly said, "I need to talk to you first."

32

Brett and Josh walked into the open room of desks and filling cabinets where the rest of the Homicide Department and Anti-Vice were waiting. Chief Black leaned against Josh's desk on the left side of the room and looked over at the duo walking in. Josh noticed the folded arms of the chief and remembered that she was never happy when she looked at you with her arms folded in front of her.

"Sorry we're late," Brett threw out at the group. He took off his bulky coat and placed it over his chair.

"Did you find anything else?" Black asked them.

"Nothing of importance," Josh explained, "The scene looks like Doyle had just happened to walk into the attack on the gang member. Doyle got a shot off at him and then got shot back. What doesn't make sense is that Doyle's got great aim. So why isn't there any other blood besides Doyle's and the gang member?"

"Could he have taken the shot in a struggle and missed?" Russell asked.

"No, there were no signs of a struggle. The prints in the snow were uniform. No slipping or sliding," Brett answered.

"What if Hermes had protection? I mean after the shootout in the bus garage, he'd have to. No way anyone's lucky enough to not get shot from a few feet away," Russell offered.

"That would make sense as to why Melvin and them couldn't find Doyle's fired bullet," Fernandez stated, "That fucker took it home with him in his vest."

"Actually, before we continue with this discussion, can someone buzz Lucky to come down and join us?" Chief Black asked, "I want to go over what he found." Luis raised a hand and picked up his desk phone, dialing the crime lab's extension.

"Now, I want everyone on this Hermes case. If you're working something else, put it on the back burner for now until we catch this guy. Commissioner Price has our back on this too. Just don't push your luck. In the last 24 hours, we've started to get more complaints regarding gang activity. Looks like the Latin Soldados and the Jackals are starting their own search for this Hermes vigilante."

"Great," Luis muttered, "We're racing against the gangs now?"

"That's what it looks like. Where are we with getting this kid downstairs to talk?"

"We're letting him stew with the criminals down stairs," Josh told her.

"Not anymore," Emerson reported, "Sergeant Hines just told me that Julio Jimenez and some lawyer just walked in a few hours ago and bailed the kid out."

"Wait a minute, Julio has him?" Brett asked, standing up. This was not good news. He wondered if anything else could go wrong.

"There goes that lead," Luis added.

"Someone contact the kid's family and see if they know where he is. If he's out there, someone must know," Black stated.

"I'll get on that," Josh said. He punched a few keys on his keyboard to look up the phone number for the Perez family.

"I just say let the gangs find this Hermes guy," Kylee said, "It'll save us the trouble and maybe he'll take out some more gangbangers in the process. Two birds with one stone."

"You don't really believe that, do you?" Brett asked her.

"She's got a point though," Josh agreed.

"What? No way. This guy killed Doyle, for crying out loud," Orlando argued, "We need to take this mother down now."

"Honestly, look at it this way," Josh continued, "He's taken down more gang members in the past two days than we have in the past two years."

"Screw you," Luis said, angry, "These guys are clever and know the rules that we have to abide by. You think it's so easy, you take them down."

"Exactly," Kylee said, "He doesn't have the law to hold him back. I say let him finish the job. Then you can catch him and put him in jail afterwards."

"And allow him to become a hero to these people? What if several innocent people get shot in the cross fire? Sorry, I'm with Brett on this one," Black interjected.

"Kylee's right," Russell said, "I'm not happy about it but from what we've seen this Hermes is taking care of business."

Luis laughed. He looked over at Fernandez and asked, "Why don't you give him his balls back, so he can actually think straight."

"Bite me," Kylee shouted back.

"For the record, she doesn't have my balls," Emerson said, pointing a finger at Luis, "and I'd be more than happy to show you how big they are by kicking your ass here in front of everyone."

"Enough, the both of you." Brett tried to disarm the argument. He couldn't believe that Hermes was creating tension between them as well. He certainly did know what he was doing. The scary thought was who *would* come out on top once this was all over?

33

Lucky walked into the argument with his results from the casing search and wondered if he had a chance to slowly back up and hide downstairs until it was over. He took a step back, but Chief Black looked over and saw him. She waved him over and Lucky cursed to himself about his bad luck. He awkwardly walked over to the group and raised a hand in greeting. The group stopped arguing and looked over at the short tech.

"Thank you for coming down, Lucky," Black said to him, "What did you find?"

"As most of you already know, I've identified that there were two guns that were used at the garage shootout and I'm guessing that I'll find that some of the bullets fired match the bullet that killed Detective Doyle. The first gun came across as a Spectre M4 that was involved in a Bronx gang murder back from 2001. That disappeared but I'm guessing that it was passed around gangs since and has found its way here. The second gun used by the shooter is a Glock 17C. Both use 9mm Parabellum bullets. This one is registered to an Anthony Hughes, ex-Anti-Vice detective, retired back in 2010."

"Wait, a cop is doing this?" Luis asked.

"No," Lucky explained, "Detective Hughes passed away earlier this year from a heart attack."

"Ok, so it's not Hughes that's killing them," Brett stated, "What about the wife?"

"Nah, can't be the wife," Luis said, "Doyle would never allow himself to be killed by an old lady, unless it was in bed."

"What about kids?" Josh asked.

"Records show that he had one son. Could be him," Lucky guessed.

"Or maybe the wife sold the gun?"

"Couldn't have," Lucky explained, "If that were the case, then the gun would have been registered to whoever bought it. Hughes is still listed as the owner."

"Bergen and Page were sent to the widow's home to ask her about the gun," Chief Black explained, "So while they're talking to her, I'm going to need everyone else out there and keeping an eye on the Jackals and the Soldados. If it is the son, we need to keep this quiet. It does not leave this room. No chatting with reporters, no discussing it with anyone else in this precinct, not even with your loved ones. I want him taken without any other interference from the outside."

The group separated, and Brett and Josh walked downstairs to the main entrance without a word said. They stopped at the door, looking out at the thick snow that was now falling sideways from the wind.

"So, you honestly believe what you said up there?" Brett asked his partner. Josh looked over at Foster and saw that he was serious. Raghetti sighed loudly.

"I'm not agreeing to the vigilante idea," he explained, "I'm just saying that all the rules that are being made for us is tying our hands to take down these gangs."

"Those rules are there to prevent guys like us from becoming guys like him."

"I get it. I'm not implying that we should be allowed to roam freely taking people out that we don't like. I'm just saying that the whole red tape thing sucks."

"You're right about the red tape sucking," Brett agreed, "But there's reasons it's there."

"You're blowing this out of proportion. I'm not gonna team up with Hermes on this. I'm just making an observation."

"Observation noted. Now I'm going to go out there and protect people. Feel free to join me if you're in the mood." Brett zippered up his coat and headed out the door to the car, leaving the statement hanging in the air over his partner.

34

Lyndsey and Danica arrived at the home of the late Anthony Hughes. The first thing Danica noticed was the number of Christmas decorations covering the entrance and the windows of the home. It sunk in that they were nearing the holiday in a matter of days.

"Crap, with all that's been going on, I forgot that Christmas is Friday," said Danica.

"You haven't started your shopping yet, have you?"

"No and I'm always so good with that. I'm completely slacking in the personal life department."

"I take it that the thing with Ben is over?" Lyndsey wondered.

"Oh no, he's been so understanding these last few weeks. He really deserves something nice and I'm totally dropping the ball."

"Let's go tomorrow to the mall and do a run and grab?"

"Sounds good. Thank you."

"That's what partners are for," Lyndsey smiled.

"You know I'm still getting used to this happy you. Kinda odd after all that time you spent with Mike being miserable."

"Get used to it, it's the new me."

The female detectives got out of the vehicle and cringed at the attack of wind and snow. Danica wrapped her coat tighter around herself and ducked as she walked over to the front door of the home. Lyndsey arrived right behind her and they knocked hard on the door, hoping that the occupants heard them. Lyndsey's hair whipped to the left of her face and made it even harder to see. A form appeared behind the small window in the front door. Danica held out her badge and smiled at the woman as she slowly opened the door. She wore her hair up in a grey bun with a red and green apron covering her torso. The few fresh stains on it told Danica that they had interrupted her Christmas baking.

"Excuse me, we're with the Hoboken Police Department and are looking for a Martha Hughes."

"I'm Martha Hughes," the woman said, "Is Travis ok?"

"Sorry, who?"

"Travis, my son."

"This has nothing to do with Travis," Danica explained loudly, "We have a few questions about your husband."

"Oh, that's fine, please come in, you'll get sick if you're out there any longer." The woman seemed puzzled by the statement but still let the two ladies into her home to see what it was about. She offered them a seat and they accepted.

"Is this about a case that Tony worked?"

"No ma'am, we have some questions about your husband in general."

"Well I will try to answer them as best as I can. Would you like some hot chocolate? It'll warm you up from the cold."

"That would be very nice, Mrs. Hughes," Lyndsey said. Martha stood up slowly, grunting from what appeared to be old joint issues. She hobbled into the kitchen and turned the stove burner on to heat some water for the drinks. Lyndsey and Danica sat and looked around the living room that they were in. There were pictures that told stories about a life long gone. A wedding picture of, Danica believed, Martha and Anthony Hughes caught her eye. The two were very happy in the photo and the house seemed quiet now that it was only Martha.

Martha returned a few minutes later with two coffee mugs of hot chocolate. She handed them to the ladies and smiled.

"I'm sorry dears, but I'm all out of the ones with the marshmallows. Travis likes to have them when he visits."

"It's fine without them, thank you."

"So," Martha said, sitting down at what seemed to be her favorite chair, "What did you need to know about Tony?"

Lyndsey took a sip of the hot chocolate and began her questions, "When your husband retired, he had kept his service weapon, correct?"

"Oh yes, that thing. He did. I told him we didn't need it, but he was all about the job. If I didn't force him to retire he would have ended up having that heart attack on the job."

"Do you still have the weapon?" Danica asked, hoping for some lead that would help them locate the identity of the vigilante known as Hermes. She had been hoping that this trip would get them something, for Doyle's sake.

"No, I'm sorry," Martha told them. Lyndsey released the breath that she had been holding in, feeling a little defeated at the dead end. "But Travis took it along with some of the other things of Tony's for keepsakes. I told him that I wasn't comfortable with that thing in the house."

"So, Travis still has it?"

"As far as I know. He hasn't really mentioned it since he took it."

"When did he take the weapon?"

"Oh, that was a few months ago. It was sometime in September because I remember all the back to school flyers in the mail that I was getting. I told him about that when he was taking Tony's things."

"Travis looked up to his father?" Danica asked her.

"He did. He wasn't fond of the job for taking his father away from him all the time, but he always admired Tony and what he did for the neighborhood."

"Mrs. Hughes, is there a way to get a hold of your son? We just want to see if he still has the gun."

"Is something wrong?" Martha Hughes asked. She was starting to get suspicious as to why two detectives were asking about her dead husband's gun. They couldn't reveal too much if the son was indeed the vigilante. She would contact him before they would be able to reach him. It was a tricky game to play to get what they needed and not raise suspicion.

"No, we're actually working on a case that may be linked to one of your husband's cases. We just need to confirm something in order to close the case. Any help you and your son could provide would be of great assistance." Martha paused for a moment, thinking of something or contemplating whether or not she should answer. Then she stood up again.

"I've got his number by the phone. Let me write it down for you." They followed her into the kitchen and waited for her to copy Travis's number onto a piece of note pad paper. Martha scribbled the number she had listed on a thin cardboard sheet taped to the wall next to the phone and handed the paper to Danica.

"That is his home phone. He works during the day at Lincoln Harbor."

"Oh, really? What does he do?" Lyndsey asked.

"He's an accountant there. He does well for himself. I've got a photo here of him if either of you are single."

"No, sorry, we're both taken."

"Oh, I see. Well, to each their own."

"Thank you very much for your time, Mrs. Hughes."

"Would you like some more hot chocolate to go? It's so horrible out there, you need something to keep you warm."

"No thank you," Lyndsey said, feeling as if the hot chocolate she already had was transforming itself into body fat as she stood there.

The detectives said their goodbyes and returned back outside and into the car. Snow had already covered the vehicle in the small amount of time that they were inside. Lyndsey decided to wait and melt the snow off with the car's heating system.

"Think her son may be Hermes?" Danica asked.

"Only one way to find out," Lyndsey replied. They'd have to take another trip through the snow and to Travis Hughes' apartment on 12th Street. She called the precinct to get the exact address and then plotted their plan once they reached his home while the snow slowly melted off the windshield. Before it had fully melted, they got the call about a house on fire.

35

Julio entered his home and brushed the snow off his coat and shoes. He hung the expensive coat on the coat rack next to the front door and looked over at the members of the Soldados that had gathered there while he was out. There were a few of the ones that he had sent out earlier that day for information on the man who killed Robbie and the other Soldados members. Hoping for some good news, he smoothed out his hair and smiled at his men.

"Good evening," Julio said to them, "I have good news. Enrique Perez is home safe. The bad news is that he's still open to an attack from the Jackals. I do not want this boy harmed in any way. I need three volunteers willing to endure the weather out there to make sure he stays safe."

Julio smiled at the quickness of the numerous hands that went up to volunteer. That was pure loyalty. He had gone to great lengths since he became leader of the gang to make sure that he could convince each and every member to be willing to give up their own blood to make the Latin Soldados happy.

He chose three of the volunteers to go and keep an eye on the Perez house. They grabbed their jackets and hats and headed out of Julio's home into the harsh weather. Julio waved the remaining members into his kitchen. It was the one place in the house that he spent the most money on renovating. The black marble countertops, the stainless-steel fridge and the white and black checkered tile floor were well worth the amount spent. It reminded him of his mother, who loved to cook. She had taught him several recipes for whenever he planned on impressing a woman. *Women love a man who can cook*, she always told him. But he always found that cooking relaxed him after a long day.

"What have you found out?" he asked in general.

"I couldn't get exactly what it is, but I've heard that Donnelly is planning something," Ryan was the first to speak, "He's still believes that the shooter was one of ours and he's looking to take out his anger on you."

Julio shook his head in disappointment, "What a fool that man is. He knows not what he's getting himself into, targeting the Latin Soldados. But let him come. He will learn."

"Oh, and this guy shot a cop tonight. Right after he took down Flaco too," Claudio added.

"So, I take it that the police are now putting all their resources into capturing this man?"

"Yeah," Claudio continued, "They're pissed. He was a long-time favorite among the police station. That cop you have in your pocket, Darren whatever? He was telling me all this."

"I'll have to send my regards. I also want someone to get a hold of Flaco's family and send them my deepest sympathies. Money is no object to make sure they are taken care of. Now what else have we learned about this shooter?" There was a pause. The quietness in the air made Julio frown. He knew the efficiency of his men and to have them hit a wall getting information on this one man told him that this was going to be harder than he had hoped.

"This guy is a ghost, Julio," Ryan finally answered.

"Ryan, I am not one to believe in the supernatural. This man has murdered several of our friends. He's very real and he will make a mistake. Make sure that you continue searching. I will not accept losing this time or any time. Now let's take a moment to gather our senses and make sure we are well rested and fed before we continue this search. I'm feeling the urge to make something." Julio walked over to the fridge and opened it, looking to see what he had that could be made into a warm delicious meal for the men that had worked so hard for him today.

Julio noticed most of the ingredients in the fridge would be perfect for a nice large serving of paella and he knew the boys would enjoy it. Pulling the ingredients out a few at a time, he placed them on the island in the center of the kitchen. Once it was all spread out, he noticed several smiles.

"It will be a short while for me to prepare this, but it shall be well worth the," but before Julio could finish his sentence, there was the interruption of a cell phone ringing. Then seconds later another phone rang. That was followed by two more. Within less than a minute there was a symphony of cell phones all ringing at once. The Soldados members all looked at their phones and began answering them. Finally, Julio's phone went off in his pocket. Confused by the incident, he removed his phone and looked at the screen. It read: BLOCKED. He answered it anyway.

There was no response from the outside line at first. There was just the whoosh of the outside wind. He thought it could be one of his men at first, in trouble. Before he could say hello a second time, a voice came through.

"One, two, three, four, I declare a gang war," the voice chuckled. There was no mistaking the voice.

"Vincent," Julio responded with disgust.

"Aw, was I that obvious?" Donnelly joked.

"What do you want?"

"Exactly what I just said."

"Do you really want to declare a war with me? Are you that far gone?"

"Ummmmm, yeah. I kinda am. You see, Julio, old chum, I know you and your gang had something to do with the deaths of Liam and the eight other Jackals. And it's time that you paid for it in blood."

"How many times must I tell you that I would never order a hit on my own? What possible motive would I have to kill my own just to take out a few of yours?"

"You're the clever one, you tell me."

"El Stupido!" Julio wasn't one to show anger but talking to this man was getting the better of him.

"Kiss-o my ass-o."

"Start this war and you and every member of your gang will know the meaning of suffering."

"Sorry, I didn't catch that last part. The bonfire is getting loud. You should really come down, we've got plenty of marshmallows to share."

"What are you talking about?"

"Hang on I'll send you a picture." The line disconnected and Julio was left standing in his kitchen staring at his phone. He was too involved in the call to notice the Soldados members all looking at him in shock. Julio saw the text appear on his phone's screen and tapped on it to reveal a picture of a house fire. The shock wasn't so much that a house was on fire, but it was which house. Julio knew that home. He had grown up on that block when he was young. He had been in that specific home too many times to count. It was Robbie Cruz's family's home. War had indeed been declared.

36

Enrique looked up when he heard the knock on his bedroom door. He had been enjoying lying on a bed that wasn't thin and uncomfortable. The smell of sweat and urine was finally fading from his nostrils and he was feeling warm again. His mother opened the door slightly, making sure it was okay for her to enter, and holding a cup of tea. He sat up and smiled. He normally wasn't the kind for tea but anything warm was welcomed.

Carmen sat down on the bed next to him and handed him the cup. He took it and held it in both hands.

"It's so good to have you home," she told him, "But we need to talk about what is going on."

Enrique knew this talk was coming and was dreading it, but he felt now that it was better to get it out of the way than to delay it further. He sipped on the tea and nodded.

"Mi Nino, I know the rule about not snitching, but the police are right. If you don't tell them what you know, you'll only endanger yourself."

"Ma, it's not about being a snitch. I just know that if I were to talk and let them know what I know, then my name will end up getting out there and the whole family will be in danger from this man."

Carmen was surprised by his mature "man of the house" answer. He was smart for his age. He was no longer the little boy she would push on the swings. It brought a smile to her face.

"Yes, but you did not think about what the other gangs would do when they found out that you saw who did this."

"But that's the thing, I didn't get a great look at his face. He was wearing a baseball cap and he had sun glasses on at first, but they fell off in the middle of the shootout. He looked right at me. I'd never seen him before, but I can't forget the look he had in his eyes."

"Would you recognize him if he walked by?"

"Probably."

"You need to go down there and talk to them. Tell them what you know. If you don't have a lot of information for them, at least they will know. The police aren't going to give your name to everyone in the state. And I'm sure the gangs would then leave you alone and bother the police instead."

"I guess," Enrique said hesitantly. Carmen looked him in the eyes and saw the debate he was having with himself. Would telling the police what he knew make it all better?

"If it helps you, I will go down to the precinct with you."

"No, that's okay. I'll go. Do you think Mr. Scott would go with me?"

"I don't see why not. Your father hired him to help you. I can give him a call to see."

"Yeah, I'd prefer that."

"We'll go in the morning. For now, just get some rest. You've had a long few days. And don't forget your tea." Carmen stood up, placed a kiss on her son's forehead and left the room with a smile. She headed downstairs where Emilio was standing waiting for her to return. The look on his face was one that almost made her laugh at him. He was leaning forward on the railing of the stairs, looking at her like a child waiting for a surprise. She considered not telling him and keeping him in suspense, but she knew better. He would just bug her until she told him what he wanted.

"Please call Mr. Scott and ask him if he wouldn't mind accompanying Enrique to the precinct tomorrow morning," she told him, knowing exactly what he was thinking.

"He's going to talk to them?"

Carmen nodded and smirked at her husband, who she could tell was sure that she would be able to pull it off and convince Enrique to talk to the police. Emilio smiled and dug into his pocket for the card that Jacob had given him. Retrieving it, he reached over the couch for the phone and dialed the number. As it rang, Emilio was pleased to know that this would soon be over for the Perez family. It was the police's problem now.

"Jacob Scott," the lawyer answered.

"Mr. Scott, it's Emilio Perez. I've got some good news."

"Enrique's willing to talk to the police?"

"Yes. My wife can get anyone to talk if she's given the chance. I should rent her out for the police to use in interrogations."

"I will keep that in mind. She could be useful in court too," Jacob joked, "That's good to hear though."

"Enrique asked if you would be with him when he talks to the police."

"I'd be happy to. I'll stop by the house to get him and prepare him for what to expect. Is 8a.m. good?"

"That would be fine. Thank you, Mr. Scott. Maybe now this will all be over." Emilio smiled at the thought. But if he had known what the morning would bring, he wouldn't have been smiling at all.

37

Lyndsey and Danica arrived at Travis' place twenty minutes later, after listening to a call about a potential arson. The female detectives decided that they were not needed and continued their investigation into Anthony Hughes' gun. The wind had died down slightly but the snow still continued to fall.

"Ok, it's official, I've had enough of this white stuff," Lyndsey complained, "It can stop for the rest of the winter."

"Channel 11 says that it's going to continue for two more days, off and on," Danica replied. Lyndsey glanced over at her partner with an annoyed look.

"Then you're driving tomorrow." She opened the door and ducked out into the snow again. The cold ran through her like a passing ghost. She felt the chill through her muscles and hurried around the car and into the entrance to the small well-kept apartment building. Danica was right behind her.

Looking over the row of buzzers to the apartments inside, they quickly found the one with a printed label reading TRAVIS HUGHES, ACCOUNTANT.

"Little full of himself, maybe?" Danica joked at the label.

"A little ego goes a long way, especially when it comes to murder." Lyndsey pressed the buzzer and they waited. After a minute, she pressed it again. There was no response.

"Why would he be out in this weather?"

"Hunting down some gang members?" Danica offered back. She took out her cell phone and dialed the number that Martha Hughes had given them. Hitting the speaker button on her phone so that Lyndsey could hear as well, they listened to the echoing ring over and over. After five rings, Travis' voice mail picked up.

"Hello, you've reached Travis Hughes, accountant for Arrow Accounting. I am unable to answer your call at this time" Danica disconnected the call before the beep arrived. She stood there for a moment and then dialed another number. Lyndsey stood and waited, peering into the hallway while she did.

"Hey Sergeant, Detective Page here, can you help me with any contact numbers for a Travis Hughes?" Danica spelled it out to Hines, "We've got the home number but he's not here. Yes. Great thank you." Danica waved her hand at Bergen for her phone. Lyndsey handed it over and Danica punched a number into it. She thanked Danny and hung up.

"Cell phone?" Lyndsey asked.

"Cell phone," Danica smiled devilishly. Lyndsey hit the dial button and let it ring. After the third ring someone answered. The detectives had some trouble hearing the caller due to the noise in the background. Lyndsey heard loud dance music and happy shouting in the background, as if he were in a club.

"Travis Hughes," the man on the other line said.

"Mr. Hughes, this is Detective Lyndsey Bergen with Hoboken police. I was hoping to speak to you in regard to your father, Anthony. Will you be arriving home any time soon?"

"What? Who is this?"

Lyndsey repeated herself a little louder this time.

"Hoboken police? What do you want?"

"We need to speak to you about some things of your father's."

"He's been dead for years. What could you possibly want now?" Lyndsey noted the aggression in his tone. There was something about it that made Lyndsey believe he was not happy with any police official. Was it caused by the police force itself or did it originate from his father?

"I'd rather do this in person if you don't mind."

"Yeah, well I do mind. I'm at a Christmas party right now and have no plan on leaving just yet."

"I can meet you there if you prefer," she offered, trying hard to set up a meeting as soon as possible. The sooner she could talk to him, the sooner she could confirm if Travis Hughes was involved with the garage shooting.

"I'm sure that would go over well with my co-workers. No thanks. Call me tomorrow or book an appointment." And with that, Travis hung up on Lyndsey. The small enclosed area became silent again and Danica sighed in annoyance.

"What an asshole."

"Well, we've got two options. We can go down to where Arrow Accounting is located, or we can call it a night and meet him here bright and early."

"I'm calling it a night," Danica replied, "I just want to crawl under my covers and put this day behind me. It's been exhausting."

"I was hoping you'd say that." Lyndsey and Danica returned to the car and Bergen drove her partner home before heading home. The entire drive home, she felt this nagging feeling in her gut that she had missed something in the call she made but no matter how hard she tried, she couldn't figure it out.

38

Angie had just served Tamara her bedtime snack when she heard the scraping sound outside the dining window that looked out onto the street in front of the house. She noticed a figure outside the short metal fence surrounding the small yard. It was hunched over and moving slowly. She wasn't able to make out any details due to the large flakes that continued to fall. If it continued, she saw Tamara's school calling her with a closure in the morning.

The figure continued moving slowly toward the stoop of the home. *Who was that?* She thought. She heard Tamara move her chair to see what her mother was so interested in outside.

"What are you looking at, Mommy?" she asked. Angie didn't have an answer for her daughter. Even if it weren't snowing, the lack of street lights and the figure's thick coat and large hood didn't help.

"Go sit back down and eat your snack," Angie told her. The mystery behind the identity of the figure was beginning to worry her. She wanted to go out and see who it was but was afraid of what might happen if she did. The figure didn't seem to be leaving but moving closer to her front door. What did they want? She had to find out.

Angie picked up Tamara and placed her back on her chair, asking her to stay there and eat. She ducked into the hall closet and retrieved one of the weapons she kept hidden throughout the house. She did that when Josh left, but now that Brett was around more often, she wouldn't need them as much. This one was a wooden baseball bat. Gripping it tightly, she held the knob of the front door, breathing deeply and preparing herself for the unknown. She quietly counted to three and threw the door open wide and raised the bat in defense. The quick flash of light and movement startled the figure outside and he dropped the shovel that he had been using to clear her portion of the sidewalk and walkway to her front door. He looked up and Angie saw Brett's shocked face under the thick hood.

"Jesus on a cross, Brett! What the hell are you doing?"

"I'm shoveling for you. And if you're looking to help, you'll need something wider than a bat to clear this snow."

"You scared the crap out of me."

"I'm sorry, that wasn't my intention."

"Well get in here, it's freezing," she told him. Brett propped the shovel along the railing of the short staircase and stomped his shoes on the mat before entering the warm home. Angie took his coat and hung it one on the hooks behind the front door. Tamara poked her head out of the dining room to see what the commotion was about. When she saw Brett, she smiled and ran over to wrap her tiny arms around his waist.

"Hi Brett! Guess what?"

"What?"

"Only 4 more sleeps until Christmas!"

"That's right!" Brett went along with the adorable child.

"How did I do in the play?"

"I think you were the best elf I've ever seen in a show."

"Mom thinks I have what it takes to take it to Hollywood! I think I'll be as beautiful as Jennifer Lopez."

"I don't doubt it."

"Come on now," Angie interrupted, "It's time for bed." Tamara hugged her mother and Brett and rushed off to her bedroom to get one more sleep out of the way. Brett smiled and missed being a kid at Christmas. He remembered seeing a snowfall like this and getting excited instead of now where he cringed at snow.

"How was your day?" Angie asked, once she knew they were alone. She leaned forward and kissed him before he could answer. He tasted the strawberry that she had eaten just minutes before on her lips and felt the stress ebb away.

"Much better now," he replied.

"If you play your cards right, it can get way better," she smiled back seductively.

"Doyle's been shot."

"What?" she said, covering her mouth with her hands. The shock in her eyes brought him back to the crime scene with the splotch of blood on the concrete where Doyle had died. His stomach twisted, and he nodded, lowering his head in the process.

"What happened?"

"We're working on the same case. He came across the suspect in the middle of the crime and was shot. He died before he could get any help."

"Oh my God, Brett, I'm so sorry." Angie hugged him tight, giving him the ability to let it out. It wasn't like him to do so, even though she had been trying to get him to open up slowly. The urge to open up was there but he wasn't quite ready just yet. He just hugged her back in silence.

"Have they caught the guy?"

"No, but we're asking tenants hoping a witness comes forward with some information or a lead. We've got a lead on the weapon, but Danica and Lyndsey are still working it."

"How's Josh taking it?"

"We, uh, got into a little argument about the case."

"Oh, Brett."

"I know. I'm not happy about it, but this case has everyone on edge. Even Kylee is affected. She's cursing even more now."

"Very funny," she said, rolling her eyes. "Have you eaten anything for dinner? I saved you some of ours if you didn't."

"No, I've forgotten to. That would help, thank you."

Angie directed him to the dining room table and headed into the kitchen to retrieve the plate of dinner for him. She placed it in the microwave and Brett sat back, finally able to relax after everything that had occurred earlier that day. He closed his eyes and focused on the whirr of the microwave's internals. When he heard the ding of the bell, he looked over and saw Angie bring him the food with a bottle of Samuel Adams. He smiled at her and thanked her before digging in. She stood there over him, rubbing his shoulders, getting him to relax. He could have fallen asleep right there, he was that tired.

Angie leaned over and whispered into his ear, "You should stay. It's not safe out there."

"Are you sure she won't mind?"

"I think she's secretly waiting to see you here in the morning to talk your ear off instead of mine. She'll be just fine, Brett."

"And you're okay with it?"

"I wouldn't have asked if I wasn't. Come on." Angie took his hand and led him to her bedroom. She sat him down on the edge of the bed and helped him out of his clothes. Then he helped her with the same. Angie gently swung her leg over his lap, pushing him down onto his back. Leaning over to kiss his chest, she could feel him getting aroused, quickly. He ran his hands over her body, feeling every inch of her smooth skin. Angie felt her temperature rise with each touch. She took him completely and they moved together slowly, enjoying every moment.

After a slow long session of lovemaking, they fell asleep together, Angie in his arms. And outside, his car sat in the same spot until the morning came.

39

Hermes grinned from ear to ear as he stood in his kitchen listening to the police scanner. They reported the house fire set by Vinnie Donnelly. That was all going to plan. The unstable gang leader had been thrown off the path of sanity and was now fully blaming Julio Jimenez for the shooting at the bus garage. His plan was coming along perfectly. He couldn't have hoped for better!

"Engine 9 has arrived," squawked the scanner, "We need to clear the way. There's too many people watching in the street."

He laughed at the amount of people in the street, knowing most of them were either Jackals or Latin Soldados members. He wished that he could be there to watch it all fall apart. He listened on, hoping that a fight between the two would break out.

The next step would make it even worse. What he had planned was something that Donnelly wouldn't be able to ignore, and it would eat at him so bad that Hermes knew by the end of tomorrow either Jimenez or Donnelly would be dead. That would leave him one left to deal with instead of two. Thinking of his next step, he realized that now would be the perfect time to gather the supplies for it and set everything in place. He knew that he would regret the late night come the following morning, but this was more important.

Hermes grabbed his café bag and placed his tools needed to obtain the supplies into it. He looked around for his lock picking tools and realized that they were in his bedroom. He hurried into the bedroom and swiped them from his dresser. As he returned to the kitchen, the police scanner went off again as two officers were conversing over the line. He listened to them talking as he rechecked everything he had placed into the bag.

"Car 15, are you over by the Perez home?"

"Yeah, Mitch, I am. Why, are they asking for someone to drive by and check on the kid again?"

"Affirmative. They just want to make sure that no one is lurking around the street now that he's out."

"You think? I mean the kid's the only one who knows what the hell happened at that shootout over the weekend. The gangs are going to want revenge."

"Yeah, this is why they want you to go check up on the family. Now stop yapping and go over there."

"Car 15 out."

Hermes froze in his spot. A witness? Were they talking about a witness? They were no witnesses! He had taken them all out. He was sure of it! There was even that one guy that wasn't even a gang member who was caught in the crossfire. Hermes thought back to that night.

The vest had been very handy. After he returned home he discovered four bullets had actually found their mark through the dozens that were fired at him. Hermes had unloaded about 7 clips of bullets from the Spectre he had taken from Finnegan's place and the gun that had once been used by a retired cop. The irony of its new owner did not escape him. It had made him laugh.

He stopped shooting in the garage and heard a muted ringing from the noise of the gunfire in the echo. He picked up the sunglasses from the concrete where they fell during the shooting and looked around. There was no movement from anything and besides the ringing, there was silence also. He lowered his arms and took a deep breath. Through the pain of the impact of the four slugs, he smiled. It was time to inspect his work.

Walking around the bodies, he noticed his aim was pretty decent. The time that he had spent at the shooting gallery these past few months had finally paid off. Before that he had never fired a gun. Now, there were some hits that had taken portions of faces off the gang members. Even though the Spectre M4 provided quick bursts to take out the most guys in the fastest time, the Glock 17C was the perfect gun to use for this set up. It had short recoil, allowing him to keep it from knocking him back. And the range of the shots could travel as far as 55 yards, which in an enclosed area such as the bus garage was perfect.

Walking around a stacked pallet of cardboard boxes towards the back, he almost tripped over the body of a middle-aged man. Hermes stopped short and looked down at the stranger. A blooming circle of red covered his chest and the dead eyes staring up confirmed the death. He knelt down and checked the man's pockets. Based on his age and his clothes, this man did not belong to either of the gangs. Unfortunately, finding no identification, Hermes came to the conclusion that this man was a worker of the garage, perhaps even the manager. Seeing no gun near the body, he knew that this was no cop or security guard. It had saddened him that this innocent man had become the first casualty of the war he was starting against the gangs.

As he stood back up to leave, his eyes ran past the back door of the garage. Not paying any attention to it, he walked back through the carnage and out the front entrance onto Jefferson Street.

The back door! Could someone have escaped out the back door during the shootout? This changed everything, Hermes thought. Was this Perez kid able to identify him? There was a reason that he had worn the baseball cap and sunglasses, to make it difficult for anyone to make note of any significant details of his face.

He paced back and forth in the kitchen, thinking of what he should do. Running through the paces of the last few days, he came to realize that if the kid had known anything, the police would have been on him by now. Hell, even Detective Mark Doyle didn't know who he was until he had taken off the hood and shown his face. If this Perez kid did see him, he would be presently sitting inside a jail cell and not standing in his kitchen.

He was too far into this now to turn back and go into hiding. He had to finish the plan to the very end or, at least, until he was stopped. Hermes turned off the police scanner and zippered up his bag. Throwing it over his shoulder, he quietly left his apartment and headed back out into the night to bring the end of the Jackals and the Latin Soldados one step closer.

40

The Perez home was in its typical chaotic mode that Tuesday morning, regardless of how close it was to Christmas. Maritza was hogging up the bathroom, doing who knew what to her face. Carmen was trying to get lunch together for Emilio as well as breakfast for the children before she headed out for her cleaning job at the W hotel. Emilio was looking for his socks and Enrique was sitting at the table, feeling the butterflies in stomach, zipping back and forth.

"Enrique, can you please get the syrup out of the cabinet for me?" Carmen asked. Enrique stood up from the table and opened the cabinet. He handed it to her and she thanked him, turning to look at him. She noticed the concern in his eyes and felt bad.

"There's no need to be scared, Niño. You will be fine. You'll be surrounded by the police!" she joked.

"I know, Ma. But what if Julio shows up again?"

"I'm sure that Julio Jimenez would think twice before walking into the police station with the crimes he's committed."

"It's ok, son," Emilio added, "Jacob Scott wouldn't let anything happen to his client. That is a good man there."

"I hope you're right about that."

"I know I am. Look, call me after it's all done, or we can talk about it when I get home. I really need to get ready right now. Do you trust me?" Emilio asked, looking his son in the eyes. Enrique nodded. "Then trust me when I tell you that you will fine. Mr. Scott will be there if you get scared."

Enrique found it funny how his parents were very positive while it was him that was about to be questioned a second time by the police about being involved in a crime that had made front pages in the local newspapers. Jacob had agreed to be there and help him with the questions, but he saw on the TV shows how the police always found a loophole for the cases. He feared that it would happen this morning. And the detective with the goatee looked grumpy during the interrogation last time. He hoped that one wasn't there today.

"Mari! I need to shave before I leave!" Emilio shouted. Then he looked to his wife and asked, "What could she possibly be doing in there for 35 minutes?" He was answered with a shrug of Enrique's shoulders and shook his head. Emilio headed back upstairs to finish getting dressed when he heard the phone ring. The ringing startled Enrique. He turned it over to look at the called ID screen. It read: SCOTT, J.

"Mom, it's Mr. Scott," he told her, handing the phone out to her. She turned and looked at him in puzzlement.

"So, answer it. I'm busy cooking."

Enrique looked down at the phone and tried to bring himself to pressing the TALK button. Carmen became frustrated by the ringing and scooped the phone from her son's hand.

"Good morning, Mr. Scott."

"Good morning, Mrs. Perez," he responded, "Is Enrique ready?"

"I'm serving him breakfast right now. He should be done and ready in twenty minutes."

"That's perfect. I'll come over now and go over what to expect before we head over to the precinct."

"Would you like me make you some breakfast too, then?"

Jacob laughed, "No, that's fine, thank you. I just had some."

"Oh, is that girlfriend of yours a good cook?"

"I think so. She hasn't burned anything yet."

"Then you are a lucky man. May I ask you something else?"

"Certainly."

"Will these police officers talking to Enrique be threatening?"

"Oh, no, not at all. I know these detectives and they will be very respectful. Even if I don't ask them."

"Good. And what will they be asking him?"

"Well, they'll be asking him about what he knows about the shootout that he witnessed. They will want to know the details, so they can get a better picture of what occurred and if he can describe the man who set up the gangs that were there." Carmen listened to his answer as she placed several pancakes onto a plate for Enrique and several more for Emilio. She placed the plates on the table at each seat and set the butter and syrup in the center of the table.

"But what if he didn't see this man's face?"

"If he is unable to identify this man from a set of pictures, they will always ask about clothing, voice, anything that he can provide to them so that the police can locate this man. The sooner they can find this shooter, the sooner this will all be over."

As Jacob was explaining himself, the front door bell rang. She glanced over to Enrique who was deep into the small stack of pancakes that Carmen had placed in front of him. She leaned out into the living room and shouted out to Emilio while she covered the bottom part of the phone, so not to deafen Jacob.

"Emilio! Can you answer the door? I'm on the phone with Mr. Scott!"

"I just got into the bathroom!" he shouted back.

"Maritza! Please answer the door!"

"I'm not even dressed yet, Mom!" Carmen sighed.

"I like the sound of that. Thank you, Mr. Scott. I will not be here when you arrive because my shift starts soon, so I will wish you and Enrique good luck at the questioning today."

"Not to worry, Mrs. Perez. I will make sure they take good care of Enrique while we're there."

The doorbell rang again.

"Mr. Scott, would you please hold? There is someone at the door."

"That's probably the police. I was told that they would be keeping an eye on your house until this search for the shooter is over."

Carmen walked over to the door and peered out through the eyehole in the center of the door. She saw a male standing there, wearing a black coat and looking out at the street, with his back to the door. She was unable to see his face but from what Jacob had told her, she expected it was a police officer.

"One moment, please." She said into the phone. Carmen placed the phone on the small change table next to the front door and unlocked the top lock. She turned the knob and opened the door with no fear.

"Hello, can I help you?" she asked the person standing on her porch. The man turned around upon hearing her voice and smiled at her. The man was not wearing a police uniform and she did not recognize him. Nor did she recognize the other three men standing off to the side of the front door. Their appearance startled her, and she took a step back.

"Good morning, Mrs. Perez," the man smiled at her, "Could Enrique come out and play?"

Even through the phone, Jacob could hear and recognize the voice of Jackal leader, Vinnie Donnelly.

41

Unable to find a parking spot, Josh was forced to double park and had to hurry to talk to Angie and ask her to take Tamara away for a couple of days. With the gang activity increasing around the town, he didn't think either of them was safe until this was all over. The nightmare that he had last night cemented his decision. In it, both Angie and Tamara were taken by Donnelly and tortured.

He knew that Angie's job most likely couldn't afford to have her away during the last few days of Christmas shopping season, but he knew that if he had her parents on his side she couldn't say no to all three of them.

He shuffled around the car in front of Angie's house and stopped short when he recognized it. It was his partner's car. And the snow was still blanketing it in its spot. He couldn't help realizing what it meant.

"Well, it's about freakin' time," Raghetti said to himself. Then he noticed that the sidewalk in front of the house was shoveled as well. *Oh, she's got him in deep now*, he joked to himself.

He rang the bell and was greeted by Tamara. Her tiny frame struggled to open the thick door that he had installed when Angie had decided that their marriage was over. It wasn't much but it had made him feel that more at ease that they would still be safe even though he was not there. Her bright smile warmed his soul. She had her mother's beauty and sassy attitude but had his style. Today she had two ponytails, one off-center on the left side of her head and the other coming straight out of the top of her head. He knew that it was of her own design.

"Looks like someone has been styling her own hair this morning," he said, opening his arms as he crouched down to greet her. She jumped out at him and into his arms.

"Hi, Daddy! Do you like my hair? I did it myself!"

"And here I thought that your mother took you to the hair salon as soon as you woke up."

"No, silly! They don't open up until later!"

"Oh, you are so right. Hey, is Brett here?"

"Yup. He had a sleepover! Come in!" She took his hand and pulled him into the house. Josh took off his shoes and headed into the kitchen with Tamara guiding him. He noticed Brett's eyes had bags under them and Angie was in her thick bathrobe that she normally wore when she was feeling lazy or tired.

"Rough night?" Josh threw out there, unable to help himself. Angie turned and gave him the annoyed stare that he missed. Brett shook his head.

"I'd forgotten that you might show up too." Foster said, unable to look up and admit of what he had been up to hours before. Josh chuckled.

"Want some coffee?" Angie asked him, changing the subject. Josh took a cup and sat down next to Brett.

"I was hoping to talk to you this morning," Josh told his ex.

"About what?"

"About you taking the next few days off."

"Wait, what? Why would I do that? We get Christmas Eve and Christmas Day off." Angie's voice had gotten higher in pitch. He knew from experience that when she was preparing to argue, she would raise her voice in pitch rather than volume, but the volume would follow shortly.

"Hear me out," Josh explained, "And I'm sure Brett will agree with me."

"So now you two are going to team up on me?"

"No, you need to listen." Angie was cutting him off before he could explain his thoughts. This was going to be harder than he thought.

"Listen to what?" Angie turned to Brett, "Does this have to do with Doyle's murder?"

Josh turned to his partner, "You told her about that?" "Yeah. It came out last night when I showed up," Brett explained, "I was exhausted, and I needed to get it off my chest."

"This does have to do with Doyle's murder!"

"In a way, yes," Foster interjected, "I know what Josh is getting at and he's right. What's going on around here and what's coming is something that isn't safe for you or Tamara."

"Then you two need to tell me what's going on if you even think I'll consider taking off right before Christmas." The two detectives looked at each other and explained about the shooting in the bus garage, the attacks on the gangs, Vinnie Donnelly's unstable mind, Doyle's death by the hand of this mystery killer who wasn't going to stop until either he took them out or they took themselves out. She sat there, taking it all in. Josh almost begged her to take Tamara away before the gang war got so out of control that she wouldn't be able to leave.

"Do you understand now?"

Angie sat there, staring at her cup of coffee, thinking about what they had just told her. She considered what she would have to do in order to call out just days from Christmas Eve.

"Where am I supposed to go?"

"Go see your parents," Josh explained, "They're only in Brooklyn and how long has it been since you visited?"

"They would love seeing Tamara. But I can't just tell my boss that my boyfriend and my ex want me to leave because of a gang war that no one else is aware of. I'll have to lie to him and I hate lying."

"I know but it's for a good reason. Think of our daughter."

Angie sipped on her coffee and remained silent. Josh hoped that his reasoning got through her stubbornness. He never could in the past. It was extremely difficult to win a debate with Angie. In the years that they were together, he had never won an argument, even when he was right.

"Fine, but we're coming back on Christmas Eve because I'm not lugging all those presents in the closet to Brooklyn."

"We're going to do everything we can to end this by then," Brett told her.

"Help her get some clothes together. I'll go get dressed."

42

Travis Hughes left his apartment earlier than most people in the building. Making money waited for no one. He yawned as he stepped out into the grey, chilled air. Piles of snow littered the sidewalk and the spaces in between the parked cars. He found two women standing there, between him and his car, waiting for him with cups of Dunkin Donuts coffee in their hands. He raised his eyebrows at the sight, wondering if his luck was getting even better.

"Good morning, ladies. Travis Hughes, accountant." He reached into his coat and removed a business card. He held it out to them to take but neither of them moved to take it.

"Mister Hughes, Detectives Page and Bergen. We'd like to ask you a few questions." Upon hearing that they were police, he changed his tune and took back the card to place into his coat again. A frown took over his face and he shifted on his feet.

"You're the one that called me last night."

"That would be me," Lyndsey admitted.

"I'm a very busy man, Miss Bergen. Perhaps we could do this another time." Hughes began walking down the street to a silver Audi A8 that beeped when he pressed the button on his remote keychain.

"I'm sorry but this can't wait any further. Now if you prefer we could follow you to your place of business and then force you to join us to the station. It's your choice," Page told him. It was her turn to raise her eyebrows. Travis sighed and opened the trunk to place his briefcase.

"Fine. But make it fast." He turned and rubbed his eye.

"You look tired."

"I told you that I was at an office Christmas party last night. I got home late. Nothing a Red Bull couldn't fix."

"Fine. We wanted to ask you about your father's old service weapon."

"What about it?"

"We spoke to your mother last night. She explained that she had given it to you. It's recently been linked to a new case that we are assisting on."

"And you think I had something to do with this case of yours? Think again. My place was broken into a month ago. The thief took a few things of value. The gun was one of them."

"Did you file a report on the break-in?"

"No. I know how the police are in this town. I grew up with one. It would have only been a waste of my time."

"You seem very angry at the police force in this town. May I ask why?"

"You want to know why? Because from personal experience, all you cops think about is yourselves. I know. My father was never around when I was a kid. He'd get up in the morning, take off, and not come back until it was time for bed." Lyndsey watched his facial features as he spoke. She had recently learned techniques to identify the tells that indicate a person is lying. It was an evening seminar that the state offered to the police. She found it very interesting in the end and knew that eventually it would come in handy. Like now.

"Perhaps he was trying to make the neighborhood safe for you and your friends to play in?"

"Fat chance. If that was the case, then Billy Mateo, a friend of mine, would have never gone missing back in 1981. Look that case up. Couldn't find him until he showed up dead in the dumpster of the old ShopRite supermarket. And they never found the person that killed him either."

"I'm sorry to hear that, Mr. Hughes, but do you mind if we take a look around in your apartment? Just to make sure you didn't misplace it."

"No way. You want to snoop around my apartment, get a search warrant. Until then, leave me alone. I didn't shoot anyone."

"We've never accused you of shooting someone."

"I know how you cops think. You're looking for my father's gun for a reason. And it ain't to scratch your ass with. Now we're done here. I'm leaving."

"Before you go, Mr. Hughes," Lyndsey said, stepping forward and brushing the front of his coat with her hands, "Just know that we will be speaking again."

"That a threat?"

"Oh, no. Not at all." Lyndsey smiled and stepped back.

Travis Hughes opened his car door and got in. Danica and Lyndsey stood there and watched him drive away. He even had the audacity to lower the window and wave goodbye as he traveled down the block.

"Total dick," Danica stated.

"Total lying dick," Lyndsey corrected her.

"You saw that too?"

"The eye twitch? Couldn't miss it. He's hiding something. What though, I'm not sure."

"Wanna go visit one of the judges and get ourselves a search warrant?"

"Not just yet. I want to learn a little more about Mr. Hughes. How about we take a drive over to Lincoln Harbor and do a little looking around Arrow Accounting?" She took her hand out of her coat pocket and held up the business card that Travis originally offered.

"Did you just pull a magic trick on me?" Danica smiled.

"A little something that Hines taught me when I first came on the force."

"You'll have to teach me that."

"Now, now, a magician never reveals their tricks." Lyndsey winked at her partner and got into the passenger side of Danica's Saturn.

43

Vinnie Donnelly rushed Carmen Perez and knocked her back into her house. The three other Jackals were right behind and spread out into the house like roaches, scurrying as if a light had been turned on. Carmen's scream of surprise alerted everyone in the house. Enrique dropped the fork in his hand and stood up from the table. Emilio threw the bathroom door open and rushed down the stairs, worried about his wife's health. Maritza opened the bedroom door and poked her head out to see what the commotion was. Emilio was met at the bottom of the stairs with the barrel of a gun. He stopped short, shocked. The second Jackal yanked Enrique into the living room while the third Jackal dragged Maritza behind him by her hair. Once everyone was in the living room, Vinnie Donnelly closed the front door behind him and smiled.

"Good morning all. You may not know me. I'm Vinnie Donnelly, rival gang leader to the Soldados. You may be wondering why I'm here. Funny story, actually. It's come to my attention that your son was the only person to walk out of a shootout. He's the lone witness to who murdered my good men. I'm not too happy about that and I'm willing to offer you good money to get the answer that I'm pretty sure I already know. But confirmation is a good thing. So whadda say? Name your price and you'll get it as long as your son sings like a canary." Vinnie held his arms out at his sides and waited for an answer.

"This family doesn't deal with criminals," Emilio spat at the insane gang leader.

"That's funny considering your son was in jail for the last few days.

Maybe I should give you a little incentive?" Vinnie helped Carmen from the spot on the floor that she had fallen. He wrapped one arm around her shoulders and with his other hand, he squeezed her mouth into a pucker.

"I'm sure that your wife is the glue that keeps this family together. Am I right? It would be a damn shame for something bad to happen to her." Vinnie pushed his coat to the side, revealing his own weapon on his hip. It was a survival knife tucked into a forest green sheath. To Enrique, it looked more the size of a machete than it did a knife.

"If you so much as hurt anyone in this family, I will hunt you down myself," Emilio replied.

"Oooooooo, scary!"

"Robin, call Brett Foster!" Jacob shouted across the room. He had not put the phone down since the conversation with Carmen Perez had begun. He was able to hear most of what was going on at the other side of the call and was afraid that the police would not get there in time. He couldn't bear to disconnect the phone and not know what happened to the Perez family. He had been told that Vinnie Donnelly had become unstable recently. And what was going on right now confirmed that.

"What's going on?" she asked, worried.

"Vinnie Donnelly is at the Perez house right now! We've got to get someone over there before he hurts or kills someone!"

Robin scrambled for her cell phone and swiped Brett's card from Jacob's hand. She listened to the ringing and after what seemed like minutes, Brett's voice mail took the call.

"I've got his voice mail, should I leave a message?"

"Yes, and then call the precinct to let them know. Ask for Orlando, or even Emerson. Tell them I'll meet them there."

"Wait, you're going over there, now?"

"Someone has to stop this." Jacob threw on his coat and slipped his shoes on before rushing out of the house, the cell phone never leaving his ear.

Maritza and her captor were off to the side next to the stairs. No one was looking at them. The Jackal had one hand gripping her neck and the other holding her right arm. The leader was so focused on her parents that she was sure no one was paying them any attention. Looking past her father and the Jackal that was holding a gun at his face, she saw that other than the main couch, she had a clear line to the front door. If she could get the Jackal to let go of her, she could pass her father, jump over the couch and get out the front door before anyone would realize what was happening.

She wiped the tears from her eyes and looked down. She saw that the Jackal holding her wore low top sneakers. It gave her an idea that her gym teacher had taught her class back in September during a self defense class that city hall promoted through the schools.

Maritza wound up, slowly bringing her knee up in front of her, and then slammed her heel into the front of the Jackals' ankle. She heard a slight crunch under the howl that he released. His grip immediately went loose, and she didn't hesitate. She ran straight for the couch and placed one foot on the seat of the couch to push herself over the back and right over to the door. She landed a foot from the door and grabbed the knob to twist it. But the leader of the Jackals was just as fast as her. He grabbed her by the neck and slammed her face into the door. Releasing the knife from its sheath, he poked the tip of it into her cheek. Getting in close to her, Vinnie could smell her fear and took it in.

"Bad move sweetheart. But maybe I should start with you first? What do you say Daddy? I can make her prettier." Vinnie turned in time to see Emilio land a punch in the other Jackal's face. He grabbed the gun that was pointed at him and directed it, towards the bay window that looked out to the street in front of the house. The gun went off in the struggle, shattering the window, and it startled everyone in the room. Emilio took advantage of the moment and screamed to his son.

"Enrique! Run!"

Enrique brought himself back into the moment, pulled his arm from the Jackal's grip, and turned to escape through the back door. The Jackal watching Enrique recovered quickly and went after the boy. He grabbed the teen's shoulder to turn him around and away from the back door. As Enrique turned, he grabbed the fork he had been using to eat his breakfast and plunged it into the Jackal's hand. The Jackal screamed and let go of his prey a second time. Enrique threw the door open and raced out into the yard.

* * *

Jacob jumped so hard at the sound of the gunshot through the phone that he almost dropped it onto the floor of his car. Recovering quickly, he scooped it back to his ear and could make out Emilio screaming for Enrique. *Was the boy shot?* he thought. Jacob pushed down on the gas pedal and honked his way through the intersections. He just hoped that he would make it to the house before it was too late.

    Vinnie grimaced. He wrapped his arm around Maritza's throat and brought the knife up to where one of her arteries lay just under the skin. He poked the tip into her skin hard.
    "Move and she ruins all the furniture in this room. Got it, Daddy?"
    Emilio froze at the statement. He had done what he needed to get Enrique away. They didn't want anyone else and knew that they'd leave to follow him. He held up his hands and gave in.
    Donnelly turned his head to the Jackal that was trying to remove the fork from his hand. Gritting his teeth, he ordered, "Go after him or I'll kill you myself. Devon, go bring the car around. Now." The Jackal limped out the front door.
    Donnelly walked Maritza over to Emilio, never releasing the knife from her neck. He leaned forward towards Emilio's ear. Then in a low deep tone, he said, "After we catch him and make him tell us what we want to know, and he *will* tell us, then I'm going to kill your son. And that will be your fault."

44

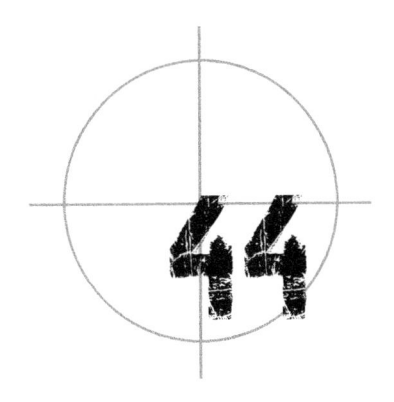

Orlando, Fernandez and Emerson were already at the precinct waiting when Foster and Raghetti had walked in. They were thirty minutes late, after driving Angie and Tamara to the PATH station down by the NJ Transit Terminal. Orlando was ready to explain everything that had happened since their discussion last night.

"Wogle's working overtime with the boys going over all the evidence from the fire last night. They're thinking arson all the way but they're making sure. And we pretty much know who's responsible. It was Robbie Cruz's home."

"Donnelly," Brett said.

"Exactly. But it gets better. Julio called me last night, right after he got word of the fire. He received a call from Donnelly who told him about the fire. And that wasn't all he told him."

"What else did he do?"

"He declared war against the Latin Soldados."

"Holy fuck," Raghetti said, "We are so screwed."

"That's the same fuckin' thing I told Russell," Kylee added.

"What's the chief have to say about this?"

"That everyone is going to working overtime for the next few days," Black said, walking in behind them, "At least until this Hermes is caught."

"Sorry for being late," Foster explained. He told them about seeing Angie and Tamara off until this was all over.

"That's fine," the chief told them, "There's more that I have to tell you all. Commissioner Price just called me asking for some men to keep the peace at City Hall this afternoon."

"Oh no," Emerson realized, "Seriously?"

"What?" Luis asked.

"He's having a press conference, isn't he?" Brett asked. Chief Black nodded.

"I'd rather have a police baton shoved up my ass," Kylee provided her opinion on security watch.

"You kinky vixen, you," Josh joked.

"Don't worry, none of you will have to be there but he's asking for ten to twelve of our uniformed officers to help. And this means that we're going to be short out on the streets. So, we'll need you guys out there."

"What the conference for? The gang war?"

"No, but close. Price is pushing his End the Crime campaign. He's also going to make mention about Doyle's death to help push it." "Douche bag," Kylee coughed.

"So, any word on Doyle's autopsy?"

"Aaron confirmed that it was the bullet that killed him," Russell explained, "And his family is having the funeral tomorrow morning. They want us all there to pay our respects."

"Consider us there," Brett said, speaking for everyone in the room.

"Where's Bergen and Page?" Raghetti asked.

"They're still following up on Travis Hughes, Detective Hughes' son. They just called in and told me that Travis said he doesn't have the gun anymore because his place was broken into and it was taken, but he's refusing permission to go look around his apartment without a warrant. Right now, though, they're following him to his place of business to talk to some of his co-workers before they go down to City Hall and request a warrant."

"How's the Perez kid?" Russell asked.

"I've had the night shift do a routine drive past the house every hour. It's been quiet. But his lawyer, Jacob, notified us that he's gotten Enrique to come in this morning to finally talk to us."

"That's great news!"

"Yeah, so Brett, you and Josh are going to have to stick around until they get here. Scott said they'd be here around 10."

"Maybe we'll have this fuck in time for dinner," Orlando smiled.

"We can only hope. But this is a step in the right direction. Then we could put an end to this gang war," Black finally managed to smile.

"I take it Donnelly is no where to be found?" Luis questioned his boss.

"No one's seen or heard from him since he spoke to Julio last night, but I'm sure that it's only a matter of time before he pokes his head out the hole he's hiding in to cause more trouble. I want you all out there watching for the Jackals."

"What about the Soldados?"

"Nah, Julio knows that a gang war is not something that will help him in the long run. He won't be causing trouble," Luis told them.

"Well, that's a relief," Raghetti said, sarcastically.

"Still," the chief added, "He's not going to let Donnelly and his men take out his guys and just sit there. I don't want any of you getting caught in the crossfire, understood?" They nodded.

Before Chief Black could dismiss them, Hines came running into the department. The look on his face was one of panic. He stopped and tried to catch his breath. He took several deep breaths and finally said, "Chief, we just got a call from Jacob Scott's assistant. She said that there's an attack on the Perez home. I just sent a couple of cars to the location."

Everyone froze in shock from the news. Black looked over and pointed to Brett and Josh.

"Go," she told them.

The two detectives were out of the station and driving down the block, heading to the Perez home in two minutes - a new record.

45

"Go, go, go!" shouted Vinnie. The injured Jackal pressed on the gas as his leader threw himself into the passenger seat. Donnelly hadn't even allowed the driver to wait for the last Jackal to leave the house. The long green Cadillac's engine roared down the block, slowing briefly to turn the corner so that they could circle around and catch Enrique before he reached the end of the line of backyards.

"Who knew that they were going to fight back? I think that little bitch broke my ankle," complained Devon.

"Shut up and drive!" Vinnie punched the dashboard several times in anger. This was supposed to go according to plan. He would have no choice now but to torture the family and make Enrique tell him what had gone on at the bus garage that Saturday night. Vinnie knew what had happened, but he wanted the kid to tell his gang that he was right - that Julio set up the meeting to take down a good amount of his Jackals. But the Jackals would make a comeback. And Vinnie would prove to his men that, even without Liam, he was still stable enough to run the show. He just had to make sure he knew which ones to trust.

They didn't think he could hear them talking about his supposed instability, but he did. But they didn't know it wasn't instability or insanity, it was anger. Anger that the Latin Soldados were still around, after all these years. He had wanted them gone for what they had done to him and his friends all those years ago. He would never forget. He built the Jackals with Liam because of that.

Donnelly was shocked back into the present when the car jerked to the side, taking another corner. He reached out and grabbed the ceiling strap by the door, keeping himself from falling into Devon. The noise of the Cadillac brought the morning people to turn their heads towards them or to peek out their front windows. Donnelly ignored them and focused on the task at hand, finding Enrique Perez.

"Do you see him?" asked Devon.

"No. Not yet. He must be trying to hide in one of the backyards. Turn the corner again and stop there."

"Why?"

"Because I'm going in after him, you moron."

Devon nodded and did what he was told. When they reached the side street, the last Jackal made his way around the opposite corner and met up with Vinnie. Donnelly got out of the car and walked over to Louie. The Jackal still held the gun that he had been pointing at Emilio Perez as if it were a cell phone while he focused more on the welt forming under his eye.

"Did you see him?"

"Nah," Louie told him, "Benny chased after him. They headed in this direction."

Donnelly looked out into the line of backyards and couldn't see anyone over the line of fences. He hated doing the job himself, but he knew that if he didn't there was a chance that Enrique would escape his grasp.

"Wait here," he told Louie. He tucked his gun into his coat and hopped the fence into the end backyard. There were no signs of anyone in that yard, so he moved ahead. The next two yards had been untouched as well.

When he got to the third yard, he found what he was looking for. Unfortunately, it wasn't the way he wanted to see it. Vinnie had found Benny. He was there in someone's backyard, lying on a pile of snow, face down. The snow around him was sprinkled with red dots and lines. Vinnie bent down to turn Benny over and heard the crinkle of Benny's coat. Benny had been stabbed in the stomach and bled out. Donnelly wondered if this was the work of Enrique Perez. The kid seemed too scared to fight this viciously, but appearances were deceiving when someone is fighting to live.

Vinnie looked around and saw tracks in the snow that led to the fence of the backyard that adjoined the other side of the block. Donnelly climbed over the fence and looked through that backyard, seeing tracks as if someone had stumbled. The trail led through the alley of the house to the front where Vinnie and Devon had driven past, frantically. Donnelly could not believe that he had missed seeing the kid in the alley as they drove past.

Donnelly followed the trail to the sidewalk on the opposite side of the block and lost the trail onto the street. Enrique must have waited for him to pass and then crossed the street. But where was he headed was the question. The trail was headed away from the police station and directed to the west of Hoboken. Vinnie thought of what was in that direction. There was Columbus Park and Hoboken High School. The high school was closed for the holiday, but he could be going to a friend's house. It would be impossible to find him before the police covered the area.

"Fuck!" he shouted at the top of his lungs.

He turned quickly to his right and shot a fist out at the closest thing to him, an old wooden fence. The fence splintered under his clenched fist. The anger in him was unleashed on the fence. Throwing punch after punch until his fists were bloody. Once he started feeling the pain, he stopped and caught his breath.

Vinnie returned back to the car where Devon and Louie were still waiting. The bruise around Louie's eye was blackening by the minute. He was leaning on the driver side of the car, smoking a cigarette, and talking to Devon. Angered by the way his plan had fallen to shit, Vinnie walked over to where Louie was standing. Louie looked up and Vinnie raised his gun and fired a bullet into Louie's skull. The point-blank impact turned the back of Louie's skull into a firework explosion of miniature pieces of brain and skull. Louie's body slumped to the side of the car and Devon screamed in shock. Donnelly opened the driver's door and pushed Devon over to the passenger side.

"We're getting out of here," Donnelly told the scared Jackal. He threw the car into drive and sped out of the area just as police arrived from the other direction.

46

"Excuse me, Julio, there's some woman here to speak to you," said Oscar, a long-time member of the Soldados. Julio looked up from his desk in his den. The den had become his place of solace when strategies needed to be formed. And after the fire last night, that was exactly what needed to happen.

Julio had taken a few of his men to the Cruz home to see if anyone was in the house when the fire started. He found Rosa Cruz, Robbie's mother there staring at the blaze with tears streaming down her face. Jimenez was not one for showing emotion but the sight of her like that floored him.

"I promise you, the person responsible for this will suffer," he told her.

"No, please Julio. No more violence. Do you see what that brings? I have lost enough already. My Roberto and my home. You have Carlos, too. At least leave me my dignity."

Julio couldn't believe that she had pushed him away. After all he had done for the Cruz family. But in a way, she was right. This was his fault. He allowed Vinnie Donnelly to exist in his town even though he knew the danger of doing so. It was time to make things right. If Donnelly wanted a war, then Julio Jimenez was going to give him one. He would have revenge on the man who had attacked his family.

Sitting down at his desk, he went over his options. If he handed Vinnie to this vigilante, known only as Hermes, he could keep his hands clean and then hand the vigilante to the police. Everyone would be happy, and the town would be all his. His contacts in the police department would keep him protected from those police that still attempted to "make the city a better place" by removing all gang crime. But he knew that if he were taken down, someone else would just move in and take over. Someone worse.

"What woman?" he asked Oscar.

"I don't know," Oscar said, shrugging, "But she looks like a cop."

Julio paused, wondering what female police officer would come into his home to speak to him. He had no females on his side in the police department. The curiosity got the better of him and he waved her in to Oscar. Oscar turned and motioned for the woman to come forward and enter the room. The woman was tall, with brown hair that fell over her shoulders. Even covered by a winter coat, he could see the workout curves of her body. *Not bad,* he thought. *Maybe I should have some females on my payroll.*

"Hello."

"Mr. Jimenez, may I have a moment of your time?" she asked.

"But of course. Excuse me though, you have the advantage over me."

"How is that?"

"You know who I am. But I have never seen you before in my life. And trust me, I would remember you."

"Amanda Fenton, ATF." Fenton moved her coat to the side, revealing the badge on her hip. He nodded and motioned for her to sit.

"I'll stand if that's alright with you."

"Whatever pleases you. So, what can I do for you, Agent Fenton?"

"I want to talk to you about the shooting at the bus garage on Saturday night."

"You do realize that the local police have already questioned me? I've given my statement and have witnesses that will testify as to my whereabouts at the time of the shooting."

"I prefer to speak to you one on one."

"So be it. Would you like something to drink?"

"No, thank you. What do you know about the shooting?"

"Same as everyone else. A third party set up my men and several of the Jackals, murdering them in cold blood. He goes by the name Hermes and the police are in the dark as to where to find him."

"We can play this game all night, Mr. Jimenez. Or you can be straight with me and tell me what else you know. The things that the police don't."

Julio smiled. He liked her fierceness and her street smarts. He could sense something else hiding under the surface. He would continue to work himself into her head to find out her secrets.

"You are a smart one. But why should I reveal my information to you? What part do you play in this investigation and hunt for the truth?"

"My partner was there that night. He was killed as well."

The news came to a shock to Julio. He was unaware of that. There was no information that any officers were there that night. This made Julio even more curious.

"My apologies for the loss of your partner. May I ask what he was doing?"

"Not until you give me something in return."

He paused, considering what to reveal, whether to give her anything. Looking into her eyes, he was sucked into her story. He wanted more from her. He craved more from her. It was all about information and hers was a tasty carrot dangling over his head.

"Fine. The boy is the key to ending this."

"Tell me something that the police don't already know."

"You don't get it, Agent Fenton. Enrique has seen this man's face. He's kept it from everyone, but I know. I see the fear in his eyes. Hermes' face haunts his dreams."

"I guess he's told you about who the vigilante is?"

"No, he's a stubborn boy. Like his uncle. It runs in his blood. But I knew his uncle. And I know what it will take to get this information."

"You have no intention of providing that information to the police?"

"Ah, ah. I have revealed to you. It is now your turn. Why was your partner there that night?"

"One of the Jackals is a CI. He tipped my partner off to the meeting."

"I'm not surprised that it was a Jackal to squeal. But if your partner was tipped off, why did you not accompany him?"

"I was visiting family at the time in Pennsylvania."

"Interesting. Now, let me explain something. I lost seven men in that shooting, friends and family members of my surviving crew. They are looking for vengeance. I cannot deny them that by handing this man to the police. I have to keep them happy in order to keep them loyal."

"I understand that. I'm looking to get my hands on this man as well. And I will do what I need to."

"I respect you for that, Agent Fenton. My question is, are you willing to go to the same lengths I am?"

"If need be, Mr. Jimenez."

Julio felt the statement bore more than it seemed. There was still something that the ATF agent was not telling him. He didn't want to push too much only to have her shut down. It was a dance and he had to keep leading in order to get what he wanted.

"I have a feeling that Hermes will be coming for me."

"Why do you think that?"

"Because he started this to get the gangs to fight each other, but I am too smart to fall for that. Vincent Donnelly, on the other hand is too ignorant to recognize the clues."

"But why not just take out Donnelly and put the blame on you?"

"This vigilante is a smart man, I will give him that. He knows I'll beat any charges. He'd have to come to me in the end because I will be the last one standing."

Fenton stood silent for a long moment before saying, "You know who Hermes is."

"Maybe I do. Maybe I don't. We will all learn who he is in the end. Who will get to him first is the question you should be asking. Now I do have things to take care of, if you'll excuse me." Julio stood up and walked to the doorway of the den. He turned to see Amanda out. Fenton took the hint and left the den. She was met by Oscar, who led her back to the front door of Julio's home. She hadn't learned anything of importance, but she did get the feeling that Julio knew more about Hermes than the local police did. Oscar opened the door for her and as she exited, Julio spoke out to her one last thing.

"Good luck with your search, Agent. May we all get what we wish for this holiday."

47

Chief Black stepped out of her office, looking to see who had remained behind. Luis had followed Brett and Josh to the Perez home. Danica and Lyndsey were still looking into Travis Hughes. Russell and Kylee were at their desks filling out the paperwork from yesterday.

Black had remembered when the two had first become more than just partners. It was pretty obvious from the way they acted and how they spoke to each other. She didn't see the connection at first because they were very different personality-wise but after a few weeks she saw the couple aspect of their relationship.

"Fuckin' mouse! It's not working again!" Fernandez yelled, slamming the computer mouse on her desk. The fiery attitude of Fernandez made Christine Black laugh to herself. She had remembered dealing with Kylee when she was younger. The girl had a hard upbringing, being orphaned at the age of five. Being moved from foster home to foster home was tough for any child, but Kylee had still been able to rise above it all and when she became old enough, she moved out on her own and applied for the police force.

Her tough exterior was her way of keeping the bad of the world away, yet Black had seen the inside woman. Fernandez had a heart for children as well as for the underdog. There was an underlining sweetness to her that Russell had brought to the surface. Even though Black knew that partners in the station house that end up in bed was always frowned on, there was no better team than the two before her.

"Ahem."

Kylee and Russell looked up from their computers and saw Chief Black standing there.

"Hey Chief, need anything?" Russell offered.

"Hines just got a call from someone who lives in the apartment building that Mark was killed behind. They've decided to come forward and that they saw part of what happened to him. I'd like you two to go interview the witness and see if they have anything on the vigilante. Name's Emily Trenton. Here's the address and apartment number." The chief handed the piece of paper to Russell. He slipped the paper into his shirt pocket and grabbed his coat.

"I've got to run. If you or the others need anything, ask Sergeant Hines."

"Hot date?" Kylee asked.

"I wish," Black responded, "I have to head over to City Hall to be there for the Commissioner's press conference."

"My apologies," Russell joked.

"We'll go talk to the witness and then we'll patrol for the gangs," Kylee told her.

"Oh, and see if the guys in the lab have any updates before you go, please."

"Got it, boss lady. Knock 'em dead out there." Kylee winked at her boss. Black smiled.

"Thanks, you two. Well, I'll see you when I get back." The chief put on her coat and headed downstairs to the front entrance. Fernandez stood up and adjusted her breasts in the new bra she had bought and winked at her partner. Then the two headed down the hall to the crime lab. The three techs were all busy hovering over their own workspaces. Melvin's satellite radio belted out Stone Sour's 'Tired' and Russell chuckled at the irony of the scene, as they had all been working through the night.

"Morning, boys," Kylee said, walking into their space. Melvin and Lucky jolted up, unaware that the short Puerto Rican firecracker was even there. Wogle looked up and paused from what he was doing.

"Hey, you two. What's new, what's happening?"

"The chief asked us to come up here and see if there was any progress," Emerson explained.

"Well, it's official," Wogle told them, "The fire was, indeed, arson.

Traces of gasoline over the majority of pieces we collected from the house. And considering that the house was owned by Rosa Cruz, it doesn't take a Jeopardy contestant to figure out who was involved."

"Vinnie Donnelly," Kylee and Russell said in unison.

"Most likely. Anyway, that's what I have. Melvin's been working on locating where the bullets used at the shooting were purchased. And Lucky over there is going back over all the pieces from the shootout. We want to make sure we didn't miss anything the first time around. I honestly hate to say it, but this vigilante guy is very careful. There's no prints on the casings, the front door, or on the clothing wore by any of the victims. No foreign fibers, saliva, or skin. It's like he's a ghost."

"Or maybe someone familiar to police procedures," Russell wondered.

"Who isn't with all these crime shows on television?" Kylee rebutted.

"Yes, but most people always make a mistake. But this guy? He knows what he's doing," Wogle said, agreeing with Emerson. Russell looked over at Kylee and smirked. She rolled her eyes at him.

"This vigilante could be a cop? Or maybe related to a cop?"

"If you're reaching, it's possible. You have someone you're looking at?"

"Bergen and Page do. They're looking at Tony Hughes' son."

"Travis? Really?"

"Lucky confirmed that the gun used at the shootout was Tony's. Tony's wife gave Travis the gun after Tony died. They're over there now trying to talk to him because he blew them off last night."

"Wow, I knew Travis when he was a kid. Tony used to bring him in every now and then. Seemed like a good kid."

"They always do. Until they do something like this."

"We've got to get going," Fernandez told them, "Someone may have seen something last night in the alley where Doyle died."

"Good luck, you two," Wogle said to the duo, "We'll let you know if we find anything else." Russell thanked Mike and the two left the lab techs as Five Finger Death Punch began to play.

The two headed downstairs so they could get Kylee's coat. Fernandez stopped as they passed the bathroom. Russell stopped and looked back at her. A sly smile grew across her face.

"What's the look for?"

"Tonight, Momma needs some lovin'."

"You're insatiable. Fine."

"And I'm on top. And don't forget the nipple play. They're not there for decorations." The comment made Russell smile. He not only loved his partner for the great sex, but he loved her for who she truly was.

"I love you," he told her. Kylee looked at him and stared into his eyes. She could feel the love and thought of the feeling she got when wrapped up in his arms. It was one she never thought she would find, but she was glad that she had and would fight to the death to keep it.

"I know," she told him.

48

Kristie Marks pulled into her parking spot in the lot of the Meadowlands Convention Center in Secaucus. Today was the big day and she was feeling the need to vomit the breakfast that Dean had made her. After studying non-stop for the past two months, she was finally there and ready to take the Bar.

Since helping Jacob on the case for Doug Martin, Kristie had decided to make more of a difference than she had before. And with that difference, came the looming monster that all lawyers fear: The Bar. The biggest exam in a lawyer's life that was ten times worse than the SATs she took back in high school.

Kristie closed her eyes and took a deep breath. She told herself that she was doing this for herself and for Connor. She wanted him to have a good life and not have to worry about money for the two of them, even though she now had Dean in her life. Having met him shortly before the murder of the lawyer she had worked for, Dean Williams helped make life as a single mother bearable. The fact that he had stayed with her after being shot by an assassin while trying to protect Connor made him Man of the Year to her. She would never forget the day she had met him, even though it had been rather embarrassing.

And as for her son, Connor, he was her life. Now in the second grade, he was growing into his own personality. And she was learning that he was quite the heartbreaker in his class, hearing stories about girls coming up to him and giving him a quick peck on the cheek. According to him, though, there was one girl that he already planned on marrying.

"Her name's Ruby and she's the most beautiful girl. Other than you, Mom." The comment had made her, and Dean laugh.

Marks looked into the rearview mirror and fixed her hair, telling herself, "Ok, Marks. This is what you've worked hard for. This is your moment to shine. Get in there and kick that exam's ass."

Kristie grabbed the yellow pad and the several sharpened pencils on the passenger seat and got out of the car. She looked over at the Convention Center and made her way across the lot to the front entrance. With every step, she went over the topics that would be covered in today's portion of the exam.

The Bar in New Jersey was a two-day event. The first dealt with essays on Contracts, Torts, Criminal Law, Property and Evidence. Those taking the exam had a full 8 hours to complete it. Allowed only a quiet snack and some writing utensils, the test takers were locked in the large room with several people keeping watch on them. And after the first grueling day, they were forced to return the next morning to cover the Multi-state portion of the exam, with another 8 hours to complete that part.

Kristie looked at the long-term goals that she could complete once this was over. She would be able to be a real part of the Hoffman and Delgado firm that she had started in a couple of years ago. Then, and only then, would she be doing her part in courtrooms of New Jersey.

A woman sitting at one of the long white covered tables waved her over. Kristie smiled at the woman.

"Name?" she asked Marks.

"Kristie Marks." The woman ran her eyes down the list that she held on her clipboard. Finding the name halfway down, she placed a check next to Kristie name. She pulled a form from under the list of names and handed it to her.

"Please sign this and hand it to the man over by that door." The woman pointed to Kristie's left. Kristie took the form and thanked the woman. Almost immediately, the woman waved another person over. Kristie read over the form, reviewing the rules of the exam and then signed and dated it at the bottom.

She walked over to the man at the door and smiled. He took the form and nodded thanks to her. Kristie walked into the wide area and scanned the room to find a seat that suited her. She noticed another woman her age sitting off to the side. Kristie decided to sit near her. She placed the pencils and the protein bar that Dean had given her on the table and sat down. The woman, wearing short blonde hair and glasses, looked over at Kristie and smiled.

"Good morning," the woman said. Kristie could see the stress on the woman's face and imagined that she looked the same.

"Morning," Kristie smiled back.

"I really hope I'm not the only one here that's ready to throw up from the nervousness."

"Oh, no," Kristie replied, "I've had that feeling since I woke up this morning." The woman laughed gently.

"Good. I'm Trish, by the way." She held her hand out to introduce herself. Kristie took it and shook.

"Nice to meet you, Trish. I'm Kristie."

The conversation was interrupted by the man standing at the head of the room with the microphone in his hand. He thanked the room for being there and went over the rules once more as two women walked around handing out pamphlets. Minutes later, Kristie was beginning the first page of the exam, putting everything out of her mind besides the volumes of information she had studied.

49

Jacob found Carmen and Maritza on the porch cold and in tears when he finally arrived at the house. The lawyer double parked, not caring about getting a ticket or even blocking the street. He knew that the police would be right behind him and they would most likely do the same. He ran to the porch. Carmen was holding her daughter tight and pointed into the house for Jacob.

"Are you okay?" Jacob asked. He looked them over. Carmen seemed ruffled, but he noticed the dot of blood on Maritza's cheek. "Did they hurt you?"

"Help him," Carmen asked him hysterically, "Help him save Enrique."

"They, they went after Enrique. My father chased after him," Maritza explained.

"How many were there? Did they have any weapons?" Jacob needed to know everything before he went into the house after Emilio and Enrique. He understood how upset they were, but every second counted. The Jackals could have already captured Enrique and began torturing him for information. He hated the thought, knowing Enrique was more concerned with protecting his family than himself.

"One had a gun. The leader had a big knife. I didn't see if the other two had anything," Enrique's sister told him.

"Okay, stay here," the lawyer told the women, "The police will be here any minute. I called them."

"Please! Make sure they're alright! Enrique!" Carmen cried out. She grabbed Jacob's arm, the fear and worry pouring from her eyes. Jacob tried to comfort her and rested his hands on her shoulders.

"I'll go make sure they're okay. Just stay here." She released her grip and Jacob headed into the house.

The silence was deafening. Jacob saw the living room in disarray. The table next to the door was knocked over. He saw the phone that Carmen had spoken to him minutes before lying on its side. The back door was left wide open, blowing the cold wind into the house. He approached the kitchen, keeping an eye on his sides, in case one of the Jackals had returned.

Jacob stopped at the doorway, looking down. He saw the drops of blood staining the linoleum tile. But whose blood it was, he did not know. To the side of the back door was a bloody fork. He hoped it had been used on a Jackal.

Looking out into the backyard, he saw the Perez' pet dog sniffing the fence on the right side of the yard. Creeping quietly towards the dog, he held out his hand, hoping to keep the dog from barking. The dog turned and sniffed his outstretched hand before giving it a warm lick. Jacob scratched the dog behind the ear as a reward and slowly looked over the solid fence. He saw tracks leading through the adjacent yard and signs that the chase had continued into the yard beyond.

Jacob climbed over the fence as carefully as he could; realizing he should had put on his sneakers instead of shoes when rushing out of his own house. Hopping down into the next yard, he continued following the tracks. It wasn't until he peered over the fence into the fourth yard, that he saw the Jackal, lying face up dead. The gang member's eyes were staring up into the great sky where the lawyer knew the Jackal would never go. The blood on the Jackal's belly had dripped down his sides and turned the snow under him red.

"Enrique!"

The shout jarred Jacob back to reality. He knew the voice. It was Emilio, and he was close. Jacob followed the tracks in the snow to the fence on the west side of the neighbor's yard. He saw through the yard, down the alley and onto the opposite street. There was Emilio, throwing his head from side to side so fast that Jacob was sure he was bound to give himself whiplash. Jacob climbed the last fence and headed through the alley to reach Emilio. Only feet away from the panicked father, Jacob reached out to touch Emilio's arm. As soon as he did, the large man spun around as fast as he had ever seen someone move and pull back to hit the lawyer. Jacob threw his hands up in defense and Emilio saw that it wasn't one of the Jackals. His shoulders immediately slouched in relief.

"Oh God, Mr. Scott, I am very sorry."

"Don't apologize, Emilio. Did you find Enrique? Is he safe?"

"I don't know. Dear God, Jacob," Emilio said, his eyes pleading, "Help us. We just got him back. And now he's gone again. The Jackals have taken him from us. Please get him back alive."

Jacob didn't know what to tell Emilio. If Enrique had been taken by the Jackals, he couldn't lie and tell him everything would be okay. Because it wouldn't.

50

"Get every weapon you can carry and take it with you. We are hitting Julio where it hurts," Donnelly ordered his men. He wasn't wasting any time now. He knew that his rival had taken out Benny in the backyard and now had the teen. It was time for retribution. If Jimenez wanted a war, then he would know what it meant to feel Donnelly's wrath.

The seven men there scrambled, opening up spots in the room where the guns had been hidden in the event that the police raided the place. There were rifles, shotguns, and pistols being pulled out of every nook. He smiled at the commotion. Regardless of the question of his sanity, his Jackals were loyal to the end. They knew better than to defy him.

Devon walked up to Vinnie and handed him his favorite rifle. He looked down at the gift and took it with one hand. The other hand patted Devon on the arm, in thanks. The leader of the gang was ready. The rifle was all he needed.

"What we are about to do, we do for our fallen brothers. We show our love and respect through violence. Why? Because we are," Vinnie leaned his head towards the men before him.

They raised their guns and shouted, "Jackals!"

"You're damn right, we are. Now let's show these spic fucks how we do things in this town." Vinnie opened the door and stepped to the side, allowing his men to exit and enter the three cars in front of the hang out. Vinnie closed the door behind him and walked to the Hummer in front of the other two vehicles. He raised his rifle in the air and smiled at his men. Then he climbed into the passenger side and gave Devon the thumbs up. Devon pulled out of the spot and Vinnie threw his fist out the window and up in the air. The morning quietness was broken by the excited honks of the three horns. An attack was coming, it spoke. And there was no stopping it.

Amanda sat in her car that was still parked on the other end of the street across from Julio's home. She had kept watch on the house since she was escorted out thirty minutes ago. Julio had yet to leave and from the number of cars out front, there were a fair amount of gang members in there with him.

The ATF agent didn't enjoy the conversation with Julio, but she had to find out who was responsible for Tommy's death. The murder of Mark Doyle didn't make it any better. She had liked the older detective, he had reminded her of her father. She had wished at that moment that her family was closer to her than they actually were. Although, if it weren't for her having to go home to deal with a family crisis last week, Tommy wouldn't have been alone that night and he would still be alive.

The guilt ate away at her since the moment she walked back into the Trenton office. Her boss had let her settle in before telling her about Tommy's absence after talking to him that Saturday afternoon. She knew right away that something had gone wrong. There was no logical reason why her partner would have remained quiet since the stake out. That wasn't like him.

She had last talked to her supervisor hours ago. Neil Jones answered his phone with the same gravely voice that he had since she was assigned to the Newark branch of the ATF. She had seen him as a father figure since her own father had been gunned down.

"Hey Chief," she said with a smile.

"I hear the smile, Fenton. What do you want?"

"I'm just hoping to get some more information on the conversation that Tom had with that Finnegan guy."

"What more are you looking for?"

"Anything that will help the police here to figure out who's been shooting the gang members."

"The police or you, Amanda?"

Jones was observant that way. He knew her better than she knew herself. And he knew that she would be looking for revenge.

"Can you find anything or not?" she snapped.

"Let me see what I can do. But snap at me again and I'll have you yanked back here and find someone else to cover this case." He hung up on her. She quickly regretted getting angry at him. She knew that he would come through for her.

So, while she waited for that, she sought to find out more on the gangs and who may have had a grudge against them. Talking to Julio, she managed to get a feel for the gang leader: clever. The way he spoke and carried himself showed that he was more of a business man than a gangster. This was more about the money and respect for him than it was the crimes.

Her phone buzzed on her leg. Looking down, she saw she had a text from her boss. Attached were several pages of documents that Tommy had filled out to document the conversation between himself and Finnegan, his CI. As she read the words on the screen, she missed the three vehicles slowly pulling up to Julio's house. She ignored the sounds of numerous car doors opening, too focused on the pages.

It wasn't until the first shot was fired that she noticed the eight Jackals standing in the street, firing guns at Julio Jimenez's home. Her head shot up. The blasts were deafening on the small block, echoing off the houses around them.

Amanda immediately dropped the phone and took her weapon from its holster. She ducked and crawled across the seats to the passenger door. Opening it, she pulled herself out of the car and took cover. She peeked over the hood and saw that all the Jackals had their attention towards Julio's house, unaware that she was there.

"Freeze, police!" she shouted. She aimed her gun over the hood. With the low visibility, it was difficult to see them clear enough for a good shot. The two words stopped everything. Vinnie Donnelly and his men turned to look at her. Vinnie gave her a "what-are-you-thinking?" look. Then he motioned for two of his men to take care of her. They didn't even aim; they just blasted her car to pieces. She kept down until the bullets heading her way came to a stop.

The few seconds that she had gotten their attention with was plenty of time for the Soldados to burst out and retaliate. Several members came from around back and ducked behind the short concrete fence that surrounded Julio's snow-covered yard. They fired back at the Jackals. Bullets flew through the thick snowflakes, missing all their targets. It was a constant boom throughout the street.

Donnelly was done hiding behind the Hummer. He stepped out in front of the vehicle and walked around, fearless. Holding up the rifle he aimed and took out one of the Soldados members when they poked out of their spot to fire. Fenton saw that the two Jackals that were shooting at her had turned their attention back to Julio's house.

Amanda took the moment and stood up. She aimed and hit one of the Jackals in the left shoulder blade. *Wow,* she thought, *nice shot!* The gang member went down. The Jackal beside him turned quickly and gave off a few shots. She managed to dodge the first few, but the last took her off her feet forcefully.

* * *

Julio stood between the front door and the side window. The constant firing from all seven Jackals made it difficult to return fire. He peeked out the front door and was met with pieces of flying wood splinters from the doorway. It was impossible to do anything but stay hidden, but Julio was not one to hide from an adversary.

Then suddenly the firing stopped completely. The silence only lasted seconds, then the street was overcome with revving engines. *Just like a coward,* he thought of Donnelly. Shoot and run. He swung out of his stance and ran out of the house to the sidewalk. By the time he reached it the vehicles were already half a block away.

Jimenez lowered the Desert Eagle in his hand and gritted his teeth. Donnelly would pay dearly for this personal attack. And it would be up to Julio to collect.

"Julio!"

Ryan ran up to Julio with a fearful look on his face. Julio knew that it would not be good news. He was waiting to find out how many more Soldados members were killed.

"How many were injured?" he asked Ryan.

"I don't know. But it's worse. Your abuela, Julio. She was sitting at the window upstairs when they showed up. We couldn't get to her in time."

Julio's jaw dropped. He had been letting his grandmother stay with him because he refused to keep her in a retirement home. He had hired someone to daily come by and make sure she was kept clean and fed. She had lived a long life and Julio actually enjoyed having her there. The rest of his family had shunned him for what he did. She didn't, though.

Julio looked up into the grey sky and closed his eyes, muttering a prayer under his breath. Once he was done, he looked over at Ryan. Ryan could feel the anger through the stare.

"I want each and every Jackal dead. But not Vinnie. Vinnie is all mine. He will die slow and painful. This, I vow."

51

"Do we know for sure that the Jackals have Enrique?" Brett asked. "Is it possible that he could have gotten away? Maybe run to a friend's house?"

Emilio sat, defeated, on his porch. A blanket had been placed over his shoulders to keep him protected from the cold and the shock of the attack on his family. He shook his head slowly, unsure of whether or not Enrique could have gotten away. Brett was afraid of the dead stare in the father's eyes. He had seen that a number of times in the eyes of parents that have had to identify the bodies of their children. Foster tried to give Emilio some hope that his son was not dead. Brett had a strong feeling that the boy was still out there, hiding from Donnelly and his men.

Josh came out from inside the home and they saw Orlando walk down the street with an impressed look on his face. Raghetti watched as he came closer. Luis looked up at the two once he reached the front step of the home.

"We've got two Jackals dead. The first one is in a neighbor's backyard and the other we found around the corner. I think Enrique may have taken out the one in the backyard. From what witnesses are saying, Donnelly took out his own man. Which means good news."

"How does that mean good news?" Raghetti questioned.

"Because Donnelly would only take out his own man in anger. And if he's angry, then that means he doesn't have Enrique," Brett explained.

"Exactly. The kid's still out there."

"We've got to find him before someone else does."

"Maritza," Emilio said to the detectives.

"She's inside, Mr. Perez."

"No, Maritza. Ask her. She knows who Enrique's friends are."

Brett looked over at Luis and he nodded. Heading into the house, he approached Maritza and sat down next to her on the couch. Carmen was in the kitchen making coffee for the officers. Even though she had just been in a traumatic moment, she was still holding it together for the family. Maritza had a distant stare in her eyes. She was still recovering from the incident that had her stunned. Luis leaned in close, hoping to get her attention.

"Maritza, can I ask you a few questions?"

Maritza's eyes refocused and she looked over at the Anti-Vice detective. Looking right at him, he still had the feeling that she wasn't really all there.

"I'm sorry that this happened to you and your family, but we're trying to locate your brother. He got away from the Jackals, but we don't know where he would have run to. Are there any friends nearby that you know of? Ones that he might have felt safe to hide with?"

"There's Miquel, or Mikey, they call him. He's three blocks over right off of Willow and 10th. He and Enrique are always hanging out. There's a couple of others but I don't know where they live. And there was Tiela. Some girl he was interested in, but they never hooked up. She was different. I think that's why he was so interested."

"Different how?"

"She was into punk. She always was dyeing her hair a different color every month. I thought she was just a weirdo. I don't know where she lives but I know where she hangs out."

Orlando took out his little pad and pen and handed them to Maritza, asking her to write down the names and places he could find them Enrique. She gently held the pen and wrote out the information and handed him back the pad. He thanked her and left her to the Emergency response crew to help take care of her.

Brett and Josh were still outside, talking to Jacob Scott and a uniformed officer on the sidewalk. Luis walked over to them with the information that Maritza gave him.

"Okay, we're headed over there now," Brett told the officer, "Make sure that the Perez family is taken care of."

"What's going on?" Orlando asked.

"Donnelly went from here to Julio's house. He and several of the Jackals just shot up the place. Agent Fenton was there also and was shot."

"Shit. Well, I'll stay here and follow up on finding Enrique. You two go see if anyone else was hurt."

Once they pulled up to the block, Josh and Brett could see the aftermath as clear as day. The entire front of Jimenez' house was falling off and looked as if monster termites had attacked it. They stopped at the corner and got out, showing their badges to get past the police barricade.

The first thing Brett noticed was the number of shell casings that littered the packed snow. He saw the red car on the opposite side of the street that had also been shot. He knew right away that it was Fenton's car, and not just from the bullet holes.

There were four ambulances along the street, taking care of those who were lucky enough to survive the attack. Josh noticed Amanda Fenton sitting on the back of one of the ambulances with her leg stretched out in front of her. An EMT was examining her leg and applying pressure to her thigh. The two detectives wandered over to her.

"You do know, it's easier to show up *after* the shots are fired," Raghetti joked.

"It wasn't by choice," she replied, flinching at the EMT's examination.

"What were you doing here?"

"I was keeping an eye on Jimenez. I have a feeling that he may know more that he's letting on about the bus garage shooting."

"Why do you say that?" Brett wondered.

"He seemed too laid back about losing his guys. He wasn't sending his gang out to get revenge. Like he was waiting for just the right time to strike."

"That's Julio's style," Josh told the ATF agent, "He acts like nothing gets to him, but it does, and he does everything on the low end so as not to bring any attention to himself or his gang. The amount of crap the Soldados is actually responsible for is enormous. They're responsible for at least 12 murders this year, but it's all for the sake of the neighborhood."

"I'm sorry. That wasn't what I got the feeling for."

"When you deal with someone for as long as we do, you can foresee their moves before they're made."

"Well, when I spoke to him, it seemed like he wanted to tell me something."

"Wait," Brett interrupted, "You spoke to him? When?"

"About twenty minutes before this all happened."

"Please tell me you didn't reveal anything to him."

"No, Detective Foster. I'm actually good at my job, even if you think otherwise."

"That's not what I was getting at, Agent. Julio has a way with making people comfortable when around him. Just making sure he didn't con you into letting something slip."

"Sorry to break things up but the agent here is going to need stitches for this," the EMT said, "We'll have to take you to the hospital. You can meet her there."

Fenton climbed into the back of the ambulance and was taken away a few minutes later. Brett felt frustrated, knowing that this case was putting everyone on edge. If they didn't stop this before it was too late, Christmas would be ruined for everyone in this town.

52

Bergen and Page pulled into the huge lot at Lincoln Harbor. They had followed Travis Hughes into the riverside area and drove slowly, looking for a place to park. At this time in the morning, most people travelling to New York City were already at work and they had left their cars in Lincoln Harbor to catch the bus to Port Authority.

"This is going to be like finding a needle in a haystack," Lyndsey said.

"This is only because I'm driving today," Danica complained.

"Wait, there's a spot!" Lyndsey pointed out with excitement. Then she realized that the spot was too small because someone was double-parked.

"We should so key his car when we find a spot," her partner joked. Four minutes later they managed to find a spot and parked the car.

Once at the entrance to the silver office building the detectives hurried inside and looked over the listings of business located above the main floor. Arrow Accounting was on the third floor.

Taking the elevator up, they followed the signs to the lobby of the accounting firm. Behind the front desk was what Lyndsey and Danica thought of as the typical secretary. She had long blonde hair, bright and long nails and a perpetual scowl.

"Wanna bet on her name?" Danica asked in an evil but playful way.

"Twenty says it's Tiffany or Judy," Lyndsey said, playing along.

"I'm thinking she looks more like an Ashley or a Candi." The females approached the desk and smiled.

Lyndsey flashed her badge and said, "Good morning, we're detectives Bergen and Page. Do you mind if we ask you a few questions, Miss?

"Oh, you mean like that old show my mother watches? Cagney and Lacey?"

Danica fought the urge to roll her eyes and nodded. "Yeah, something like that."

"Sure! I'm Ashley. What information were you looking for?" Lyndsey grimaced at the loss of her twenty while Danica smiled.

"We were just looking to get your opinion on one of the accountants here. A Travis Hughes."

"Oh, Travis," Ashley's smile melted away at the sound of the name, "He's a creep, if you ask me. The way he tries to sleep with every pretty woman in here. It skeeves me out."

"So, besides the creep factor, does he seem dangerous? Is he violent towards anyone here?"

Ashley shook her head no. Danica was afraid that the girl would lose any remnants of a brain by doing so. "Not really, other than the creepy perv factor he seems pretty harmless. He's been grumpy lately but that could be because of the long shifts this month but he doesn't get into a fight with anyone. He did get a little hands-on with Brittney from our legal department at the Christmas party on Friday night. But Arthur chased him off." Lyndsey and Danica stopped short and looked at each other.

"You said the Christmas party on Friday? Was that the company party?"

"Yeah, the owner decided to have the party on Friday so that everyone had the weekend to recover before they had to be back yesterday."

"There was no party here last night?"

"No, we actually closed early last night. Everyone was out of here at 4 o'clock yesterday."

"Were you here on Saturday?"

"Yeah but we're only open until three on Saturdays."

"Was Travis here last Saturday?"

"No, he took the weekend off."

"Thank you. And if you don't mind my asking, how long have you been with the company?"

"It'll be a year next February."

"Thank you, Ashley. We'd ask that you please don't mention our conversation to anyone here."

"Is Travis dangerous?"

"Probably not, we're just checking."

"Um, okay. Have a good day and Merry Christmas!" The two ladies nodded and wished her a Merry Christmas back before turning to leave.

Lyndsey dug into her pocket and handed over the twenty that she had lost. Danica smiled and examined the twenty in the light over the elevator.

"What do you think about the lie he told us?"

"I think he's hiding something," Lyndsey said, "He definitely could have been at the bus garage shooting. No alibi for Saturday, lying about his whereabouts last night and he owned the weapon last. I think we may have to talk to Travis again."

"How we stop for lunch first? My treat!" Danica said, waving her newly won twenty.

53

Kylee carefully walked down the hall to the apartment 30. Russell had already reached the door and smiled at the sight of his partner holding her stomach. Whenever she skipped lunch, she regretted it with strong hunger pains.

"I'm really going to need something to eat after this. A snack or something," Fernandez complained.

"What would you like for dinner?"

"The biggest friggin' burger you can find me in this town. And fries. The fat thick ones, not those anorexic McDonalds ones."

"Ask and you shall receive."

Emerson knocked on the door firmly while grinning from ear to ear. He could hear someone behind the door, shuffling closer. He noticed the shadow under the door, someone was peering through the eye hole in the door. Russell held his badge up by his face. The chain on the lock shifted and the door opened. Inside, a young woman with blonde hair and glasses smiled.

"Hello, there," she said, with an English accent.

"Good morning, we are Detectives Emerson and Fernandez. We're following up on a call that we received about the shooting that happened last night in the back alley. Are you Emily Trenton?"

"Yes, please, come in." The young woman opened the door wide, allowing the couple to enter her home. Kylee went for the couch, feeling more at ease now that she was sitting comfortably. Russell sat down next to her. Emily walked over to her kitchen.

"Can I offer you something to drink? I just made some coffee."

Russell declined the offer, but Kylee accepted a cup. Emerson figured that it was better to get this over with by asking her the first question as she was pouring the coffee.

"Did you see or hear what happened?"

"At first, no," Emily explained, "I didn't know anyone was out there. I was sitting here watching some telly while I was waiting for my husband to come home. He works the evening shift at the gas station over by the Lincoln Tunnel. I didn't know what it was, but I heard a big pop, like a firecracker. I didn't know if it was usual for anyone to set off fireworks on Christmas, so I went to the window here." Emily pointed to the living room window to the detectives' left. Russell stood up and looked out the window. He noticed that it looked directly down to the crime scene.

"Were you able to see everything after that?"

"Well, it was snowing, and the wind was howling so I couldn't hear anything from here. Although, I was able to see most of what happened after the first man was shot. There was a man in a dark coat with a hood ~~on it~~. He was holding his gun down and the older man was aiming his gun at the man in the hood. It looked like they were talking about something, but I couldn't hear them from here."

"Then what happened?" Russell asked. He was hoping that she might have been able to see the vigilante's face or any identifying marks that would be able to help them to catch the killer.

"Then the man with the hood tried to raise his gun but the older man shot him first. The hooded man fell down and I thought it was all over but not even a minute later, the hooded man got back up like he wasn't even hurt." Kylee jotted down BP VEST? on her pad.

"Of course, the older man was just as shocked as I was. That was when the man took off his hood to show his face to the older man, right before he shot him. He stood over the older man and then touched his face before he walked away. I was too scared to do anything in case the hooded man saw me at the window."

"Were you able to see his face, this hooded man?" Fernandez asked.

"Not really. The snow didn't help, but I know he had short dark hair.

And he was white." Russell glanced over at Kylee, who was writing as fast as she could.

"Was there anything else that the man with the hood did that you can remember? Anything unique or odd?"

Emily paused and thought hard about that incident she saw. Putting a finger to her mouth, she suddenly realized something, and her eyes went wide.

"Not the hooded man but the older man."

"What about the older man?"

"When he saw the hooded man's face, he looked surprised."

"Like surprised scared?"

"No, like he knew him."

"Are you sure?"

"That I did see. The area was well lit. They installed flood lights in the back alley last summer because someone was mugged back there. And before the older man could say anything, the hooded man shot him in the chest."

"There's nothing else that you can remember?"

"No, that's all that happened. It seemed like it took hours, but it was fast. I'm sorry that I couldn't tell you any more than that."

"It's a big help. Thank you, Ms Trenton." Kylee finished her cup of coffee while Russell handed Emily his card if she remembered anything else and said goodbye.

"Fuckin' Doyle knew Hermes?" Kylee asked her partner, once they were outside the apartment.

"Sounds like it, but I think I may have an idea about this." Russell took out his cell phone and dialed a number. Kylee stood there listening to Emerson's side of the conversation.

"Hey, Danny, it's Emerson. I've got a question for you. Did Tony Hughes ever work with Doyle? Yeah. Ok, Thanks. No, I was just talking to a witness to Doyle's murder and there was something she said. Right. Ok, talk to you later. Thanks Danny."

"You're thinking Travis Hughes, aren't you?" Fernandez asked.

"Both Tony and Doyle were part of the police department at the same time. Hughes retired the year before we came onto Homicide, but Danny just told me that Hughes and Doyle did work a few cases together throughout the years and were pretty good friends. Who else would Doyle be surprised to see Hermes be than the son of an old cop friend?"

"Another cop?"

Russell didn't know how to respond to that question. And he hoped that he wouldn't have to.

54

The press had huddled outside Hoboken's city hall on Washington Avenue and Don Price could not have been happier. The press conference was only eight minutes away from beginning and the butterflies in his stomach were fluttering like crazy. The sky couldn't wait until after the conference to start snowing again. The flakes were light and small, but everyone was hoping that the snow was going to end. The mayor's assistant thought wrapping bright LED Christmas lights around the columns of the City Hall would add a feeling of togetherness. It had made Price want to be somewhere else, honestly, but his assistant knew what worked and what didn't.

"You two look great," Mayor Ray Victor said to Price and his son, Ron. Ron asked to be there with his father and they had decided that his being there would give a nice family feel to the whole conference.

"He's a chip off the old block," Don said with a smile. He gave Ron a proud pat on the shoulder.

"Just following in the steps of a great man who loves his hometown," Ron gushed.

"No tears of joy just yet, gentlemen," Jon Charloni, Victor's assistant told them, "Save it for the cameras."

"Nah, Pop isn't one to shed tears," Ron explained, "He's too old school tough for that."

"What can I say? He's right," Don laughed.

"Okay, so I'll start it off by giving the news of Mark Doyle's death and then I'll pass it on to you to announce and promote what we've got going for the ETC initiative," Ray told Don.

"I've got it," Don confirmed. Then he looked around, "Where's Christine?"

"Sorry, makeup was taking longer than I thought they would," Chief Black said, walking up to Don from behind, "I hope that's not a sign of my age."

"Says the youngest police chief in the state," Raymond laughed.

"How are you, Ray?" she asked.

"Cold and bored, Christine. I'd rather be out there talking already." Mayor Victor was one to be out and getting things done instead of sitting behind a desk talking on the phone. He had even personally unveiled the new Pier C Park located on the riverfront.

"I'm surprised that Pittman's not here, soaking up the spotlight," Black said, referring to the governor.

"I made sure that this was set up while he was busy with something else down by Bel Mar. He's far enough from here so that we can actually take a breath from explaining every little thing."

"Two minutes, Mayor," John said to Raymond.

"Showtime, everyone." Victor approached the podium with the Hoboken seal posted on the front for all to see. The seal was a portrait of the city from the early days, looking at the town from over the Hudson River at the birth of the major transferring point that allowed those from New Jersey and Pennsylvania to travel over to New York City via trains and ferries.

Don waved Ron over to him and the commissioner's son took his place behind his father's right shoulder. Christine Black stood to the left of the mayor. She was not expected to speak, but her appearance there was to show unity with the police force. She, otherwise, would have preferred to be out there with her detectives tracking down this vigilante.

Mayor Victor cleared his throat and smiled at the press, who were taking over the steps leading up to him. Then he began, "Thank you all for coming out into this wretched weather. I'd like to start this by giving my great sympathies to the family of Detective Mark Doyle, who was gunned down last night in cold blood while trying to stop a crime. I did have the chance to meet Detective Doyle and I can say I am extremely honored to have known him. Mark Doyle was one who thought more of his friends and family than he did of himself. And I want to keep that going by announcing the Mark Doyle Police Fund. This fund will be mainly focusing on helping to support those looking to be a part of the outstanding police force in this town." Victor read off the number for more information about it.

"And now I'd like to pass it along to Police Commissioner Donald Price to announce and explain our new End to Crime initiative." The mayor stepped to the left side and shook Don's hand before allowing him to begin.

"Thank you, Mayor Victor," Price began, "I'd also like to thank you all for being here as well. Today we are beginning our End to Crime initiative to help make this city safer for all the families that call it home. To do so, we are adding an additional twenty new police officers to our force. This will help in times of strife or gang activity. And speaking of which, we have begun a crackdown on all gang activity in the town limits in regard to drugs and gun control.

"But in order to have this be effective, we are reaching out to the public. We have launched a phone app this morning called The ETC App. This app allows the public to contact our emergency services with just a tap, in the event of a crime or accident. The app is completely confidential, very user friendly, and does not take up a lot of memory. And it's completely free. There is a video on how to use it located on the city's website as well as their Facebook page. If we work together, we can make this town safer for ourselves and future generations." Don finished and took a step back to wave proudly at the crowd. The reporters below him began throwing out questions about the initiative and the new phone app. He smiled at the response and knew this would go over well.

Price leaned over to Raymond and patted him on the shoulder, "I think we just jumped up 20 points in the ratings."

A voice from the crowd cried out. It was louder than the others and got everyone's attention. Price and Victor looked out over the sea of reporters and picked out the one man in the back with the megaphone. Chief Black cursed under her breath when she saw who it was. The reporters stopped everything and turned to see the new unplanned part of the press conference. The whole thing was going live on both Channel 78 and several of the New York City news stations were filming for the evening news.

"Attention, big wigs of the city!" the voice called, "Us cockroaches would like to retort your statement, puh-lease." The man speaking stood on the top of an unmarked van, waving to those at the top of the city hall steps.

Mayor Victor looked over to Price, who was looking towards Chief Black. She was talking to the officer next to her, getting him to send word over the police channel to have all present officers to converge on the man with the bullhorn and take him down immediately.

"What the hell is this?" Raymond asked Don.

"I'm not quite sure. Christine, who is that?"

"A major problem that we've been dealing with for the past few days is who."

55

Feeling helpless just sitting at the Perez house, Jacob had joined Luis in the search for Enrique. Orlando welcomed the company. Especially now that the snow was beginning to fall once again.

"I've had enough of the snow," Orlando grumbled.

"How much more snow is expected to fall before Christmas?"

"Weather network said at least another foot and a half," the detective replied, "More than we need if you ask me."

Most of the roads had been cleared by the city since the snow stopped early that morning but with more snow on the way, driving was only going to get worse.

"Can I ask you a question?" Jacob blurted out, trying to change the topic.

"Shoot."

"What's with you and Chris Delgado?"

Orlando laughed, "It's a bit of a long story but I'll try and shorten it up for you."

They were interrupted by the ring of Jacob's cellphone. Worried it might be bad news, the lawyer looked down at the screen and saw that it was Robin calling. He realized that he had forgotten to call her once he reached the Perez home. She had no idea what had happened.

"It's Robin," Jacob told Luis, setting him at ease behind the wheel. He answered the phone with some effort to sound hopeful.

"What's going on? Is everyone okay?"

"No one was seriously hurt, besides two of the Jackal gang members."

"Oh God, that's a relief. I hadn't heard from you, so I thought something bad had happened."

"No, I'm sorry, that was my fault. With everything going on here, it slipped my mind."

"Did they manage to fight off the gang?"

"Well, kind of. Emilio and his daughter distracted Vinnie Donnelly and his guys so that Enrique could escape. The problem is, we don't know where Enrique ran off to."

"He's a teenager, why not text his phone."

"It's not so easy. He left his phone on the kitchen table in the middle of the attack. I'm with Detective Orlando right now and we're checking his friend's home to see if he ran there. I'll be back to the office soon as we can find him."

"Okay but please be careful out there. You're no action hero."

"Maybe not but you do have to admit there's a resemblance to Gerard Butler." Luis burst out laughing at the comment. Jacob looked over at the detective and furrowed his brow.

"I am going to go with that and I'll talk to you later."

"I love you," Robin blurted out at the last minute. It took Jacob by surprise because at this point of the relationship, those three words were not often said. He knew she was worried.

"I love you too," he replied before hanging up. He looked out the windshield through the snow and saw their destination in front of them. One block from the high school Enrique attended, the small brick apartment building stood out among the two-story houses like the abnormally tall kid in gym class.

"Now remember to let me do the talking because Sparta this ain't," Luis joked.

"I'll keep that in mind as you try to get the ladies with that beard of yours."

"Don't dis the beard. Mock all you want but keep the beard out of it."

They walked up to the entrance of the building and pushed the button for Miguel Santos's family. Luis had been unable to call ahead as he usually did, so it would be a surprise visit. The speaker garbled a response and Orlando explained that he was there to speak to Miguel. There was a hesitation and then the buzzer went off, allowing access to the inner sanctum of the apartment building. Jacob followed Luis in and before they could reach the stairs to get to the second floor, Orlando's cell phone went off.

"What now?" Luis complained. He stared at the phone's screen and clenched his teeth together.

"What is it?" Jacob asked.

"They've called me in to help out at City Hall. Apparently, our little friend, Vinnie, has been keeping himself busy. He just interrupted the press conference. Do you mind following up with the best friend while I take care of that?"

"Anything I can do to help find him."

"Okay, if you find out where he is, bring him to the precinct right away. If not, then I'll meet you at your office and we can put our heads together and figure out where he may have run off to."

"Sure. Did you want me to check with this Tiela girl also?"

"Yeah, why not?" Luis handed the paper Maritza gave him to Jacob and headed out the door to his car. Jacob watched him drive off, realizing that he was now stranded and forced to walk through the cold weather back to the Perez home.

Heading up the stairs, he was met by a man and woman standing in front of one of the apartment doors. They stared at him in puzzlement, thinking that he was the deep voiced cop that announced himself on the intercom.

"Are you the police officer?" the man asked.

"No, he was just called away on something else. My name is Jacob Scott. I'm a lawyer and was hoping to speak to your son. We're looking for a friend of his who may be in danger."

"What friend?" the father asked in defense, as if his son had no friends to speak of.

"Enrique Perez."

"That boy is nothing but trouble. Miguel is not allowed to deal with gangsters."

"Pop, he's not a gangster. It's not the 30's anymore. No one calls them that," said a teen from behind the two. Miguel Santos stepped out of the apartment and joined the adults in the hall.

"Miguel, your father told you to stay inside," his mother argued.

"I'm sorry for my over-protective parents. I'm Enrique's friend, Miguel." The teen reached out and shook Jacob's hand. This was the second time this week that he was surprised by the maturity of some of the kids in this town. The kids that he normally dealt with were through the law firm and they didn't tend to be the most respectful.

"Have you heard or seen Enrique today?" Jacob asked, hoping that the teen was actually hiding in Miguel's bedroom.

"Sorry, but I haven't seen him since school let out last Friday."

Jacob felt his body sag and the words sunk. That was the last thing he wanted to hear. He believed that the longer that Enrique was unaccounted for, the more of a chance that he was in danger of being caught by either Julio or Vinnie.

"Do you know where he may be if he was in hiding?"

"Did he do something?"

"No, he's being chased by some bad people and we're hoping to find him before they do."

"I dunno," Miguel said, "He's been hanging with the Latin Soldados lately. Mostly because he heard that his family was having money problems and he wanted to help them keep their house. Someone told him that money isn't an issue with the Soldados. I told him it was a bad idea because once you become a part of them, they never let you go until you're in the ground."

"I'm hoping to prevent that."

56

Once they had finished their lunch, chicken wraps at the local health restaurant, Lyndsey and Danica headed over to Kevin Finnegan's place to check something out and idea Lyndsey had had. They slowed down on the turn to Finnegan's block and were startled by an oncoming UPS truck. Danica hit the brakes and worked on keeping the car from fishtailing out of control. Lyndsey grabbed for the dashboard, keeping herself from being knocked around. The UPS truck came to a quick stop and Danica's car came to a slow stop inches from the bumper of the delivery truck.

"Asshole," Danica said through gritted teeth. After slowly moving back and finding a spot two blocks away to park, the Homicide detectives returned to the building where Kevin Finnegan had once lived. The UPS truck had moved on to scare another driver.

Lyndsey hit the bell to the superintendent and waited for him to appear from his apartment on the ground floor. The older man poked his head out from the doorway to see who was bothering him this time. He rolled his eyes and said something to himself at the sight of the two women, who were holding their badges up to the glass door between them. Shuffling out to open the door, his frumpy look brought smiles to their faces.

"Whatta youse cops want now?" he whined.

"Good afternoon," Lyndsey said, introducing them, "We were wondering if you had seen this man in or around your building in the past few days."

Danica held up her phone, showing the superintendent a head shot of

Travis Hughes that they had taken from his Facebook page online. The almost cartoonish elderly man squinted at the screen and pulled back.

"No. He doesn't live here."

"But have you seen him visiting anyone in the building?"

"No. I just fix things. I don't get involved in these peoples' lives."

"Okay, do you mind if we ask some of the residents?"

"Fine. Go. I've got Stranger Things to watch." The superintendent waved his hands shooing them away. They thanked him and headed up to the floor where Finnegan lived. Danica started by knocking on the door to the left of Finnegan's apartment. The couple there did not know anything about Finnegan, other than that he was loud, and they were glad he was gone from the building. The single mother across the hall from Finnegan's apartment was too distracted by her children to even look at the photo of Travis. It wasn't until they began speaking to the elderly Hispanic woman to the right of Finnegan's place that they had hit pay dirt.

The woman came to the door in a housecoat with a bandana tied over her hair. The squinting smile on her face made the women feel at home talking to her.

"Hi Ma'am, sorry to bother you but we were hoping that you may be able to help us. Have you seen this man around here?" Danica asked her, holding the phone screen close to her face. The woman leaned in closer and examined the head shot of Travis Hughes. Then she looked up at Lyndsey and Danica and smiled.

"Yes, dear. He was here a couple of nights ago."

Lyndsey and Danica looked at each other with happy surprise. They continued asking her about when she saw Travis.

"It was late. I was just about to go to bed and I was putting my garbage on the side here. The husband of the sweet couple over there," she said, pointing to the door of the first apartment they had tried, "He is nice enough to bring it down for me in the morning. This body doesn't take steps as good as it used to. But when I opened my door, that man was knocking on the door next to me. He didn't seem angry, but he did seem like he was in a hurry."

"And you're sure that it was this man?"

"Yes, he looked right at me and smiled."

"Thank you. You've been a very big help." Lyndsey handed the woman her card in case she saw the man again. She smiled at them and returned back inside her apartment.

"So, in total," Lyndsey stated, "We have Travis lying about his whereabouts on the night that Doyle was murdered, we have him being the last known owner of the gun used in both the garage shooting and the murder of Doyle, and we have him at Kevin Finnegan's apartment before or on the night of his death."

"I'd say that's plenty to take to the judge for a search warrant on his place." Danica smiled with her devilish grin.

"Merry Christmas, Travis Hughes, you're busted."

57

The Hoboken University Medical Center was a tomb the days before Christmas Eve. The occasional holiday-related injury was the highlight of the Emergency Room. There was a patient in curtain 1 with shards of a fragile Christmas ornament in their foot; Curtain 2 held a child with freezer burn on their tongue after being dared to lick a stop sign pole; Curtain 3 was empty. Then, the aftermath of the Castle Point Terrace shootout arrived. Shooting victims poured in by the car load.

Relaxed nurses and interns were suddenly running back and forth, treating the worse injured first and asking those with flesh wounds to please be patient. Amanda Fenton, due to her leg wound and the fact that the EMT had already helped her at the scene, was asked to please bear with them. She had no choice but to sit and wait.

Brett, Kylee and Russell walked into her small room, off to the side of the ER. Foster had received a call from Chief Black, asking for assistance at City Hall. Using their traditional Rock, Paper, Scissors, Foster had been lucky to avoid the political havoc, but Raghetti was forced to go help out.

That was when Emerson called Brett to inform him of what they had found at the Trenton residence. Brett had sent the information on to Danica and Lyndsey, who also had good news. Foster was actually able to smile with the progress of the investigation; it was only a matter of time until the gang war was over.

"Sorry," he joked to Fenton, "But we've run low on bed pans. Would you mind sharing?"

"That was horrible and yet hilarious at the same time," Fenton replied, "There just may be hope for you yet, Detective."

"How are you doing?"

"In a lot of pain, but stuck waiting for someone to come see me. What is it like out there?"

"Like a TV drama about an ER. Rushing nurses, shouting back and forth, cries of pain and blood everywhere."

"You think someone can go get me some Advil or something to kill the pain?" Russell and Kylee offered to go look and left the room. Brett leaned against the side of the bed and gave her the lowdown that she had missed on the way to the hospital.

"So, this Travis guy looks good?"

"Yeah, he's looking pretty good. Look, I'm sorry about snapping back at Julio's place. This whole case is getting crazy and we're being pressured by the commissioner and the mayor now into getting this closed as soon as possible. Translation: now."

"As a fellow officer of the law, I understand and forgive."

"What did Julio tell you when you went to see him?"

"Not a whole lot but he did seem like he knew something that we didn't, but he was in a rush and told me to leave. I figured if I sat outside his place long enough, I'd find something interesting."

"Well, you certainly did," Brett joked again.

"I'm disappointed though because I had just gotten the paperwork from my supervisor about the talk that Tom had with Kevin Finnegan. I didn't get to read too far into it to see if there was anything of interest."

"Well, you're in luck." Foster pulled a cell phone out of his coat pocket and held it out to Amanda. The screen was not cracked or shot. She smiled and took it. She was looking for a name or some information about the garage meeting that may help them in the investigation.

"I don't see a Travis Hughes anywhere, but there's another name. He said that this guy was looking to get rid of some weapons that had fallen into his lap. I've never heard of him. Does it seem familiar to you?" Fenton handed the phone back to Brett. Brett looked at the screen and froze. The name couldn't be right.

"I do know that name. Can you please email me that to my work address?" Brett pulled a card from his wallet and handed it to her, "I have to run but stop over at the precinct once you get out."

"Um, sure," Fenton told him as he rushed out of her room, his biggest fear realized. Seconds later, Russell and Kylee returned with some pain killers for the ATF agent.

"Where's Brett?" Russell asked.

"I showed him a name Finnegan gave my partner about that meeting at the bus garage. Then before I knew it he asked me to email this to him and he ran out. Do you know this person?" Fenton showed the couple and both their jaws dropped.

"No fuckin' way," Fernandez muttered. Then the statement that Emily Trenton gave them about Doyle knowing his killer made so much sense.

58

"This is not happening now!" shouted Don Price. The officers littered throughout the crowd converged on the van. On the corner stood Vinnie Donnelly, dressed in his forest green trench coat. In his hand was a bullhorn, and on his face, a big smile. Under him was a van that held a dozen of his men.

"Hello Mister Mayor!" the leader of the Jackals hollered through the bullhorn, "I'm just here to call shenanigans on your whole plan to clean up the town. No matter how many times you fumigate, there will always be some roaches lurking in the corners waiting for the smoke to clear."

"Get him down from there and shut him up," Ray Victor said to Christine. Christine grabbed her mike located in her coat pocket and called the officers to pull him down from the top of the van.

"Be careful not to use too much force," she told them, "We need to remember that the press is here."

"Good point," Don Price commented. Ron placed a hand on his father's shoulder, making sure that the older man knew that he was there to help.

Vinnie saw the cops closing in on the van and stomped on the roof twice with his boot. The driver took the signal to move and put the van in gear. The shift in the van nearly made Vinnie lose his balance, but he gained control and crouched down.

"Catch me if you can!" he laughed through the bullhorn. The van turned north on the closed off portion of Washington. The cops in the crowd followed. Donnelly slapped his hand on the roof and the driver reversed the van towards the officers, who immediately backed off. When the van slowed down, they moved in again. Vinnie held up the bullhorn and howled into it.

Just then, from around the back of city hall, a dozen Jackals emerged and began tossing eggs at the civilians and press members. Don Price ducked when one came flying his way.

"We should head back inside," Ron suggested.

"Not a chance," Ray replied, "I'm not hiding from this tool." The mayor approached the microphone while watching for any flying debris.

"Donnelly! You think you're making us look bad when you're only showing everyone who lives here that you need to go."

"You can try all you want, Mayor!" Vinnie replied, "The Soldados tried to get rid of me and they failed. You'll do the same. You can't get rid of me! You can't kill me! I'm immortal!" Then he raised his middle finger at the leader of Hoboken.

Christine was sending a massive text alert to anyone who was available. She wanted more bodies in the crowd to help get rid of the Jackals. Another egg came flying from the south side of the steps. Ron saw it and stepped forward, getting in-between the egg and his father. The egg found its mark, hitting Ron in the shoulder and cracking open. The oozing inside dripped all over his wool coat.

"You should step back," Don said to his son.

By now, the cops in the crowd were focused on taking out the egg throwers, leaving Vinnie all alone. Donnelly leaned over the side of the van and reached down towards the passenger side window. He then stood up holding something large in his other hand. Several people noticed the object and screamed.

"Gun!"

Ray Victor's security guards rushed forward and grabbed the mayor's arms. They pulled him back to the safety of the front entrance. Victor squirmed in protest, not wanting to hide. Don and Ron moved quickly to the side, taking Christine with them.

Vinnie laughed as he raised the paint gun in his hand and began shooting the video cameras. One by one, he covered the cameras with globs of paint, preventing the cameramen from continuing to film the chaos.

In the air, the sound of more police cars approached. Vinnie knew that his plan to make the mayor's press conference a joke had worked. He leapt off the side of the van and pulled the back door open. Jumping inside, the van took off.

"You need to get that son of a bitch," Price growled to Chief Black. She looked over at him and nodded.

It was an hour later that both Josh Raghetti and Luis Orlando managed to leave the front of City Hall and travel over to the law firm of Hoffman and Delgado. The snow fall was getting thicker again, and visibility was diminishing. Luis was curious about whether Jacob had learned anything about Enrique's whereabouts. He had contacted the precinct and was told by Hines that Scott and the teen had not shown up at all. So, he took Josh with him over to the law firm where he had asked Jacob to meet him.

"Hi, I'm hoping to meet Jacob Scott here. Do you know if he's back yet?" Luis asked Abby.

"No, sorry, Mr. Scott hasn't been in this morning. I haven't heard from him either. But his assistant, Robin, is in if you'd like to speak to her."

"Actually, yes, please." Abby called over to Jacob's office and asked Robin if it was okay for her to send through the two detectives. She looked up and nodded while saying goodbye. Luis thanked her and headed in to the office to talk to Robin. When he walked in, he saw the worried look on her face. It was the familiar look of wondering if a loved one was hurt or dead. In his line of work, the notification to family members was the worst part of it all, but this time it would be good news.

"Is Jacob okay?"

"Yes, we were just supposed to meet here with any information."

"Oh, good," Robin said, breathing a sigh of relief, "What information were you needing?"

Luis explained the attack on the Perez house and the search for Enrique. As Robin listened to the story, Delgado and Ron Price walked over to the office with Jacob behind them.

"What's wrong, Detective," Delgado asked, "All the donut shops closed?"

"No, I was just showing my colleague the truth to the joke I told him earlier."

"And what lame joke is that?"

"The fact that donuts and your head have something in common. There's empty space in the middle of both."

"Your humor lacks the same intelligence as your detective work."

"At least I'm not the babbling one when approaching a judge's bench."

"I do not babble. And what would you know about court? You're only in court is to make a mockery of everything."

"Like that hairdo?" Luis said, pointing to the top of Delgado's head.

"How a person with a child's mentality like you was promoted to detective is the problem with today's law enforcement." Delgado huffed and walked quickly away. The others laughed.

"Okay, please tell me what happened to have you two at each other's throats," Jacob asked again.

"It's a long story I had to testify on a case and Delgado was the defendant's lawyer. He tried to turn my words around on me to help get his client free, I cracked a joke at his expense in front of everyone and because they all laughed at it, he's had it in for me ever since. Now I just do it because it's fun."

"Please continue," Robin told him, smiling for the first time that morning.

"I've got bad news," Jacob reported, "Miguel has no idea where Enrique is."

"Damn," Josh added, "I was afraid of that."

"Who's Enrique?" Ron asked them.

"He's my client. He saw a shooting happen over the weekend and now the gangs are after him to find out who shot everyone."

"Does this have to do with what happened at the press conference earlier?"

"Unfortunately, it does," Luis confirmed, "That was Vinnie Donnelly, leader of the Jackals. They're one of the gangs in Hoboken."

"So why not just have this Enrique give you a description of the shooter, and just arrest him?" Ron asked.

"It's not that easy. Enrique's gone missing and no one knows where he is. Without him, this gang war is only going to escalate, and then more innocent people are going to die from it."

"Did you want me to talk to my father to get you some help?"

"No, please," Raghetti said, "He's done enough by pressuring us into to get this case closed."

"My father can be rather pushy. He's always been that way. Let me know if there's anything I can do to help. I've got to get back to my office, I've got that Hansen guy arriving in about twenty minutes. Just want to make sure that I have all the facts down."

"Thanks Ron," Jacob said and looked back to the two detectives, "I honestly don't know what to do now. He could be anywhere. Hell, he could be in Manhattan at this point."

"Let's hope he's still local. This is his home. This is where he's most comfortable. I doubt he would have crossed the river to hide. He's a teenager. Kids know all the nooks and crannies of their neighborhood. If we keep turning over stones, I'm sure we'll find him."

"We just need to find him first," Josh added.

"Right, and I'll contact his parents again to have them call us if he tries to contact them. And trust me, he will. It's too cold out there and he's a smart kid."

"I just hope we find him before Donnelly does."

59

"This is bullshit. I haven't done anything wrong and you have no reason to keep me here," shouted Travis Hughes, still angry about having been taken out of his office at Arrow Accounting. Danica and Lyndsey showed up there willing to keep things quiet in front of his co-workers, but their appearance at the accounting firm only made him aggressive. They decided to take him down to the precinct in covered handcuffs, hoping he would make less of a scene, he didn't.

"Mr. Hughes, look," Lyndsey tried to explain, "We've found probable evidence of your involvement in the shooting at the bus garage. We're just looking to get some information from you to help you out."

"Yeah, right. Keep lying to the cop's kid because I don't know how this works. Gimme a break."

"Okay, we can do this two ways," Danica told him, leaning in closer to be intimidating, "You can answer the questions and get yourself off the hook, or you can dig yourself deeper and we'll just make your life miserable. Your choice."

"What questions? I told you already that I had nothing to do with that shooting."

"If that is the case, then we can just wrap it up after this talk is over. How does that sound?"

Travis sat silent for a minute, plotting his options before answering, "If this will get you off my back, fine. But when I'm done giving you your answers, we're done. Got it?"

Danica held her hands up in acceptance, "Fine by us."

"Now where were you last night? And don't tell us that you were at the company Christmas party, because that was on Friday."

"I was at the strip club in Secaucus, all right? Happy now?"

"Can someone confirm you were there?"

"Sure, the stripper that gave me a lap dance at the same moment you called me. Dancer name's Sparkle. Don't know her real name. Didn't really care."

"I see your father would be very proud."

"Hey, listen, bitch, there's no reason to bring that piece of shit into this. Now, let's get this over with before you regret it."

"That a threat, Mr. Hughes?"

"No. And that counts as a question. Next."

Lyndsey smiled. She had dealt with jerks like this before.

"Why are you so hostile to us, Mr. Hughes? Is it because we're women? Or is it because we're cops like your father?"

"Try to mind bend me all you want, sweetheart. It's not going to work."

"Can we check out your apartment to make sure your father's gun isn't still there?"

"No."

"Can you tell me where you were on Saturday night?"

"Home watching TV."

"What were you watching?"

"TV."

"Nothing specific?"

"Nope."

"Anyone with you to confirm that you were home on Saturday night?"

"Nope."

"So, there is a chance that you weren't home and were out somewhere else?"

"Nope."

"Can we walk through your apartment with you to look into the location of your father's weapon?"

"I'm going to answer that with one word: lawyer." Travis leaned back in his metal chair and folded his arms across his chest. Believing he had won the argument, a smile spread across his face, but this was exactly what

Danica and Lyndsey had been hoping for. With his hostility and refusal to help with the case, it he had given them the icing on the cake. They were now able to request the search warrant without much of an argument from a judge, and Hines had told them that Judge Germaine Irwin was available for warrants today and tomorrow.

"Ok, thank you for your time," Lyndsey said, smiling back. She and Danica stood up and walked out the door, leaving Travis Hughes alone in the interrogation room. It wasn't until then that they heard the shouting down the hall by the entrance of the building.

Brett entered the precinct, furious. He was there to get answers, no matter what the cost. Foster looked around, breathing heavy from running through the parking lot up the stairs. Danny Hines stood behind the front desk, staring at the red-faced cop. He wasn't sure if he wanted to say anything to Brett for fear of being attacked.

"Hey Foster, you okay?"

"Where is he?"

"Where's who? Raghetti? Haven't seen him."

"No, Sheridan."

"Oh, I think he in the break room getting, but before Hines could finish getting out the word "coffee", Brett was off, headed straight for the break room. He threw the door open hard, slamming it against the wall, startling everyone. Uniformed cop Darren Sheridan turned as he continued stirring his coffee. Foster headed straight for him, knocking the coffee cup from his hands.

"What the hell, Foster?" Darren complained, but Brett didn't stop there. He grabbed Darren by the shirt and slammed him against the wall, pinning him with a forearm across his neck.

"Where were you Saturday night?" Foster asked through clenched teeth.

"Let go of me, dammit."

"Answer the question!"

"Why the hell do you care?"

"Because I have something that puts you at the bus garage on Saturday night. Now tell me where you were."

"I was on patrol that night. Check the sign-in sheets!"

"Were you here at the time of the shooting?"

"I dunno. I may have been out getting something to eat at that time, but I was covering Washington on Saturday. Ask Hines." Brett thought about what Darren was saying. Things weren't making sense. Why would Finnegan give Ketchum the name of a cop as the one trying to sell off guns to gangs? Brett knew that Darren was a bit on the dirty side, but he had no motive for taking down both gangs and ruining his extra income.

"Why did Finnegan give the ATF agent your name as the one setting up the gun sale?"

"What? The hell if I know! I had nothing to do with that whole incident on Saturday night!" Foster saw the surprise in Darren's eyes at his accusing statement. He seemed like he really didn't know anything. Foster released the pressure on his neck and Darren took a deep breath. Brett said nothing, he just walked for the door. Darren followed him.

"Wait, Foster. Who else thinks I had something to do with that trap on Saturday?" There was a worry in his voice. Darren was scared that the gangs that he also worked for would think he double crossed them. Brett believed then Darren had nothing to do with the shooting. *But then why was his name thrown into the mix? Was it a fake lead created by Hermes? And if it was a fake lead, how many others were there?* The amount of unanswered questions worried Brett; Hermes was truly making the police force of Hoboken look like incompetent fools.

60

Night had finally fallen over Hoboken, but it didn't keep the Jackals from having some fun. The snow had started falling again and the cold wind had come along, keeping those who had done all their shopping inside where it was warm. A number of Jackals decided to go out to Shaunessey's, a bar located near the end of Willow Ave, blocks from the tracks leading to the Train station that separated Hoboken from Jersey City.

The Irish pub was alive this evening, with the Pogues being played from the stereo system installed. The bartender poured several glasses of Guinness and handed them to the four Jackals sitting at the bar, while another two played pool towards the back. There was an aura of happiness untouched by the events that occurred outside.

"Hey Murphy! Twenty says you miss that shot," laughed Cassidy from the bar, known for his pale skin and bright red hair.

"Cassidy, you pale vampire! You're on!" Murphy aimed the pool cue and conversation in the bar fell silent. All eyes were on Murphy and he felt them watching. He couldn't screw up because he knew of the mocking that would follow if he did.

Murphy focused all he could into the tip of the pool cue and let the energy out of his arm and into the cue ball. The ball rolled across the green felt and bumped into the 9 ball, sending it into the corner pocket as planned. The crowd in the bar roared with excitement and Murphy stood up straight, smiling at Cassidy. Cassidy grimaced and dug into his pocket to retrieve the twenty-dollar bill that he had just lost.

"That'll teach you to doubt me, boyo," Murphy laughed. He snatched up the twenty and smelled the bill as if it were a rose, then placed it on the bar.

"Lenny, one pint of Beamish Stout, please. Only the best for a winner!"

The front door of the bar opened quietly. No one in the pub had noticed the four men that entered. If they had, they would have immediately seen the guns in their hands and the black bandanas on their heads. The men stood together in a wide line and raised the weapons. It was then that Lenny, the bartender looked over and saw them.

"Guns!" he shouted.

There was a moment in the bar where everything stopped, giving the customers the chance to absorb the alert, but it wasn't enough for anyone to react. The four members of the Latin Soldados opened fire, spreading bullets wide throughout the pub. Glasses shattered, wooden tables and booths splintered, and bodies jerked left and right. The noise of the automatic guns drowned out the screams and cries of the victims.

Lenny ducked behind the bar and reached for the unregistered shotgun he had hidden for moments like this. He waited for what seemed like minutes until the gunfire from the Soldados members ended before even considering making a move against them. He was afraid to look at the destruction of the pub his father had built there over forty years ago.

It's now or never, he thought. Lenny stood up as quickly as he could, swinging the shotgun in the direction of the front door. Without aiming, he fired a shot at the four men. One of the members of the Latin Soldados was knocked backwards from the force of the gun shot, slamming into the door frame of the entrance. The remaining three reacted with cat-like speed and opened fire on the bartender. Lenny's torso and face were riddled with bullets, as were the bottles and the wide mirror behind him.

Once the Soldados were sure that all in the pub were dead, lifted their friend from the grimy floor and dragged him outside to be placed into one of their black vehicles. From another vehicle exited Julio Jimenez. He walked into the pub, frowning as he looked around Julio walked over to one of the Jackals lying on the floor. He nudged the body with the tip of his shoe, it shifted and then remained still. He reached into his inside coat pocket, retrieved a card and placed it on the Jackal's forehead. Standing back up, he made the sign of the cross and walked out.

Outside, the vehicle that had held the downed member of his gang was already gone. It was headed to the office of a doctor in Jersey City who provided medical assistance to Julio and his crew on his off hours. Julio walked through the snow and tightened his coat to protect him from the icy wind.

"How is he?"

"He's breathing but he took the shot to the chest. I don't know if he's going to make it but he's on the way to the doctor."

"Please keep me updated on his health."

"Yes, Julio."

"Good." Julio turned back to look at the neon sign of the pub. "Well then, let's move on to the next spot." The Soldados member opened the door of his vehicle and Julio climbed in. Then the remaining two vehicles pull away from the pub and drove off, headed to the next Jackal hangout on the list.

61

There was nothing but silence after Murphy heard the vehicles leave the block. But then again, he was unable to hear anything after the barrage of gunfire that tore through the pub. There could have been people talking right over him for all he knew, all he could hear was ringing. He squirmed his way out from under Cassidy. Seconds before Lenny had seen the gunmen, Murphy had caught them in the mirror behind the bar. Those few seconds save him as he ducked around Cassidy and hid behind his friend's body.

Despite the ducking, one of the bullets had ended up in his calf. The pain burned up his thigh and he was unable to put any pressure on it. The coppery smell of blood was now stuck in his nostrils, and what he saw around him would stay with him for the rest of his life.

The scene before him looked like something from a gory episode of CSI. There was blood and broken glass and wood everywhere. The remains of the people he had once called friends were nothing but bloody pulp. Murphy couldn't help but vomit all over his shoes and what was left of Cassidy.

Wiping his lips, he reached into his pocket to find that his cell phone had survived the attack. His brain told him to contact the police, but he knew that calling Vinnie first was crucial. He speed-dialed Donnelly's number and closed his eyes while he waited for him to pick up.

"Murphy? What is it?" Vinnie answered.

"Vinnie, the Soldados. The Soldados hit Shaunessey's. They killed everyone in here." Murphy stopped talking and waited for a response. He heard nothing and thought that the call had dropped. "Vinnie?"

"How many of ours did he get?"

There were eight of us. I'm the only one left. I got lucky, but they hit me in the leg."

"Stay there. I'm on my way."

"But what if they come back?"

"Stay there and kill whoever they send back. Do you understand?" Donnelly asked him. Vinnie was uncomfortably calm about all of this, Murphy thought.

"Um yeah, ok. But hurry, my leg is killing me."

"I will kill you if you don't act like a man and shut up." Donnelly disconnected the call and left Murphy alone again. Looking around, he realized that he had to get out of there or else he would only vomit again. Murphy stepped over people and headed for the front door. Once he reached it, he slowly poked his head out into the cold night, making sure all was clear. He didn't see any cars or people out on the street. Murphy stepped out and realized as the cold wind hit him that he had left his coat back inside. Knowing what was back in there, he chose to leave the coat there and suffer the weather.

Looking around, Murphy waited for Donnelly to arrive. Looking Suddenly, north up the street, through the snowflakes, he noticed a hooded figure standing under a street light on the opposite side of the street. The figure wore all black. It had to be a Soldados member left behind to watch for live bodies, Murphy thought.

"Shit," he whispered.

Murphy turned the other way and ducked around the corner, limping as fast as he could to get away from the rival gang member. The neighborhood had gone quiet, which was strange to him. Normally, he would have seen another person on the block. He guessed that the weather may have had something to do with it.

Looking back every few steps, he didn't see the figure following him. Knowing that it didn't prove his safety, Murphy continued down the side block. He wasn't going to chance stopping, only to get jumped from another direction. Murphy looked back once more. There was no one else on the street. He took another step and turned to face forward.

That was when he saw the hooded figure a foot in front of him. Stopping short, Murphy twisted his injured leg, causing him even more pain than before. He yelped and stumbled backward. The light of the street lamps was not bright enough to illuminate the hooded face, making the figure more mysterious and frightening.

"Jesus, man! What the hell's the matter with you?" Murphy yelled.

"Your kind is what's the matter," the figure replied, "Both gangs have been a blight on this town for too long. It's time you were all removed."

"Look, look, I'm sorry about all this. It's Donnelly. He's nuts. If we were to disagree with him, we'd be shot."

"I know."

"I promise, you let me go and I leave this all behind. I swear."

"I saw what you did. You hid like the snake you are. Do you really think I would believe your lies? You're more a fool than I thought."

The figure revealed a knife from his side and with one quick move, he ran its cutting edge across Murphy's neck, slicing the skin deep and piercing the left artery. Blood shot up and out from his neck wound, raining on the snow-covered sidewalk.

The hooded figure was not yet finished with Murphy. He took a cigar from his pocket and placed the Montecristo Eagle into Murphy's mouth, leaving a message for Vincent Donnelly and his remaining Jackals.

62

Hermes arrived home, pleased with the day's results. He placed his bag on the couch in the living room and sat down next to it. The apartment, dark as the night outside, was inviting to him. The quiet was peaceful and soothing. He needed to relax after a very busy day. Everything was going according to plan. The war between the Jackals and the Latin Soldados was in full swing.

He hadn't expected Julio to react as quickly as he did after the attack on his home but was glad he did. It saved him time. It was almost poetic how Julio had come down on the Irish pub. Hermes had watched the entire thing from outside. He heard pop after pop of the four automatic weapons. And the shotgun blast was a bit of a surprise, but exciting.

Hermes was just about to leave the scene in case the police arrived quicker than he expected when Brian Murphy of the Jackals stumbled out of the pub, still alive. The vigilante paused and pondered about leaving Murphy to go back to Donnelly, but when the Jackal looked over at him under the street lamp while he spoke to Vinnie on his phone, Hermes knew what he had to do.

The cigar bit was genius in his eyes. He had thought of it days before, right after the shooting of the gangs at the bus garage. It was a dangerous task, yet he knew how effective it would be. Yesterday afternoon, when Julio had left for an hour, Hermes had taken advantage and snuck into his home. Searching the den quickly, he located the humidor of Montecristo Eagle cigars that he was known to enjoy. Hermes took one and tucked it away to use at the right moment.

Hermes stood up from the couch, smiling over the bit on TV that he had seen from the press conference. The news had a perfect shot of Donnelly standing on the top of the van shouting at the mayor and police commissioner through a megaphone. And the police officers, trying to climb the van to pull him down, were reminiscent of one of those old Keystone Kops shorts. He had never laughed so hard.

The gangs were a virus in the town where he had grown up in. A virus that the police were unable to fully rid his home of. He had never tried to become a cop, yet he knew that he had what it took to do what they were supposed to do. And yes, he realized the dangers of what he had done, but he was making more progress in the week that he had started than the police had made in years. Take that, Commissioner Price and Mayor Victor.

Hermes threw his head back to drink down the cold Pale Ale that he had taken from his fridge. The feeling of it running down his throat was unbelievable. There was always a time to celebrate a victory.

The solo celebration was stopped when Hermes heard a noise down the hall. He stopped drinking and placed the bottle on the kitchen counter. His first thought was that someone had followed him. He had been found out! The vigilante pulled the knife he had used on Murphy out of its sheath. Crouching low, he slowly made his way around the kitchen and down the hall. He placed his feet down quietly with each step. There was no noise other than the bump and thump from the end of the hall.

As much as he had wanted to run down the hall to see who it was, he knew it was better to have the element of surprise. So, he was forced to take his time. He just hoped that whoever it was didn't come to the bedroom's doorway before he got there. A knife was never useful from a distance, but he knew shooting a gun in the apartment would only bring more attention than he wanted.

With the doorway to his bedroom only a foot away, Hermes got down even lower and carefully peeked in – the bedroom was empty. Then it came to him. He knew the cause of the noise. Standing up, the vigilante walked into the bedroom and over to the closet door. He paused briefly to listen. He opened the door swiftly, surprising the person in the closet. His captive looked up at him, fear pouring from its eyes.

"Ah, it's just you. You should stop fidgeting, you might hurt yourself," he said. Hermes knelt down to examine the person tied up inside. Turning the head from side to side, he was pleased that they were still fine.

"You're fine. Behave and I'll get you something to eat later. Got it?" He didn't wait for an answer and closed the closet door, leaving Enrique Perez tied up and locked away once again.

63

"He's just arrived home," Brett said into the phone. Josh sat next to him behind the wheel of Raghetti's car. They were parked across the street from Travis Hughes' apartment building. On the phone was Chief Black, who had ordered the two to keep an eye on the suspect. They had not minded as Josh's new car kept the heat in and the cold wind out. Huddled in their coats and gloves, they sat, sipping on fresh coffee from the local Dunkin Donuts.

Black had returned to the precinct after the debacle of the press conference very unhappy. The evening news had turned the conference into a joke and she was getting heat from the mayor and the commissioner. Lyndsey managed to calm her down with their latest news with the information that Kylee and Russell had gotten from the witness to Doyle's murder. It brightened her night and she asked that everyone work overtime to help make completely sure that Travis Hughes was their man.

Bergen and Page had tried reaching out to Judge Irwin for the signature of the search warrant, but the judge had left the courthouse early and was unreachable. Black explained that they would just have to wait until the morning after the funeral. Orlando, along with Fernandez and Emerson, were sent to investigate the shooting at Shaunessey's. They had been met with trouble as Donnelly and several of the remaining Jackals had beaten them to the scene.

"Don't take your eyes off him," Black replied, "If we can catch him in the act, case closed."

"Got it, Chief. I'll be in touch."

"Thanks Brett."

"It would be nice to bury Doyle in the morning with some closure for him," Josh said to his partner.

"It would," Brett agreed while staring at his phone and flipping through something.

"What are you doing?" Josh asked, looking over.

"I'm just searching the Internet for more info on this Hermes character. I was hoping that it may help to understand how he sees himself. Any information could be helpful and used to trap him."

"What have you found?"

"Pretty much the same as we already knew. But it says here that in some myths, Hermes was a trickster, able to outwit the other gods for either his own satisfaction or for the sake of humankind. That would explain giving Darren's name to Finnegan as his own. He knew that would stir up the pot."

"Yeah, I heard about the scene you made in the break room."

"I'd rather not talk about it. This case is starting to get to me."

"So, what, he sees us as the other gods?"

"Could be. It does make sense, though, if it really is Travis Hughes. He's the son of a cop, making him the same by blood. And if he sees himself as a cop, then he'd be among the other gods."

"But he thinks he's smarter than us."

"Pretty much."

"Does it say anything else?"

"Not really," Brett said, scrolling through the information, "He was known for wearing a winged cap and winged shoes, was known to seek things lost or stolen, son of Zeus, invented several sports, and was mostly known to be amoral. That pretty much sounds like Travis. He sees his father as Zeus and isn't really concerned with the difference between right and wrong."

"Wonderful. We have to nab yet another nutcase."

"Not quite. He is smarter than the average nutcase. So far, we've gotten lucky. It may be tougher to get him to slip up. After all, he is familiar with our procedures."

"Yeah, but he's taking on Raghetti and Foster. This momo doesn't have a chance."

"Momo?" Brett asked with raised eyebrows.

"Whatever. Don't mock the Italian, Jersey City boy."

"Heaven forbid."

As they argued, a young woman wearing a black bandana on her head walked down the block and stopped at Travis's apartment building. She dialed a number on her cell phone and looked up to the third floor.

"Whoa, what's this?" Brett wondered, noticing her. Josh looked over and peered through the small stadium binoculars that he had brought with him.

"Black bandana on her head. A Latin Soldados?"

"Damn, has Julio found out we're watching him?"

"Hang on," Josh said, placing a hand on Brett's chest, "Let's see where this goes before we go jumping out with guns blazing."

The young woman spoke excitedly to whomever was on the other line. A minute later, she placed the phone back in her coat. She stood there, looking back and forth, as if she was hoping not to be seen there. She stepped back and forth, keeping herself warm in the cold.

"What are you doing?" Brett wondered aloud. The two detectives remained in the car, ready to jump out in the event that more Latin Soldados members appeared.

Suddenly, the three of them noticed someone at the front door of Travis's apartment. A man opened the door and waved the young woman in. Josh heard a happy squeal as the woman ran up to the door and placed a mouthy kiss on the man. Then she ducked inside as the man poked his head out of the entrance to look around the street. Comfortable that no one was watching, Travis Hughes stepped back inside the apartment building and closed the door.

"What the fuck?" Raghetti said, stunned.

"Is he dating a gang member?"

"I think he is. Son of a bitch is tasting the menu that he's cutting in half."

"Is this how he's doing it? Is he sneaking his way into the gangs to get info? Then using that info against the gangs to get them to go to war?"

"I'm not sure, but I do know one thing. Lyndsey and Page need to get in that apartment to see what the hell is really going on."

64

It was a perfect day for a funeral. The sky was as gray as the mood that morning in the white field that was the Palisade Cemetery in Union City. Everyone in the office was there to pay their respects to the fallen comrade Mark Doyle. Doyle's daughter and son-in-law were there in the front of the group, sitting in front of the casket. Through the strands of her dark brown hair, Brett could see the resemblance in her kind watery eyes.

The priest spoke the regular funeral speech with pride, as he had also known Doyle through the neighborhood they shared. Doyle had requested that the priest provide the funeral service if he were to go first. Father Petrullio promised that he would send the detective off in style. And now, he was holding true to his promise.

"All of you here have been given a flower that you can place on the casket before we commence in the lowering. Mrs. Delbert, would you like to go first?" Petrullio held his hand out to Doyle's daughter. She nodded and stood up. Her husband, Adam Delbert, rose with her and stayed by her side as she said goodbye to the man that she had looked up to all her life.

"You were a stubborn old-fashioned man, but I wouldn't have anyone else as a father. I love you, Daddy. Rest now." The moment had brought several tears to the eyes of the women there. Josh handed Lyndsey a tissue from his pocket and she smiled at him. Chief Black stood stern, fighting back the emotion, trying to be strong in front of her crew. Russell held Kylee close to him, as she hid her tears with his chest.

Patricia Delbert sat back down, and the priest motioned for the rest of the group to line up and pay their respects before Doyle's body was lowered into the ground. One by one, the group placed their flowers on the top of the casket and said goodbye to a great cop.

When Luis approached the casket, he stopped and placed a hand on the top while he dug inside his coat for something else. Revealing a wrapped meatball sub, he pried the casket open slightly and slid the dead detective's favorite sandwich inside.

"I know you didn't get a chance to eat your sandwich that night, so I hope this makes up for it. Thank you for being the best partner I ever worked with and for helping to make me a better cop. I'll miss you, buddy."

Once everyone had had their chance to say goodbye, the cemetery servicemen lowered the casket into the ground and the crew began to disperse. Josh and Brett walked over to Luis to see if he was okay. He choked back a lump in his throat and smiled at the two.

"You okay?" Brett asked.

"Yeah man. I'm just going to head back to the precinct and change. Then I'm going out to find Enrique. He never came home last night, and no one knows where he is."

"Sounds like a good idea. We'll meet you back at the precinct," Brett said, seeing Patricia getting ready to leave. He walked over to say goodbye to her before it was too late.

"Trish?" he called out to her. Trish turned and saw Brett coming near. She smiled, remembering the detective from the last birthday party she had held for her father.

"Hi Brett," she said, giving him a hug, "It's good to see you."

"I just wanted to make sure that you knew about tonight."

"What's tonight?"

"Your father's friends are all getting together at a bar by the precinct for a traditional cop toast. We'd love to have you there."

"That sounds like fun. I'd love to, thank you."

"Just call the precinct this afternoon. I'll have the desk sergeant give you the time and directions." Brett gave her a hug and watched her get into the limo and drive away. It wasn't until then that he noticed Julio Jimenez standing off in the back near one of the trees. Brett cursed under his breath and walked over the gang leader.

"Good morning detective," Julio said, holding a hand out in a peaceful gesture. Brett denied him the response he was hoping for.

"What the fuck do you think you're doing here?"

Julio held up his hands in defense. "I was just paying my respects to your friend. He was a good cop."

"He was killed trying to save one of your men!"

"I understand that, and I thank him for that."

"You're a piece of shit, you know that? If it wasn't for you and Donnelly, this vigilante would never have started this, and Doyle would still be alive."

"I'm sorry you feel that way detective. I wish there were something I could say or do to change your mind."

"You could go crawl off and die. Let me tell you something, if it comes down to it and I'm the only one who can save you, you can kiss my ass. You'll never get any help from me."

"I understand. I do respect the police force and have no intention of causing any more harm to you or your fellow men. That's what I wanted to tell you."

"Tell me what?"

"Donnelly killed a member of my actual family, not a Soldados. He pierced my heart with his spear. And because of that, I have no choice but to see Vincent Donnelly removed from this world."

"You were behind the Shaunessey's shooting last night."

"I was no where near any bars last night. You do realize that, don't you?"

"Doesn't matter. You had several of your men do it. I'm sure it was your order they were following."

"My men have minds of their own. I do not order them like an army. Nor can I stop them if they get something set in their mind. Contrary to your beliefs, I'm not Jim Jones or David Koresh. I'm just a man with many friends."

"Talk all you want," Brett told him, sticking a finger in Julio's face, "You will go down. It may not be today or tomorrow, but you will. And when it happens I will be there to watch it."

"Please refrain from the hostilities, Detective Foster." Julio turned his face to the side to avoid the waving finger.

"Hey," Josh said, placing a hand on Brett's shoulder from behind. Brett turned to see his partner and the others watching him from afar. He stopped and lowered his arm.

"Again, I'm terribly sorry for the loss to your team." Julio walked around Brett and Josh and wandered out of the cemetery to where his ride was waiting.

"What was that about?" Josh asked.

"He just told me that Donnelly going to be taken down, sometime real soon," Brett explained.

"You okay?"

"Yeah," Brett said, looking over at the hole was now partially filled with his friend's casket, "I'm just dandy." Then Foster walked away, wishing that Angie was still here to help him through this.

65

The main lobby of the courthouse was located in the lower floor of the city hall. The city hall building, built in 1883, stood tall and historic just a few blocks from the famous Hoboken waterfront at the end of Washington Street. Danica and Lyndsey entered the dark wood finished area and walked over to the security desk. Behind it sat Deb Chopin, a no-nonsense woman with glasses and short blonde hair. She looked up at the women and nodded.

"Morning ladies, what can I do for you?"

"Hi, Deb, is Judge Irwin in?" Danica asked.

"She's in her chambers. Just got here about twenty minutes ago. Are you two working on the whole gang war thing, too?"

"The whole stationhouse is."

"That incident yesterday at the press conference turned this whole place into a circus. We were on lockdown for an hour. Any idea on when it'll be over?"

"At this time, it's anyone's guess. But the sooner we can find the guy that started it all, the sooner we can resolve the war."

"That's insane. Well, good luck."

"Thank you," Lyndsey replied. They walked down the hall on the right to the thick door that read HONORABLE GERMAINE IRWIN. Lyndsey knocked and waited for a response. The words, "come in" were heard from the other side. Lyndsey opened the door to see the judge sitting behind her wide desk, drinking her morning coffee. Judge Irwin was not the type of woman that you would expect to see in the black robe. Her face had a glow of friendliness and the hint of a smile but underestimating her is where most people in court went wrong. Germaine Irwin was a stern judge and stuck to the letter of the law. Her short brown hair and wire-rimmed glasses gave her a professional and serious look, but her chambers were a different story. Along the walls and her desk were photos of her large family. There was more of a warm homey feeling to it.

"Good morning, Detectives Bergen and Page, your honor."

"Ah yes, the ladies with the search warrant. What do you have for me?" she asked, getting right down to business. Irwin held out her hand, motioning for the two detectives to have a seat. Danica handed over the paperwork for the search warrant. Judge Irwin skimmed through the first page and looked up. "Wait a second. This is for Travis Hughes? Tony Hughes' son?"

"Yes, your honor."

"This is a joke, right? I hope it is, because Tony Hughes was a damn good cop and to accuse his son of a crime is like spitting on his grave."

"Your honor," Lyndsey interjected, "We had a hard time believing it too but there's too much evidence to ignore."

Germaine looked at the two of them and leaned back in her chair, "Okay then, wow me. What is this evidence?"

Danica and Lyndsey shared the evidence with the judge, explaining the lies, the lack of an alibi and the fact that Tony's gun was confirmed as the weapon used in the bus garage shooting. With each piece given to the judge, Germaine Irwin found it harder to believe that Travis Hughes was as innocent as she believed him to be.

"And it was Tony's gun that killed Detective Doyle also?" the judge asked.

"Our forensics team confirmed that it was a match. A witness to the crime also confirmed that it appeared that Detective Doyle knew the vigilante."

"Oh my God, Tony would be rolling in his grave if he could see this. You've built a solid case. As much as I don't want to do this, I can't deny you after that."

Judge Irwin took a pen from the kid-crafted pen cup on her desk and signed her name to the search warrant. "Please keep me update on this case. If it is or isn't Travis, I'd like to know either way."

"Absolutely, your honor," Danica told her.

"Good luck detectives," Judge Irwin said, handing the search warrant back to them. Lyndsey folded it back up to place in her coat pocket.

"Thank you for your time, Judge Irwin," Lyndsey said. The two detectives left the chambers and Danica immediately dialed Chief Black's number.

"Hey Chief, we've got the search warrant and we're on our way over to Travis' apartment. Can you send over two officers to help out?"

"I'll send Kassen and Schiebal. Let me know what you find the moment you're done."

"Will do, boss lady." Danica hung up and looked over to her partner, "Let's go take this jerk wad down."

66

Jacob Scott stood in the elevator, debating whether or not to go into the office at all today. The feeling of exhaustion and a fogged mind would only make the day harder to get through. Robin had tried to help him get sleep last night but no matter what they did, his mind always fell back to Enrique. He had tried calling the Perez home last night and learned through Emilio that Enrique had still not returned home. The police had put out an APB on the teenager in hopes of finding him before Donnelly or the vigilante.

The doors opened and revealed Abby sitting at her desk. She looked and smiled, then her smile turned to concern.

Jacob realized that it was pointless to stand there and took a step off the elevator. The doors closed behind him, making it impossible to turn back.

"Are you okay?" Abby asked.

"Yeah, just some stress from a case," he told her.

"I always find that a nice container of chocolate ice cream always makes the stress go away. Unfortunately, it also packs the weight on my rear too."

"I will keep that in mind. Thanks Abby."

"Hope you feel better, Jacob."

Jacob walked past her and saw Allan Hoffman coming his way. Hoffman smiled at the younger lawyer and nodded.

"My," Hoffman said, "It was either a really good night or you've got problems."

"Just a case I'm working on," Jacob explained.

"Well, tell me about it." Hoffman turned direction and began walking with Jacob to his office.

"I've got this case where the father hired me for his son. Son's a good kid in a bad situation and the situation just got worse. Now the kid's missing and I'm afraid the wrong people have him."

"I see," the mentor said. Hoffman chewed the inside of his mouth, which he normally did when he was thinking. Jacob looked over, hoping for some advice. After a minute, Hoffman spoke again, "It's important to give 100% to a case but there are times when even the best of us lawyers are helpless. It seems that it is up to the police now, but I will say that sometimes things can be right under our noses and we don't even notice them."

Jacob stopped walking to think about what Hoffman just said to him. Perhaps Enrique was still there, waiting for the excitement to die down before coming out of his spot.

"Allan, thank you. I think I may know where to find him."

"Glad I could be of help. Oh, have you heard from Miss Marks? I am curious on how her first day was."

"She sent a message to Robin last night. She thinks she covered everything in her answers but she's afraid that she might have missed something."

"I remember when I took the bar. It was in small room with school desks. There were only 7 of us there that day and it only took half a day to complete it. That was so long ago."

"At least it paid off," Jacob replied, "Look at you now."

"All you have to do is want it and work hard and this can all be yours one day."

"That would be nice. For now, I think I'll just stick with helping people one person at a time."

"Words like that make me happy that you're working for us. Now go find your client. Best of luck." Hoffman patted the young lawyer on the back and walked back to his office.

The talk had given Jacob the small bit of hope he needed. Reaching his office, Robin had already arrived and was in the middle of working on setting up his day. When he walked up to her desk, she glanced up to see his face. The small smile forming told her that he had either learned something or had an idea.

"I take it you have an idea to find Enrique?"

"I just might, thanks to Allan."

"Did he give you one of his little inspiring talks again?"

"He did, and it worked. I've got to call his mother. I'm hoping she's home because I may need to talk to her."

"Do you think she'll know where he is?"

"No, but she could help me figure it out." Jacob rushed into his office, dialed the Perez home and told Carmen that he was on his way over. When he hung up, he stopped to get a good luck kiss from Robin as he headed for the elevator.

67

Vincent Donnelly being alone and on the loose was something that Liam Dillon had tried to prevent. Despite the best efforts of the remaining Jackals, this morning Donnelly had gone out alone. He just simply walked out of his place before any of the others had a chance to follow him.

Vinnie's state of mind, since the shooting on Saturday, was quickly deteriorating. He was no longer taking the medication that he had started years ago, which kept his mind focused and his mood docile. With Liam no longer here to make sure it was taken every morning, Vinnie had decided it would only fog his mind. He needed to keep sharp in the war against Julio and the Soldados.

On the morning of Doyle's funeral, Vinnie Donnelly was driving himself southbound on Washington Street. He was still furious from the attack on Shaunessey's Pub. When he and a few others reached the pub, they had found Murphy dead around the corner with the Cuban cigar that Julio was known for smoking in his mouth. That with the blank prayer card that was left on the forehead of another inside the bar was more than enough proof for Vinnie. This had Julio's name all over it.

This was fine by Donnelly, it just made him angrier. And with that anger, he would bring the town to its knees, proving that screwing with him was the worst idea anyone could have. That was why he was out alone: to show that even if all his men were taken down, that he alone could take out all the people that fought against him.

"Fuckin' Julio," he said to no one, "Thinks he can get the better of me. No one can."

He slowed down for a bus and his attention wandered off to the sidewalk on his right. His thoughts moved from driving to what he would do if he found and members of the Latin Soldados. He thought of slowly torturing them, or even carving their faces off. He even fancied a beheading with the results left on Julio's lawn. He had just wished that he would come across any of the Soldados.

A quick glance over made his wishes come true. Walking up Washington Street were two Latin Soldados, bundled in black feather-down jackets and talking casually. Donnelly smiled and put the car into park. The car directly behind him noticed the parking lights and honked their horn. The noise didn't faze Vinnie as he focused his eyes on the two rival gang members. The two looked over at the noise of the car horn to see what was going on. They immediately saw Donnelly coming for them.

"Shit, it's Vinnie!" one shouted.

The second Soldados member reached around their back for the pistol tucked into his pants waistband. Donnelly didn't even give him a chance to draw it. Vinnie raised his gun and fired into the second member's chest. Two holes opened in the front of the jacket, spitting out a few feathers into the cold grey air.

The first Soldados member took initiative and turned to run. Donnelly expected this and moved his arm to the left in the direction that the gang member was running. Vinnie fired as Jose of the Soldados was pushing past a couple walking by him. Donnelly's bullet lodged itself in the shoulder of the man in the couple, knocking him back and onto the snow covering the sidewalk.

Jose's balance was lost in bumping into the couple and he stumbled to the ground. It allowed Vinnie to close the distance between the two. Jose turned his head back to look and Vinnie could see the fear in the Soldados member's eyes. It was pure irony, which brought a smile to his face. Jose stood up to keep running. Vinnie fired once more, and this time hit his target. The side of Jose's skull exploded outward, leaving a gaping hole over Jose's right ear, and he slumped to the ground.

Those nearby began screaming and running. Donnelly walked over to Jose's body to make sure he was dead, but at the sight of a uniformed officer in front of him. Donnelly raised the gun fast and pointed it at the cop. The female officer held her hands out in front of her in surrender.

"Okay, okay," she said to Vinnie, "There's no need to hurt anyone else. I'm not going for my gun and you won't get any fight-back from me. Just put the gun down and we can talk this through."

Donnelly just stared at her, saying nothing. Officer Stacey Colton felt herself begin to sweat in the cold, wondering if she would even get to spend Christmas outside a hospital bed. Then Donnelly took a step. Colton took a step back and Vinnie pointed the gun out further, telling her to stop. He came closer and in the end, held the gun two inches from her face. She could smell the burnt gunpowder from the barrel and feel the tiny bit of heat it had created.

"You cops are nothing," Donnelly told her, "Julio thinks he's going to take me down. He's wrong. He can't stop me. You can't stop me. I won't stop until they're all in the ground. Just like you."

Vinnie pulled the trigger and released another bullet into the cop's face at point blank range. The bullet shattered her skull and wiped away any bit of a face that she had once had. Donnelly had been right. They weren't going to stop him easily. *Merry Christmas*, he thought, walking back to his car.

68

"He's out of control!" Josh said out loud. It had been twenty-five minutes since Donnelly's car pulled away from the scene. Half of the block had been cordoned off and Josh, Brett, Kylee and Russell were investigating the scene. Brett was on the phone with Chief Black, explaining the scene, while Raghetti expressed his opinion loud enough for even the chief to hear him clearly. Kylee and Russell were questioning the witnesses who bothered to stay until the police arrived. Agent Fenton has just arrived, looking to help in any way she could.

"He's right," Christine told Foster, "Donnelly needs to be brought in as soon as possible. He's only going to escalate from here on. No one is safe."

"It's going to be tough. With Julio already looking for him, he's not going to out for a stroll any time soon."

"Then we put out an APB on him. And with this new 911 app that Price launched yesterday, we should be able to locate him with the public's help."

"Will anyone even use that app?" Brett asked, weary of the number of downloads it would get, even after a month.

"Don't knock it. That's how we were told about your crime scene there. Someone sent in a text report."

"Really? I guess he does know what he's talking about."

"They don't just hire someone off the street for that position, Foster."

"Anyway, what's the time for getting someone from forensics down here? The EMTs are waiting to move the bodies and there's a crowd forming already."

"He should be there any minute. Just make sure everything is taken care of down there. I'm going to talk to Sloan over at the servers to have an alert sent out through the app. The faster we get word out there that he's out there as a danger to the public, the sooner we can get him put away. And Brett?"

"Yeah, chief?"

"I know you're doing what you guys can, but Christmas Eve is in two days. We need to end this now or no one is going to be enjoying Christmas this year."

"I've got it, Chief. We won't let you down." Brett hung up and looked at his partner. Josh was allowing Fenton under the yellow tape, providing her with an update of what had happened. Brett understood his boss's request, but he knew that ending this gang war wasn't going to be as easy as the Mayor and the Commissioner were hoping but taking down Donnelly would be a good start.

"Hey Foster," called out Mike Wogle. He wasn't alone. A middle-aged woman with shoulder length black hair was at his side. She was holding a black case in each hand.

"Mike, sorry to pull you away."

"Don't worry about it. I've called in some help. Meet Jan McClune. She's with the Manhattan offices of the FBI. We met at a Forensics convention at the Jacob Javits Center back in September."

"'Hello Detective," Jan said, setting down the cases and holding out her hand, "Good to meet you and I'm glad I could help. I have a few days off from my job and I was getting so bored that I jumped at the chance to help Mike when he called."

"Right now, any help is welcomed," Brett replied. She picked up her cases and began gathering evidence. Brett looked over at Wogle and Mike smiled back at him. Then Mike followed Jan over to the bodies and began processing the scene.

"I wish I could do more," Amanda told Josh, "It doesn't help that I'm not familiar with the area."

"The fact that you're here is plenty of help," Raghetti replied, "Have you gotten anything back on where those bullets came from?"

"No, I faxed the paperwork to my office to have one of my fellow agents look into it," Amanda reported, "I'm hoping to hear from her some time today. I'll let you know the moment she calls."

"Thanks again on that," Brett said to her.

"Like I said, it's the least I could do."

"Black's sending out an APB on Donnelly. She agrees that the sooner we get him, the faster this gang war ends."

"And this Hermes guy?" Fenton threw out into the air between the three of them.

"Enrique hasn't surfaced. That scares me, but if we get Donnelly, we can rule him out."

"I'm just going to make a phone call," Fenton said, turning and taking a few steps away from the two cops.

69

The ringing ended when Julio Jimenez answered on the other end. Amanda looked back to make sure no one else could hear her before she began speaking. She knew that the homicide detectives would never understand the need to get into the dirt to get things done. That's how they did it in her office and it had worked year after year. The bullet search wasn't the only thing she had requested from her office. Her co-worker also looked up the home number of the Latin Soldados's leader.

"Julio, Agent Fenton calling."

"Ah, Agent Fenton. I was wondering when I would be hearing from you again. I think I may know what you're calling about this morning."

"I'm sure you do. Everyone is talking about one thing."

"Vincent Donnelly."

"Yes. And I know that you have a good feeling where he is right now. Provide us with that information and I'll make sure he pays for his crimes against your gang."

"What he has done to my gang is nothing compared to what he has done to my family, Agent Fenton. Let me make something clear. Vincent Donnelly is mine and mine alone. I know how the police in this town work and by the time they figure out where he is, he'll be a rotting corpse. And that's if I leave a body to be found. Now unless there is something else you would like to talk about, this conversation is over."

"I can help you with this," she told him, trying to keep him talking.

"I highly doubt you can, Agent. But you will have my assistance in locating this vigilante, only because I know he is responsible for the murder of Thomas Ketchum, your 'partner', as you put it. I only give you that as thanks for helping to stop the attack at my home yesterday morning. We will then be even."

"What do you mean by that comment about my partner?" Fenton asked, wondering if Julio knew more than he was letting on.

"That is a conversation for another time. Good day, Agent Fenton. And good luck." Julio disconnected the call. Amanda was left staring at her phone, wondering if the gang leader had learned about Tom Ketchum and who he really was. She hoped not. That was her one secret she planned on taking with her to the grave.

70

With smiles on both their faces, Lyndsey Bergen and Danica Page walked into the lobby of Arrow Accounting looking for Travis Hughes. Behind them were officers Kassen and Schiebal. They were there to help 'keep the peace', as Chief Black liked to put it. Lyndsey thought that it made them more serious looking. She knew that Hughes would give them a hard time, even with the search warrant, but the girls were willing to do it the hard way if they had to.

She just hoped that they weren't too late to prevent him from removing any evidence from his place. Even with the watchful eye that Chief Black had placed in front of his building for the past 24 hours, there was still a chance for him to have removed the gun and placed it elsewhere. Danica had been able to confirm that he had no safety deposit box or even a P.O. Box, but that didn't mean he didn't have other places of hiding.

"Hi again," Danica said to Ashley. The bubbly blonde looked at the detectives and officers in confusion.

"Um, Can I, um, help you?"

"If you could just direct us to Mr. Hughes' office?"

"Sure, but he never came in this morning." Ashley looked at them blankly. Danica and Lyndsey looked at each other. Lyndsey turned to the uniformed officers.

"We need to get to his apartment now."

* * *

Both the police cruiser and the unmarked vehicle arrived at the building in 5 minutes. It was a new record for Lyndsey and it helped to have the uniformed car with them. She flipped off the switch for the flashing light on her dashboard and the cops in front of her turned off their lights and siren to keep from alerting Travis any earlier than needed.

Without even stopping to look for a spot to park, they both made their own parking spots and jumped out of the car. Lyndsey and Danica went in first with the uniforms right behind them. Lyndsey knew that something was up when they found the second inside door propped open. She heard conversation above them. Removing her pistol from the holster tucked against her ribs, she slowly crept up the stairs. The four were completely silent and once they reached the second floor they could make out what was being said.

"The sooner we get this out of here, the better," Travis Hughes said to someone else.;

"Dude, I'm not going down for you. You're cool and all but there's no real friendship here," explained a second voice. Lyndsey turned to those behind her and held up two fingers and then pointed up, notifying the others how many were actually there.

"If you want more of this, then I suggest you help me." Hughes sounded aggravated. Lyndsey poked her head up, looking across the level of the third floor. There was no one in the hall but she saw Hughes' apartment door open. Just before she could turn back to the others behind her, the other man with Hughes stepped out of the apartment with a potted plant. He locked eyes on her immediately and froze in place. She didn't know what to do but brought a finger to her lips, asking him to keep quiet. In a perfect world, the man would have calmly walked out of the apartment and left quickly.

"Fuck!" the man yelled, dropping the plant. He jumped aback into the apartment and slammed the door, locking it. Lyndsey could hear him, "Travis, there's some chick on the stairs!"

"Damn," Lyndsey heard Danica say behind her. Stepping from their spots, the four approached the door to Travis' apartment and Danica pounded on it with the side of her fist.

"Travis, make this easy on yourself and just open the door. We have a warrant. Your choice, open the door or we break it down. Either way, we're coming in."

"Why couldn't you have just left me alone?" Travis said through the door, "I told you that I had nothing to do with those shootings!"

"Evidence says otherwise. Just let us in and we can get this over with. Any lack of resistance will be seen as cooperation."

Lyndsey and Danica waited for a minute, wondering if he was contemplating giving them access or was making a run out a window. Then the lock on the door was undone and the knob turned. All four of the officers outside in the hall got into a stance, in the event that he rushed them. The door slowly opened, and Travis stood there with his hands up in surrender. Lyndsey handed him the warrant and they all walked in past him. Lyndsey and Danica found the other man sitting on a couch with his hands behind his head. Danica picked him up and went to take him out into the hall.

"I swear I have nothing to do with the stuff in here," he told her.

"We would have let you go if you had kept quiet," Lyndsey replied.

Lyndsey and Danica pulled on plastic gloves with Officer Kassen while Officer Schiebal kept the second man company outside the apartment. They began in the living room and Officer Masson headed into the small enclosed kitchen to look through the drawers and behind appliances.

"Do you want to make this easier on us by saving some time?" Danica asked Travis, who was now sitting on the couch with his head in his hands.

"I'm telling you that my father's gun isn't here. I wasn't lying about that. Someone broke in a few months ago. There was a bunch of stuff taken and when I went through my stuff, I saw that several things had been taken from the box of my father's stuff. The gun was one of them."

"Then why all the lies and giving us a hard time?"

Travis sighed heavily. He pointed around the corner of the area by the bathroom, located on the side, between the living room and the kitchen.

"What, your bathroom's untidy?"

"No, past the bathroom. Door on the right."

Lyndsey and Danica looked at each other, wondering what he was directing them to. They were unsure of what was in there and were weary of going in alone.

"What's in there?"

"Something my father wouldn't be proud of."

"Care to elaborate?"

"Just see for yourself. And I'm sorry."

Lyndsey decided to let Danica take point on this one. Danica shook her head and gave her the sign of Rock, Paper, Scissors. Lyndsey rolled her eyes and went along with her. Lyndsey threw out a scissors while Danica held her hand flat, revealing paper.

"Never lose," Lyndsey smiled. Danica took out her gun and walked up to the door that Travis had indicated. Looking back, she glanced into Lyndsey's eyes. Lyndsey could see that Danica wasn't up for dying today, but Detective Page took hold of the door knob and slowly opened the door into the brightly lit room.

71

Hermes arrived at his apartment for a late lunch. Even though he was hungry, that wasn't the main reason for him being here. He had been wondering about the teen tied in his closet and wanted to make sure that he was still there and was fed. He had hoped to avoid anything like this but with every plan there was always a need to expect the unexpected. Just like the boy in his closet that knew more than he should.

He walked into the apartment and opened the freezer. Inside, he had a number of microwavable dishes that he had purchased for this exact reason Hermes hoped that the boy would learn something from this; maybe he would rethink being part of a gang.

Hermes popped the small cardboard container in the microwave and then he poured milk in a plastic cup - he wasn't about to give the kid glass.

When the food was ready, he took a spoon from the drawer and brought it all into the bedroom. Opening the door, Enrique squinted looked up and squinted in the bright light. Hermes smiled and pulled Enrique out of the closet.

"I am going to feed you now. Do not try anything stupid or you will be punished. Nod if you understand."

Enrique nodded faintly. Hermes smiled and pulled the gag around his mouth down so that he could eat. He scooped a spoon full of the pasta noodles in a meat sauce. Enrique leaned forward, eager to have something in his belly. Enrique savored the feeling of food on his tongue after the dry cotton-like feel he had had all morning.

"Not too fast," Hermes told him, "You'll get a bad stomach." He scooped up another spoonful and held it back, waiting for Enrique to finish the first mouthful.

"You do realize that I'm not going to kill you. This is only to make sure that you don't ruin the plan before I can complete it. You'll be home before Christmas. I promise."

"Why?" Enrique asked.

"Why what? Why am I doing this?"

"Yes," Enrique said weakly.

"It's simple. I'm doing this to save the city that I love and grew up in. I take it you were born here in Hoboken?" Enrique nodded, "Right. And do you remember what this was like when you were little?"

"I remember some."

"And is it completely different now compared to then?"

"I guess."

"Let me explain something, Enrique. When I was a kid, there were no gangs or drugs or drive-bys here. It was a fun place to be a kid. Nowadays, this place has become a slum. I mean sure, the mayor is cleaning up the river side, but this town isn't just a river view drive. There's a home here for many families. The mayor and the police commissioner don't understand that, though. Just like they don't understand that the gangs work under different rules than the police do. This is why I'm taking out the gangs. I'm doing it to take back this town for the families that still live here as well as the families that may live here someday."

Enrique tried to laugh, "You sound like the Punisher."

"Who's that?"

"Comic book character. He kills all the mobs because they murdered his family."

"Well, there was no one murdered in my family so it's not quite the same." Hermes put the spoon by Enrique's mouth again and Enrique took it gentler this time. The vigilante put the spoon down and held up the cup of milk. He tilted it slightly against Enrique's lips, making sure not to spill it on him. Enrique drank half the cup in one gulp.

"I'll get you more once you're done," Hermes told him kindly, "Now can I ask you why you were there that night? Why are you part of the Soldados?"

"I needed some money and Julio offered me more than just a regular job at McDonalds."

"It shouldn't have to be that way. I know you're still learning. You are in school still, right?" Enrique nodded. He hoped that he would be able to return back to school, as odd that sounded to him. He was good at drawing and had been considering going into architecture. His counselor at school told him about the college in Newark that specialized in the field. Enrique figured that it was close enough to home that he would be able to live there while attending.

"I know it sounds like a commercial, but school is important. You don't want to end up like Julio Jimenez."

"At least he doesn't keep me locked in a closet," Enrique replied.

"Do you really think I want this? I don't like it any more than you do. But for the sake of my plan, it's necessary. Now finish eating." Hermes held out another spoonful of pasta. Enrique leaned forward and instead of taking the spoon, he opened wider and bit into the side of Hermes' hand. Clenching down hard, he gritted his teeth, drawing blood. Hermes screamed in pain and dropped the spoon. He grabbed Enrique's jaw with his other hand and squeezed, hoping to get the teen to release him. Enrique held on tight.

"Let go!" Hermes shouted. When the boy refused a second time, the vigilante had no choice but to slam a fist into the side of Enrique's head.

Enrique opened his mouth and moaned at the throbbing pain in his head now. Hermes' blood slowly dripped from his mouth. Enrique spit out the blood onto his shirt, removing the coppery taste that overtook the flavor of the cheap rubbery pasta.

"After all I've done. After telling you that you would be able to see your family again, you do this? Maybe you are like Julio after all. You're just another criminal for me to take down. Let me walk away now before you end up like all the others that were at the garage that night." Hermes grabbed the gag and tightened it across his mouth, making Enrique choke on the taste.

Using his foot, the vigilante shoved Enrique back into the closet and shut it tight before placing a padlock on the latch and squeezing it closed. Looking at his hand, he went into the bathroom and ran it under the cold water from the faucet. The bite wasn't so bad looking once the blood was washed off, but he knew that it would bruise.

He opened the medicine cabinet with his other hand and took out some bandage and tape. Wrapping the hand gently, he tried to figure out how to explain this to his employer or anyone else he knew that would notice it. The thought of his kindness being returned like this made him angry. He didn't want to, but he considered taking the boy out to save him the further trouble, but it would be a last resort.

Once the wound on his hand was dressed, he returned to the kitchen to fix himself something to eat before leaving to return to his other job. *I'm not a bad man*, the vigilante thought, *just misunderstood*.

72

Hines hated days like today. On top of everything ~~all~~ that was going on, he still had to deal with smaller issues. For example: Dave Bennett, who was standing before him with a baseball bat in one hand and the collar of a Jackal's shirt in the other. The main problem was that the owner of the shirt was still wearing it. And the Jackal was bleeding from the head.

"Mr. Bennett, I thought we discussed this," Danny began, "You need to leave catching criminals to us."

"If I did that, then this douchebag would be somewhere far away with Old Lady McFarlane's money and credit cards."

"Still, we are going to have to take you downstairs. You broke the laws, too."

"You know that's complete bullshit!"

Hines waved a couple of uniformed officers over to take both Bennett and the bleeding Jackal to a holding cell, minus the bat. Shaking his head, he looked over at officer Hoy.

"Who was that?" she asked.

"That was Dave Bennett, bringer of justice and local nutball. He actually lives right next to Doyle in Anti-Vice." Danny then caught himself, "I mean, he lived. Damn, I'm going to miss that crotchety old bastard."

Lyndsey and Danica walked into the precinct with Travis Hughes in tow. Even though they weren't smiling, they were welcomed with a small cheer. Lyndsey held her hand up for silence, but that just elicited a high five from Raghetti. She threw him an annoyed look and took Travis over to Officer Belanger to be brought downstairs into one of the holding cells.

Chief Black stepped out of her office while Officer Kassen and Schiebal delivered the evidence they had retrieved from Travis's apartment to the other side of the building.

"Why the long faces?" Black asked the women.

"He's not the vigilante," Lyndsey told them. Her comment was returned with confused faces.

"But I thought that he had the gun that was used?"

"The search revealed that he was telling the truth about his place being broken into and the gun being one of the things that were taken. We even examined the lock on the front door and saw that it was jimmied open."

"But why did he give us a hard time about where he was and allowing us to look around his apartment?" Russell asked.

"The reason behind that is being taken down to evidence by Kassen and Schiebal as we speak," Danica cut in, "He had small marijuana growing hot house in one of the bedrooms. He was pretty professional with it too. Lighting and ventilation was all set up and the window was sealed up with a big laundry hose that ran up to the roof. That kept the smell from getting through the building."

"Clever thinking," Raghetti joked.

"So now what?" Black asked.

Amanda raised her hand as she stared at her phone. She said, "My office just got back to me about the bullet casings at both scenes. They were able to confirm that the bullets were purchased in a store up in Englewood."

"Seems sensible," Brett said, "Buy them a fair distance away to prevent any alarms nearby."

"Exactly. But that's not all. Even though he paid for it with one of those preloaded credit cards, he still signed for it."

"We've got a name?" Josh asked, excited.

"What a dumbass," Fernandez laughed.

"Not quite," Amanda said, "The store owner sent over a scanned copy of the receipt which was all he had due to the fact that his security footage is taped over every week." Fenton held up her phone for the group to see. Leaning in, Brett saw that the name it was signed from was "Harry Ermes." He shook his head in disappointment.

"Who's Harry Ermes?" Danica asked.

"Harry Ermes is H. Ermes," Russell explained, disappointed as well.

"This guy is slick," Lyndsey said, "Annoying, but slick."

"So, what, we're back to square one?" Black asked.

"Again," Russell added.

"We've got to be missing something. He couldn't have been this careful. Lyndsey, you said that this Hermes broke into Travis' apartment to get the gun? Did you check for prints?"

"There were two sets on the front door. One we believe is Travis' and the other was just brought upstairs by Officer Kassen. We'll see if the lab boys get any hits."

"Here's the thing," Brett explained, "Hermes knew that the gun was in Travis' apartment. And I'm sure that he knew that the gun belonged to his father, Tony. But the question is, how did he know?"

"I told you," Kylee said, "This fucker's gotta be a cop."

"Ok, so if he's a cop and if he's familiar with the town, then he has to be one of us. And how do we figure that out?"

"Bring in Internal Affairs?" Danica guessed.

"No," Josh added, "They would take too long, and the town would have fallen to crap by the time they realized who."

"We find out who Travis knows from the police force. Whoever Hermes is, they knew that the gun was no longer at his parents' house. This means that our vigilante had to have known either Tony or Travis."

"What if it's the neighbor?"

"No, not with the way this guy's been playing us. He has something to prove. Let's not forget the fact that he threw Darren's name out there to the Jackal that set up the meeting. He knows more that the average citizen."

"I'm sorry," Kylee piped up again, "In case I didn't say this earlier, maybe he's a cop." Brett rolled his eyes at the short homicide detective. It was at that moment that Luis came running into the squad room.

"Stop everything!" he shouted, "I've just gotten a call. One of the Jackals has given me Donnelly's hideout location. Who's with me to go get him?"

Luis had never seen so many hands shoot up in the air so fast.

73

Vincent Donnelly sullenly ate a terrible cup of noodles prepared by two incompetent Jackals. It was bad enough that he was stuck hiding out in this shithole. He was just waiting a couple of hours and then when it was dark enough, he would make another move at Julio's home. This time though, he would be making his way inside instead of just standing out front.

The two-story home that he had taken as a secret hangout for the gang was located on Newark Street, about forty feet from Gateway Park, which sat just outside the row of train tracks going to and from the Hoboken Train station. It was a bit noisy for a hangout but only those higher up in the gang knew about it. Unfortunately, the house had not been kept up in the past few months and the cold wind made its way in through old window frames and the uninsulated attic. The TV was an old 18-inch with rabbit ears that provided every local channel with a slight static. The couch that he sat on was old and seemed like they had found it at a yard sale held by an old folks home. He was disgusted and couldn't wait for tonight.

"Go get me a Heineken," Vinnie demanded. Richie, the first Jackal, looked over at the other, Harry. Harry shrugged and stood up. He walked into the pale white kitchen and opened the old fridge, which smelled of the rotted cheese sandwich someone had left there the last time the house had been used. Harry took two Heineken bottles and brought them back to the living room. He handed Vinnie one of the bottles and cracked the other open himself.

"Where the hell is mine?" Richie asked.

"You didn't ask for one and you ain't in charge. Get it yourself." Harry didn't even look his way. Richie flipped him the bird and got up to get a beer.

Vinnie looked out the uncovered front windows, facing Newark Avenue. Anyone walking by could have seen three of them huddled around the small TV. It would be embarrassing to be seen hiding out here. He was Vincent Donnelly, leader of the Jackals. He was destined for big things. He was going to take down the Latin Soldados on his own, for Christ's sake!

"We need to leave," he said out loud to no one specific. Richie looked over at Harry for some response. Harry didn't know what to say, but he had heard about what happened to Louie when he spoke up.

"Where did you want to go?" Richie asked.

"Anywhere but here. I deserve better than this shithole. I'm Vincent fuckin' Donnelly!"

"Okay, I'll give Colton a call and see where we can take you," Richie said, reaching for his phone. Vinnie smacked it from his hand.

"No, we go where I say we go. Do you hear me?"

"I'll go start the car, Vinnie." Harry headed for the front door, digging the keys from his pocket. Before he could even reach the door, one of the front windows shattered inwards. A cracked brick landed on the floor in front of Vinnie. Then, the front door was kicked in and two Latin Soldados members rushed in. One, carrying a shotgun, aimed his gun at Harry and fired it into the Jackal's chest. Harry was knocked backwards into the wall, leaving a smear of red behind. Vinnie tried to run for the backyard entrance, but he stopped when he saw another member of the Soldados in the kitchen, blocking his path.

Richie froze where he stood. Donnelly was trapped between the rival gang members. His face turned into a scowl when he saw Julio enter from the front doorway. The leader of the Soldados was in his long black wool coat. A red handkerchief sprouted from the chest pocket, and his shoes tapped softly as he walked across the old wood floor. He stopped in front of Vinnie and smiled.

"Finally," was all he said. Vinnie stared into his eyes, not blinking. Donnelly was damned if he was going to give his enemy any pleasure.

"You just saved me the trouble of going to your house," Donnelly told him, "By the way, how's Grandma?"

Julio looked down for a moment, disappointed. Then, with no

warning, he brought his right hand up and backhanded Vinnie across the face. Vinnie's head flew back, and he lost his balance. As he fell to the floor, Richie stepped back in surprise. Donnelly looked up in defiance, wiping the thin streak of blood from his mouth.

"Don't get up, you dog," Julio told him, "I want to remember you like this."

"Funny, I'm sure this is the same view your mother had when I made her beg."

"You never learn, do you Vincent? This is why you never had a chance against me."

"I'm sorry, Julio," Richie said, "If we're good, I'm going to leave him to you." Vinnie's head shot around, and he looked up at Richie in anger.

"You! You sold me out? You fuck! I will find you. No matter where you hide, I will find you!" Donnelly shouted.

"Will you PLEASE SHUT UP!" bellowed Julio. Vinnie stopped talking. Julio looked at Richie and then to the member of the Soldados that had shot Harry, "Pay the man so he can leave."

Richie smiled, happy to have gotten away with the betrayal. The shotgun man nodded to Julio and raised the shotgun.

"No, wait. You said," Richie said before the shotgun blast cut him off by shredding his stomach. The room then fell silent and Vinnie, against anyone's wishes, stood up.

"This is how you're going to do me? Unarmed and outnumbered? I always knew you were a coward."

"Mister Donnelly, my grandmother died without a fighting chance. My best man's family had their house burnt down without a chance to save it. Are you that out of your mind that you think I would allow you a fighting chance to get away? You're even crazier than I thought," Julio laughed out loud. "But you know what, you have a point. I think I will give you a chance to fight back." Julio turned to the man who entered from the backyard and held out his hand. The gang member nodded and pulled a hand gun from his coat. Julio took it in his hand and took two shots to Vinnie's knees. Donnelly screamed as he collapsed to the floor. Then he took one more shot to Donnelly's outstretched left hand. Vinnie pulled in his hand and cradled it against his stomach.

Julio snapped his fingers and the three Soldados members rushed out of the house through the front. Less than a minute later, they returned with full jugs of gasoline. The three men uncapped the jugs and began pouring the gas over everything in the house. Once they were done, Julio walked over to Richie's corpse and retrieved his cell phone; he couldn't allow this to be traced back to him. Julio walked over to the shattered window and placed the cell phone on the windowsill.

"I wish you luck, Mister Donnelly." Julio waved his hand and his men left the home, returning to the car across the street. Julio took a Montecristo Eagle cigar from his pocket, snipped the end and flicked his lighter. He walked to the front door and stopped. Turning, Julio smiled at the man he knew as a rival for the past four years.

"Oh, one more thing," the leader said, "Give the devil my best wishes." Julio flicked the lighter once more and dropped it on the couch. The gasoline whooshed, and the couch was immediately covered in flames. In seconds, the entire first floor of the house was engulfed.

Two minutes into the fire, several unmarked cars with flashing lights screeched to a halt in front of what Donnelly had just minutes ago called his hideout. Brett jumped out of Josh's car before his partner could put it in park. He took several steps closer to the inferno before the heat forced him to stop. Foster felt a chill through his body as he heard the cursing screams of Vincent Donnelly from inside the house. He couldn't quite make out the words that the Jackal leader was saying but he was sure that Julio's name was mentioned.

"Holy Fuck," Kylee said, stunned.

"Oh my God," Luis followed.

"Was this Hermes?" Russell asked the others.

"This is pretty brutal, but it could be," Lyndsey said.

Josh looked around, wondering if the vigilante was hiding somewhere watching them from afar. It wasn't until he looked on the other side of Newark Avenue that he saw Julio standing behind his car that was quietly running. Julio was looking right at them, admiring his work. The gang leader stared into Josh's eyes and told him everything without even saying a word. Then without a noise, he got into his car and slipped away into the night. Josh was the only one to have seen him. The others were too busy staring at the fire and Brett was on the phone with the fire department.

"They're on their way," he told the others around him.

"It'll be too late for Donnelly," Danica stated the obvious. Brett had noticed that the screams had stopped. The fire had finally gotten to the gang leader.

"This wasn't our vigilante," Josh said.

"How do you know?"

Josh told them.

74

Jacob yawned, it was time to call it a night. He had spent most of the afternoon at the Perez home, where Carmen had welcomed him in with an open-door policy.

He had asked to look around Enrique's room, in hopes of finding some clue as to where he might have gone. Carmen had joined him in his search, but several hours later, they hadn't found anything.

Jacob apologized for taking up her time and returned to the office. Robin had several messages from other clients that she had had to apologize to throughout the day.

"I'm sorry about that," he said to her.

"I know that you're worried about Enrique, but it'll only be so long before Delgado is on your case about the amount of time you're spending with the police on this one."

"You're right, it's just I know this kid is stuck between a rock and a hard place, and he doesn't have anyone outside his family to talk to."

"That's what I love about you," she told him, "Your talent for being the good guy."

"I have many other talents as well, you know. I can juggle like no one's business." The joke made her laugh and he finally smiled after a long day. "Why don't you head home and pick out something nice to wear. I'll finish up here and meet you in a little bit. Then you, me, and a nice dinner out."

"That's it?" she asked, "Just a nice dinner?"

"Well, desert may be on the menu too." He said, winking.

"Can I get whipped cream on that this time?"

"Yeah, sure." He kissed her gently and smiled, happy to have her to help cheer him up and make life better.

"Don't be too late," she told him, grabbing her coat and closing down her computer.

"I promise."

Jacob walked into his office and sat down, taking a deep breath and looking over the papers on his desk. Trying to figure out where to begin tomorrow, he was interrupted by a knock on the door. He looked up and saw Kristie Marks in the doorway.

"Hey, student Marks, how was the exam today?"

"I am SO relieved that it's over." Kristie replied. She sat down in one of the chairs in front of his desk and relaxed.

"The hard part is over, remember that. Now it's just a matter of waiting for them to mark it. That, unfortunately, could take a while."

"How long is a while?"

"I had to wait four months before they told me."

"Four months!?!" Kristie said, surprised, "I can't wait that long!"

"You have no choice, you're at their mercy now."

"Wow. I need a drink."

"Go home, relax and celebrate that the exam is over."

"I think I will. How are things here?"

"Not too bad, just working on a case with the gang war. Lots of fun and a missing witness, to boot."

"I think I'll take the exam over that."

"Oh, just wait, your time will come. Now go on home to see your family. Tell Connor I said hi and I'm waiting to take him on again in a sword fight."

"Oh, he's been practicing. Be afraid. Be very afraid." Kristie got up and said good night before leaving the office. Jacob was alone once again and got to work, setting things up for tomorrow.

Enrique knew that if he didn't try to escape, after what he did to his captor earlier, he would not make it to Christmas. As the hours passed, he made several attempts at loosening the rope that kept his hands tied behind his back. There were a few times that he ended up losing feeling in his arms from the awkward angle, but he would just shake it off and try again after a few minutes.

The vigilante had made a mistake by revealing his face. On the night of the garage shooting, Enrique hadn't gotten a clear view, but now, he had studied it. He would use that information to get retribution.

The teen pulled on a piece of the rope until he felt the tightness of the knot relax a little. That gave him hope that he was working it right and that if he kept at it, it would release its grip on his wrists. For what seemed like two hours, he continued to tug and twist. Finally, the rope became loose enough that he could slip one of his hands out. When he was able to see his hands in front of him, he felt like crying in triumph, but he wasn't sure if the man was home or not.

There was only one way to confirm that. Enrique kicked at the closet door, trying to get someone's attention. He waited a minute and then kicked again. After several attempts, he knew that there was no one else around. So, he leaned his back against the back of the closet and put every bit of energy he had left into kicking the door as hard as he could. The kick caused the wood in the door to crack slightly on the side. On the second kick, he managed to get the door to give even further.

"Only one more," he said to himself. Enrique slowly pulled himself to his feet. The blood finally rushed through them and gave him a tingling sensation. He decided to put his whole body into the next hit. He moved back as far as he could to get momentum and pushed off. His shoulder hit the door first, followed by the rest of his torso. The door finally gave way and he stumbled out of the closet. Jumping to his feet, he realized that he had done it. He was free!

He knew that the man could return home at any time and he had no concept of what time it really was. The apartment was dark. Enrique felt around the walls for a light switch. He saw that he was in a bedroom with the window painted black, preventing any light from coming through. The teen made his way down the hall to the living room where he saw that through the window, it was night. With the help of a street lamp, he could see that it was snowing again, but the weather was the least of his concerns.

He rushed to the front door of the apartment and fumbled to open the top lock - his fingers still recovering from the lack of blood flow. Beyond the door was a rundown hallway in the center of an apartment building. The floor was silent. But Enrique's eyes fell on the staircase that led down.

He rushed forward and ran down the stairs. When he reached the bottom floor, he charged the front entrance and found himself out in the street.

The cold crept into his body as he looked around, trying to find out where he was. A street sign on the corner read Colden and Varrick. He had never heard of the streets and wondered if he was even in Hudson County, let alone Hoboken.

Enrique heard an engine and looked to his right. A bus was heading towards him, its LED sign read EXCHANGE PLACE. The words gave him hope. He remembered Jacob Scott telling him that his office was at Exchange Place. Running out into the street, Enrique waved his hands to get the driver to stop the bus. The driver, an older man with graying hair and a thin mustache, opened the door and said, "Son, you shouldn't be out here without a coat. You'll freeze to death."

"I need help," Enrique explained, "Sir, I don't have any money, but I need to get to Exchange Place."

The bus driver noticed the raw skin around the teen's wrists and looked into the boy's eyes, seeing the distraught soul inside.

"You sure you don't want me to get you the police?"

"No, my friend at Exchange Place can get them for me. I just need to get there."

"Well, okay. Have a seat and relax. I'll get you there as soon as I can." The driver closed the door, turned up the heat and put the bus back into drive.

75

Seeing Amanda Fenton on his front steps was not what surprised Julio. What surprised him was the look on her face. Annoyance. He smiled at her as he approached the house. When he came close enough, she stood up, as if to tell him that she had been waiting to be let in. He did not hesitate and opened the door. She gave him the opportunity to enter his own house first before following him in.

"Hello, Agent Fenton. And how has your evening been?"

"Cut the act, Julio. You know why I'm here and I know you have what I'm looking for."

Julio stopped for a moment and looked up and down the street that he lived on. He did not see a single person outside his house, which he was grateful for.

"If you wish to speak to me, you need to either come inside or come back later when you are calmer. That's your choice." Julio stepped out of the doorway and waited for her to decide. Amanda stood there, deciding on whether or not she wanted to play by the gang leader's rules. Realizing that the information was too important to her, she stepped inside. She didn't notice the smile on Julio's face as he closed the damaged door.

"Why do you smell like smoke?" she asked.

"It is a long story," he replied, "Please."

He led her into the den and offered her a seat. He walked around the wide and remained standing. Fenton noticed the act of authority he was trying and wasn't impressed, but she continued the meeting.

"What do you know about the vigilante?"

"As difficult as I'm sure it will be to believe this, I have not learned anything as to his identity. He had become a rather formidable opponent."

"Both you and I know that is total bullshit. You may not know everything, but I have a strong feeling that you're closer to identifying him than the police are."

"Wouldn't that include you too, Agent?" he asked, jabbing back at her verbally.

"Enough with the dancing," she told him, standing up as well, "You know what my group can do to your gang's income. Do you really want to get me started?"

Julio stopped and looked down. He normally did this when he was trying to remain calm. Of course, after what he had just done, his blood was pumping quickly through his limbs. Julio knew better than to get into a fight with someone in law enforcement. There was a reason why he had been leader for this long. His mind was as sharp as new blade. And he wasn't going to allow a woman to ruin all he had built.

"I know you'd rather not let the police get to him first, because then you'd never get your hands on him."

"My dear Amanda, you're wrong there. What you fail to remember is that my grasp knows no bounds. Do you honestly think if the police got this man first, that I wouldn't be able to get my revenge? Your disadvantage is not being from around here. I've got my hands in everything in this town. I can guarantee that I would be able to get inside the police station, kill the vigilante and walk out without them being any the wiser."

"That's quite the ego you have there," she smiled. Fenton knew how a man like Julio Jimenez worked. Threaten his manhood and he would release his claws and his calmness would disappear. That's what she was going for. She figured that if she kept it up, he would eventually let something slip. Of course, there was another reason for doing this, but she would tell him that at the right time.

"Agent Fenton, your attempts to anger me are not working, and I'm disappointed you would try. I will tell you once more, I understand your determination to get your hands on this Hermes before your fellow police detectives do. After all, he killed your partner, Thomas Ketchum. I suppose I will have to show my hand to convince you that there is no ace up my sleeve. One moment, please. Excuse me, Ryan! Can you come in here please?" Julio stood and waited for his new right-hand man to come to the den.

"What can I do for you, Julio?"

"I would like you to tell Agent Fenton here what we know about Hermes. And do not worry, you can tell her everything. I'd like her to hear it from you."

Ryan stood there, unsure of what he was supposed to say. He looked at Amanda and then back at Julio. Amanda wondered what was going on.

"What should I tell her?" he asked his boss.

"Tell her everything we know about this vigilante," Julio said with a tone of a father egging his child to be brave and do as he ask.

"Did we learn something about him? I didn't think we were able to figure out who he was," Ryan said with a bit of sadness in his voice. He seemed like the son that had just disappointed his father and was depressed about it. Amanda was amazed by the control Julio had over his men.

"No, that's exactly what I've been trying to tell her. I just thought hearing it from you might help her believe it. Thank you though, Ryan. You can go." Ryan nodded and smiled at Julio then threw a look at Amanda and left the den.

"Satisfied now? I told you. Now is there something you would like to tell me?"

"What are you talking about?" she asked, confused.

"You know, the reason why you go by the last name of Fenton when you were actually born Amanda Ketchum?"

76

It had been five years since she had first met Thomas Ketchum, a full year after she had first learned about him. Her father, Roy, had sat her down and told her about him.

"I know you're going to get angry at me for keeping this from you and I deserve it, but I needed you to be old enough to understand."

"Dad, I'd never get mad at you. What's wrong?" She looked at him, innocently. Roy knew that that innocence was short-lived; she had told him a few months before that she was applying for the police academy.

"Sweetheart, you know that your mother and I struggled lots around the time you were born. And it wasn't you, please remember that. It just was the time and the situation."

"Dad," Amanda said, "Please, just tell me."

"You had just turned one and I was strapped for cash that I couldn't give you the birthday party that your mother had wanted. We had an argument and I stormed out of the house. I ended up at Partner's, the bar down the block. I had a few drinks. Then I had a few more. Before I knew it, I had gone home with one of the girls in the neighborhood. We, we did some things. I'm not proud of it and I won't blame the alcohol, but I tried to hide that from your mother."

Roy stopped talking for a minute, trying to get the courage to finish the story. It took him a minute, but he was able to continue.

"Almost a year later, I came home from patrol one night and your mother had a friend over for coffee. It was the woman I slept with. And she was just about to give birth."

Amanda's mouth dropped open wide and tears began to form in her eyes. The sight broke Roy's heart and he felt his heart scream. He didn't want to lose his baby girl to a mistake he had made so long ago. Yet he couldn't hide it forever. His wife had told him that he needed to tell her, or she would.

"I took responsibility for my actions. There was no way I couldn't have. I love your mother too much to let her go. Your mother asked me to keep him away, but she's realized now that it wasn't fair to you. His name is Thomas. And he is your half brother."

From that day forward, Amanda had held some anger in her heart for her father, but there was also fear. She was afraid to learn anything about the brother she never knew she had. Would he hold resentment towards her for getting to keep the man she called father in her life?

Months went by and it was the weekend before Easter; that's when everything had changed. Her father had been assigned to a task force to raid a place in Hoboken where a stash of guns had been dropped off for a local gang. During the raid, Roy had been pinned down by opposing gunfire. He was shot in the back in by surprise. She learned from her father's friends on the ATF force that it was the new leader of the Latin Soldados who had obtained the guns – Julio Jimenez.

"Ah, I remember that," Julio spoke finally. Amanda stared into his eyes the entire time she told the story. He watched her snarl the last part of her tale and it explained everything about why she had come to him in the first place. She wanted closure.

"I finally got the courage to go see Thomas. And I'm glad that I did. He also became part of the force and to make sure that we could team up, like a brother and sister team-up, I changed my last name to my mother's maiden name, Fenton. I told him everything. Even the vow I made to find the man that killed our father. I had just hoped that he could have been there with me."

"I am fully aware that you are armed, but I also know that you do realize that if you try anything, you will not leave alive."

"I know that it's not the right time. I can wait. I've waited five years. What's a few more?"

"You are an enigma, Agent Fenton. And I await the day that we meet again. I wish you luck in finding the man that killed your brother. Good night. You can see yourself out. I have work that needs to be done." Julio sat down and opened the laptop on his desk. Amanda stood there, not moving. There was a slight chance that she could take him out right there and still make it out alive, but the moment didn't feel right to her. There would be another time that was perfect. And then Julio Jimenez was all hers.

77

"I'm sorry but I'm really starting to side with this Hermes guy," Kylee joked. The group returned to the precinct to inform Chief Black the events of the evening. She expected the bad news when she came out of her office and saw the looks on their faces.

"I really hope you're joking about that," Brett replied.

"Oh Christ, give it a rest boy scout," she threw back at him.

"Enough, both of you," Black demanded, "Now can we link Julio to the crime other than him just being there?"

"Not until the fire dies down and the Arson guy checks it over. That could take days. A week considering the holiday," Danica told her.

"Okay, so what do we have on Hermes? Did he play a part in this?"

"Yeah," Josh said, "This was his plan the entire time and it worked perfectly."

"So, his plan is complete?" Black asked. She was trying to get them thinking. She had seen this frustration many times before and knew exactly what was needed to motivate them in the right direction. She didn't gather this group together just to have a team of detectives. She had seen how they worked off each other. And now was the perfect time to get them to be a team, not a group. Not a sports fan, she did like the symbolism of it being the final quarter with only minutes left to the game.

"No, he's still got Julio left to take out," Russell said matter of factly.

"So, you have Julio then. What else?"

"Enrique Perez, but no one can find him."

"Then he's out of the equation. That all?"

"We've got the gun that belonged to Tony Hughes, the mystery link to Travis Hughes, the fact that Hermes knows a little too much about how we work, and how he gave Darren's name to the Jackal that set the meeting up in the first place," Brett provided.

"Don't forget the fact that he calls himself Hermes. That's gotta be something," Luis offered.

"Great. Now what do we get from that?"

"A walking hemorrhoid."

"Seriously guys," Chief Black said, "All of this is from one man. There has to be something that we're all missing. What is it?"

The team fell silent and thought of all the events that had happened from Saturday night to that very minute. Black pulled her short brunette hair back into a pony tail and waited for a light bulb to come on. Brett looked up at her with a sense of nervousness.

"I hate to admit this, but Fernandez may be right when she says that it may be a cop," he said.

"It does kinda make sense," Lyndsey agreed.

"Then go with that, but tread lightly. We don't want to make waves accusing the wrong person. This is one of our brothers we will be accusing." Black smiled. Her team was on the move again.

"Fuck yeah," Kylee shouted, "Booyah, bitches!"

Hermes returned to the apartment after a long day. He had been in the car listening to his portable police scanner. He even decided to risk driving past the burnt remains of the house where Julio had burned Vinnie Donnelly alive. He had to see the way his plan had played out in the end. It was majestic.

He was now in the last act of his fateful play. All the pieces on the board had been set in place and now all he had to do was set up the final attack. But the main problem of what to do with the teen, Enrique Perez, was the only thing left to figure out. He didn't want to kill the boy, but he had seen Hermes' face. He couldn't convince the boy to stay quiet. Or could he? The boy did have a family. Perhaps threatening their lives could work to keep him quiet. But that may only work for so long. He would have to think about that more later.

The vigilante climbed the stairs after having to park two blocks from the small apartment building. He had chosen the building after coming across a bar that was on the other end of the block.

He showed up at the bar that one night when he had started planning everything. Sitting alone at the bar, nursing a Maker's Mark on the rocks, the seat next to him was suddenly filled by a man that already gotten a buzz and was looking to commit to a total blackout night. After a few drinks, the man became chatty and started a conversation with him that Hermes was not in the mood for. But the moment the man started talking about his dead ex-cop father and the gun that his mother had forced him to take, Hermes then believed that the man was put there for a reason. After a few more drinks the man revealed his address. Hermes made note of that and waited for the right time to break in. He made it seem like someone had just broken in for money, then left the gun at the crime scene, creating the perfect distraction for the police.

Hermes froze when he reached the floor that his apartment was on. His eyes fell on the front door that was wide open. He rushed across and into the living room.

"No, no, no. Dammit, no!"

Running down the hall, he almost tripped over the closet door on the floor. Enrique had escaped! How could this have happened? Hermes began to panic. How long ago did he escape? Had he managed to make it home? Had he already told the police? No, he thought. If Enrique had gone to the police, they would have been here already. He didn't have a whole lot of time. He ran back to the kitchen and retrieved the cleaning supplies. He needed to wipe the apartment down of any prints. Then he needed to gather all his utilities and weapons and remove them all. He wasn't concerned with linking the apartment to him as he had signed all the paper work using a false name and ID.

The detectives of the Hoboken force weren't dummies. He knew that if he took too long they would figure everything out. The fact that he knew how they operated was a major asset, but it was also a hindrance because it pointed out how he knew.

He had to get Julio tonight or else the plan would never reach its end. The layout of Julio's home was still in Hermes's bag, along with the gun that he had taken from Travis' place. He knew that after what Julio did tonight, he would most likely be in his den or the master bedroom upstairs, relaxing and enjoying the fact that the Jackals was no longer an issue.

Twenty minutes later, he had finished wiping everything down and he headed into his bathroom. Inside the bathroom closet was the small chest that held the weapons he would need to finish off Julio and the remaining Soldados. He placed the bag on top of the chest and carried it out of the apartment. He stopped to close the front door behind him so not to alert the neighbors to any suspicious activity. Then he carried the chest down the stairs and looked outside before leaving the building. As he walked the two blocks back to his car, he thought of perhaps driving past the Perez home to see if Enrique had made it. Maybe, he thought, he could force the teen to join him for the final act. It seemed only fair that he be there to see the finish as he had been there to see the start.

Three

An End to Crime

78

Thirty minutes after getting to the office, Jacob was finished with setting up his schedule for the last work day of the week. Hoffmann and Delgado had decided to give the firm the following four days off. It gave the offices some holiday morale, considering most of the lawyers there were feeling overworked. Jacob certainly was. He sat back and closed his eyes. If Robin hadn't been expecting him, he felt that he could probably fall asleep in the chair at that moment.

Jacob fell into the relaxed state a little deeper, trying to recover some energy that he had spent in the past few days. Knowing that the night would end enjoyably, he tried to meditate for a few minutes. The thought made him smile because he had never meditated before and honestly did not know how. He didn't even know if the "ohm" sound was for real.

But the phone on his desk told him that another minute of meditation was impossible. He opened one eye, looking at the caller ID. The word SECURITY flashed on the small screen on the side of the phone. Wondering what it could be, he decided to answer it anyway.

"Jacob Scott," he answered.

"Mr. Scott? This is Oscar downstairs at the security desk." Oscar had been the afternoon shift's security guard for the entrance to the building. He was a portly middle-aged man with a personality that no one could ever truly get mad at. His nice and thoughtful attitude at life had somehow gotten him the job that required him to be stern and aggressive to those who didn't have access to any of the floors.

"Hey Oscar, you caught me just as I was about to leave. What's up?"

"Oh, I'm sorry about that, Mr. Scott. It's just that there is someone here asking to see you. I was seeing if you were still here."

Jacob looked at the clock on the wall. It read 5:53PM.

"Sorry Oscar, I've got dinner plans. Can you please ask whoever it is that they can stop in tomorrow morning and one of the lawyers can see him then?"

"Um, he seems very persistent. Are you sure?"

"Look, Oscar, please give him my apologies and let him know that I will personally make some time for him tomorrow morning. Just have Todd call him up tomorrow. I really have to get home."

"Okay, Mr. Scott. I'll let him know." Jacob heard the phone move to the side and Oscar told the man that he would have to come back. There was some arguing and then Jacob heard the phone get jostled and dropped. The electronic crack of the phone hitting the desk made him cringe. Then he heard the man yell into the phone.

"Jacob! Help me!"

Jacob froze and his mouth open in surprise. He knew the man that was there to see him. It was Enrique.

79

As always, there were no parking spots on the block, so Hermes had found one in front of a fire hydrant that was located right across the street from the Perez home. He kept the car running in the event a cop was to come along. He sat in the car for a minute, thinking of some kind of strategy to get Enrique out of the house if he was even there.

"Come on think," he said to himself. Time was running out and he needed to finish this as quickly as possible. He didn't want to hit Julio's place without knowing where Enrique was. The fact that the boy was out there with knowledge of his face was enough to scare him into making a mistake. He couldn't risk it because there was so much riding on this plan. He just couldn't be caught. This town needed him to get rid of the criminals that the police were unable to. He had a duty to his fellow neighbor to make sure that they felt safe in the city that they called home. The mayor and police commissioner had ideas that weren't as effective as his.

Hermes stepped out of the car and walked through the falling snow across the street and found that he was able to look into the bay window at the Perez' in their living room. The father was on the couch and had a worn look on his face. Hermes could tell that he was worried about his son. Could Enrique have not even made it home? The thought gave him hope. It also gave him another idea.

He noticed a young girl, slightly older looking than Enrique – a sister. She had her coat on and was on her way out the door when she was stopped by the mother, a short cherub-faced woman. He could see that the mother didn't like the idea of her daughter leaving the house. The father stood up from his couch, he was a tall burly man. The vigilante hoped that he wouldn't have to go fist to fist with the man. The father gave the daughter a hug and held her in place while he spoke to her. Most likely, he was telling her to be careful.

"Come on, let her leave," Hermes said to them. He took stance behind the pickup truck that was parked right in front of the house. The daughter said her goodbyes and opened the door. She looked outside at first and made a face at the snowfall. She zippered her coat up to her neck and headed out onto the sidewalk. Hermes looked over and saw that neither parent was looking out the window to see if she was okay. Perfect, he thought.

"Excuse me," the vigilante called out to the girl. The call startled her, and she turned around fast, ready to run back into the house. He held his hands up to calm her.

"I'm so sorry. I didn't mean to scare you. I was just hoping that you could help me." Hermes pointed to his car that was still running. "I was just trying to drop food off to my grandmother. She lives right over there," he said, pointing to a house further down the block, "I parked in front of the hydrant because I was only going to be a minute. She can't leave the house with her hip and asked me to pick her up some groceries. Anyway, I'm stuck in the snow. Could you maybe give it some gas while I push it out of the spot?"

"I'm sorry, but I don't know you."

"Hey, good for you," he told her, "You don't see that these days. Look, here's my card. You'll see I'm legit. And I'll give you ten dollars for your trouble. You'll save me the trouble of a ticket." Hermes handed her his card with a folded ten-dollar bill under it. The girl looked at the card and examined the words on it. She looked up at him and he gave her a desperate please face.

"Okay, fine. But no funny stuff."

"Oh, thank you. Just put it into Drive and be gentle on the gas. I don't want to hit any of the parked cars too." Hermes got behind the car and prepared to push with all his might. The girl walked around the front and opened the driver's door to get behind the wheel. She pulled the shift into the Drive position and tapped gently on the gas pedal while turning the wheels out of the spot. Hermes gave a push and the car gently shifted out from in front of the fire hydrant. Once the front of the car was in the center of the street, the girl pulled the shift back into Park and got out. Hermes stood up and smiled at her.

"That was easier than I expected it to be," he told her, "Thank you so much. It's good to know there are some good kids out here on the holidays."

"I've got to go."

"Yeah, sure. I appreciate it," Hermes said to her, making like he was going to get into the car. At the last moment, he shifted his body sideways and clenched his hand over her mouth while his other arm wrapped around her waist, pulling her closer. She immediately squirmed against him, trying to escape. He held her tight and pulled her backwards towards the trunk of the car. While he was pushing the car out, he had popped the trunk open and bumped it open now. Then with one heave, he picked her up and dropped her into the roomy trunk. Then with speed, he slammed the trunk closed before she could scream for help.

He looked around and saw that the street was still dead silent. No one was outside or even looking from their windows. He took that as a good sign and took off before it was too late. What Hermes didn't notice was Emilio throwing the front door open in an attempt to save the daughter he had just seen kidnapped.

80

"Foster! Raghetti!" shouted Danny Hines. He ran into the squad room with Jacob and Enrique behind him. Everyone in the squad room dropped what they were working on and moved over to where Brett and Josh were. Even Chief Black came out of her office to see what the matter was. Enrique was sat down, and Brett looked over his wrists and his face.

"What the hell happened?" Brett asked.

"Where has he been?" Josh asked.

"Why didn't you come straight to the police?" Danica asked.

"Okay," Black interrupted, "Everyone settle down. Let's allow them to sit for a minute before we all question him."

"He showed up at the office," Jacob tried to explain, "He was kept captive by Hermes."

"You saw his face?" Brett asked, excited.

"Yes, I know what he looks like now," Enrique answered faintly. Kylee left the room to get him some water and Russell grabbed the first aid kit from the locker room. The others backed up a little to give them room.

"If we got someone who can draw, would you be able to describe him?" Chief Black asked. Enrique nodded. She turned to Luis and asked him to go check to see if Lucky was still in the lab. Luis headed out into the hall and ran to get the tech.

"How'd you escape?"

Enrique told them about freeing himself from the closet and then getting a ride to the law firm when he saw the bus outside. Brett was amazed to even see the boy there, let alone alive. He had almost believed that Donnelly had gotten to him. It was a relief that he wouldn't have to make the house visit to tell his parents the horrible news.

Josh looked over at Jacob and said, "Good job, councilor. We've got it from here."

"I'd like to stick around if that's okay. He is still my client."

"Yeah, no problem. Have a seat," he said offering his chair.

"I'll actually be right back. I've got to make a phone call."

"Try the break room. It'll be quieter."

"Thanks." Jacob began dialing Robin's place as he walked over to the break room. He would have to tell her the good news that would ruin the dinner plans they had, but he was sure she would understand.

"Do you remember where he kept you?" Brett asked.

"It was in Jersey City. There's an apartment building on the corner of Colden and Varick. He had me in an apartment on the second floor. I didn't notice what number. Sorry."

"Hey, that's more information than we normally get. Great job," Brett told him. He turned to the chief and asked her, "Do you mind if Josh and I go check out the apartment?"

"Take Bergen and Page for backup. You don't know what he'll have waiting for you if he's there."

Brett assured Enrique that those remaining there would take good care of him. Then he promised the teenager that he would find Hermes. Enrique smiled gently and thanked the detective. Josh, Lyndsey and Danica followed Foster out of the room.

Kylee and Russell had returned with the water and first aid kit, and Luis walked in with Lucky behind him. The lab tech had a laptop under his arm.

"Thanks for the help, Lucky," Chief Black said.

"Anything to help," he smiled back. He sat down at Brett's desk and turned to talk to Enrique, "Now just sit back and relax. I find that the more comfortable you are the better you'll be able to remember. Okay?"

"Okay," the teen replied. Lucky opened the program that he used to create accurate depictions of criminals and clicked on one part of the screen that opened a window that showed a blank head. To the right were small thumbnails of options.

"Let's start with the shape of his face. Was it round? Did he have a sharp chin? Or was his jaw wide?"

Enrique went through the thumbnails and examined each one to see which was closer to the shape of Hermes' face. Lucky then went through the options of noses, eyes, ears, mouth and hair. Within twenty minutes, they had a picture of Hermes' face.

"Does that remind you of any of our cops?" Black asked Russell and Kylee.

"No, but he does look kind of familiar," Russell said.

"Yes, he's no cop here but I've seen him before."

"Is there anything that may not seem right to you?" Lucky asked Enrique.

"Like I said, that looks like him. But whenever I saw him he was wearing that cap. I never saw what his hair was like."

"That's fine, Enrique," the chief assured him, "I'm sure that when we send it out to the all the police on patrol right now, someone should be able to recognize him. Lucky, can you submit that to the servers now?"

"Sure can. It'll take a minute to upload but all the cruisers will receive it in about five minutes."

"Here we come, fuckface," Kylee smiled. Then she noticed Enrique looking at her. "Oh, sorry."

81

Taking Luis Munoz Marin Boulevard all the way down to the end, Brett and Josh turned onto Grand Street, going north. The boulevard was named after the man who had been called the Father of Modern Puerto Rico. He was most known for being the first elected governor of Puerto Rico. Josh wondered aloud why a street in Jersey City, NJ was named after a foreign politician. Then Brett pointed out where they were. Most of the neighborhoods in Hudson County were predominately Hispanic.

Once they reached the corner Enrique had mentioned, the two pairs of detectives parked and headed into the building. A younger woman with a basket of laundry was exiting and allowed them access inside. They headed to the second floor and took a look at the doors. All the doors looked the same.

"Okay, let's split up and take a door each," Brett thought up. Each of the four chose one and knocked.

Russell placed his hand on Enrique's shoulder. The boy was exhausted from the day he had had. There was nothing he wanted more than to go home and sleep for days. The homicide detective was able to read him from the look in his eyes. He felt that the teenager didn't deserve what he had been through since he walked into that bus garage on Saturday.

"Hey, why don't you come kick back in the break room? There's a couch and a TV in there to keep you occupied. I'll go make a call to your parents to let them know that you're okay."

"Do you have anything to eat? He didn't feed me much."

"Would you mind a burger from one of the local places?"

"Anything is good."

"Okay, I'll have one of the officers downstairs grab some stuff for you."

"Thank you." Enrique got up and headed into the break room where Jacob was still on the phone.

Kylee picked up the ringing phone on Brett's desk while Russell went to get food. Upon answering it, she found that it was the desk sergeant.

"What's going on Danny?"

"I've got a kidnapping on the phone," he reported to her, "I thought from the name you might want to take it."

"What name?"

"Perez. Maritza Perez."

"You've got to be shitting me," Fernandez replied.

Danica and Josh's doors were answered by people. Danica's resident explained that she didn't socialize with the other people in the building. Josh showed the picture on his phone that had been sent to him a minute before. Brett and Lyndsey had gotten no response.

"Yes," the man talking to Josh told him, "I know that guy. He lives in that apartment. He pointed to the door that Lyndsey had knocked on.

"Are you sure?" Josh had to ask.

"Yeah, that's pretty dead on. Is there something going on?"

"Sir, I need to ask you to return inside and stay away from the door, please." The man did what he was told and went back inside. The four gathered around Hermes's door. They stood to the side and took out their guns, expecting all hell to break loose.

"Ready?" Brett asked the others. They all nodded, and he knocked on the door once more. "Police, open the door!" he shouted. The wait for a reply was long.

"Try the knob," Lyndsey said, "Maybe he's not back yet?"

Brett took hold of the knob and slowly tried turning it. The knob clicked and turned with his hand. The door opened slowly, and they found the main room dark as night. One after another they headed in. They spread out and turned on all the lights making sure that there was indeed no one in the apartment.

"Kitchen's clear."

"Bathroom's clear."

"Bedroom's clear and I've found where Enrique was kept."

The four gathered in the living room and looked around. They all noticed the same thing. Everything was white. The walls, the floor, the furniture and the couch were all white.

"This place looks like a sterile lab from a sci-fi horror movie," Josh said.

"You think we'll find any prints in here?" Danica wondered.

"Won't know until we try."

Brett felt his phone buzz in his pocket. He took it out and glanced at the screen. It read: HPD. He held a finger up in the air to ask the others to wait for a minute. He hit the speaker button and answered.

"Brett, it's Kylee. The Perez family just called the front desk. I've got bad news."

"What is it?"

"Looks like our boy decided to take their daughter in exchange for Enrique."

"Why?" asked Lyndsey.

"He's trying to get Enrique to keep quiet. It's a little too late for that," Josh figured.

"Are they still on the phone?"

"I've got them on hold right now."

"Okay, go back to them and let them know that Josh and I will be down there in a few minutes. Then go ask Wogle to send someone over to this address." Brett read her the address and then said, "Make sure they bring a finger printing case. I'll have the ladies stay here and keep an eye on the place until they get here."

"Gotcha. I'll see you later." Kylee hung up and Brett returned the phone back to his pocket.

"This is getting better and better," Josh said, sarcastically.

Enrique sat down next to Jacob who had just gotten off the phone with Robin. She told him that she would change quickly again and head down to meet him at the precinct. He thanked her and told her that he loved her. The teen sat next to him, with his head resting on the back of the couch and his eyes half open.

"Are you sure you're okay?" the lawyer asked.

"What I wouldn't give for an energy drink," the boy joked.

"I could go find you one if you want."

"No that's okay, the detective guy with the glasses and the really short hair went to get a burger for me."

"Good, then I'll veg out here with you. I've been helping your parents try and find you."

"How are they?"

"Worried out of their minds, but they were determined."

"My mother could convince a junkie to give up their dope if she tried." Jacob laughed. He looked over at the television and saw that the news had come on. He got up and walked over to it.

"I'm sure you could do without the boring news," he said to Enrique. He reached out to change the channel but froze when the teen yelled at him to stop. Jacob moved back from the TV and turned back.

"What's the matter?"

"Him!" Enrique yelled, pointing at the TV screen, "That's him! On the news!"

Jacob looked back at the TV and saw the video that was playing. There were several people on the screen and he wasn't sure who Enrique was pointing out.

"Which one?"

Enrique got up and ran over pointing out a specific person on the screen. "That guy! He's the one who kidnapped me."

"Are you positive?"

"Hell yeah," he said with confidence.

Jacob couldn't believe it. If Enrique was right, which Jacob believed he was, then shit was inches from hitting the fan.

82

Emilio was standing in the window, waiting for the police to show up when Brett and Josh arrived. They parked in front of the fire hydrant to keep the street cleared for passing traffic. Brett left the police card on the dashboard in the event any unknowing police stopped by while they were talking to the Perez family. He didn't like ignoring the rules, but time was of the essence.

"Why are they taking my kids?" Emilio said the moment they reached the door.

"Mr. Perez, Enrique is okay. He just showed up at the precinct with your lawyer. He informed us that the vigilante had taken him captive in order to keep him quiet about seeing his face. As for Maritza, I believe the reason he took her was that he was trying to keep Enrique from giving us a description of his face. Unfortunately, he's too late for that."

"Does this mean he'll kill her?"

"No, it's just that the reason he took her was leverage and that he doesn't have anymore. We know what he has planned so it's just a matter of time that he tries to accomplish the final part of all this and we'll be waiting."

"How long will it take for us to get her back?"

"We don't know right now. But let me show you this," Brett took out his phone and showed Emilio and Carmen the sketch that Enrique created with Lucky. "This is the man that Enrique says kidnapped him. This is the vigilante that shot the men at the gang meeting. He's also responsible for creating this gang war between the Jackals and the Latin Soldados. Does this look like the man that took Maritza?"

Emilio studied the phone's screen and nodded, "Yes, that looks like him. I can't be completely sure, it's dark out there."

"That's fine, I understand."

"What about the car?" Josh asked, "Could you describe it?"

"It was silver. It was one of those newer slick models."

"Was it two-door or four-door?"

"It had four doors. He threw her in the trunk and then took off fast. Too fast for me to chase after him."

"It's better that you didn't Mr. Perez, we don't know how dangerous he is. He could have been armed."

"Detectives," Carmen said, stepping forward, "Please, help us end this. We've done nothing wrong to anyone, we don't deserve this. Please bring her back." Her eyes became red and teary. Brett hated moments like this. The worst cases were when kids were involved. Fifty percent of the time, they were never returned to the parents safely. He couldn't bear to have that happen just three days from Christmas.

"Mrs. Perez, I promise you that I will do everything I can to make sure Maritza is brought home safely. We're very close to catching him now, thanks to your son. Just be ready for her to come home, okay?"

"Thank you, detectives. May God bless you for all that you do." Carmen stepped forward and wrapped her short arms around his muscular frame. He was taken by surprise but tried to hug her back in return.

"We'll get the description of the car out there so that all the patrols will be on the lookout for it. This should help us locate him faster," Josh told Emilio.

"You two get some rest and we'll have Enrique brought home very soon. He's looking forward to coming back. We just need to get a few more details that may help us in the search." Brett was once again interrupted by his phone. "Excuse me, please."

Josh stood, listening to Brett's side of the conversation, wondering who he was talking to.

"Hey. Yes. What? Wait, are you kidding? That can't be right, is he sure? Wow. This changes everything. Yeah, ok. We'll be right there." Brett hung up the phone and looked at the three who were staring back at him in suspense.

"What was that about?" Josh asked him.

"That was Kylee," he told Josh then explained to Emilio and Carmen, "She's one of our other detectives. She just said that Enrique just saw Hermes, the vigilante, on the news."

"What? What was he doing on the news?" Raghetti interrogated his partner. Brett continued to speak while still stunned.

"She never said, but she told me who he really is."

"Who?"

Brett divulged the name, which Emilio and Carmen did not recognize.

"Are you friggin' kidding me?" was all Josh could say.

83

Hermes had never realized how difficult it was to travel across the small town on the edge of the Hudson without hitting so many red lights or stop signs. The girl in the trunk banging and screaming for help did not help, either. He knew that he should have pulled over to gag and tie her down, but he was in a hurry. The one plus was that he had already removed the car's emergency escape tab before taking Enrique from the neighbor's backyard.

He turned onto Washington and drove an entire block before another red light stopped him. He sighed in frustration and hoped that the banging was muffled enough to not be heard by people walking along the sidewalk. Staring at the red light, he willed it to change, but nothing happened. Instead, something he hadn't hoped for, did.

A police cruiser pulled up next to him at the light. He cursed to himself and tried to ignore it. He couldn't believe his luck. The light was not changing. He wondered if the light was even working at all.

A car honked, and he jumped, looking in the rearview mirror to see if the girl had escaped from the trunk. There was no one behind him. He looked over at the cruiser and saw the officer looking in his direction. The officer had a poker face and Hermes was not sure if he had noticed him and was looking to get him to pull over, so Hermes rolled the window down and smiled at the officer.

"Yes, sir?" the vigilante said.

"Hey, I saw you on the news. That was crazy," the officer said with a smile.

"Yes, it was even worse being there."

"I'm sure it was!" the cop laughed. Hermes relaxed a little knowing that he was safe once again. Then the cop looked down at his computer screen that rested between the two seats. Frowning, he hit a few keys and hit the switch for the lights on top of the cruiser. *Damn*, Hermes thought. *He knows.*

The cop looked over, nodded and drove through the red light headed somewhere else. Hermes sat there, surprised and relieved. He knew that he would have been forced to fight with the officer if he had tried to arrest him. Even though he would not have wanted to, the plan was too important.

The light had finally turned green and Hermes pressed down on the gas pedal and drove through the intersection. He continued on for a few blocks, listening to the thumps and thuds coming from the back of his car. After a few blocks, the noise began to irritate him. He decided to have a bit of fun. Making sure that no one was behind him still, he stomped on the brakes, sending Maritza rolling forward into the back of the rear seats. He heard her hit with a thud and smiled. She stopped banging.

Hermes made a few turns and then pulled over. He took a look around and made sure that the police were nowhere in the area. It was time for the final act. This was the most important because it was all him this time.

Now that Donnelly was taken out by Julio, he needed to finish the job and take out Julio. This was dangerous as Julio was a smart man. That was the only reason he was never overthrown by one of his own. No one knew what he was thinking, and no one knew what his plans were until they were completed.

He got out of the car and went around to the trunk. He pushed the button on his keychain and the trunk opened with a pop. Maritza was silent. He pulled up the hatch and looked down at the girl. She shivered in fear and had pushed herself further back.

"Listen," he told her, "I'm not going to hurt you, but I will hurt your family if you talk to the police about me. You will get out of this alive. I just need to go take care of something. You'll be parked on a side street, but I want you to remain quiet until you hear the police or until I get back to the car. Do you understand?"

Maritza nodded at the stranger, not wanting to ask why he was doing this even though she knew it had to do with what happened to her brother. There was one thing she needed to know, though.

"Is Enrique okay?"

Hermes paused, unsure of how to answer that now that he was on the loose and God knows where.

"Yes, and he will continue to be fine as long as you do as I say. Now behave and be quiet." He closed the trunk and got back into the car.

"Now or never," he told himself. Then Ronald Price, son of police commissioner Donald Price, drove the car around the corner and onto Julio's block.

84

Brett and Josh returned to the chaos that was the squad room. Everyone had just learned who Hermes was and people were shouting over others, and running back and forth, trying to get organized. Josh looked over at Brett and they wondered what they had walked into. That was when Chief Black stood up on a desk and yelled for everyone to stop what they were doing.

"I'm sorry but this is not the way we do things. We need a little order and I'm going to provide that. When you hear your name and your job, go do it professionally. Now, I know it's a shock to all but any information in this room right now stays in this room until we've captured Ronald Price. I don't want the press getting word of this until its official.

"Let's start with a photo of him and a description of the car he drives. I want that out there to every cop in this town and the surrounding ones in the event that he's running. Next, Bergen and Page, what did the search of his apartment bring?"

"Unfortunately, nothing," Lyndsey was disappointed to say, "The FBI examiner that Captain Wogle brought in to help found no prints. He must have wiped down the apartment before we arrived."

"Fine, Foster and Raghetti, what have you found out from the Perez family?"

"The father saw him take the daughter," Brett explained, "And he confirmed it was him from the sketch that Lucky made with the kid. We've got him on kidnapping at the least."

"We need to find the car," Russell added, "He's most likely got any weapons and evidence on him. Maybe he has some kind of tracking device placed on it in case it was stolen."

"Good idea, Emerson. You and Fernandez look into that. Orlando, I want you to use your contacts in the Latin Soldados to keep track of Julio Jimenez. We know that Ron is targeting him, so I want to know if he makes an attempt. Finally, Bergen and Page, I want you two to contact DOT and see if they can keep track of all the local traffic cameras. Maybe we can catch him driving around. Anyone who finds him, try to take him in easy. No roughing up, understood?"

"Excuse me, Chief," Josh called out, raising his hand.

"Raghetti, this isn't school. Put your hand down."

"Sorry, but has Commissioner Price been notified?" Black looked down. She had been trying to delay it for as long as she could, but she knew that Donald should hear it from her and not some rookie cop. Sometimes, she hated her job.

"I'll be handling that. The rest of you get out there and look for him. Now go."

Jacob pushed his way over to Brett and Josh. Enrique had been sitting in the break room for the past thirty minutes alone after he pointed out Ron Price. Jacob had been keeping an eye on him while the police were gathering intel.

"Hey, is there anything I can do to help?" he asked the two detectives.

"You worked with him, right?" Josh asked him.

"We worked in the same firm, but I didn't really know him."

"What about your bosses? Would they know anything that might help?"

"I can call them and see if you want."

"Wouldn't hurt," Raghetti said.

Jacob called the main office line and then pushed Delgado's extension. He knew that if anyone was still there, it would be Chris. After the third ring, Delgado did answer.

"Hey Chris, it's Jacob. I need your help if you have a minute."

"What is it about?"

"I'm trying to get a hold of Ron. I think he may have accidentally taken one of my case folders. Do you have any way of contacting him?"

"Of course, I do," he said, "Give me a moment and I'll find his number." Jacob nodded to the two and gave a thumbs up. Brett scooped a pen of a desk nearby and handed it to the lawyer.

"Ok," Delgado said, "Here it is." Chris read off the cell phone number that he had on file.

"Thanks. See you in the morning," Jacob said before hanging up.

"Good thinking," Foster said. Jacob handed over the number and Brett dialed it.

Christine Black sat down at her desk and made sure her door was closed before she called Don Price. As the phone rang, she tried to think of how she was going to give the news to him. She knew that if it were her son, she would be devastated and would wonder what she had done to make him that way. Before she could decide, the commissioner answered.

"Christine, tell me you've got good news on this vigilante case," he said. She could hear the happy tone in his voice. This was going to be harder than she thought.

"Don, I have something to tell you and I need you to sit down for this, please."

Price could sense the trouble in her voice and it sent a shiver though his bones. "What is it, Christine?"

"The teenager that survived the shooting on Saturday was brought in this evening."

"Oh no, is he dead? I'll be more than happy to talk to his parents."

"No, Don. The boy is fine. It's just that he finally was able to identify the vigilante."

"Christine, that's no reason to be so morbid. What is it? Please tell me it's not one of our own that went vigilante."

"It's worse. It's Ronald, Don."

"What? That's impossible. Is this kid on drugs? Ron couldn't have done what this maniac has done."

"That's where the evidence points. We're doing everything we can to see if it really is, but he's also kidnapped the boy's sister. The father saw the whole thing."

"No, I refuse to believe that. You get him to look again. Ron would never do anything like this. Christine, get your men to go find the real vigilante and don't call me until you have him in custody." Don slammed the phone down, nearly breaking it. Christine Black hung up her phone gently and then turned to open the bottom drawer on her desk. She pulled out the small bottle of red wine that she kept hidden away for moments like this.

"Dammit," she said before taking a drink from the bottle.

Ron Price sat in the car outside of Julio's ruined home, trying to build up the nerve to go in and end the legacy of crime in Hoboken. The phone beside him had rung four times already. He knew now that the police were aware of him. Why else would a homicide detective call him at almost 9PM? He just let it go to voice mail. Ron turned back and took hold of the two guns that he had resting on the back seat. There were several clips that he packed into his jacket. There was no way that he would run out of ammunition if there were more Soldados in there than he had expected.

The phone rang again, and he glanced down at it. It was his father. Now he knew that the police knew and were after him. But was his father leading the witch hunt? He picked it up and hit TALK. Then he allowed his father to begin the conversation.

"Ronald? Are you there?"

"What?" he said in a dead tone.

"The police think that you're the vigilante. I told them that they were insane."

"Cut the crap, Dad. They're right. Just accept it."

"But why? What would cause you to do this?"

"Do you really have to ask that? Then you really have buried your head in the sand since Mom died."

"What does this have to do with your mother?"

"It has everything to do with her! When we learned that she had cancer, where were you? Out saving the world like the great cop you were. I tended to her while she withered away. I watched the life go out of her eyes that day. And how did you cope with it? You dug yourself more into the job. You threw me to the side. And for what? So, you could put this city first with your plans of a better world. Meanwhile, I tried to show you that I was here, that I could be just as good as you. I was valedictorian in law school. I aced the bar and got in with one of the greatest firms in the Tri-State area, but that wasn't enough for you to notice me because you were too busy being the big police commissioner. You even came up with that lame End to Crime initiative. That's gone over *so* well! Guess what?

I've figured out how to really end crime. No legal ties, no red tape. Just complete effectiveness. How did I do, Dad? The son has finally surpassed the father. I've rid this town of more criminals than you or your group ever have."

"But you killed Detective Doyle," Don cried, "You killed one of our men. That makes you just as bad as the men you killed."

"I had no intention of shooting him, but I knew he'd never let me leave that alley. I was just getting started. I got rid of one of the gangs already. Vinnie Donnelly and his Jackals are no more. You're welcome."

"Ron, please, just give yourself up. We can talk about this."

"Too late, Dad. I've got to finish this now. For Mom. For me. For this town that you love so much. There's just one more vermin to exterminate. Then I'll give myself up." Ron hung up before he even said goodbye. His father didn't deserve a goodbye. He had never said goodbye to his mother.

Ron got out of the car with the two guns. *Showtime*, he thought.

85

Julio smashed the small butt of the cigar he had just finished into the ash tray and finished his work. Even though the holiday was right around the corner, there was no rest for the wicked. He still had to keep the customers happy. Even if he was being hunted by a mystery man bent on taking down the empire that he had worked so hard to build.

But the one thing that made him smile right now was knowing that Vincent Donnelly and his gang were no more. They were what had been preventing him from expanding. With both Vinnie and Liam gone, the Jackals had no real leader to guide them into the new year. He knew that the lackeys had no sense of business like he did, and the new year would bring nothing but opportunities for him and his men. Christmas had come early.

A knock on the door caused Julio to look up from his laptop. Ryan Mendoza stood in the doorway, waiting to be allowed in. Julio smiled and waved the Soldados member into the den.

"Ryan, please come in. I'm glad you're here. I was hoping to talk to you a little more about what we discussed last night."

"Okay, but I just want to let you know what was going on with the renovation schedule and the funeral home."

"Yes, absolutely. Sit and tell me." Ryan sat down in the chair across from Julio.

"The funeral home has scheduled the funeral for Friday morning. I gave them the request for the lilies to be placed around her casket during the wake and they said they would be able to have that ready."

"Good, Abuela always loved lilies. Especially during Easter."

"And the renovation company that you suggested are unable to start the repairs until right after Christmas because they're backed up right now."

"Give them another call back and advise them that we are willing to pay double their price in order to be bumped up on the wait list."

"I'll call them first thing in the morning."

"Thank you, Ryan. This is why I selected you above all the others."

"Thank you, Julio. I can show you that you chose the best candidate for the job. I won't let you down."

"So, let's talk about what I have planned," Julio started to say. Then the phone besides him rang. He shook his head at the interruption but answered the phone anyway.

"Good evening," he said.

"Julio Jimenez? It's detective Luis Orlando calling."

"What a wonderful surprise, detective. Do tell me that you're calling to inform me that this vigilante mess is over."

"I'm sorry but it's not. We believe that he's actually coming for you. Possibly tonight. Is there somewhere that you can go for the time being?"

"Detective Orlando, I just had my house shot up, several of my friends and employees murdered and lost my grandmother. Now you're telling me that one man is coming to kill me? Please. The security and amount of protection I have is more than enough for just one man."

"You don't understand," Luis said, "He's clever and he's got nothing to lose. We know who he is, and he is aware that we're looking for him. He may not care if he's walking into a trap. Actually, he's probably expecting it."

Julio laughed, "I have dealt with men like that before. I assure you, detective, this man will never get the best of me. I've got men who have been trained by the best. Do you hear any worry in my voice? No, because I am a man who does not worry. I am a man of action. Now, you can either say goodbye and goodnight, or you can come here to remove his remains from my house after I protect myself. But while I have you on the phone, I do have something important to speak to you about."

Julio paused when he heard the doorbell ring. He placed his hand over the mouthpiece and asked Ryan, "Could you please have someone answer that? I still need to talk to you." Ryan nodded and got up while Julio returned to his conversation with Luis Orlando.

Ryan stepped out of the den and hollered up the stairs for someone to answer the door. Ricardo, one of the new and young members of the gang, came to the top of the stairs and told Ryan that he would. Ricardo waked down the stairs and looked himself over in the cracked mirror located to the right of the front door. He always tried to look good every moment of every day. It was all about the ladies for him. Ricardo had a lot to learn, but for now he figured it was best to have fun before he got older and had to be more responsible.

The doorbell rang again, and Ricardo rolled his eyes. Some people were just so impatient.

"Hold on, I'm coming," he called to the person just outside. Ricardo opened the door and was met with a gunshot to the head. Ron Price stepped over his dead body and into the home of Julio Jimenez.

86

Ron made sure that his clips were fully loaded before ringing the doorbell. He had taken out the two outside guards quietly with a sharpened steak knife from his apartment. He had hesitated to kill the first guard, but he had closed his eyes and plunged the knife into the side of the guard's neck anyway. After the first kill, he felt alive. It was a feeling that he had never felt before. The second one was easier. There was no hesitation then.

Ron had waited on the side of the front door, in case they were expecting him. The moment the door opened, he shoved the gun into the small opening and fired one bullet into the face of the gang member who opened it. The shot was deafening inside the echoing front entrance. He knew that it would alarm everyone in the house, so he rushed in and scoped the entrance area as quickly as he could. Finding a small inlet where a coat closet lay, he ducked inside there and waited for them to come. He would have to be quick to keep from allowing Julio to escape from the back.

Two Soldados members came running from different directions. Neither had seen him tucked away, but both had seen their fallen comrade.

"Oh shit," the thin one said, "Ricardo's dead! Julio! Someone shot Ricardo!"

"Shut up, estupido!" the other shouted in a whispering voice, "You're going to give away where he is. Look around." The thin one stepped over the body of Ricardo and looked outside to see if whoever had killed his comrade was still around. Ron took advantage and took out the other Soldados. Then, before the thin one could pull his head back in from outside, Ron shot him in the chest. Three down, and who knows how many more to go.

Ron stayed low to the ground as he ran across the entrance and peeked into a room on the left side. He found himself extremely lucky - inside was Julio's den. And behind the wide desk was the leader of the Latin Soldados, himself. Julio smiled gently and stood up. He raised his hands up to shoulder height.

"Good to finally meet you," Julio said, "Ron Price, isn't it?"

"Who told you?" Ron asked.

"A plump little bird," he replied.

"You know what this means."

"Yes, I do, but I need to ask. How have I wronged you that you would do this to me and my men?"

"You exist."

"Surely there has to be more. There's a little old man down the street. He exists. Are you going to shoot him next?"

"That's not the same."

"Well, of course not. This is why I asked you. What did I do to you to bring you to this savage plan of yours?"

"It's because of you that my mother died without her husband by her side."

"Correct me if I'm wrong but your mother died of cancer, right?"

"Yes, how did you know?"

"Although I am thought of as a criminal, I'm not a monster. I sent flowers to your father as a sign of respect when she died. I have the receipt tucked away to prove it. What you and most others fail to realize is that at heart, I am a businessman. The only difference between me and those on Wall Street or sitting at the top of a skyscraper is that as they hide their illegal activities, where as I do not. I'm not a sneak. You could say I'm actually quite honest. Now, I do understand your anger. I'm sure that my activities kept your father busy as your mother was dying and I apologize for that. I really do. But don't you think your anger is being misplaced? It's not like I twisted your father's arm to chase after me at the time. Am I right?"

"You're not going to brainwash me into thinking that you're all goody two shoes," Ron told him, "both reptiles and devils have forked tongues."

"Very true. And here's another thing that's true. You can do all you want to me. Kill me, behead me, shoot me and bury me in the ground, never to return. But you know what happens to the empty hole that I once filled? That will be filled in by another. And they'll keep the business going. And if you kill them too, someone else will come along and jump at the chance to do what I do. You can't stop crime without stopping the human race."

"I will do what I have to in order to clean this town up to the way it used to be."

"Even kill me and my men?"

"Yes," Ron said outright.

"Just like Detective Doyle?"

"What happened to Detective Doyle wasn't supposed to occur. But I knew that he would have never let me leave that alley freely."

"Just a matter of having to break a few eggs to make an omelette, I take it?"

Ron looked at him, trying to figure out what game Julio was playing with him. Or was he just delaying the inevitable?

"It's over now, Julio. Time to finish this once and for all." Oh, one last thing, in regards to my last comment, I wasn't quite right on the whole honesty bit. Do say hello to Detective Luis Orlando." Julio pointed to the phone on his desk. Ron noticed that the phone receiver was off the hook and resting on the desk.

"Ron? It's Luis. This isn't worth it, man," said the speaker on the phone.

Julio had played him into admitting everything while the police were on the phone, listening. Ron raised the gun and fired once.

87

The dimly lit street was silent as a cemetery. Brett and Josh pulled up to the home of Julio Jimenez. Foster thought that the silence was a bad sign. Lyndsey and Danica pulled up right behind them. They all gathered around the front yard. Josh pointed out the dead man lying in the shadows of the tree that was located right on the edge of Julio's property.

"Here's Price's car, too," Josh told them. He placed a hand on the vehicle and patted it.

"This is not good," Brett said, "I don't like the quiet. Either there's someone waiting in there for us or it's all over."

"What if Julio's talking Price's ear off?" Danica asked, "You know how he loves to hear his own voice."

THUMP

"Or maybe Jimenez talked him to death," added Lyndsey.

"Did you hear that?" Josh asked them.

"Hear what?"

"I heard a noise."

"I don't hear anything."

THUMP THUMP

"There it is again," Josh said. He leaned over the trunk and heard a whimper from inside. "Hang on." Josh walked around to the driver's side and opened the door. He looked down and found the trunk release latch on the floor to the side of the seat. He pulled it up and the trunk popped open. Brett opened it all the way and found Maritza shivering inside.

"Maritza!" he called, reaching in for her. She recognized the cop and reached up to wrap her arms around him.

"Oh God, I thought he was going to kill me. Is he gone?"

"Don't worry, we have you now. You're safe. Hey Bergen, can you get her in one of the cars and turn up the heat."

"Where's Enrique?" she asked.

"He's safe," Brett explained, "He's at the station with your parents. They're waiting for you."

"Come on over here. You need to keep warm." Lyndsey guided the girl over to her car and let her in the front seat. She started the car and turned up the heat and the radio.

"I'll call in EMTs for her," Danica said, dialing her phone.

Josh's phone buzzed at the same time. It was Luis.

"Hey what's going on?"

"Ron's at Julio's," he told him.

"Yeah, we know we're outside."

"Yeah, but he's with Julio now. They were talking, and I heard the whole thing. Got it on tape, too. Julio got him to admit to killing the gang members and Doyle."

"Good job. So, what's going on now?"

"I don't know. He didn't really say much about if he was heavily armed or what. I heard a gun go off and the line dropped. I'm thinking he shot the phone."

"Okay, we've got it from here."

"Be careful," Orlando told his friend, "He sounds out of it."

Josh thanked him and hung up. Then he looked at the others and said, "We've got trouble."

Amanda Fenton crept over the fence into Julio's backyard and slowly walked along the shadowed side of the yard, around the inground pool and up to the back entrance. Unaware of those in front of the house, she was there for one reason, revenge. There was no reason that Ronald Price should have all the fun tonight. She wanted the two men that were inside the home. One had killed her father on purpose while the other had killed her half brother by accident. They were both scum and deserved to die.

Fenton took hold of the knob and pulled it ever so gently towards her. The door opened without a sound. Inside she heard movement. She slid in head first, making sure that there was no one near. The door led into the kitchen. It was dark, but she could see with the light coming through the doorway from the other end of the kitchen. There was no one there. Once she was fully inside, she closed the door but left the latch undone so that she could slip out quickly and silently.

A noise came from further inside the house. She could hear someone dragging something or someone up the stairs. *Great*, she thought. It would be more difficult to get close to them without being seen, but she wasn't leaving until she got what she came for: blood.

88

"Get up and walk," Ron scolded Julio. He was pulling the gang leader up the stairs to the second floor of the house. He wanted some space between him and the police when they showed up. He would be able to hear them making their way up the stairs before they got too close.

Annoyed that the police had heard everything that he had said through the phone, he had shot the phone. The shot had surprised Julio and he jumped back in defense. Ron took advantage of it and grabbed Julio, pulling him out from behind the desk.

"Let's go," he told him, "It's only a matter of time now before they show up."

The surprise had cut his time dramatically. Ron wanted to savor the moment he had with Julio. Now he would have to just kill him off and escape. But he wanted to at least make sure he had some time before they were on him.

Julio stumbled on the top step and fell forward, almost taking Ron down with him. He placed the gun's barrel on the back of Julio's head. Julio froze.

"Stop playing around and get your ass up into the bedroom. NOW."

"Can't we just discuss this like gentlemen?"

"You're no gentleman, Julio. You're slime. Better yet, you're the frothy film on the edge of slime."

"Now you're just being mean, Ronald."

Ron had had enough and yanked Julio to his feet by his slick hair. Julio howled in pain and grabbed at his head. Price waved the gun in the gang leader's face and Julio stopped moving, covering his face with his hands.

"Okay, okay, just don't shoot me in the face." Julio stopped fighting back. He was guided into the bedroom chosen by Ron Price and was tossed to the bed. "Now what?"

"Now the fun begins." He took a pair of cuffs from one of his pockets and tossed it on the bed next to Julio. He pointed the gun to it and said, "Cuff yourself to the headboard."

"Isn't that a little kinky?" Julio said, mostly trying to get a rise out of the vigilante.

"Shut up and do it or I'll gag you, too."

Julio wrapped the cuffs through a hole in the headboard and closed each one around each of his wrists. Once he was done he held his hands up and wondered what was next but didn't say a word. Ron leaned over and pulled a knife from his boot. Then he smiled and took a step towards the bed. That's when he heard one of the steps on the stairs creak.

Josh and Lyndsey quietly went in first. There wasn't a sound to be heard other than the whistle of the wind coming in from the front door. Josh pointed over to the den. Lyndsey nodded, and they crept over, pushing themselves up against the wall near the doorway. Josh held up one finger, then two and finally three. Lyndsey swung in around the corner and into the den, ducking down with the gun out in front of her. Josh came in behind her and checked the right side. One of the Soldados was coming out of a cabinet in the corner. Lyndsey and Josh aimed at him and watched as he got out and brushed himself off. He had no idea that they were there until he looked up.

"Yo!" he said, surrendering immediately.

"Where are they?" Josh asked.

"They went upstairs," he told them without hesitation.

"Get your ass out of here and do it quietly."

The Soldados nodded and ducked out of the den and out through the front door to where Brett and Danica were waiting with the EMT that had just arrived.

"Doesn't get any more fun than that," Raghetti joked to Lyndsey.

"I'm sure it could," she said, smiling at him.

"We still on for dinner once this is all over?"

"I never go back on a promise."

"Anywhere specific you'd like to go?"

"Surprise me."

"Okay, you asked for it, though."

"If you take me to Johnny Rockets, I swear I will dump your milkshake all over you and then beat you with the glass it came in."

"Well, if you're going to feisty like that," Josh said, leaving it hanging in the air. She shook her head and followed him to the stairs.

Josh took lead and took the first step onto the outside of the stair. He had learned the trick in police academy. The outside is stronger because it is attached to the foundation and less likely to make noise. He turned back to Lyndsey and pointed to his foot to show her where to follow. She gave him a thumbs up and he climbed to the next step, being as quiet as possible.

They went one step at a time making sure that there was no noise from their footsteps. It was grueling, but he wanted to make sure that Ron wouldn't hear them. The closer they could get before he knew they were there, the better. They might be able to take him by surprise. As long as Ron didn't walk over to the stairs as they were making their way up, they would be fine, Josh hoped.

They were now halfway up the stairs and so far, so good, but it was taking too long. Josh wanted to just jump up the stairs and across the landing to wherever they were.

He took another step with success. Looking up, he saw that he was almost able to peer up onto the landing. If he could make the next few steps he would be able to see the second floor.

His foot on the next step, he gently placed his weight down. The stair creaked under the sole of his shoe. Josh cringed and cursed to himself. They were so close, and he had made a noise. He looked back at Lyndsey, who threw him an angry look. He shrugged his shoulders in apology. Then he turned back and looked up. There was no one at the top of the stairs. He softly breathed a sigh of relief and moved up the next step. He was able to look at the landing now.

As he lifted his head, he saw something go flying over it, hit the wall at the top of the staircase and continue bouncing down the stairs like a tennis ball. It hit each stair until it came right at him. Then he saw that it wasn't a ball.

"Shit," he told Lyndsey, "Grenade!"

89

Turning around and thinking as quickly as he could, Raghetti wrapped his arms around Lyndsey's torso and rolled her over the edge of the railing to the floor below. He twisted her around as they fell, protecting her and making sure that he hit the floor first. Brett would later tell him that he was proud that his partner was making some progress in being a better man. Josh would later be proud of himself, too, but he would never admit it.

Josh's shoulder hit the floor first, popping his arm from its socket. He gritted his teeth through the pain and lost his breath when Lyndsey's slim, yet athletic frame landed on him.

"Duck," he told her, and they remained on the floor, tucked against the side of the staircase near the entrance to the kitchen. They listened to the grenade bounce off several steps, making its way down to the bottom.

"Why the hell isn't it going off?" Bergen asked him.

Before he could answer, the grenade hit a step and exploded. Wood fragments shot out in every direction. The sound of the blast woke the entire neighborhood and caused both Lyndsey and Josh to lose their hearing for a matter of minutes.

Outside, Brett and Danica ducked at the sound of the blast, thinking they were in danger of losing their partners.

"Lyndsey!" Danica yelled at the house.

"Stay here," Brett told the EMT. Then he and Page ran for the front door. Once they reached it, Brett disregarded protocol and continued into the house without assessing the situation inside.

"Josh! Josh!" he shouted. The smoke of the blast made it difficult to see anything. He looked over at Danica to see if she had found them. She shook her head, her eyes filling with tears. She had just celebrated the two of them being partners for the past 4 years. She had considered Lyndsey to be the sister she had always wanted, even through the annoying moments.

"Dammit Raghetti, tell me where you are!"

Brett then heard a cough. It was followed by an "ow." He headed into the house further, homing in on where he had heard the voice. He had almost tripped over the two of them before he noticed them on the floor. He helped Lyndsey up to her feet and Danica hugged her partner, happy to know that she was still alive. Brett reached out to help Josh up.

"Be gentle," Josh told him, "My shoulder popped out."

"That's what you get for rolling around on the floor in the middle of a war," Foster joked.

Fenton had not been ready for the grenade flying through the air. She was already upstairs in the bathroom on the other side of the landing, but she used the blast to make her move. She ducked and rushed from the bathroom into the bedroom where Julio and Ron had hidden in. Ron was not expecting anyone to enter the bedroom right after the blast and couldn't get the gun in his hand up fast enough. Amanda had hers, though.

"Don't move," she said. Her gun was aimed right at him. He stopped moving and stood still. An angry look appeared on his face. Amanda knew that it was because he was now unable to finish what he had started. She enjoyed that fact but didn't show it. From the corner of her eye she saw Julio smiling. "I wouldn't be smiling either if I were you, shit for brains."

"Now is that anyway to talk to a man in distress?" Julio said, showing her the handcuffs that had kept him on the bed. Fenton threw him a look that would have decapitated him if it could.

"So now what?" Ron Price finally asked.

The four detectives looked at the remains of the staircase. The bottom ten stairs had been obliterated. The first step was now five and a half feet from the floor they were standing on.

"How the hell do we get up there now?" Danica wondered.

"I'm wounded, you go," Josh said to Brett. Brett looked him and rolled his eyes.

"This is going to be trouble." Brett walked over to the edge of the hole in the stairs and tried to grab a hold of the stair. His fingertips touched the edge, but he was unable to get a grip on it.

"Is there another way up?" Lyndsey asked.

"Maybe a ladder in the basement?"

"No," Foster said, "We don't have the time. He could have killed Julio already." Brett looked up at the top of the stairs and had an idea. He wasn't the negotiator of the group and didn't want to force Ron's hand into doing something regretful, but he had to try.

"Ron? Ron Price?" he called out to the second floor, "This is Detective Brett Foster. We've met before, but you may not remember. Do you mind if we talk? You don't have to come to the stairs. Actually, it's better that you don't.

"I know that you're doing this for the good of the town but it's the wrong way to go about it. There's no coming back from killing a man. I don't like to admit it, but I know how it feels. I was forced to protect myself and I ended up shooting another person. You're not the same after that. It took me a long time to get over it.

"If you work with us, we can take Julio down the right way and we can help you with the charges that they'll be looking to put on you. What do you say? Why don't you come over and let's discuss this now?" Brett looked up and hoped that Ron would appear at the top of the stairs. He hoped that he would at least say something.

"Ron?"

Brett's question was answered with a gun shot.

90

"Are you okay?" Brett shouted up to the second floor, "Ron!" The four of them stood there, unable to check on anything. They all felt helpless. Brett cursed under his breath and took a few steps back. Josh looked at him and wondered if he was planning to jump for the steps.

"What are you doing?"

"Someone's got to get up there to see what the hell is going on. Now step back and give me some room." The women did as they were told but Josh took a step forward, blocking Brett's running path.

"No way. What if he's waiting for us up there to take us all down with him?"

"There's no need," said a voice above them. Brett and Josh looked up to see Ronald Price standing there. His hands were in the air and he was unarmed. "I'm giving myself up."

"Can you make it down?"

"I'll try, just please, don't shoot or hit me. I'm giving myself up." Ron climbed down the top half of the steps, keeping to the railing. Brett went over to the side and reached up to help the vigilante down. Ron lowered himself and Brett helped him the rest of the way. Once he was on the ground floor, Brett took Price's arms and cuffed his hands behind his back. He passed Ron to Lyndsey and Danica, who began to read him his rights and brought him out to their car. Josh looked over to Brett and saw his partner staring up at the second floor.

"You're not still thinking of going up there, are you?"

"I have to know," Brett told him.

"I'm sure Ron shot him. That's what he came to do."

"That's not enough." Brett placed a foot on the edge of the remaining part of the stairs and pushed off the wall, jumping up to grab the railing that was left. Getting a hold of it, Brett struggled to pull himself up and after a minute or two was able to climb the stairs up to the second floor.

He took out his gun and made his way around the landing. There was no one in the bathroom or the guest bedroom. But when he peered into the master bedroom he found Julio Jimenez. Julio's body was twisted oddly on the bed. Brett turned on the light in the room and walked closer. He kept the gun aimed on the figure that was not moving. *You could never be careful enough*, he thought.

Brett lowered his gun and took hold of the gang leader's chin, lifting his head. A stream of blood ran down Julio's face, originating from the hole in the center of his forehead. The hole was about the size of a bullet. The exit wound on the back of his head was much bigger.

Ronald Price had completed his plan. He had won.

91

Carmen and Emilio paced back and forth in the living room. They worried about Maritza. Why had the police not brought her home yet, they both thought. It was bad enough that Enrique was sitting there, staring at the floor, wishing that he had never gone with Wilfredo to that bus garage. He knew that it was his fault that his sister was in danger. No matter what his parents told him, he believed he had made the worst choice.

Jacob walked out of the kitchen with some hot chocolate he had made for the Perez family. He had wanted to do something for them in their time of need. He passed out the three mugs and Emilio took the bottle of beer tucked under his arm.

"Hot Chocolate doesn't do the job," he told Jacob.

"Thank you, Mr. Scott. You have been a Godsend to this family," Carmen told him, smiling through the stress.

"It's the least I can do for you," he replied.

Jacob looked out the bay window and into the street. There was nothing out there but darkness and silence. Just as he was about to turn back to the family, he saw a car heading down the street. He stopped to watch it. The car came to a stop in front of the house. Emilio and Carmen took notice and watched as the passenger door and the back door of the car opened. Both Lyndsey and Maritza emerged from the vehicle.

"Mari!" Carmen screamed with joy. Enrique finally looked up from the floor and saw that everyone else was looking outside. He stood up and saw his sister coming to the house. He smiled and thanked God in silence for bringing his sister home to them.

Enrique ran for the door and opened it without caring how hard it hit the wall. He ran onto the porch, shoeless, and hugged his sister. It had been the first time in years that he had done so, but it was about time that he did. Carmen and Emilio followed and joined in the hug. Jacob greeted Lyndsey on the side.

"Did they get him?" he asked her.

"Yeah," she said, "He gave himself up. After killing Jimenez."

Jacob dropped his head in disappointment. He had hoped that they would have been able to stop him from doing so. Too many people had died as it was. One more just put it over the top for him.

"Could you give me a ride back to the precinct?"

"Sure, we're headed back there now."

The detective and the lawyer left the family in their embrace. Enrique spoke as the car pulled away.

"It's all over now," he told them, "We'll be okay."

Brett took a drink from his coffee that Luis had brought them. Josh sat in the back of one of the ambulances having his shoulder tended to. An hour after the attack on Julio's house, the street was a party of police and onlookers. There were at least a dozen police cruisers and a handful of ambulances in the street, blocking access in and out.

"Hell of a night, huh?" Luis asked with a smile.

"Fuck you, Orlando," Josh called out from inside the ambulance.

"I second that," Brett said, "But thanks for the coffee."

"Looks like I miss the best part," said Amanda Fenton, from behind Luis. The two detectives looked over at her and nodded.

"You certainly did," Foster reported. He gave her a cliff note's version of the night.

"Well, I hope I was of some help."

"You did what you could for us and I appreciate it." Brett held out his hand and she shook it.

"It was the least I could do to help bring my partner's killer to justice. And again, I'm sorry for the loss of your partner, Detective Orlando."

"I'm definitely going to miss that old grump."

"I leave you gentlemen to your celebration. I'll be checking out of the hotel in the morning. The funeral for Tom will be right after Christmas if you're interested in coming. You're all more than welcome."

"Will do," Foster said.

"See you, Amanda," Josh said.

"Later, Ketchum," Luis said.

Amanda stopped and looked over at Orlando, shocked by his comment. She quickly recovered, nodded to him and walked away. Chief Black said hello to her as she left the area in a hurry.

"What the hell was that about?" Brett asked Luis.

"I'll tell you about it later." Luis replied, still watching Amanda walk away. He was still trying to figure out if Julio was telling him the truth about Amanda's past before he was interrupted by Ron.

92

Unsure of why they placed him in an interrogation room, Ron Price sat at the table. The cuffs around his wrists were linked to the chain bolted to the concrete floor. Ron wondered if there was anyone staring in behind the mirror. He sat there for several minutes before the door to the room opened. Jacob Scott walked in. He avoided contact at first and placed a pen and pad onto the table in front of him. He took off his suit jacket and placed it over the back of his chair.

"What is this, Jacob?" he asked.

Jacob continued to prepare himself before saying anything. Once he was, he sat down and looked Ron in the eyes.

"Ron."

"What?"

"What the hell were you thinking?"

"I'm sure you'll read all about it later. So, wait until then."

"Come on, really. What did you think you were going to accomplish with all this?"

"Exactly what I did. I helped clean up the city. Because of me there are no more gangs threatening the families that live here. Is that what you want to hear? Or would you rather swim through my head. Because that comes with a price. One that you could never pay."

"I spoke to Delgado. He's planning to drop you like a stone to keep you from leaving a black mark on the firm. I, on the other hand, thought you deserved a chance, but I can't help you if you don't let me."

"Then I guess you're wasting your time then, Mr. Scott."

Jacob looked at Ron with disappointment. "You know, you're acting like a child. I'm leaving, but I'll give you some advice, my treat. Eventually you'll need to grow up because you're playing with the big boys now. And take any help that is provided to you. Because if you don't, then one day, you'll need it and it won't be there." Jacob stood up, took his things and walked out of the room, slamming the door behind him.

Ron sat there, fuming. He waited for a cop to come and bring him down to the holding cell. There, he was given his own cell for his protection. He sat in it all night, thinking about two things that he couldn't figure out. The first was why Amanda Fenton had let him go. The second was if anyone else would learn that he never pulled the trigger that killed Julio Jimenez.

EPILOGUE

MERRY CHRISTMAS TO ALL.

Jacob Scott walked into the squad room on Christmas Eve and looked around for Brett Foster and Josh Raghetti. He found Brett at his desk filling out paperwork. Making his way through the others in the room, he knocked on Brett's desk and the detective looked up.

"Hey, how's it going?" Brett asked.

"Good now. How's the paperwork?"

"As good as paperwork will ever be, which is crappy."

"I just wanted to stop by and give you and Detective Raghetti personal thanks from me and the Perez family. Mrs. Perez gave me these to give to you." Jacob handed over a wide Tupperware container. Brett opened it up to see a selection of different Christmas cookies.

"Wow, that's a lot."

"You should see the container she gave me."

"I will accept these cookies, but please let her know that we are just doing our jobs."

"Where is Detective Raghetti?"

"Oh, he's out on a dinner date."

"Well, just give him my thanks. I have to head back to the firm, there's a surprise party that's going to happen in an hour." The party was for Kristie Marks. Hoffmann had used his contacts to learn about Kristie's bar exam score without having to wait for several months. He told Delgado and Jacob that she had passed with flying colors and he wanted to welcome her to the firm as their new lawyer.

"Merry Christmas!" Brett said to Jacob as he left. He looked down at the cookies and closed the container. He decided to bring them back to Angie's now that she and Tamara were back. In the past 24 hours, he had decided that he would give her the gift that she had been hoping for. He was going to tell her that he wanted to move in with her. It was time to become serious about their relationship. And he knew that Tamara would love to have him there.

"Okay, so there's mistletoe somewhere on my body and you have to find it and then kiss the body part it's on," Kylee told Russell as she pulled him past Brett's desk and towards the bathroom. Russell smiled and shrugged his shoulders at Brett. Foster shook his head and laughed.

Josh guided Lyndsey down the sidewalk while covering her eyes with a blindfold. The two of them had gotten dressed for a night that Josh had planned all on his own. He wanted to not only impress Lyndsey, but he wanted her to feel special.

"Josh, if I fall I will beat you with these heels."

"Don't worry, even with one arm, I'll still catch you."

The man at the door saw that Josh had his arm in a sling and opened it for the both of them. The EMT had been able to pop the shoulder back in but the doctor had advised him to take it easy for the next few days.

"Okay, you can take the blindfold off," Josh told her. Lyndsey removed the blindfold and looked around. Her mouth opened wide in surprise.

"Is this Alicia's?" she asked him. Alicia's was a famous ritzy restaurant that was the perfect spot for any romantic dinner date in Hoboken. Josh had been given a heads up from Danica that Lyndsey had always wanted to eat there but could never meet a guy that would go to those lengths.

Josh led her to their table, located in the back. He helped her sit down and then sat down as well. On the table were two glasses of champagne. He held his up and waited for her. She clinked her glass against his.

"To tonight being the first of many lovely dates," he said.

"You keep this up and you'll get that wish," Lyndsey smiled.

A young man walked into the precinct and made his way through, heading to the stairs. He had dressed himself in preppy clothes to make himself look harmless, even though he hated the clothes. Once he reached the stairs he had realized that it did make him invisible. No one had even said anything to him.

He headed down the stairs as he was coached and turned right towards the holding cells. Just as planned, Darren was sitting there waiting for him. The dirty cop nodded and pointed to the end of the row of cells. The young man handed him a roll of bills and walked down to the last cell.

In the cell sat a man who was waiting for his time in court. He looked up and saw the young man standing in front of his cell. He was hesitant at first, wondering what he wanted.

"I've got what you need to get out of here," the young man said to the man in the cell.

"What are you talking about?" the jailed man asked.

"Just come here and take this." The young man held out his hand. In the palm was a jail key. The man didn't know what to make of it. "Come on, we don't have a whole lot of time. You want out or what?"

Thinking quickly, the jailed man stepped forward and reached out for the key. As he was about to take it from the young man's palm, the young man took hold of the jailed man's outreached hand and pulled him into the cell bars.

"What the hell?"

The young man leaned in to the bars and whispered into the jailed man's ear.

"This is for Julio and Robbie, motherfucker." Then he plunged the makeshift knife into the man's belly. He did this several times, twisting the knife each time. The young man then let go, stepped back and watched Ronald Price slowly slump to the floor. When he knew that Price was dead, the young man left the holding cell area and walked out of the precinct the same way he came in.

Outside, the young man found a black SUV sitting in the parking lot waiting for him. Next to the SUV was an older man, waiting. The young man approached the SUV and nodded.

"It's all done?" the older one asked.

"Bitch is dead. Cop was paid too."

"Good job. You keep this up and you'll be going places. Hop in." The younger man, known to his friends and family as Carlos Cruz, younger brother of Robbie Cruz, climbed into the back of the SUV. The older man looked around to see if anyone was watching. When he knew it was safe, Ryan Mendoza, the new leader of the Latin Soldados, got into the SUV, closed the door and the two drove off into the snow-covered town of Hoboken.

ACKNOWLEDGEMENTS

An author can never write a book all by himself. There are so many factors that go into the final product that you have just read besides someone coming up with a story. There's the research, the editing, the cheering, the inspiration, the donating and the publishing. So please allow me to thank those that helped in making this book see the light of day and bookstores.

A big thanks to Christopher Diaz for his assistance in getting all the legalese in this book accurate. I know who to come to now in the event that I carjack someone and get caught…..kidding.

Thanks to those who donated to my GoFundMe account to assist with the publishing fees for this novel: Jan Valin, LouAnn Torres, Maura and Eric Valentin, Mark Schiebal, Ginny Fusaro, Christine Mendoza, Joan Griffen and Kristie Mahieux. Your donations have gone a long way and are all appreciated!

Thank you to my editing team of Katie Leishman-Peirens, Kristie Mahieux and Nicolle Roy. If not for you, then this book would have been the grammatic disaster that the first draft was.

Thanks to Michelle Carville, Elli Banks, Heather Carter, Kevin Diaz and the others at Authorhouse who helped give my story the paper flesh that it now has!

Thank you to my cheerleaders who helped by pushing me to that finish line. I'd still have a half written story if not for Ray Victor, Bill Porter, Shania Casson, Ali Norouzi, Katie Leishman-Peirens, Jan Valin, Eric and Maura Valentin, Josh Rau, Kristie Mahieux and Jess Walton.

I'd like to thank John Sandford, James Patterson, Brad Parks and

James Grippando, whose books I've read, studied and dissected to in order to eventually be one of the thriller greats.

Thank you to Phyllis Lennon, who helped bring this book to life by bringing me to life! I owe you more than you know.

Thank you to my son, Alex, who has taught me more about being a parent than I could teach him about being a kid.

And last but definitely not the least, thank you to Lisa Lennon, whose love and inspiration have pushed me to my limits and beyond. You are forever my muse.

CPSIA information can be obtained
at www.ICGtesting.com
Printed in the USA
LVHW11s2108221018
594456LV00001B/2/P